STUDIES IN WEST INDIAN LITERATURE

CW00494678

Theatre

Judy S. J. Stone

Series Editor: Kenneth Ramchand

MACMILLAN
CARIBBEAN

First published 1994

Published by THE MACMILLAN PRESS LTD
London and Basingstoke
Associated companies and representatives in Accra, Auckland, Delhi, Dublin, Gaborone, Hamburg, Harare, Hong Kong, Kuala Lumpur, Lagos, Manzini, Melbourne, Mexico City, Nairobi, New York, Singapore, Tokyo.

ISBN 0–333–60078–9

Printed in China

A catalogue record for this book is available from the British Library.

ACKNOWLEDGEMENTS

The author and publishers wish to thank the following who have kindly given permission for the use of copyright material:
Amber Lane Press Ltd for an extract from *Strange Fruit* by Caryl Phillips.
Marion Boyars Publishers Ltd for extracts from *Les Femmes Noirs* and *Redemption Song* in *Redemption Song and Other Plays* by Edgar White.
Farrar, Straus & Giroux, Inc., for extracts from the Prologues of *Dream on Monkey Mountain* and *Ti-Jean and His Brothers* from DREAM ON MONKEY MOUNTAIN by Derek Walcott. Copyright © 1970 by Derek Walcott.
Mustapha Matura for extracts from *As Time Goes By* and *Play Mas.*
Reed Book Services for extracts from *The Nine Night* and *Ritual by Water* by Edgar White published by Methuen London Ltd.
Mrs Joy Scott for extracts from *Terminus* and *Sir Gawain and the Green Knight* by Dennis Scott.

Every effort has been made to trace all the copyright holders for the photographs and text but in some cases this has proved impossible. The publishers apologise for any infringement of copyright or failure to acknowledge original sources, but upon information will be pleased to make the necessary arrangement at the first opportunity.

CONTENTS

ACKNOWLEDGEMENTS

Apart from my obvious debt to my publishers and to Professor Ken Ramchand, who initiated this project, I owe two Caribbean theatre people in particular for contributions of incalculable value to my work. Ken Corsbie, one-time recording angel of the Caribbean's Theatre Information Exchange, has lent his enthusiastic support and unparalleled regional experience of today's West Indian theatre to active assistance with various aspects of my research. Professor Errol Hill has generously made available to me the results of decades of his own scholarly research into and writings on the West Indian theatre of yesterday. Both have remained with this project throughout, Professor Hill having most kindly given his time to reading and commenting on the final manuscript.

In addition, I am particularly indebted to Alwin Bully, who has helped in countless ways, and to Nigel Scott. I am grateful to Bruce King for access to his research on the St Lucia Arts Guild. A special thank you goes to my assistant in Jamaica, Sonia Wilson, for her tenacious ferreting on my behalf, and another to James Lee Wah for varied assistance, in particular his meticulous textual correction of the draft manuscript, and his invaluable advice.

My thanks are also due to the many who have directly aided this project in one way or another, such as Michael Anthony, Stella Beaubrun, Holly Betaudier, Joanna Butterworth of the Lyric Theatre, Pat and Lisa Henry Chu Foon, Clara Rosa De Lima, Guyana Director of Culture Francis Quamina Farrier, Bro. Matthias Farrier, Patrick Gibbon, Rawle Gibbons of the UWI St Augustine Creative Arts Centre, Irma and Laurence Goldstraw, Electra Harris, Jeff Henry, Brenda Hughes, Ken Jaikaransingh, Horace James of Trinidad & Tobago Television, Barbara Jenson, George John, Errol Jones, Judy Daish Associates, Romeo Kaseram, Belize Director of Culture Lita Hunter Krohn, Carol Lawes, Stanley Marshall, Norline Metivier, Roger Michell, Henry Muttoo, Rex Nettleford, Elliott Netto, Monica Olivier-Rawlins and her staff at the Trinidad Public Library, Bruce Paddington, Patrick Prendergast of the Groundwork Theatre Company, Esmond Ramesar of the UWI St Augustine Extramural Studies Unit, Claude Reid, Ernest Rodriguez, C.A.P. St Hill, Joy Scott, Eintou Pearl Springer and the West Indian Reference Library, Sally Stollmeyer, Clairmonte Taitt, Jeremy Taylor, Rowena Tindall, Ruth Tompsett of the Middlesex Polytechnic, Kathryn Topham, Harclyde Walcott of the UWI Mona

Creative Arts Centre, the staff of the UWI St Augustine West India Library, and numerous others.

I am especially grateful to all the playwrights who took the time to contribute, including Cynthia Allen, Learie Alleyne-Forte, Douglas Archibald, Dermot Atkinson, James Baisden, Elliot Bastien, Lennox Brown (who is to blame for it all), Vincent Browne, Zeno Constance, Felix Cross, Pat Cumper, Azard Daniel, Basil Dawkins, Michael Denton, Devindra Dookie, St Clair Wesley Dorant, Victor Edwards, Felix Edinborough, Hall Anthony Ellis, Melville Foster, Norvan Fullerton, Roy Galt, Tony Gambrill, Lois Gayle, Michael Gilkes, Stafford Ashani Harrison, Ronald John, Freddie Kissoon, Ginger Knight, Earl Lovelace, Dexter and Dani Lyndersay, Mustapha Matura, Marina Omowale Maxwell, Paloma Mohamed, Dorbrene O'Marde, Raoul Pantin, Caryl Phillips, Michael Reckord, Clifford Sealy, Sistren, Derek Walcott, Roderick Walcott, Lester Efebo Wilkinson and Cynthia Wilmot.

And I would like to thank the countless others whose less direct contributions have made this book possible, including members of the Trinidad Theatre Workshop and the thousands of theatre people with whom I have enjoyed the privilege of working during more than thirty years in Caribbean theatre.

I also thank in advance for their patient understanding all those writers whose contribution to the literature of West Indian drama has been, for reasons of limited space or my own limitations, less adequately documented in this study than they may deserve.

Finally, I could not have undertaken the project without the support and understanding of friends such as Sonya Moze and Satu Ramcharan, and of my family, particularly John Stone and my father Peter Stone, my brother Paul, and most of all my young son Kairi, who bears the Amerindian name for the island of Trinidad, and to whom I dedicate this work.

Judy Stone
1993

SERIES INTRODUCTION

Kenneth Ramchand

The purpose of this series is to offer a new history of West Indian Literature, including the theatre. The history is intended to be new in several senses. Firstly, it is written from the perspective of the 1990s, a perspective that includes the following: the results, at least, of the quick run of critical theory through Structuralism, Deconstruction, and the various 'Posts'; the widening of outlook brought about in men as well as in women by the feminist movements and the feminist thinking of the last two decades; the dissolving of genre boundaries, as well as of distinctions between the languages of fiction and non-fiction, a process encouraged by a growing reluctance to take either fiction or non-fiction at their word or at face value; the impact on the writing and reading of literature of the forms taken by the fictions and non-fictions of the electronic media and the immediacy of response generated by these; a renewed sense of the connections between orality and writing, especially in formerly colonised territories where the oral and folk traditions are held to be the source and preservers of the self that avoided penetration by the colonising process.

This history is new, too, in the sense that it wants to present the theatre and the short story, not as appendages to poetry and the novel, but as important branches of the literature of the region in their own right. The authors of these two volumes have been granted the space to provide basic information that has been sadly lacking, to trace significant patterns, and to establish links between these two genres, and the poetry and prose that have been better served so far by commentary and criticism. Ramchand's book on the short story is an examination of the evolution of West Indian prose from scattered sources in the seventeenth, eighteenth and nineteenth centuries, through the great period of the island periodicals in the 1930s and 1940s, to the rediscovery and redeployment of the form in the 1980s and 1990s. The book looks critically at some of the consequences of the migration of West Indian writers in the 1950s and 1960s, and wonders whether the return of West Indian writers to the short story in the 1980s is not a return to a more indigenous and instinctive form.

It needs to be explained that the writers of the separate volumes in this series have not been given a format to follow, and there has been no attempt to impose uniformity of any kind. Each book does what the available material, the state of knowledge and comment, and the bent of the writer dictate. There is not very much information in print, let alone in one place, about theatrical activity, about the plays, or about the playwrights in the different islands. In many cases before 1950, some plays are known only in fragments, or by report or review. Judy Stone's work on theatre, as a consequence, has had to take on the provision of basic information as one of its main tasks, becoming a history of scripts and texts rather than the history of actors and performances that it now makes possible.

Ramchand and Stone attempt to treat their subjects in relation to the region as a whole. In his account of West Indian poetry, Stewart Brown faces up to the fact that since the break-up of the West Indian Federation in 1962 and the granting of independence to the islands one by one in the 1960s, differences between the islands have emerged, and differences have been uncovered. Some of this is reflected in the discussion of the theme of African-Indian relations in Ramchand's volume on the novel, but it is a structural principle in Stewart Brown's work on the poetry, where a recognition of the diversity of post-independence voices leads to the writing of separate chapters on Jamaica, Trinidad, Guyana, Barbados, and then on the remaining islands.

Stewart Brown's declared intention is to give an overview of the major trends, voices and directions in the West Indian poetry that exists in the form of writing. The strict chronological arrangement allows him to trace the evolution of West Indian poetry along with the evolution of West Indian society, a conjunction that links the processes of political and mental decolonisation with the growth into West Indianness of West Indian poetry. The chronological arrangement also allows him to follow the movement towards a fusion of oral and scribal traditions, a fusion that the volume sees as offering one major defining characteristic of West Indian poetry. In each chronological phase that Brown covers, calypso, dub, rap, or performance material appear as legitimate aspects of West Indian poetry. The discussions and analyses of work and writers before the sixties are useful for themselves, but they lead in the middle of the book to what is the heart of his argument, a chapter each on Derek Walcott and Edward Brathwaite.

Ramchand's coverage of the novel differs from Stone and Brown in that the work is organised according to topics like 'Orality and the West Indian Novel', 'The Vision of the Women Writers' and 'The Achievement of Roy A.K. Heath'. In this work, the West Indian novel since 1970 is fully represented, and the novels before 1970 which formed the subject of *The West Indian Novel And Its Background* are revalued in the chastened light following the collapse of the Federation, the emptiness of independence and the re-colonising of the region through structural adjustment programs imposed by the World Bank, the IMF, and other international money-lending agencies.

Although the authors of the separate volumes in the series take different approaches and organise their work in their own way, the four books focus again and again on certain issues: the relationship between oral and scribal, and the making of the language of West Indians; the relationship between literature including theatre, and popular cultural forms; the emphatic emergence of the women writers in poetry, drama and prose fiction in the 1980s; the problematics of West Indian writing overseas, with special reference to Britain and Canada where there are distinct immigrant West Indian communities; and as ever, the social orientation of West Indian literature. These common topics result in a remarkable cross-referencing and collaboration between the works, all the more significant for not having been designed by editorial prescription.

Throughout the Series, the term 'West Indies' is used to refer to the territories that were part of the British Empire; 'the Caribbean' refers principally to the geographical region that includes all the territories associated with European powers, for which the terms 'Dutch West Indies', 'French West Indies' and 'Spanish West Indies' are used.

INTRODUCTION

Kenneth Ramchand

Judy Stone's book on West Indian theatre is Volume I in this four-part series because it is the most necessary. It is preceded in criticism by Kole Omotoso's *The Theatrical Into Theatre* (1982) and Ken Corsbie's introductory *Theatre in the Caribbean* (1984); and it defers to the immense scholarship in the field of Professor Errol Hill. But this is the first attempt to put together in one place all the existing information, from the earliest documentable period, on drama in the English-speaking West Indies.

Ms Stone is very clear that this is neither a history of performers and performances nor of the drama as theatre. The work is part of a literary history, and it is based mainly upon written texts, relying where the text no longer exists, upon reports and reviews. But it is sufficiently informed by the author's knowledge of theatre and performances to lessen considerably the weight of the second of her disavowals. Her discussions of the texts are everywhere given point and poise by her sense of theatrical possibilities.

This point is reinforced by the position immediately taken in the prologue where she picks up Errol Hill's proposals for a regional theatre developed out of the folk festivals of the Caribbean, as they are elaborated in his seminal *The Trinidad Carnival: Mandate for a National Theatre* (1972). Stone's book is constructed around the proposition that there are five streams of theatre in the West Indies and in the Caribbean, and her technical concern for the discovery and elaboration of forms of theatre appropriate and indigenous to the Caribbean is apparent throughout. By the time we come to the end of her book, it becomes clear that the subtext to this informative history is a long theoretical discussion with Errol Hill.

Her account of theatrical activity in the islands before 1900 prepares us for some of the heart-breaking attitudes to serious theatre that exist in the islands even today. The description of the work of the pioneers of West Indian drama in the second chapter, among whom she ranks C.L.R. James and Marcus Garvey ('the controversial Jamaican visionary who introduced the West Indian theatre to the masses' as a means of raising social consciousness) ends with an extended and informative evaluation of the work of Errol Hill. This is an apt invocation because those who work in and for the theatre at the present time are in almost the same difficult situation as the pioneers, and because in any account of West

Indian drama, Hill as theorist, practitioner and preserving scholar is of the essence.

The five streams of theatre the book indicates are: the theatre of social realism, theatre of the people, total theatre, classical theatre and the theatre of ritual. Ms Stone makes an explicit connection between the drama of the late 1940s and 1950s and the phenomenon which is referred to in discussions of West Indian novels and West Indian poetry as 'the literature of the yard', a connection that ensures there can be no confusion with 'the later experiment of yard theatre, formally undertaken in Jamaica, Trinidad and Barbados, which promoted the staging of West Indian plays in the outdoor performing space of a yard.' Ms Stone is able to relate the theatre of the yard to the immediate socio-economic context, and to point justly to its limitations to one segment only of society, a limitation which makes the less accomplished of these plays seem dated and sentimental today. At the same time, she shows the continuity into the later twentieth century of the tradition of social realism first embraced in West Indian literature and drama in the literature of the yard. The work of Errol John, Samuel Hilary and Douglas Archibald is thus properly seen as lying behind that of later playwrights working in a socially realistic mode in all the islands. In this section of the book Ms Stone includes extended essays in the career of Errol John and then Trevor Rhone and Alwin Bully, a function of her willingness to see drama as an art of community without losing sight of the role of the individual talent.

The two chapters on forms of popular theatre bring into the field, in an informative and challenging way, a whole range of performances and performance pieces, all of which have in common the fact that they have larger audiences than the more sophisticated and thought-provoking forms of theatre. The first of these chapters, called 'Theatre of the People' includes a long overdue acknowledgement of the work of Trinidadian Freddie Kissoon and his Strolling Players; a description of the work of the Jamaica-based Sistren Group in encouraging working women to participate as actors and performers in the dramatisations of their own lives; and a convincing analysis of the work of Jamaican, Pat Cumper as individual artist and as communal collaborator. Ms Stone recounts these activities in such a way as to make obvious the connections and overlaps (subject matter, participants, themes) between these woman-centred theatre activities in Jamaica and the production of poems and prose fiction by Caribbean women going on at the same time. The next chapter 'Total Theatre' (a theatre even more popular than theatre of the people) goes into the total appeal of the musical. This chapter also focuses on the work of Earl Lovelace and Roderick Walcott as attempts to evoke a response similar to the response associated with total theatre while injecting serious themes.

Chapter 6, a virtual monograph on the dramatic career of Derek Walcott, answers all the questions anyone could ask about the output of the playwright and the different phases of his involvement in the theatre. Coming boldly under the heading 'Classical theatre' after the two chapters on popular theatre, it raises questions not just about the artist's need to discover a mode of address and a subject matter that would not drive away the ordinary person, but about the societal pressures and the educational system that produce a popular audience that is happy enough to take its theatre simply as entertainment. The discussion continues in Chapter 7 'Theatre of Ritual' where the bearing of the work of Dennis Scott, Rawle Gibbon, and Earl Warner with the Caribbean Lab established by the Jamaica School of Drama is acutely analysed: 'In the last couple of decades, principally in Jamaica, a small corps of theatre activists and playwrights has been conducting intensely intellectualised experiments in the creation of a mentally stimulating theatre peculiarly West Indian not only in form, but in every aspect of its genesis and presentation. The larger body of work coming out of these experiments is based on West Indian ritual, in a tangential development from Errol Hill's more performance-oriented Carnival Theatre . . . '.

Ms Stone's capacity to provide basic information and at the same time to analyse without dogma, is evident again in the discussion of black British playwrights, where some interesting perspectives on the theatre are developed while handy discussions of the work of Edgar White, Mustapha Matura and Caryl Phillips are conducted.

This is a formidably learned and painlessly informing book, concerned with appreciating what is there while hoping for and working towards the richest possible evolution of the West Indian drama: 'It may well be that just as Japan has both the Kabuki and the No theatres, so the West Indies too, will develop two unique theatres – the one perhaps a total theatre with a folk orientation, playing for the entertainment of the popular audience, the other a serious and more socially conscious theatre of ritual, drawing form and symbolism from the same folk heritage, but created out of a more considered craftsmanship, and affording greater intellectual reward.'

It has been a pleasure working as Series Editor with Ms Stone, and learning from her as she made a book I expect to have a long, useful life.

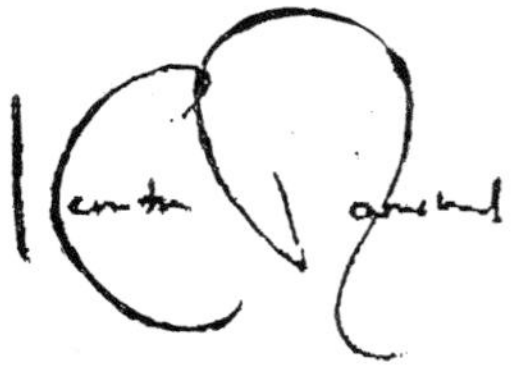

PROLOGUE

'This society is Elizabethan', wrote the poet Wayne Brown (*DE*, 13.2.91),[1] describing twentieth-century Trinidad, and by extension the greater West Indies. 'In its exuberance and volatility, its ribaldry and ostentation, above all in its turbulent love affair with language – language as self-creation, as in the Midnight Robber; language as scourge, as in the tents; language as proof of, and resistance against, the ultimate absurdity of the human condition, as in that promiscuous derision and rage of punning which constitutes an Old Mas band – in these it recalls the flair and angst of Shakespeare's world.'

Aptly, Brown's Shakespearean parallels are drawn from the theatre of the West Indies. The Midnight Robber, the calypso tents, the Old Mas bands, these are all traditional elements of Trinidad's Carnival. This Carnival is in itself an extraordinary street theatre; it is also a major resource of the more conventional West Indian theatre. But what, exactly, is West Indian theatre?

Trinidad's pioneering historian of West Indian theatre, Professor Errol Hill, was the first dramatist on record to suggest that, just as plays by West Indian playwrights do not *ipso facto* constitute a West Indian theatre, neither do plays set in West Indian settings, with West Indian characters who voice West Indian concerns in authentic West Indian dialogue. To be truly, uniquely, West Indian, the regional theatre must evolve its own indigenous form.

Hill's own proposal, published in 1972 as *The Trinidad Carnival: mandate for a national theatre*, was for a form of theatre to be developed out of the folk festivals of the Caribbean. As Hill envisioned it, this form would draw on the essence of the behaviour, speech, movement and dance of traditional masquerade characters. His proposal has borne fruit in the work of a number of serious dramatists, as well as in the generally lighter total theatre which incorporates music and dance and other arts.

Though total theatre, and in particular folk theatre, has the greatest mass appeal throughout the region, it is only one of a range of theatre forms flourishing in the West Indies today. The form most widely recognised internationally, for instance, is the theatre of the Nobel Laureate Derek Walcott, of St Lucia.

For the purposes of this study, these various theatre forms have been grouped into five streams, with a chapter devoted to each stream, rather than to each West Indian territory. This approach, to use an image of the Guyanese poet

Martin Carter, collects our scattered bones of time and place, of islands and ancestry. With its skeleton knitted together, the region can be seen as a single entity with a common history, a common culture and common concerns. Individual achievements can be seen in clear perspective against the background of parallel developments in theatre across the West Indies.

The first chapter, 'Setting the Stage', records the earliest theatre in the West Indies, up to the close of the nineteenth century. European theatre became firmly established in the region soon after the arrival of the British and French colonists. What little original writing for the West Indian stage has survived from this period was modelled after contemporary or classical English styles. The theatre was seen as no more than a hobby of the 'thin upper crust', as Richardson Wright terms colonial high society in his early theatrical history, *Revels in Jamaica*. The rare use of the vernacular was designed principally for upper crust amusement. Meantime, however, ever richer sources of material for a future West Indian theatre were gathering in the islands, as slaves and free men of different African tribes, indentured workers from India, and immigrants from many other parts of the world, gradually introduced to their new home the traditional rituals of their various cultures.

Chapter 2, 'Curtain Rise', covers the first half of the twentieth century. This was a period which saw a regional surge in writing for the stage. There was a number of pioneering movements in the West Indian theatre, most notably the nationalist movement, with its mandate to improve the self-image of the black man. This chapter looks in some detail at the work of such playwrights as Jamaica's Marcus Garvey and Una Marson, Guyana's Norman Cameron and Trinidad's C.L.R. James, and in particular Errol Hill. It touches on calypso theatre, and on Hill's Carnival theatre.

'Theatre of Realism' is the first of the five chapters each dealing with a stream of contemporary West Indian theatre. The other four streams considered are given the titles of 'Theatre of the People', 'Total Theatre', 'Classical Theatre', and 'Theatre of Ritual'. Each stream is considered both in general, and through the particular work of one or more representative playwrights. Chapter 3 opens with a discussion of the yard play movement of the fifties, and of the work of Trinidad's Errol John, author of the classic yard play, *Moon on a Rainbow Shawl* (1958). It then follows the continuing development of realistic theatre, with a closer look at the work of Jamaica's Trevor Rhone and Dominica's Alwin Bully.

Bully is one of several writers who have worked in more than one stream of theatre. Both Rhone and Bully are prime examples of a common West Indian phenomenon, the playwright who perforce also acts, directs, designs, produces, and generally fills in for any job that needs doing in the theatre. For many such playwrights, in their early years at least, running their own theatre company is the only way to get their plays staged. Such activities seriously encroach on their time and energy for creative writing, but that is the reality of West Indian theatre. On the positive side, the playwright who is also a theatre practitioner learns his craft in depth, from aspects not available to the desk-bound writer.

The next two chapters are devoted to popular theatre. The first, 'Theatre of the People', touches on all aspects of the popular form other than the musical, or total theatre. It looks briefly at the output of such representative writers as Trinidad's Freddie Kissoon and Ralph Maraj. In rather more detail it examines the work of Jamaica's Sistren movement, and of Patricia Cumper.

Cumper is a product of the West Indian playwright's commitment to his society. The strong communal sense apparent in the work of most of the region's leading writers extends, in many cases, into their private lives. Playwrights such as Jamaica's Dennis Scott have not only acted as mentor to upcoming young writers, they have made time to visit schools and open the students' eyes to the arts. It was through a series of such visits that the school-age Cumper became drawn to the theatre.

'Total Theatre' covers the various forms of the most popular theatre of all, the musical and total theatre such as the Ram Leela pageant, developments in Carnival theatre, the Little Theatre Movement's Jamaican national pantomime, and the government-sponsored 'calabash' theatre. The chapter focuses on the work of St Lucia's Roderick Walcott, and the plays of Trinidadian novelist Earl Lovelace.

Jamaica boasts the region's only School of Drama. Elsewhere in the region, the support of West Indian governments for theatre, as for all the arts, has traditionally remained minimal, and channelled to the easily-controlled amateur. Though many such projects have been planned, and some even inaugurated, there is not today a single fully operational national or regional theatre company in the West Indies.

The opposite face of this political indifference generally balances lack of government support with lack of government interference. Even so, in 1991 Trinidad's theatregoers were shocked by an unprecedented incident. A posse of heavily armed police stormed the stage during a scene of Godfrey Sealy's unexceptional drama on domestic violence, *Home Sweet Home*. The play had enjoyed an uneventful premier run in 1989, but two years later the leading actor was arrested on stage for using obscene language, as scripted, during his portrayal of marital rape. The following year, during the revival of another Sealy play, *One of our Sons is Missing* (1988), cast and crew were again intimidated by a police posse backstage during performance, but no arrests were made.

With or without direct government support, there is a slowly increasing number of institutions offering vocational assistance to playwrights, as to other artists. These institutions include the Jamaica School of Drama, the Creative Arts Centres and Extramural Departments of the three main campuses of the University of the West Indies, a few private sector foundations, and various national festivals, conferences and competitions.

The Caribbean Festival of Creative Arts is the premier regional cultural event of the four major language areas of the Caribbean: English, French, Spanish and Dutch. Because of its cost Carifesta, as it is better known, has been staged only sporadically in different territories since its genesis in Guyana in 1972. Even so, this Arts Festival has proved to be invaluable as a vehicle for Caribbean integration. It brings the West Indian peoples, as well as their playwrights and artists, 'together under the discipline of our arts', as Lovelace has written in Trinidad's *Sunday Express* (19.1.92), '. . . discovering ourselves to ourselves for ourselves'.

Among the benefits which have resulted from Carifesta has been a greater appreciation of the regional mutuality of goals in the development of a West Indian theatre.

Chapter 6, 'Classical Theatre', is devoted to the *oeuvre* of Derek Walcott. Long recognised as one of the world's finest English-speaking poets of this century, Walcott is exceptional among West Indian playwrights by reason of his inspired use of language and his breadth of vision. He is the pre-eminent example of Brown's West Indian Elizabethan.

However, the extended length of this chapter is due not only to the unique literary quality of Walcott's plays. A study of the evolution of Walcott's sweeping range of dramatic voices, in particular his search for a poetic form with the rhythms of West Indian dialect, realised most memorably in *Dream on Monkey Mountain* (1967), is a representative study of the long regional quest for a characteristic West Indian literary voice.

Walcott is one of the region's few playwrights to have his works published on both sides of the Atlantic. Many of the works discussed, however, have not been published, yet are seminal to the writer's development. With the increasing international interest in West Indian theatre, it is to be hoped that not only Walcott's unpublished works, but a range of the best West Indian plays still in manuscript, will be published before they are lost.

'Theatre of Ritual' covers the last of the five streams of theatre, a highly intellectualised, and often surrealistic, experimental approach to the creation of a West Indian theatre. The greater part of this writing is based in the rituals of the West Indies. The chapter draws reference to the work of the Caribbean Lab at the Jamaica School of Drama, and studies in particular the plays of Dennis Scott, Trinidad's Rawle Gibbons and Guyana's Michael Gilkes.

The final chapter, titled 'Black British Theatre', looks at the theatre of exile, epitomised in the work of Montserrat's Edgar White. There is a sizeable body of West Indian playwrights living and working in England, where they are developing a forceful black theatre. The other playwrights studied in this chapter are Trinidad's Mustapha Matura and, from the younger generation, the St Kitts-born Caryl Phillips.

White, Matura and Phillips are all, like Rhone and Derek Walcott, published playwrights in their own right, apart from any inclusion in collections. Their major scripts, unlike those of many West Indian playwrights, are readily available to the reader. However, when studying the text of any play, it should be borne in mind that, unlike any other form of literature, a playscript is not complete in itself. A novel is a finished work of art. A script is no more than a blueprint for a work of art, the realisation of which depends not on the writer's vision alone, but on a synthesis of the creative talents of numerous artists: playwright, director, designers, actors, perhaps a composer or musical director, choreographers, musicians, dancers, singers, and others. Dialogue is not the only element, nor even necessarily the principal element, in a theatrical production. Dennis Scott has written of 'the parity and indivisibility of a play's three languages – the playwright's word, the actor's body, the symbols they create'.[2] 'The performance is the work of art', Professor Hill pointed out in 1971, adapting an analogy borrowed from American scenographer Lee Simonson. 'The printed book is the corpse.'[3]

West Indian theatre, in all its forms, is exceptionally vital and performance oriented. Even the most realistic performance styles, reflecting the natural ebullience of the West Indian people, are more active, vigorous and full-throated than their counterparts in, say, Canada and England. When a Trinidad Theatre Workshop actor performed in a Minneapolis production of Walcott's *Pantomime* (1978) a role that had been written for him, and that he had performed many times in several West Indian productions to considerable acclaim, the American director found it necessary to tone down his performance to make it more acceptable to American audiences. When the leading American actor from that *Pantomime* performed on exchange in Trinidad, critics and audiences alike found his acting style overly restrained.

The West Indian is indeed, as Brown suggests, an exuberantly Elizabethan society, whatever its chosen form of theatre. Surely Shakespeare himself would have delighted in the intrinsic vigour, the brawling wit, the compassion for the curiosities of the human condition, the intellectual challenge, the metaphors of masquerade, and the fresh-minted, image-laden language of the best West Indian writing for the stage.

NOTES

1. For key to abbreviated publication titles, see Selected Bibliography, 9. Periodicals and newspapers.
2. Dennis Scott, 'Introduction', in *Sir Gawain and The Green Knight*, USA: Anchorage Press in association with National Theatre of the Deaf, 1978.
3. Errol Hill, 'The Emergence of a National Drama in the West Indies' *CQ*, Vol. 18, # 4, 1972.

1

SETTING THE STAGE

Theatre in the West Indies to 1900

One sultry evening in 1729, a number of planters and their families, and others of the 'thin upper crust' of Barbados society, took their seats for an amateur performance by some of the Gentlemen in their midst. In their tight bodices and hooped regency gowns, the Ladies glowed genteelly, surrounded by a general hubbub of strident greetings and chattering excitement at the unusual Diversion. The stage was set for John Crowne's *Sir Courtly Nice*, the latest popular comedy from England. It was also set for the delivery of two additional speeches, the earliest surviving indigenous work in the theatre of the West Indies.

How theatre came to the West Indies

Unusual as the above diversion may have been, theatre was not unknown in the region at this date. Of all the English-speaking West Indian territories, Belize can claim the oldest legacy of theatre. As Robert A. Johnston notes in *The Theatre of Belize* (1973), there was theatre there some two thousand years ago, during the time of the ancient Mayan civilisation.

In Belize today, as in only two or three other parts of the Caribbean, the Black Caribs of Stann Creek still stage the traditional ritual dances that must have been the earliest form of theatrical expression common throughout the West Indian islands, wherever there was an Amerindian settlement. From the great-grandfathers to the babies in their mothers' arms, the entire community takes part in these dances.

The original purpose of the ritual dances was to control the phenomena of rural life, such as the weather and the harvest. In the normal course of events, these rituals could have been, as those of other nations have been, the primary source for the development of an indigenous theatre. But the Amerindian culture was virtually obliterated under the Spanish colonisers, who followed in the wake of Christopher Columbus.

In this century, however, a few West Indian playwrights have begun to draw on the Amerindian experience for their inspiration. F.E.M. Hosein's miracle play, *Hyarima and the Saints* (1931), is a product of colonial tutelage. Recent plays that explore the subject with a more sensitive perception include Michael Gilkes's *Couvade* (1972), and Raoul Pantin's *Hatuey* (1980). Guyana's Amerindian playwright, Basil Rodrigues, is best known for his comedy, *Kanima at Sun Mountain* (1977).

Soon after the conquests of Columbus, Spain found itself rejoicing in its golden age of theatre, and of the Spanish arts and literature generally. Yet available records show only, literally, a single word concerning theatre in the West Indies during the two centuries of Spanish occupation. A 'theatre', as listed by Frank Cundall in *Historic Jamaica*, was one of the notable public buildings of Sevilla Nueva, the brief-lived capital city founded by Jamaica's first Governor in 1509. In the absence of further records, a parallel may be drawn with the later experience of early colonists in the neighbouring islands. It seems probable that the sixteenth and seventeenth century Spanish communities of the West Indies would have staged occasional amateur theatrical entertainments for their own amusement. If so, they would have drawn on traditional Spanish forms, and any original material, perhaps based on their pioneer experiences, would naturally have been in the Spanish tongue.

Historians may have ignored the Spanish theatre of the West Indies, but West Indian playwrights have not ignored the Spanish experience. Plays such as Pantin's *Hatuey*, Charles Shanahan's *The Spanish Warrior* (1853), Lewis Osborne Inniss's *Carmelita, the Belle of San Jose* (1897), Douglas Archibald's *Defeat With Honour* (1952), Derek Walcott's *Drums and Colours* (1957), and a number of historical pageants, are either wholly or in part set in the era of Spanish occupation. There are also works such as Walcott's *The Joker of Seville* (1974), which draw on the parang, the traditional Christmas music which is part of Trinidad's Spanish heritage.

It is not until nearly the end of the seventeenth century, twelve years after Jamaica was officially ceded by Spain to the English, that we find the first positive record of plays being performed in the West Indies. Frank Hanson, in his *Account of the Island and Government of Jamaica*, lists, as one of the 'Recreations' of this 'flourishing' island around 1682, 'Plays at a Publick Theatre'. Hanson does not identify these plays. However, the English having initially captured the island in 1655, it may safely be assumed that after nearly thirty years of English rule these plays originated from England. They were probably staged by resident amateurs.

The next reference to theatrical activities in the West Indies returns us to our Gentlemen friends in Barbados, with the earliest record of the actual plays produced. In 1728 the Gentlemen Amateurs gave their debut performance in, and, according to Samuel Keimer in *Caribbeana*, 'General Satisfaction with', their staging of *The Royal Convert*, by England's leading writer of tragedies, Nicholas Rowe. The English theatre was to remain the dominant form of recognised theatre throughout the West Indies well into the twentieth century, and still exerts a powerful influence.

During the eighteenth century most of the region's theatrical productions, with the exception of those in Jamaica, were staged by the resident amateurs of each territory. With extraordinary perseverance, under the most challenging conditions, group after group of amateur players would form and perform, for a few nights, months or decades, eventually to drift apart, only for another group to form, perform and drift apart in their wake.

The earliest productions were staged in the open air, in barns, halls, hotels, houses, estate houses, coffee-houses, court-houses and, Jose Bodu mentions in *Trinidadiana*, even in an old police station. In nearly every case, it was the amateur players of each territory who were the principal force behind the construction of the first buildings designed primarily for the staging of theatre. It is remarkable how many of these playhouses, throughout the region, were nostalgically and perhaps optimistically named after London's Theatre Royal. Guyana, then British Guiana, opened the colony's first theatre, the first Theatre Royal, in Georgetown in 1810, and by 1813 had another Theatre Royal in New Amsterdam. The newly-formed English Amateurs of Trinidad opened their Theatre Royal in 1818; the existing group of French Amateurs apparently had no theatre of their own, and briefly joined forces with the English. St Lucia's Theatre Royal was opened in 1832 by the combined efforts of English and French amateurs, assisted by a theatre company from Martinique. Jamaica's Kingston Theatre was renamed the Theatre Royal in 1842.

As early as 1771 the Virgin Island, St Croix, then under the umbrella of the Danish West Indies, had two theatres, one in Frederiksted and one in Christiansted. In Antigua a group of amateurs, together with the band of the locally-stationed 69th Regiment, opened the island's first theatre in 1788. In Barbados a public theatre, built by subscription, opened in 1812.

The region's amateur companies sometimes presented several new productions each month. Up until the early nineteenth century these actors routinely performed with scripts in their hands. And as late as 1870, Joel Benjamin notes in *The Early Theatre in Guyana*, 'young men generally had to play the parts of women, and audiences were extremely pleased when a "real" actress appeared on the stage'. Though the tradition dated back two and a half millennia to the classical Greek theatre, and though even in England women on the stage had been a rarity until the later seventeenth century, after the Restoration, the transvestite actor on occasion caused considerable displeasure to his West Indian audience. Guyana's *Royal Gazette* of 7 August 1810 carries the comment, '. . . whatever merits the Gentlemen Amateurs might have possessed, yet it must be acknowledged that their want of Female Performers certainly was of a nature both unnatural and disgusting'.

However, in the stylised Indian theatre of Ram Leela, for instance, the transvestite actor continued to perform until late in the twentieth century. In Trinidad's *Sunday Guardian* of 14 October 1990, Kamla Tewarie writes, 'No females were given parts, and even the role of Sita was portrayed by men because of social and cultural constraints. It is only in the last decade that women have been playing the role'. For very different reasons, evolving from a form of slave protest, and probably with roots even further back in African ritual, certain masquerade characters, such as John Canoe's 'lady' in Jamaica, were played by men costumed with exaggerated female characteristics. In Trinidad such burlesques are a favourite component of the ribald old mas bands that parade during the pre-Carnival season and pre-dawn on J'Ouvert morning. Carnival's Dame Lorraine too is still performed in the transvestite tradition, much like the dame of British pantomime.

In the English theatre of the early nineteenth century it was the common practice to present a double bill, composed of a full length play followed by a short farce or burlesque. The West Indian amateurs selected their scripts from the classics, and from the best of England's contemporary repertoire. Plays were also selected if the subject matter was thought to have particular relevance for the colonial audience. Shakespeare was a frequent choice, though it was not until after Emancipation that *Othello* was considered suitable for presentation in the colonies. Some fifty years after Emancipation, a rare reference to theatre in Tobago is given by Anthony Froude in *The English in the West Indies*, describing a production of *The Merchant of Venice* staged for the visiting Governor by 'a party of villagers'. Of contemporary offerings, *The West Indian* (1771) by Richard Cumberland, a comedy about a young Jamaican planter in London, was a regular favourite. Other playwrights whose works were often staged were Mrs Centlivre, William Congreve, John Gay, Oliver Goldsmith, Richard Brinsley Sheridan and Rowe.

The professional troupes originating from England, and later from America, offered similar fare. Whenever opportunity offered, the local amateurs would take part in a visiting production. Considering the difficulties of travelling at the time, there is on record a surprising amount of movement between the islands of actors and productions, amateur as well as professional. The earliest record of professional productions in the West Indies is Jamaica's 1733 season of plays presented by a visiting English troupe. Thereafter, companies from England used the island both as a base and as a springboard for America.

Professional theatre became firmly established in Jamaica from 1755, with the first visit by Lewis Hallam's American Company of Comedians, which was originally from England. On this visit the American Company remained in Jamaica for three years, during which time Hallam died. David Douglass, an English actor-manager resident in Jamaica for the previous ten years, took over the management of Hallam's company, merging it with his own. In 1758 the new American Company returned to America, where it continued to tour until the outbreak of the War of Independence. In 1775 Douglass brought the American Company back to the safe refuge of Jamaica. During the ten years of the company's second West Indian sojourn, several of its members wrote original plays which the company staged.

Among these original works, the comedy *Scandal Club* (1781) is the first known full-length play by a West Indian writer to have been performed on the West Indian stage. Written by an anonymous 'West Indian Lady', the comedy apparently drew heavily on Sheridan's *School for Scandal.* Of the other plays, John Henry's four-act drama, *School for Soldiers, or The Deserter* (1781), seems to have been particularly successful. It was published in Jamaica two years after its première, and went into a second edition.

Margaret Cheer Cameron's farcical afterpiece, *A West Indian Lady's Arrival in London* (1781), is notable for the controversy it aroused over the heroine's use of 'dialect peculiar to a few in this island'.[1] This controversy marks the earliest recorded introduction of the vernacular on stage. The author's intention was to amuse, but Jamaican society feared itself ridiculed. Jamaican society did not wish to be associated with the vernacular. For another century or more playwrights in the West Indies wrote for their upper crust audiences in the standard English of the time. Before long, however, the occasional use of the vernacular became acceptable to the colonial theatregoers as in itself quaint cause for merriment. In these early days the vernacular was also used as a device to stereotype black characters, usually in a demeaning manner. During the nineteenth century, however, after Emancipation, as theatre became more realistic, and as West Indian playwrights became more concerned that their work should be relevant to the region, the vernacular began to find a more genuine expression on stage.

Apart from the one attempt at the vernacular, and occasional Jamaican references, the original works staged by the American Company were indistinguishable in style and content, though possibly not in quality, from the English plays on which they were modelled. Such indistinguishableness was to remain the ambition of most West Indian playwrights, whether foreign or native born, until well into the twentieth century.

How playwriting began in the West Indies

The American Company's were not the earliest plays to originate from the West Indies. Nearly a century previously, the region's first recorded playwright, the precocious teenager William Walker, who was born in Barbados and educated at Eton, acted in the 1698 London production of his own first play, *Victorian Love*. Five years later his comedy, *Marry or Do Worse*, was also staged in London, and later published. Walker in due course abandoned the stage to return to the West Indies where he became, eventually, Attorney-General of Barbados.

Attorneys, doctors, and other intensively educated professionals, not surprisingly comprised a large proportion of the early West Indian writers. Matthew Concanen, Attorney-General of Jamaica from 1732 to 1744, was the author of a comedy called *Wexford Wells*. It had, Richardson Wright notes in *Revels in Jamaica*, 'a brief career', from which we may assume at least a single performance.

'A famous and beloved physician', Wright tells us, was the author of the original dialogue delivered by our Gentlemen friends in Barbados. The prologue and epilogue written by Dr Richard Towne for the Gentlemen's 1729 production of *Sir Courtly Nice* are preserved in *Caribbeana*. In thirty-six lines of iambic pentameters in rhymed couplets and triplets, the prologue refers to the warm reception of the Gentlemen's previous production, apologises for the inadequacy of the performers, flatters the ladies of the audience as having 'Charms unrival'd by the *British Fair*', and touches on the disputations of current politics. The epilogue 'was thought to contain a good deal of Humour'.

For a further century after Dr Towne, some fifty years after the strivings of the American Company, there is little else on record of indigenous work for the West Indian stage. A melodrama written by 'a gentleman of this city' was staged at Jamaica's Kingston Theatre in 1822. Benjamin mentions that at least one original skit, *The Demerara Hobby*, was performed in British Guiana in 1817 by a Mr Franklin, who may have been the author.

Also in British Guiana, in the 1890s, the Revd P. Giddings published a collection of ten sketches, *Quid Rides (Why do you laugh?)*. Norman Cameron, in *Drama in British Guiana*, describes these sketches as characterising 'various foibles of the people, especially a tendency to use words of learned length and thundering sound'. The pseudo-learned character, who knows the sound of words but not their sense, has since become a stock figure of West Indian comedy. Derek Walcott has immortalised the character as Mi-Jean, in *Ti-Jean and his Brothers* (1958). There is, Benjamin writes, a long-lasting tradition in Guyana of short humour sketches based on close observation of local life. A similar tradition, of even shorter sketches, is reported by Johnston for Belize. Trinidad's calypso theatre, which is discussed in the following chapter, may be seen as a parallel evolution.

In Jamaica a similar tradition of humorous social commentary developed through the one-man performances of reciters and storytellers. The Jamaican Raphael J. de Cordova wrote a body of comic monologues, which for some thirty years, from 1859 to 1888, he recited with great success on tour around America. Periodically he returned to Jamaica to perform in his native island. Six of his 'lectures' were published in 1939 as *The Wit and Humour of the 70s.* Henry Garland Murray, a professional storyteller who was a contemporary of de Cordova, also wrote his own comic material. However, Murray, who was a reader of enormous popularity all over Jamaica, was black, whereas de Cordova was white. It is Murray's work that is the more significant for the purposes of this study. A newspaper editor and proprietor, he died in 1877, having spent only the last eight years of his life writing the humorous stories that he referred to as 'Manners and Customs of the Country a Generation Ago'. He wrote for the people of Jamaica, and he wrote, says Errol Hill in *The Jamaican Stage 1655–1900*, in a 'simple and natural' vernacular style. 'His appeal was immediate and electric. Nothing like that had ever been offered to audiences before, and they never tired of hearing him.'[2] Murray's two sons carried on the tradition after his death.

During the nineteenth century it was fairly common practice for the newspapers to publish dramatised commentaries on topical events. These commentaries were intended for the reader rather than for performance, but several of them showed genuine dramatic potential. Two of the earliest on record are the satires, *A West India Scene* and *A Jamaica Comedy*, written by an anonymous Jamaican planter and published in 1824–25 in the *Jamaica Journal and Kingston Chronicle.*

A West India Scene was written at a time when colonists generally were dreading and vociferously resisting the approaching emancipation of their slaves. This commentary takes the form of a witty and, in the circumstances, a surprisingly objective dialogue between a planter and his 'negro driver'. The planter proposes a number of reforms on his estate, including abolishing whipping. The driver, who speaks authentic vernacular, pours the cold water of common sense on the scheme. Hill writes in *The First Playwrights of Jamaica*, 'This is the first Jamaican play on record to deal directly with an issue affecting the lives of thousands of Jamaican people. While couched in a humorous vein and written from the point of view of the planter class, it unwittingly reveals the silent resistance of black slaves to their condition. The play also explains why, with freedom won, former slaves were unwilling to continue working on the estates as paid labourers.'

Other published dialogues are for the most part political in character. Of particular interest is Trinidad's 1881 satire, *The Old Regime vs. The New, or, Colonial Prejudice*, featuring the notorious Inspector of Police, Captain Arthur Baker. Baker's mishandling of Carnival that same year had provoked the bloody Canboulay riots. The inspector, newly out from England, had banned the traditional torch-lit Canboulay processions. As a result, for the six hours between Dimanche Gras midnight and J'Ouvert dawn, intense pitched battles were fought between the police and groups of defiant Canboulay revellers. Over the ensuing century the episode, and Baker himself, have acquired a mythical quality in the island's folklore, symbolising the clash of cultures under the colonial system. Among several modern dramas that have drawn on this source are *Warrior Bois* (1982) by Ronald Amoroso, *Canboulay* (1990) by Norvan Fullerton and Stephen Landrigen, and most notably *I Lawah* (1985) by Rawle Gibbons.

We now meet 'The Bard of Trinidad', whose works were performed in the early 1830s. Edward Lanza Joseph was a Scotsman who arrived in Trinidad about 1820, and remained till his death in 1840. He wrote a history of Trinidad, a biography, poems, and a number of plays.

His musical farce, *Martial Law in Trinidad* (1832), is an important milestone in West Indian theatre. The plot is set against a background of Trinidad's annual Christmas muster of troops. In style the farce is patterned after the witty comedies of Sheridan. Its satirical lyrics, such as the 'Humbug Song' ('In writing we say, "dear sir", to those whom we mean evil, / We subscribe "obedient servant" and wish them to the devil'), are, as Hill has remarked, suggestive of the D'Oyly Carte operas to come. But here for the first time was a locally written full-length play whose concerns were relevant to contemporary life in the West Indies, which attempted to create a range of recognisably local characters, and which treated an occasion characteristic of the West Indies.

Martial Law's comic treatment of military procedures has a parallel in the parodies of the militia that were to be seen in Trinidad's military Carnival bands even before Emancipation, as Michael Anthony records in *Parade of the Carnivals of Trinidad.*

The obverse of parody is homage. During the early twentieth century, the region's intellectual movement increasingly came to appreciate that recognition of West Indian heroes was a vital factor in the building of nationhood. The first known play to pay such tribute was written by a young reporter of the *Colonial Standard and Jamaica Despatch*, Charles Shanahan. Shanahan's only previous work had been a one-act farce, *The Mysteries of Vegetarianism* (1853). His full-length historical drama, *The Spanish Warrior*, also produced in 1853, celebrated the exploits of the fifteenth-century explorer and coloniser of the new world, Vasco Nunez de Balboa. Hill believes Shanahan may have modelled his play on Sheridan's *Pizarro, or The Death of Rollo.*

Among the relatively few subsequent Caribbean works to honour heroic lives are *Hatuey* on the Amerindian war chief; C.L.R. James's *The Black Jacobins* (1936), Aime Cesaire's *La Tragedie du Roi Christophe* (1963), Derek Walcott's *Henri Christophe* (1950), and Denis Martin Benn's *Toussaint L'Ouverture* (1968), all on the Haitian revolution; Pacheco Domacasse's *Tula* (1973), on Curaçao's slave rebellion of 1795; Roger Mais's *George William Gordon* (published 1976) on the martyr of Jamaica's Morant Bay rebellion; Douglas Archibald's *Defeat with Honour*, on Spain's surrender of Trinidad to the British; Freddie Kissoon's *God and Uriah Butler* (1967) on the Trinidad labour leader; Edgar White's *I, Marcus Garvey* (1987), and Walcott's panoramic overview of the region's history, *Drums and Colours*.

In the second half of the nineteenth century, an increase in amateur dramatic activity, particularly in Jamaica, coupled with pioneering efforts in drama productions by schools, resulted in an increasing number of original works for the stage. For the most part these were works of foreign influence, but at least two, *In Stormy Days* and *A Las Armas*, were of compelling Caribbean relevance.

In Stormy Days, or, The Vow That Saved Jamaica was written by one of the nuns of Jamaica's Alpha Cottage, a Roman Catholic orphanage for coloured children. The play, writes Hill, 'recalled an event in early Jamaican history when a large contingent of French forces from neighbouring Hispaniola, led by Jean Du Casse, attempted to capture the island then governed by Sir William Beeston. The colony had been enfeebled by the devastation caused two years earlier by the great earthquake of 1692. The French forces made several landings on the island, were engaged by local militias, and were eventually driven back, but not before they had inflicted severe destruction to life and property. The play even had the Governor captured by the invaders and rescued through the efforts of a gypsy queen'.[3] The several reviews of this ambitious production, acted by an all-girl cast of orphans, were exceptionally enthusiastic. They praised the dramatic power and high literary quality of the writing. They also pointed out the possibilities the play opened up for a serious national theatre.

The Cuban *A Las Armas*, which is of unknown authorship, was staged in Jamaica in 1898 by a group of Cuban refugees. A defiant celebration of the ongoing Cuban struggle for independence from Spain, this fervently patriotic one-act drama was played, reports a reviewer, with 'an intensity of realism never before achieved on the Kingston stage.'[4]

As the century drew to a close, one other Jamaican playwright attempted to capture a West Indian character. *Malcolm and Alonzo, or the Secret Murder of Leonard* (1880), by John Duff Spraggs, is a revenge melodrama written in rhyming couplets. Its comic relief is supplied by Tobie, a labourer, who speaks in the vernacular. Though played for comedy, Tobie's dialogue is drily acute:

> Me work fe true an true, but pay is small,
> Money is mek, but massa keep mose all.

In the same period, Guyana saw its first published plays, including Father

C.W. Barraud's two 5-act historical dramas in the Shakespearean manner, *St Thomas of Canterbury* and *St Elizabeth of Hungary* (1892), W.M.E.P.'s *Abassa* (1883), and Walter J. Veecock's verse drama, *Phileron: The Tragedy of a Poet Soul* (1896). None of these works had anything to do with the West Indies.

For the centenary celebrations of British rule in Trinidad, Lewis Osborne Inniss wrote a four-act historical romance, *Carmelita, the Belle of San Jose* (1897). Set in Trinidad at the time of the English conquest, and enlivened with Spanish dancing, bandols and chac-chacs, this love story between a Spanish Indian girl and a young Englishman is, observes Hill in *The Emergence of a National Drama in the West Indies*, 'sentimental and exotic, two fashionable characteristics of English drama in the early part of the nineteenth century.' The dialogue is uninspired, and Inniss took some historical licence in his treatment of the noble savage betrayed by the Spanish conqueror. He took a similar licence in a subsequent play, *Mura, the Cacique's Daughter*, which was produced in 1898 for Discovery Day.

Carmelita is perhaps of most interest as an example of a phenomenon still apparent sixty years after Emancipation, the virtual exclusion of the African population from its cast of characters. At the time the play was set, more than four-fifths of Trinidad's population was of African descent. In a play celebrating the nation, most of the nation was ignored. There was indeed a great deal of work ahead for the coming West Indian playwrights.

Not all playwrights were as blinkered as Inniss. The anonymously written *The Violet of Icacos* (1897), set in a south Trinidad fishing village, included African labourers in the cast. Hill suggests that these would have been played by 'whites in black-face',[5] as was the common practice. However, as far back as 1800 Henry Bolingbroke recorded, in *A Voyage to Demerara*, that 'in the French islands, negro performers have been enlisted to take parts . . . but there are few Moorish characters on our stage, except Othello, Juba, and Oroonoko, which they could personate with propriety'.

The principal role of the enslaved black in formal West Indian theatre, Edward Brathwaite tells us in *The Development of the Creole Society in Jamaica 1770–1820*, was to reserve his master's theatre seat by sitting in it till the master arrived. Such slaves would then be allowed to watch the play from an upper gallery. One result of this practice was the development of farcical versions of scenes from Shakespearean and other plays, these parodies being presented by the Actor Boys of Jamaica's Jonkunnu festival. Segregated seating was advertised to the general public by the Jamaican theatre of the early nineteenth century, and even before full Emancipation an apprentice is known to have demanded his rightful entry to the theatre. However, the cost of a theatre ticket would have been beyond the reach of most members of the black public at this time. And the plays then staged in the formal theatre were as far removed from the black experience of the day as are the American soap operas screened on today's Caribbean television. There are records of black drama groups forming soon after Emancipation, but these were not long-lived. The poor organisation of national education for the century after Emancipation allowed few black West Indians to awaken to the potential of formal drama. The masses continued to see theatre as the hobby of the privileged few, an attitude traces of which linger up to today.

But the black masses had their own theatre for all that. Rituals brought from Africa survived in one form or another. Traces of the egungun masquerade, for instance, out of which the Yoruba travelling theatre developed in the seventeenth century, clearly inform the street masquerades of the region's carnivals and Jonkunnu. Over the years, such rituals adjusted to the artificial *mélange* of different tribal cultures, colonial influences and the folk heritage of other immigrant cultures. With Emancipation, Trinidad's Carnival became the people's festival. Other popular festivals, such as the flower festivals, developed in the other islands.

There were also other ethnic theatres. In British Guiana, for instance, Benjamin records, there was a Dutch theatre by 1828, a Portugese theatre from 1854, Chinese theatricals from 1877, and the Hindu epic outdoor theatre of Ram Leela. Trinidad, which also stages Ram Leela, and in addition Hosay, saw Yiddish plays during the Second World War. Apart from Ram Leela and Hosay, the ethnic theatres did not survive long, but the rich diversity of cultural experience is still there to be tapped by the new generation of West Indian playwrights.

NOTES

1 Richardson Wright, *Revels in Jamaica 1682–1838*, New York: Dodd, Mead & Co, 1937.

2 Errol Hill, *The Jamaican Stage 1655–1900*, Amherst, USA: University of Massachusetts Press, 1992.

3 *Ibid.*

4 *Jamaica Post*, 1 July 1897.

5 Errol Hill, 'The Emergence of a National Drama in the West Indies', *CQ*, Vol. 18, #4, 1972.

CURTAIN RISE

The Pioneers of West Indian Theatre 1900–1950:
Errol Hill

As the sun rose on the twentieth century, the educational provisions instituted after Emancipation were beginning to show results. Mass illiteracy was gradually receding around the Caribbean, and the early playwrights were emerging in increasing numbers. It was to be a long, painstaking struggle for mastery of their new element, and at first the writers lacked direction. Though theatre, amateur or professional, had been active in the colonies for the last two hundred years and more, up to the end of the nineteenth century the scattering of plays that had originated in the region had been European in style and for the most part alien in perception. The image of conventional theatre as a pastime of the colonial elite would take another century to eradicate from the public mind. However, with the progressive opportunities for schooling, and the consequent development in each island of an educated middle class consisting largely of the descendants of slaves, as the decades passed more and more of the new playwrights were of non-European origin. Even so, the comedies and melodramas were still modelled on Victorian theatre. Not until the thirties did the West Indian stage begin to reflect the influence of the black nationalist movement gaining ground in the thrust towards independence. Not until the forties did drama seriously attempt to take on the uniquely West Indian character identified by the literary movement of the previous decade. Not until the fifties were there coherent signs of the search for a West Indian form of theatre.

During the first thirty years of the century there were few Caribbean playwrights of note. In British Guiana a comedian of Portugese descent, Sidney Martin, enjoyed popular success with his *Mrs Farrington's Third Husband* (1916) and other comedies. Norman Cameron, in his *Drama in British Guiana*, also pays tribute to the 'brilliant' work of a later comedian, G. Ingham Goring, who wrote comic sketches such as *Perseus Drops a Brick*, and *Mortgage on the Old Guiana Home.* In Trinidad Cecil Cobham wrote and staged several melodramas, including *Sold But Not Lost* (c.1926), *Retribution* (c.1928), and *Suspicious Husband* (c.1929). In Jamaica the plays of the period included two historical dramas, Tom Redcam's *San Gloria* (pub.1951) and *A Soul's Sacrifice* (1921) by Alexander MacGregor James, and the earliest work of Ranny Williams. Williams was a comedian whose popular farces drew large crowds to Marcus Garvey's Edelweiss Park in 1929 and 1930. Twenty years on, as playwright-performer, Williams played a key role on the team that shaped the unique annual Jamaican pantomime.

A Soul's Sacrifice is a conventional melodrama set in seventeenth century Jamaica shortly after the British conquest. The story, true to the stereotypes of the time, is of upstanding British settlers, a dastardly Spaniard, a buried treasure, and thwarted love. Errol Hill comments that the play is interesting mainly for its range of characters, and for the use of dialect by Fidelle, a black housemaid, and Choto, an evil Maroon obeahman.

Tom Redcam is the pen-name of Thomas Henry MacDermot, who in 1933 was posthumously created Poet Laureate of Jamaica. His *San Gloria* is a long and ambitious work based on an incident on the coast of Jamaica during the third voyage of Columbus. As a piece of writing the play is a ponderous pastiche of Shakespeare and the Bible. As a piece of theatre it is so disappointingly lifeless, with the central man of action having little to do other than pray and soliloquise, that it has apparently never been produced. But in his attempt to blend prose and verse in a heightened language that would ennoble one of the region's historical figures, MacDermot was breaking ground that a later poet, Derek Walcott, was to till to bounteous effect. And the Jamaican's introspective treatment of Columbus suggests that MacDermot may have been one of the first West Indian playwrights to respond in any way, however unsuccessfully, to the late nineteenth-century movement in European theatre, from mannered romance to realism.

It was Marcus Garvey, the controversial Jamaican visionary, who introduced the West Indian theatre to the masses in its new role of social responsibility. Garvey dedicated his life to raising the black man's sense of his own identity and self-worth, both in the Caribbean and in America, and eventually around the world. In the 1920s the Universal Negro Improvement Association (UNIA) that Garvey founded, with headquarters in Harlem, became the largest African-American and Pan African mass movement in history. Garvey ran his own weekly newspaper, wrote and published a number of philosophical texts, and was a major influence in the Harlem Renaissance. Many leading artists of the period found their first platform through Garvey – the performers at his movement's Liberty Hall (Marian Anderson sang there in 1922), and the writers in his newspaper, *The Negro World*.

But it was the black masses that Garvey believed most needed his help. And he came to realise that theatre had a greater potential to reach and touch the uneducated man in the street than all his publications. He wrote several plays, and became the first West Indian playwright to break the stage and film stereotypes of the 'Mammy' and the 'Uncle Tom', of the menial black, the evil black, the craven, ludicrous or beefcake black. Garvey presented the black man as a rounded human being with his own dignity.

In August 1930, three years after Garvey's deportation from America, the UNIA staged in its new open-air auditorium at Edelweiss Park, Kingston, one after the other on three consecutive nights, Garvey's 'three great dramas': *The Coronation of an African King*, *Roaming Jamaicans*, and *Slavery – from Hut to Mansion*. Hill writes:

> The first play, with scenes set in Senegal, Dahomey, the Sudan, London, Paris, Washington and New York, crystallized Garvey's world struggle for a free and independent African nation providing an ancestral home for all African and African-derived peoples. The second play depicted the life of migrant Jamaicans who were forced by economic conditions to leave their homeland and find work in the United States, Panama, Costa Rica, Cuba, Haiti, and other foreign lands. The third play described the horrors of slavery and the slave traffic, the agitation for freedom, emancipation, and progress thereafter. Garvey's view of black life was always epic and his use of the stage to delineate this view in graphic portrayals was an important part of his strategy to bring his message to grassroot Jamaicans.[1]

Garvey's life has since inspired several plays, most notably Edgar White's *I, Marcus Garvey.* And, as the black nationalist movement gained ground in the thirties, other writers followed Garvey into the theatre with plays extolling black heroes. Most prominent among these playwrights were C.L.R. James of Trinidad, and Norman Cameron of British Guiana. All three – Garvey, James and Cameron – underwent the disconcerting experience of life as a young black man in 'the mother country', England, in the early twentieth century. For Cameron, especially, the experience was seminal in the shaping of his philosophy and his life's work.

Cameron was the Guiana Scholarship winner of his year, an exceptional student who read mathematics at Cambridge University. Joycelynne Loncke, in an article titled after one of Cameron's major works, *The Price of Victory*, writes,

> the young men coming from the colonies tended to become more conscious of their colonial status, once they left their country's shores and found themselves uneasily installed in the midst of a European civilisation which they had been taught to consider their own. . . . In fact, if only by coming into contact with the often unconscious prejudice that makes itself felt in the metropolitan countries, these pioneer students were abruptly made aware of what it really meant to be a colonial subject, to be a black man coming from a subject people. In the face of this traumatic experience, the reaction of the black student was too often extreme. Cameron is one of those who was able to come out of this experience without bitterness, though he remained convinced that it was absolutely necessary to work at rehabilitating the history and philosophy of Africa, and re-instating the black man's heritage.[2]

In discussing this period of the writer's life, the Guyanese critic Gordon Rohlehr, in his essay *Articulating a Caribbean Aesthetic*, describes Cameron's 'vocation to teach in Liberia', which 'impelled him to find out all he could about that country. This awakened in him an appetite to know more about Africa itself, particularly in the pre-European period: he read all the collected works of all the early travellers. He augmented these with French translations of Arab and Moorish documents. He developed a keen interest in African art and sculpture . . . in oral traditions such as the drum and elephant horn orchestras; the praise songs and use of poetry for the recording of oral history'.[3]

Cameron returned to British Guiana in 1926 and immediately founded a private high school in Georgetown. He began writing that same year, first his long treatise *The Evolution of the Negro*, and then *Balthasar*, the earliest of his didactic epic plays honouring noble black heroes in African history. The pioneering playwright used as his model the classical grandeur of ancient Greek drama. To begin with, his themes were those of colonialism and its problems, the fight for independence, the search for a cultural identity. Later, with independence within reach, his themes became less universal, more parochial.

Balthasar was staged in 1931. Based on a version by French novelist Anatole France, it tells the story of the third Wise Man at the time of the birth of Christ. Walter Mac A. Lawrence, reviewing this play in the *New Daily Chronicle*, hailed it as the beginning of a new phase in local drama. In 1943 Cameron staged his next major play, *Adoniya*, in which he tackles colour prejudice through the story of the Ethiopian wife of Moses. *Sabaco* (1947) deals with the Nubian conquest in Egypt. *Ebedmelech* (1952) again treats colour prejudice, this time through the medium of Paradise. *Kayssa* (1959) is set in Africa before Christianity, at the time when Islam was beginning to spread south of the Sahara. *The Price of Victory* (1965) was inspired by a Yoruba legend, in which the conflict is between old and young, wisdom and progress.

This latter work, divided into two movements that span a decade, is perhaps Cameron's most ambitious in form. It incorporates a blend of dialogue, folksongs, proverbs, mime, drums, flute and dance. Rather than any traditional fixed construction, Loncke suggests, *The Price of Victory* has its own profound and essentially African unity, arising from 'a rhythmic progression based on a motif which is elaborated and developed, or syncopated, turned inside out, or repeated afresh, so that it seems to describe a circle that is fluid but always dynamic'.

For all his innovativeness, intellectual ability, high purpose and considerable output, Norman Cameron is not one of the region's more esteemed playwrights. The Nigerian writer Kole Omotoso is not the only theatre critic to point out a number of inaccuracies and distortions, beyond creative licence, in the playwright's use of African and other historical material. Cameron has also been criticised for some tedious overwriting, and for being out of touch with reality – though his *Jamaica Joe* (1946), for example, is an acceptably realistic tale of black relationships during the Second World War. Cameron himself has commented simply that in his time it was necessary to build up a literary heritage. If plays such as his had already existed, instead of the stereotypes of the day, 'I may never have written those plays'.[4]

Of sounder calibre and enduring relevance is the single play by C.L.R. James, *The Black Jacobins.* This epic is based on the Haitian Revolution, which James had researched for his historical study of the same title. The play had its première performance in London in 1936, under its original title *Toussaint L'Ouverture.* The famous American singer-actor Paul Robeson created the title role. Ivor Brown, in the *Observer*, wrote:

> Mr James' play is a careful prose record of Toussaint's tremendous struggle against the remorseless toughness of the European exploiters and the weakness and flightiness of his own hard-driven people. The pulse of righteous indignation beats

> strongly and sometimes the narrative needs trimming and tightening. The play, however, manages to be continuously interesting because Toussaint himself is interesting. Probably poetry would better have honoured the great and magnanimous figure of ebony which Mr Paul Robeson presented like some tremendous tree defying hurricanes and finally overwhelmed by the small, mean blade of French dishonesty.

The play was not to be seen in its author's homeland until 1979, nearly half a century after its initial staging. By then it had been revised and retitled for staging in Nigeria in 1967. At that time Nigeria, like the Haiti of *The Black Jacobins*, was ravaged by civil war. James's play had a remarkable impact on Nigerian audiences, who were moved by the strong parallels between their own situation and that on stage where, as Hill describes it, they saw 'black leaders struggling for their country's freedom from foreign control and then plunging it into further bloodshed through their lust for power'.[5]

In their homage to specifically black achievement, these plays of Garvey, Cameron and James, and the subsequent work of Roger Mais, with his *George William Gordon*, were, in respect of content, the forerunners of all later plays written from the perspective of black consciousness, whether of political, social, or religious thrust, whether of Black Power or black poverty, of Baptist or Rastafari. More broadly, they can be seen as forerunners of plays of multiracial Caribbean nationalism, plays which would not have been possible until the black man was accorded his rightful place on the Caribbean stage. However, unlike these early works, the later plays are for the most part written in a realistic mode.

Mais, a major novelist and poet as well as one of the most prolific and engaged of all West Indian playwrights, wrote both realistic plays and plays in a more classical form. Both *Atalanta at Calydon* and *Apollo in Delos*, according to Dr Adrianne Baytop, 'include the dramatic element of the Chorus from the Greek tradition and reflect the fatalistic vision of Aeschylus's *Eumenides*'.[6] Regrettably, apart from *Atalanta* and his box office hit *Hurricane*, a social drama in a plantation setting, comparatively little of Mais's *oeuvre* has ever been performed, not even, apparently, his epic chronicle of the martyrdom of the mulatto Gordon. This major prizewinning work of his alternates scenes of natural dialogue with verse-speaking by an unseen chorus. In their use of heightened language for their epics, whether verse or prose, Mais, James, Cameron and Garvey were also, like MacDermot, forerunners in the stream of heroic West Indian classical writing that would reach its finest expression in the works of Derek Walcott.

Despite the achievement of *The Black Jacobins*, James apparently wrote no further plays. In 1977, however, his innately theatrical novel *Minty Alley*, adapted by the poet Pearl Eintou Springer, was staged in Trinidad with some success. The milieu, characters and dialogue of James's novel are in stark contrast to those of his play. *Minty Alley*'s heroes are those of survival, its language that of the streets. The novel was a forerunner of the yard plays discussed in the next chapter.

It was in the mould of *Minty Alley*, rather than in that of *The Black Jacobins*, that another ardent black nationalist playwright of the thirties, Jamaica's Una

Marson, saw the future of West Indian theatre. Marson was a pioneering woman writer who, like James, Garvey and Cameron, suffered the intense disillusionment of the black colonial during her first sojourn in England, in the early thirties. A remarkable achiever all through her life, Marson founded *The Cosmopolitan* journal in 1928, when she was only twenty-three. She was a consistent proponent of a Jamaican national theatre, which she saw as a theatre of social realism, based on the lives of the Jamaican people. Her first play was a one-act Jamaican comedy, *At What a Price*, which she co-wrote with Horace Vaz. It had its première in London in 1933, with Marson in a leading role, to such enthusiastic reviews that it was booked for a further run. On her return to Jamaica in 1936, Marson staged her second play, *London Calling*, a full length serious drama. Her most important play, a milestone in Jamaica's theatrical history, was the 1938 *Pocomania*. Pocomania is a Jamaican cult religion derived principally from African sources. An exploration of how this socially unaccepted form of worship affected an ordinary middle-class family, Marson's was the first play to bring pocomania onto the conventional stage. *Pocomania* is also notable as one of the early experiments in incorporating both folk songs and folk dances into a West Indian drama.

Long before Springer's *Minty Alley* adaptation, Jamaica saw several popular dramatisations of West Indian novels. Ernest Cupidon adapted and staged two well-loved stories by Herbert G. De Lisser. *Susan Proudleigh* had its première in 1930, and was frequently revived. *Jane's Career* followed in 1933. Cupidon was the Cupes of 'Abe and Cupes', a comedy team whose popularity was rivalled only by the longer-running 'Bim and Bam', who worked in the black-face tradition. In Cupidon's hands, these De Lisser adaptations were little more than light entertainment. However, as recorded by playwright-journalist Archie Lindo, they unintentionally served a finer purpose, for they were among the earliest instances of plays that featured a black heroine:

> . . . a sort of shade, or 'class' bar in theatre in those days . . . was broken down with the dramatization by Ernest Cupidon and his Group of De Lisser's *Jane* and *Susan Proudleigh*. From there on there was no bar, and the stage was open to all.[7]

Lindo himself translated another De Lisser novel to the stage with such success that *The White Witch of Rosehall* (1945) ran for more than twenty performances, breaking all previous records for a straight drama. The play's popularity, says Hill, 'was due not only to melodrama but also to the fact that, like James's L'Ouverture play, it showed black slaves taking hold of their destiny and striking a fatal blow for freedom and justice.'[8]

The nationalist writers creating their black heroes were by no means the only playwrights of the period. Apart from this pioneering writing in classical theatre, the second quarter of the twentieth century saw exploratory work in what were to become three other major streams of West Indian theatre form – social realism, popular drama, and total theatre.

Among Jamaica's early writers in social realism, in addition to Una Marson, were Frank Hill, whose *Upheaval* (1939) dealt with Jamaica's labour riots of the previous year; Canadian-born Cicely Waite-Smith, whose first play, *Grandfather is Dying*, was published in 1943 and who went on to make a significant contribution to Jamaican theatre; and W.G. Ogilvie, whose *One Soja Man* was produced by the People's Theatre in 1945. Marson and Waite-Smith were prominent among the region's comparatively few female playwrights; others of the time were Trinidad's Kate Bourne, and the British Guianese propagandist Esme Cendrecourt. In Trinidad, the principal playwright attempting work of social realism was DeWilton Rogers, a schoolmaster who taught Errol Hill. Rogers wrote several plays highlighting issues that affected the lives of the disadvantaged. None of his work has survived, but records of his productions show *Blue Blood and Black* (1936), *Trikidad* (1937), and *Silk Cotton Grove* (1942). The latter dealt with the uprooting of families to make way for United States wartime bases.

Most of the successful writers of the popular theatre of the time were themselves comedians, such as Sam Chase, who succeeded Martins in British Guiana. Chase wrote broad vernacular comedies and satires on topical events, such as *The Mare and the Bonds*, which was based on an injudicious proposal by a Georgetown mayor. Chase habitually hired cinemas for the staging of his low-budget productions. Trinidad's leading playwright of the genre was the head-master of the Nelson Street R.C. Boys' School. Sometimes known as 'Obeah' Roberts, after one of his plays, Arthur Roberts wrote a number of full-length topical farces. Few of his scripts are known to have survived. Among the titles on record, as well as *Obeah*, are *Divorce*, *Fidelity*, *Is It I?*, *Romance Without Sanitation*, *That Hospital*, *Two Sides of the Picture*, and *War Gossip*. Roberts, like Chase, used to stage his plays at a cinema. His earliest female roles were played by schoolboys, but eventually Roberts was able to form a theatre group that included women among its members. The Nelsonians comprised teachers and graduates from the Boys' School, along with their friends and relatives. As in most popular theatre, Roberts used the vernacular, and stock characters such as the society matron, the gossiping neighbour and the ignorant or stuttering maid. Another popular writer in south Trinidad was Philip Gaines, whose *Mother-in-Law* and *Two Husbands* were both performed in 1945.

Trinidad was also active in musical theatre, though the musical comedies of Errol Cherrie, such as *Chamber in the Moon* (1944), and of Ralph Cherrie, such as *Music and Memories* (1944), seem to have been based on the standard Broadway product. One musical, William Archibald's *Carib Song, a musical play of the West Indies*, was actually staged in New York in 1945, but had only a short run.

One of the pioneers of West Indian musical theatre was Dominica's leading folklorist, Mabel Caudeiron. In the thirties Caudeiron arranged patois performances at Government House and on the cocktail party circuit, gaining social recognition for the intrinsic artistic value of Dominica's folklore and songs and dances. She founded the Kairi Artistic Group, for which she wrote plays and what she called 'calypsoperettas', or creole musicals, including *How Johnny Break de Spell* and *Vernie*. She also researched and staged traditional Carnival masques such as the satirical 'Pappyshow' weddings.

In Jamaica, Louise Bennett was gaining acceptance for the vernacular through her dialect performances, and the first Jamaican pantomime, *Soliday and the Wicked Bird*, written by Vera Bell, was performed in 1943. However, the musical work that made the most lasting impression was an extraordinarily ambitious church pageant, Father Daniel Lord's *Jamaica Triumphant*, which in 1937 became something of a national event. Lord, a Roman Catholic priest from America, in fact wrote only part of the script, the narration. However, he also provided the general historical outline, and the dramatic approach which included juxtaposition of scenes, a technique rarely seen thereafter until Peter Minshall's 1989 *Santimanitay* in Trinidad. The scenes of Lord's pageant were scripted by several Jamaican writers. There is little indication of the overall quality of the writing, but for size, spectacle and sheer grandeur, *Jamaica Triumphant* was not to be surpassed until Derek Walcott's *Drums and Colours* marked the opening of the Federal Parliament in 1958.

With so much focus on West Indian nationalism during this second quarter of the century, most of the ethnic theatres mentioned in the previous chapter eventually ceased activity. However, in 1945 Basil Balgobin established himself as one of the earliest West Indian playwrights of East Indian origin. His political play, *Asra*, was set in India, and had nothing to do with the West Indies. The play was staged by the British Guiana Dramatic Society, an organisation with an exclusively East Indian membership. This society was remarkably active during the thirties and forties, and even issued its own magazine.

Errol Hill

The last of the great West Indian theatre pioneers active in the first half of the twentieth century, and the one whose continuing influence is still felt throughout the Caribbean today, is Errol Gaston Hill. As a creative artist Hill is a fine actor and director, and a playwright whose works continue to be produced with exceptional frequency, particularly in the region's secondary schools drama festivals. His place in West Indian theatre is uniquely assured through his academic contribution as archivist, commentator and theorist, in particular his promotion of Carnival theatre. Hill gave West Indian theatre recognition, and he gave it form.

Born in Trinidad in 1921, Errol Hill does not remember a time when he was not involved in theatre. As a boy he performed with the Methodist church (Michael Gilkes and the Walcott twins were also raised in the strict discipline of the Methodists), with his Sunday school and with the Boy Scouts. He was still a teenager when he became clerk to the Education Commissioner for the Eastern Caribbean, a job that entailed travelling up and down the West Indies from British Guiana to St Kitts. Hill's introduction to these other territories opened the young artist's eyes to the existence of a common regional community. It was not until several years later, though, that he began to discern the existence of a common regional culture. His earliest perceptions of this pan-Caribbean culture developed while he was the member of the Trinidad and Tobago Youth Council responsible for assisting with the nurture of the steelband, the island's newborn cultural phenomenon. At the time, Hill took the opportunity to learn to play pan. It was an experience that he was to distil into his one-act play, *The Ping Pong* (1950).

It was a time when, across the region, starting with the inauguration of the Little Theatre Movement in Jamaica in 1941, new theatre companies were being formed that were to have a profound effect on the development of West Indian theatre. One such company in Trinidad was the Whitehall Players, which Hill founded in 1946 with, among others, his sisters Jean and Lydia, the poet Cecil Herbert, and future playwrights Osbourne Ashby and Errol John.

To begin with, the Whitehall Players trod the time-honoured colonial path, trained under two professional actresses, and presented the traditional fare of English comedies and melodramas. It was box-office fare, but the nationalist movement was well under way. The pioneering company of young black artists committed to excellence in theatre came under relentless pressure from nationalist writers such as Albert Gomes and Alfred Mendes. They should, the critics told the Whitehall Players, be staging indigenous plays. The Whitehall Players agreed. But where were the indigenous plays of a quality suitable for staging? They decided to write their own. John, the leading actor in the group, turned playwright with the one-act *How Then Tomorrow* (1947). Hill wrote *Brittle and the City Fathers* (1947), later to be published as *Oily Portraits*. Based on a true story told Hill by his brother, who had been a painter working on restoring portraits for the Council chamber, his first one-act play was a comedy of City Council graft, with a counterpoint bewailing Trinidad's lack of respect for the native artist.

In 1947 the two new plays were staged in a triple bill with scenes from Shakespeare. The critics were ecstatic: 'I'll stake my pygmy reputation that this evening will be remembered forever,' wrote Mendes.[9] Such untempered ecstasy was ahead of its time. Though written by a West Indian, there was little about Hill's deftly structured first play to identify it as West Indian, not even the idiom. The dialogue is mostly in standard English, the style is straightforwardly British, and plot, characters and setting could as well have been found in Bournemouth or Bombay.

Two years later Hill staged his second one-act play, *Square Peg* (1949), a melodrama that dealt in more depth with the plight of the unrecognised artist. For the brief appearance of the young racketeer Spades, Hill made a tentative, not altogether convincing essay at the vernacular, and also sprinkled a few idiomatic expressions through the dialogue of the forthright Merle, but for the rest the script is business as Britishly usual. The contrast with his third play is all the more striking. In *The Ping Pong* Hill, drawing upon the immediacy of his experiences with the steelband, achieves a brisk creole dialogue that is electrifyingly authentic, graphic and witty. The first of Hill's plays to have an unmistakably West Indian setting and plot, *The Ping Pong* can also be counted one of the earliest of the yard plays, a forerunner of the movement of the fifties.

The tightly crafted comedy is set in a backyard bamboo 'tent', the home of the Canary Steelband. An hour before an important competition, the captain's irreplaceable pan is stolen. The audience sees the theft, and the suspense that is skilfully developed from the outset of the play relies not on who did it, but on his motivation, on whether the pan will be rescued undamaged, whether the culprit will be discovered and the framed man cleared, whether the band will play in the competition, whether the Canaries will beat their rivals. The plot is one of personal as well as tribal rivalry, and the denouement, though well signalled in advance, still achieves surprise.

Totoy: Boy, you coucou burn.
Midge: You mean to say I . . . Olga making . . . But why de ooman ent tell me so sheself?
Totoy: Because you too damn louse. You bad talk she all over town, you say you done wid she. You buse everybody who bring message from she. She send Jigger tonight and what you do? You frame him.
Midge: But I didn't know . . . I in thing . . . Olga! Well I never hear dat!
Totoy: You ent know what you in for. Is chips, plenty chips. Every small cent you could rake up. Dat is why I didn't want Butts pick your pocket. You have anything save up?
(*Midge shakes his head.*)
Boy, you better beat pan tonight like you crazy if you want a piece in de prize money.

Half a century later, mature audiences may perhaps query whether the suspicion-riddled Midge would so readily have accepted the news of his paternity. Still, with the passage of time pan itself has undergone many sea-changes, and today *The Ping Pong*, while still the most popular of Hill's plays for performance by schools, has developed the patina of a period piece.

The Ping Pong did not reach the stage until 1953. Its première production was as a radio play for the BBC in 1950. At the time Hill was in London on a two-year British Council scholarship at the Royal Academy of Dramatic Art, from where he graduated with distinction in 1951.

Before he left London, Hill staged a production that he counts as the major achievement of his early years in theatre, and one that considerably influenced his thinking about pan-Caribbean culture. The play was Derek Walcott's Haitian tragedy *Henri Christophe*. Hill first directed a radio version in 1951 for the BBC, where he was working as announcer and actor. He played the title role himself. Then in 1952 he redirected the piece for staging at the Hans Crescent West Indian Students Centre, with Errol John in the title role. Fortuitously, virtually every territory in the Caribbean was represented in that production, along with black South Africa. The cast included even a future Prime Minister of Trinidad and Tobago, Arthur Robinson. The reviews were among the best the play was ever to receive.

Hill returned to the Caribbean in 1952 and settled in Jamaica, running summer drama schools, publishing his early thoughts on *The West Indian Artist* and *The Case for a National Theatre*. In 1953 he joined the Extra-Mural Department of the University College as its Drama Officer. As Noel Vaz writes in the *ACTA News* of January 1990, it is extraordinary how little recognition has been accorded the role played by Jamaica's Extra-Mural Department, and the other such departments throughout the region, in promoting West Indian arts generally, and in particular drama, especially during the third quarter of the twentieth century. Hill was allowed virtually to write his own job description. Seeing the regional theatre's most immediate need as training, he somehow overcame a total absence of budget to become 'a travelling salesman of drama',[10] circling the Caribbean basin to lecture and run workshops. He also assisted in the establishment of several community and other theatres, one of which was Jamaica's Federal Theatre Company, co-founded with Wycliffe Bennett, with Hill as the first president. At the same time, Hill was tackling the dearth of West Indian dramas by collectively creating and producing plays such as the Jamaican political piece *Sleepy Valley* (1952) and the Antiguan comedy *Priscilla's Wedding* (1953).

This groundbreaking emphasis on the West Indian, while satisfying to artists and audiences alike, drew fire from certain quarters, in particular from schoolteachers who feared that the 'subversive' promotion of the vernacular on stage was undermining their students' command of standard English. Oddly, having demonstrated his own command of the vernacular in *The Ping Pong*, and while deliberately employing dialect for his work with the young talent around the region, Hill returned to a blandly standard language for the next plays he wrote, the melodramas *Dilemma* (1953) and *Broken Melody* (1954).

It soon became obvious to Hill that creating new plays was only part of the answer for regional theatre. The scripts still had to be circulated around the Caribbean. He began the personal collection that became the most comprehensive library of West Indian theatre material in existence. In 1954 he raised money from Foyle's Bookshop in London to start publishing, under the imprint of the University College of the West Indies, selected scripts such as *Sleepy Valley*, *The Ping Pong*, and Walcott's *The Sea at Dauphin* (1954) and *Ione* (1957).

As an artist himself, and a man of innate sensibility, Hill has acknowledged a sense of awe in his admiration for the sweep of Walcott's genius. As the developing doyen of the West Indian stage, however, Hill recognised that the classically-inclined young poet was hewing his own solitary path to scale an isolated height. Hill found himself drawn ever more surely towards the belief that the true direction of the indigenous regional theatre lay along the crowded highway over the fertile plains of the folk culture. He was in the early stages of formulating his theory of Carnival theatre.

Two new vernacular plays, written by Hill in 1957, both celebrated pursuits that society then considered disreputable. Trinidad staged the première of the one-act *Wey-Wey*, which is based on the illegal numbers game brought to Trinidad by Chinese immigrants. Jamaica staged the première of the full length *Man Better Man*, based on the stickfighting sport brought to Trinidad from Africa. Stickfighting throughout history has been endemic wherever and whenever peoples have lacked access to more sophisticated weaponry, whether in Africa or India, whether with the quarter-staves of yesterday's England or the bo staffs of today's Japan. In the West Indies, stickfighting is a ritualised event which is formally staged in an enclosed arena known as the 'gayelle'.

Man Better Man is widely considered to be Hill's major work for the stage. This first version was a melodramatic revenge play in prose, without music. In Hill's view, published in a reply to Walcott's criticism of the later version, the Jamaican première was a 'rather inept' production, and the non-Trinidadian audience was 'mystified by the dialect'.[11]

Over the next three years, during which Hill received his first Rockerfeller Foundation Fellowship and attended the Yale School of Drama, he reworked *Man Better Man* according to his developing theory. By now he was envisaging a West Indian theatre form of the nature of total theatre, incorporating music, song and dance, with a strong story line. However, he was not yet seeing the form in terms of Carnival, and the relationship of his experimental musical to Carnival lies principally in the historical relationship between stickfighting itself and the festival. As he wrote and adapted Trinidad folk songs for this new version, Hill came to the conclusion that in rewriting the dialogue 'a verse form was called for to enable a smoother transition from spoken drama to sung drama'.[12] He chose the calypso verse form, as the medium closest to prose dialect, and one with which he was by now wholly familiar. At the same time, learning from the Jamaican experience, he was careful to phrase the Trinidadian idiom in a style that could be more universally understood.

Fig. 1 Errol Hill's *Man Better Man* (PHOTO: Garnet Ifill) In this scene, Tim Briscoe (Devindra Dookie) is crowned the champion of the stickfight. The 1975 production staged in Trinidad by the Drama Guild and Arawaks Dance Group was directed by James Lee Wah, designed by Stephen Davenport and choreographed by Torrance Mohammed.

The revised *Man Better Man* had its première at the Yale School of Drama in 1960. This production led to a Theatre Guild of America Fellowship for Hill. The play was staged in Trinidad in 1965, and later that same year was chosen to represent Trinidad at the Commonwealth Arts Festival in England. In 1969 it was staged by the Negro Ensemble Company in New York, and it has enjoyed numerous subsequent productions in the Caribbean and elsewhere. It was published in a Yale collection in 1964, and in 1985 in a Caribbean collection by Hill.

In its final form, *Man Better Man* appears as an ingenuous musical comedy of love. To win the favour of Petite Belle Lily, Tim Briscoe agrees to fight the stickfighting champion, Tiny Satan. The only way Tim can hope to win is with supernatural help. He has his stick charmed by the wily charlatan of an obeah man, Diable Papa, who then plots to rig the betting on the fight. Briscoe is duly felled, and seems to be at death's door. Portagee Joe fingers Diable Papa as the real culprit. Briscoe's 'spirit' is seen to harass the conspirators into returning their illgotten winnings, and all ends happily.

As examples of the contrasting approaches of Hill and Walcott, it is illuminating to compare *Man Better Man* with *The Charlatan* (1954), both of which plays developed over the same period. There are several parallels between the two pieces. Both are musical comedies. In each case the plot centres on a love story. The key figure in each is a sham obeah man (Hill's black, Walcott's white). Each has Carnival associations and incorporates calypso (also known as kaiso), with a calypsonian as a featured character. Each deals with ritual and charm, in Hill's case the authentic herb of his title, in Walcott's the tongue-in-cheek potion Man-you-must. Both pieces are written in verse, but it is in the language that the difference between the two pieces is most apparent. Walcott's sophisticated and joyous satire uses free verse, leavened with prose and the occasional couplet for specific effect. Verbally, it is a piece of intellectual bravura that, while communicating adequately for enjoyment by an audience, warrants study for full appreciation. Hill's comedy takes his subject more respectfully, and in adhering strictly to the sometimes awkward four-foot calypso line in rhymed couplets, the writer has opted for a simplicity of expression that ensures instant communication, but in effect is on occasion perhaps rather more naive than Hill intended.

Even so, when in 1965 *Man Better Man* came home to its source in Trinidad, the level of hostility it met from the local critics was surprising and, it would seem, unjustified. The good notices the musical received abroad did not entirely redress the balance. To the metropolitan critics unversed in West Indian history, *Man Better Man* was little more than a charming frivolity. Few were perceptive enough to catch the deeper resonances in Hill's message of courage, endurance and self-reliance, the protection of hardwon freedoms, and interracial harmony.

Although Hill's was Trinidad's first full-length calypso musical, it was by no means the first calypso drama. In 1968, Hill published a survey of some twenty short playlets, most of which are on record as having been performed in the calypso tents. The earliest piece of calypso theatre dates back to 1933, when Raymond Quevedo, better known as the celebrated calypsonian Atilla the Hun, played the aggrieved wife in *The Divorce Case*. Many of these calypso dramas were set in the courts of law, where the ritual dictated a simple, static presentation, and a minimum of stage paraphernalia, suited to the limitations of the tent. In addition, the details of the court cases treated in these playlets were already well known to the tent audiences, so that the plot could be sketched with only minimal selected detail, and yet be clearly understood. Most of the dialogue was sung. Spoken dialogue was not in calypso verse, and was often improvised.

Hill's list of calypso dramas ends with the 1965 *Trial of Mano Benjamin*, and little has been recorded since until the nineties, when promoters began to encourage a renewed popularity for the form with pieces such as *The Clarence Thomas Affair*, *The Mike Tyson Trial*, and *Walk With Your Bailor*. Playwright Lennox Brown is on record as believing that Trinidad will eventually develop a unique theatre directly out of the tents, written by the calypsonians rather than by any playwright.[13]

Few playwrights since Hill have used the calypsonian as more than a peripheral character, the major exceptions being Earl Lovelace in *The Dragon Can't Dance* (1986), Mustapha Matura in *Rum an' Coca Cola* (1976), and Derek Walcott in *The Charlatan* and *Steel* (1991). Ronald John's *Masquerade* (1991) is constructed in scenes that are stanzas of a calypso in the process of composition by Talker, a calypsonian who also features in the plot. But these plays employ realistic, not calypso, dialogue. One of the few playwrights to follow Hill's example in calypso couplets is Ralph Maraj, who experimented with the form in his musical *Wake It Up* (1979), and other plays.

Hill returned to Trinidad in 1962, after graduating from Yale with his BA *summa cum laude* and his MFA in Playwriting. He joined the staff of the University of the West Indies as Tutor in the Creative Arts. While he was at St Augustine, he wrote the Dimanche Gras shows of 1963 and 1964. The Dimanche Gras is an annual show which is the traditional culmination of all the national Carnival competitions other than the parades of the costume bands and J'Ouvert old mas bands. The calypso finalists, and the kings and queens of the Carnival bands, are judged during the Dimanche Gras show. Traditionally, items of entertainment in between the competitive events provide a show in the style of a revue. However, Hill saw the possibility of giving the Dimanche Gras show the more unified shape of a drama. His 1963 'carnival scenario', and his 1964 *Whistling Charlie and the monster*, blazed a trail that the Best Village competition was to follow a decade later.

During this period Hill also saw the Trinidad productions of his last two published plays. His popular one-act vernacular comedy, *Strictly Matrimony*, is a Taming of the West Indian Shrew which had premièred in Connecticut in 1960. The one-act fantasy, *Dance Bongo*, had its première in 1965. An unusual work, this last piece by Hill is another early West Indian play to draw on ritual, in this case the Afro-Caribbean death ritual of the bongo. The setting is Cedarpost village, which boasts a long string of champions of bongo dancing. These champions, however, dance for entertainment. They have lost sight of the ritual meaning of the bongo. The current champion is challenged by a stranger who claims to be the best bongo dancer in the land. He dances the bongo as it is traditionally meant to be danced, for the dead. He dances, he tells the villagers, wherever his pulse leads him, and his pulse has led him to Cedarpost. But there is no one dead or dying in Cedarpost. The stranger waits. Sure enough, before the day is out passion and guilt have run riot to the point of murder, and the stranger can begin his dance of death.

Dance Bongo has certain elements in common with earlier plays by Hill, and in particular *The Ping Pong*. Both these plays share the communal bonding of competition against an outside rival. They also share the device, exceptionally effective in the later work, whereby the play's climax is reached and the curtain closed at a point just before the key competitive performance is begun. The language of *Dance Bongo* is a more flexible development of the calypso verse that Hill introduced in *Man Better Man*. With this last play, Hill was moving even closer to his Carnival theatre theory, based on the rituals of the region.

In the summer of 1964, Hill was guest lecturer in creative writing at the University of British Columbia in Canada. The following year he took up a two-year teaching fellowship at the University of Ibadan, in Nigeria. In 1966 he obtained his DFA in Theatre History, at Yale. In 1967 he was appointed associate professor of drama for a year at Richmond College, City University of New York. He lectured at several other universities, including Leeds University in England. Eventually, in 1968, he joined the faculty of Dartmouth College in New Hampshire, USA, where he remained until his retirement in 1989. His courses there included Caribbean Drama and Theatre, Traditional Performing Arts of the Caribbean, History of Western Theatre and Drama, Black African Theatre, Black Drama and Theatre USA, Black Revolutionary Theatre, Repertory Theatre, Playwriting, Acting and Directing. He has written extensively on the theatre, both articles and books, including *Shakespeare in Sable* and *The Jamaican Stage 1655–1900*, and has edited several play collections. He has garnered numerous prestigious awards for his scholarship. He has produced and directed a comprehensive range of plays from the world's repertory.

In 1972 Hill published his milestone thesis, *Trinidad Carnival, mandate for a national theatre*. There was nothing new, he pointed out, in the idea of a national festival giving birth to a national theatre.

> The great Athenian drama grew out of annual Dionysian festivities. The drama of India originated in dances associated with fertility cult ceremonies. The earliest German comedy was a direct product of carnival celebrations. The strolling Italian players drew heavily on the carnival for much of their comedy. In France the grand court ballets of the sixteenth century with recited and sung dialogues had their origin in carnival masquerades inserted in elegant court dances. The basis of all Mexican drama was for a long time the mimetic dances performed at popular fiestas.

The Trinidad Carnival was particularly suited to make the transition to theatre, Hill felt, by virtue of the intrinsically theatrical performance of the mas players, the role played by the calypsonians, the exceptional extent to which the population participates, and the unique national ancestry of the festival. Just as the Christian church had adopted Carnival from an original pagan ritual, so in the first year of their freedom the former slaves of the island had kidnapped Carnival from the church, as a symbol of Emancipation. Hill now saw the unlimited potential of a West Indian theatre form that was not only based in indigenous music and dance, but that could in some measure incorporate, in a manner limited only by the playwright's imagination, some essence of traditional Carnival ritual. The masquerades of the Jab Jab, the Pierrot Grenade, the Dragon, the Midnight Robber, the Dame Lorraine and others, have unique and easily recognisable characteristics, signature tunes, dance steps or speech patterns, which lend themselves to symbolic as well as mimetic representation. In addition, Carnival theatre would include related performing arts such as calypso, steelpan music and the stickfight. By extension, the theory of Carnival theatre encompassed the Jonkunnu of Jamaica, and the various folk festivals of the other islands. At its broadest interpretation, Hill's theory encompassed all theatre based on folk rituals of the West Indies.

Carnival characters had occasionally before been brought onto the conventional stage, purely as spectacle, as in Vivian Comma's skits of the late fifties and early sixties. Experiments in making actual Carnival characters integral to the action of a play began a few years after Hill's thesis was published. Dominica's Alwin Bully, Trinidad's Helen Camps and Felix Edinborough, Jamaica's Samuel Hillary and Sylvia Wynter, have all worked in this field. In addition, several directors have experimented in presenting in Carnival style plays from other cultures, such as Shakespearean works and Genet's *The Blacks*. An exceptional development in Carnival theatre is Felix Cross's 1990 musical *Glory*!

Apart from the precursors of his theory, *Man Better Man* and *Dance Bongo*, Hill himself has never published a play in support of his thesis. As his academic career flourished, the curtain fell on his playwriting.

NOTES

1 Errol Hill, 'The Emergence of a National Drama in the West Indies' *CQ*, Vol. 18, #4, 1972.
2 Jocelynne Loncke, *The Price of Victory*, *Kaie*, 1977, p. 13.
3 Gordon Rohlehr, *My Strangled City and other essays*, Longman Trinidad, 1992.
4 Norman Cameron in conversation with Denis Williams.
5 Errol Hill, *op. cit.*
6 Adrianne Roberts Baytop, 'James Baldwin and Roger Mais' *JJ*, #42, 1978.
7 Quoted by Errol Hill, *op. cit.*, no source given.
8 Errol Hill, *op. cit.*
9 Quoted by Errol Hill, 'The Beginnings of Regional Theatre' Part II, *ACT*, Apr–June 1990, no source given.
10 Quoted in *The New Haven Register*, 5 June 1962, inferred source Errol Hill in press interview.
11 Errol Hill, 'Is "Man Better Man", Mr Walcott' *TG*, 3 February 1965.
12 *Ibid.*
13 Lennox Brown in interview with Judy Stone, *TG*, 18 November 1986.

3

THEATRE OF REALISM

Yard plays and the social conscience: Errol John, Trevor Rhone, Alwin Bully.

An awesome full moon shone down on the filthy, fretted eaves sheltering a cluster of hovels. Gap-toothed louvres hung crookedly in the narrow doors. A clutter of rusty galvanized sheeting and one yellowing coconut lay by the weathered step. Staccato barks punctuated the murmur of Ketch's guitar. The standpipe centre stage gushed real water.

The setting for the Trinidad National Theatre Company's 1988 production of Errol John's *Moon on a Rainbow Shawl*, with its set built by the playwright's son, was as realistic as the stuff of the play itself.

During the second half of the twentieth century, the most prevalent form of theatre created by serious West Indian playwrights, in their commitment to creating on stage a mirror of their own society, was theatre of social realism. Within this genre, following the ground-breaking novels of writers such as C.L.R. James, Claude McKay, Alfred Mendes and Roger Mais, the yard plays of the fifties formed the first coherent West Indian theatre movement.

Yard plays

For the nationalists writing in the period immediately after the Second World War, the centre of the West Indian experience lay with the grass-roots peasantry and the urban proletariat. It was a centre presented as being peopled almost exclusively by descendants of slavery.

The term 'yard play', in its purest sense, refers to a naturalistic drama with the single set of a barrack-yard, where several households, having little more in common than their poverty, struggle in forced intimacy for their day-to-day existence. Certain characters are typical of the yard plays: the earth mother, the prostitute and her American clients, the young bachelor burning with ambition, the older man who has failed and turned to drink, the innocent girl alone on the threshold of the merciless adult world, the inquisitive neighbour, the schoolchildren. There is usually a strong moral sense underlying the yard play, an unspoken outrage at the conditions in which people are forced to live, an admiration for the strength and courage with which, in their different ways, they cope, a compassion for the compromises they have to make. The themes are of self-betterment and escape from the yard, of self-respect and survival with decency, or simply survival.

By extension, the term 'yard play' also gathers under its umbrella plays that examine similar concerns and conflicts in other constrained, low-income communities, such as the panyard of Errol Hill's *The Ping Pong*, the rural village of Eric Roach's *Belle Fanto* (1966), or the slum tenement of Barry Reckord's *Della* (1954). The yard plays are not to be confused with the later experiment of yard theatre, formally undertaken in Jamaica, Trinidad and Barbados, which promoted the staging of West Indian plays in the outdoor performing space of a yard.

Occasional new yard plays continue to appear up to the present day, but as a coherent body of work the yard play movement was comparatively short-lived, being rooted in a particular time, and largely dependent on that time's particular social conditions. There was also, in the exclusive focus on one particular social class and situation, a narrowness that many later writers were to find too limiting. In the fifties, however, the arrival of the yard plays was an exhilarating regional antidote to the artifice of the still popular English drawing-room comedy. The new plays were unmistakably West Indian in every respect, as uncompromising in their natural dialogue as in their honesty, anger, comedy and pathos, and largely crafted by skilled, socially concerned writers who understood their medium better than had their predecessors.

Individual yard plays were written in most of the West Indian territories, by playwrights such as Guyana's Slade Hopkinson, whose *A Spawning of Eels* (1968) was later retitled *Sala*, and Jamaica's Samuel Hillary, whose *Departure in the Dark* (1960) is still occasionally staged around the region. The most prolific and one of the finest of the yard playwrights, whose more popular plays, such as *The Rose Slip* (1962), continue to be performed with some frequency, was Trinidad's Douglas Archibald. A civil engineer and historian, Archibald is the youngest of three playwriting brothers, the other two being William, who has enjoyed some international success in both stage and film, and Charles, whose work is less well known.

Douglas Archibald's first play, *Junction Village* (1954), won the Readers and Writers Guild prize for Trinidad's best play of 1952. It was to be another two years before the playwright could find a theatre company willing to risk a production of this vernacular comedy. The New Company eventually staged its première performance in 1954, to phenomenal audience response. *Junction Village* was pronounced the most successful local play ever written. J.S. Barker, writing in the *Trinidad Guardian*, criticised the play's construction, but accorded Archibald high praise as 'a genuinely gifted creator of living character'.[1] Archibald went on to write a further fourteen plays, both yard plays and others, including works for radio and television and his major piece *Defeat with Honour* (1952). This historical drama pays tribute to the role of the Spanish Governor Chacon in the bloodless capture of Trinidad by the British. A radio version was broadcast in 1952.

In 1971 Hill wrote:

> Archibald writes with insight, grace and understanding. He sees dramatic action in terms of character rather than plot and, like Chekhov, he has the knack of making apparently incidental actions significant.[2]

Archibald's plays have been performed throughout the Caribbean and in Great Britain. Only one yard play has received wider recognition than any of his, and that also came out of Trinidad.

Errol John

The sensitivity and compassion of Errol John made him both a fine interpretive actor and a playwright of illuminating perception. As an actor, he was born a generation too soon to find due recognition on the international stage. As the writer of numerous scripts for stage and screen, his place in the world's literary canon is assured by a single work, and that one of his earliest – the classic, prototypical yard play, *Moon on a Rainbow Shawl.*

John was born in Trinidad in 1924, and raised in the middle-class Woodbrook district of Port of Spain. His mother was from Barbados and his father from St Vincent. His elder brother George became a widely-respected regional journalist. The future playwright also, in his early twenties, earned his living as a journalist, and as a commercial artist. George John senior, the boys' father, was the West Indies' 'knight errant of fast bowling', as C.L.R. James refers to him in *Beyond a Boundary*, 'the greatest of them all', on whose memories the son was to draw for the character Charlie Adams, in his greatest play of all.

Errol John joined the Trinidad theatre as an actor. One of the first accounts of his appearance on stage is from the early forties, when he played in the cast of an Arthur Roberts revival, *Two Sides of the Picture*, a role no one else would

Fig. 2 Errol John's *Moon on a Rainbow Shawl* (PHOTO: Ed Rodway) A scene from the production staged in Guyana in 1963 by the Theatre Guild.

touch – that of an evil rent collector with St Vitus's dance.[3] One can only speculate on the influence of this character when John was shaping his own later creation of Old Mack, the landlord of *Moon on a Rainbow Shawl*. As the leading actor of the Whitehall Players, and of the later splinter group, the Company of Five, John, who also directed and designed, was acclaimed for his performances of many major roles in international works. It came as a setback, which gradually embittered him, that, with the one obvious exception of Othello, which he played at the Old Vic in 1962, in both England and the United States he was offered only subsidiary roles in film and on stage, because of his colour. In later years he refused several roles that he considered demeaning to his race. He acquired a reputation for what one of his more sympathetic obituaries described as his 'excessively unaccommodating nature'.[4] He was a man of implacable principle, for which he often suffered.

John began to write for the stage before he left Trinidad. His first work was a one-act fantasy titled *The Gateway*, which he revised as *How Then Tomorrow* for its première in 1947. Two years later came the première of *The Tout* (1949), a one-act tragedy which continues to be performed. It was published in 1966 in the UWI series of Caribbean plays, and televised in Barbados in 1972. John eventually expanded it into the screenplay *The Dispossessed*, which was published but never filmed. Even more than Derek Walcott, John continually retitled his works as he developed them.

The stage version of *The Tout* is set in a slum area of Port of Spain. The massive Muley, a one-time dock worker now paralysed from the waist down, is cared for by his retarded granddaughter, Annie. His nephew Purcy, who has already stolen Annie's savings, begs Muley for money for his passage from the island. Muley refuses. Before he leaves, Purcy becomes violent, and threatens the old man. Subsequently it transpires that Purcy has been involved in a murder, and is on the run. Annie loves Purcy, and lies to the police to protect him. Purcy returns with a seaman. Muley is powerless to save Annie from the ensuing violation, but as the tout counts his thirty pieces of silver, the cripple is miraculously galvanised to movement, and stabs Purcy to death with a kitchen knife.

John broke new ground with the dialogue of *The Tout*. In even the most realistic of West Indian plays up to that time, the dialogue betrayed evidence of the playwright's hand. John wrote lines that rang so spontaneously, there was about them a cinematic quality of realism. Clean, natural and idiomatic without obscurity, the language drives the play with exceptional economy.

Muley: What is that noise?
Purcy: What noise? (*sound of more struggling*)
Muley: Where that noise coming from, Purcy?
Purcy: I ain't hear nothing I tell you. (*rising and pacing*) Must be a cat.
Muley: 'Taint no cat. What happening, Purcy?
Purcy: Nothing.
Muley: Where Annie?
Purcy: She still in the back.

Muley: What she doing in the back so long? Purcy, what happening?
Purcy: Nothing I tell you.
Muley: What happening to Annie? (*calling*) Annie! Annie! Why she don't answer. (*looking around*) It got other people in this house – I could feel it.

John left for England in 1951, with the intention of pursuing a technical course in the study of theatre. Instead, he found himself employed, *sine* salary, as student stage manager at Bolton's Theatre, Kensington.

His first role in the metropolis was one line in a 1952 BBC radio production of *The Emperor Jones.* By 1953 he was touring with the American Negro Company as Lester in *Anna Lucasta.* Over the next few years he played in London productions of Prescott's *Local Colour*, Sartre's *The Respectable Prostitute*, Wilde's *Salome*, Julien Green's *South*, and McCullers's *Member of the Wedding*, for which he received high praise. In 1955 he played a Jamaican immigrant in the BBC television dramatised documentary, *Man From the Sun.*

But he was already chafing at the dearth of challenging roles, or any roles, for black actors. Both to protest that dearth, and to do something towards repairing it, John wrote *Moon on a Rainbow Shawl.* He titled his first full length work in tribute to Eugene O'Neill's *Moon for the Misbegotten*, a play that he greatly admired. Two years after he wrote it, the passionate, anguished slice of life in a West Indian barrack-yard won him not only the 1957 *Observer* playwriting award, from a field of some 2,000 entries, but two Guggenheim Fellowships, a West End première, productions around the world in several languages, numerous printings, adoption as a text for the Caribbean CXC examinations, and probably more revivals, according to Professor Neil Watson, 'than any other play from its period, the heyday of the so-called New Drama initiated by Osborne's *Look Back in Anger*'.[5]

John's *Moon* is set in the period immediately after the Second World War. The pivotal character is Sophie Adams, the archetypal West Indian earth mother, who lives in one of the rundown yard dwellings with her husband Charlie, daughter Esther and the baby. It is Sophie's ambition to find a decent place to live so the family can leave the yard. But Charlie has no regular work, and the little income that Sophie makes handwashing laundry is not enough even to buy the uniform Esther must have, if she is to take up the scholarship she has won to high school. Willingly and unwillingly, Sophie is privy to the intimate lives of the other yard dwellers: of the girl Rosa, who loves Ephraim and is pursued by the elderly landlord Old Mack; of the brawling prostitute Mavis, who loves a good time but longs for a ring on her finger. It is a yard of unbearable poverty made bearable by dreams. But even Rosa, pregnant with his child, is unaware that Ephraim is about to make his dream come true, on a boat to Liverpool. Ephraim's obsession with leaving the island creates much of the tension in the play. That tension is heightened when Sophie's dream turns to nightmare, as Charlie is arrested for stealing the money he cannot earn for his daughter's needs.

It is a powerful, dynamic, swiftly moving play, its complexities woven with deceptive simplicity from bitterness and laughter, violence and pathos, ribaldry and tenderness. It offers several of the finest flesh and blood roles written for West Indian actors and actresses. Doris Lessing in *The Observer* compared John's lyrical use of language with that of Sean O'Casey. Kenneth Tynan likened the atmosphere of the play to that of certain Italian films. It was *The New York Times* that measured the pulse of the play, with the comment that John had written 'with such warmth and understanding that the problems and characters of a mean backyard in Trinidad assume a validity for a multitude of teeming, troubled places on this planet'.

The first production of *Moon on a Rainbow Shawl* was a 1958 adaptation, titled *Small Island Moon*, on BBC Radio World Theatre. The following year the world première of the full play was staged at the Royal Court Theatre in London. John was so disappointed in this production that he refused all further offers of British productions until he was allowed to direct the play himself. In 1986 this finally happened, at London's Theatre Royal, and a further London production followed shortly afterwards.

In the meantime, John had revised the original text for a 1962 off-Broadway production. This was the text that by the time the playwright died in 1988 was into its eighth printing, and translations of which have been produced on stage, television or radio in Czechoslovakia, Holland, Iceland, Poland, and several Spanish-speaking countries, while in English it continues to be performed around the world. A Bengali adaptation titled *Naamjiban*, meaning 'My Name is Life', was so popular that it ran in Calcutta continuously for seven years, from 1978 to 1985. It was not until three years after the playwright's death that the adaptor, film idol Soumitra Chatterjee, acknowledged his debt to Errol John (*The Statesman*, October, 1991).

Derek Walcott's Theatre Workshop staged the play's debut production in its homeland in 1968, since when Trinidad has seen on average one production every three or four years. John himself staged a production at the Port of Spain City (then Town) Hall in 1973, for which he was producer, director and lead actor in the role of Ephraim. In 1982 a New York theatre took out an option to adapt John's play to a musical, but no production was realised. Soon afterwards in Dominica, however, a musical version of the play was staged with lyrics and score by playwright Alwin Bully.

In 1960 *Moon* was screened in an ATV London Network adaptation. Thereafter John developed a full length film screenplay which he continued for the rest of his life to polish and update, under several titles, including *They say that Carnaval is a Creole Bacchanal*, and *Caliban*. The screenplay incorporated steelband music and scenes of Carnival, and underpinned the plot with the New World symbolism in a Carnival band featuring Caliban in chains. But the central characters and story remained the same, except that Ephraim, who on stage is a driver of the now long defunct Port of Spain trolley buses, changed his vehicle to a garbage truck.

Production companies and potential investors often showed interest in making the film of *Moon*, until they realised to what extent John insisted on retaining artistic control. In 1973 an independent production team from America filmed the Trinidad Carnival for inclusion in the movie, but the anticipated financial backing did not materialise, and the project fell through. There is still a major West Indian film to be made.

Meanwhile John continued acting when he could get acceptable roles, and writing when he was not acting. He played in such films as *The Nun's Story*, *The Sins of Rachel Cade*, *PT 109*, *Man in the Middle*, *Guns at Batasi*, *Assault on a Queen*, *Odongo*, *The Games* and *Buck and the Preacher*, several of which entailed extensive travelling, to Africa and elsewhere. In 1962 he joined the Old Vic for a season, appearing in *The Merchant of Venice*, *Measure for Measure*, and as Othello, in a performance that was perhaps too introspective, and not widely admired.

In 1963 Faber and Faber took the then unusual step of publishing a collection of John's unmade screenplays, *Force Majeure*, *The Dispossessed* and *Hasta Luego*. *Force Majeure* pits a relatively naive black writer from America against his wheeling and dealing Jewish agent in London. *The Dispossessed* is based on *The Tout*. *Hasta Luego* is a poignant incident of passion and a thief's honour in a Mexican village. Also in 1963 the BBC aired John's television play *The Dawn*, followed in 1968 by *The Exiles*. The latter play, begun nearly ten years earlier, neatly expresses the playwright's own dilemma, in the dialogue of three highly literate and articulate Trinidadians lamenting the circumstances that force them to live in London for professional work which is not available in Trinidad. In 1969 the ATV London Network screened *The Insider*, but after discovering the alterations in the production text, John requested the removal of his name from the credits.

In the early seventies John sojourned for a period in Mexico, 'stockpiling writing I had to do'.[6] He continued to develop the screenplay *Force Majeure* years after its publication, and worked on numerous scripts for television and film, including the treatment and first draft screenplay of Truman Capote's *House of Flowers*. Most of these pieces were never produced. One of his last plays to be staged, based on the screenplay *Hasta Luego* and also set in Mexico on Death's Day, was *Easter! – And I'll Come for You*, which received some critical acclaim. He never, however, repeated the achievement of *Moon on a Rainbow Shawl*.

The influence of John's *Moon* can readily be seen in later yard plays as varied as *Nigger Yard* (1980) by Barbadian Anthony Hinkson, *A New Beginning* (1988) by Francis Urias Peters of Grenada, Winsome Pinnock's *A Hero's Welcome* (1986), and also in *The Dragon Can't Dance*, a yard musical adapted by Earl Lovelace from his own major novel.

Theatre of social realism

By the seventies, the face of West Indian poverty had changed, and already the yard plays seemed dated. Because of the basic simplicity of their concerns relative to the increasing complexity of the world, these plays were now often seen as sentimental. With the technological advances in communications and travel, the new West Indian writers too were changing. They were becoming more cosmopolitan in their experience and therefore in their outlook. Gradually, more and more playwrights began to pull back from the close-up portrait of a single segment of West Indian society, in order to focus on the society as a whole. Some of the new playwrights treated formerly unknown or socially unmentionable concerns that increasingly affect every level of the society, such as AIDS, drug abuse, domestic violence and urban crime. Two notable plays of this nature are the Trinidadian Dwight Arthur's sensitive and wryly funny *Behind Closed Doors* (1987) on incest, and the Jamaican Ginger Knight's exceptionally powerful piece of ghetto theatre, *Whiplash* (1984).

Prominent among the other better, and better known, regional playwrights who have worked during the later twentieth century in the field of social realism outside the yard movement are Antigua's Dorbrene O'Marde; the Bahamian Winston Saunders; Barbados's Glenville Lovell; Dominica's Alwin Bully; Guyana's Churumanie Bissundyal; Jamaica's Pat Cumper, Basil Dawkins, Trevor Rhone and Carmen Tipling; St Lucia's Stanley French; Montserrat's David Edgecombe; St Thomas's Rudolph Wallace; and Trinidad's Ronald Amoroso and Raoul Pantin.

By and large, West Indian plays of social realism continue to adhere to the traditional structure and values of modern Western theatre. The regional character of these plays depends primarily on the idiom of the dialogue, and secondarily on setting and circumstances.

Realism in other media

Many of the realist playwrights also create original works for radio, film and television, though the returns from the Caribbean markets are minimal. There is at least one successful screenplay writer, Horace Wilson of Tobago, who has never written for the stage. Wilson's greatest strengths are his natural dialogue and credible characterisation. Among his most popular works are the groundbreaking television soap operas *Turn of the Tide* (1982) and *No Boundaries* (1988–1991). The former was followed in 1985 by a feature film built around the key characters of the series.

Few of these writers for the electronic media have broken into the international market. Those who have done so are, for the most part, those who no longer reside within the region. Jamaica's Evan Jones is one example. Jones's impressive list of screenplay credits includes *The Damned*, *Escape to Victory*, *Eve*, *Funeral in Berlin*, *Nightwatch*, *Outback* and *Two Gentleman Sharing*. He has also written a number of BBC television plays including *In a Backward Country*, *The Madhouse on Castle Street*, *The Widows of Jaffa* and the 1976 series *The Fight Against Slavery*. It is perhaps revealing that Jones's achievements are largely unrecognised in Jamaica, much as Jan Carew's sizeable body of screenplays for BBC television is virtually unknown in his native country of Guyana.

Trevor Rhone

Of all the home-based West Indian playwrights currently working in the theatre of social realism, the one who has achieved the widest international as well as regional success is Trevor Rhone. Before he was fifty, Rhone was being called the father of Jamaican theatre. In Jamaica, his comedies have enjoyed record runs. Abroad, his plays are performed more frequently, and to greater acclaim, than those of any other Jamaican playwright. His films have won international recognition. He is a rare breed, the serious writer with the common touch. His gift for comedy gives his works mass appeal, and makes palatable, easily digestible, and memorable, his forthright indictments of the racism, bigotry, opportunism, corruption, idleness, and other unlovely traits that make his own Jamaican people, and by extension the human race, less than he believes they might be.

Rhone was born in Kingston in 1940, the twenty-first and last of his father's children by two marriages. He grew up in the village of Bellas Gate, and went to three different primary schools in St Catherine. He was nine when he was taken to his first village concert, where 'you paid a shilling to take off a man and sixpence to put him back up'.[7] The experience had a profound effect on young Rhone, and from then on, though he had never seen a play, he knew he wanted his life's work to be in theatre.

After the 1951 hurricane, the devastation of his own juvenile agricultural effort, a small crop of corn and sugar-cane, inspired him to writing his first dramatic piece, which was read at his school. From 1952 to 1957, during secondary schooling at Beckford and Smith's (now St Jago High School) in Spanish Town, he became intensely involved with the Secondary Schools' Drama Festival. He had a minor role in the Little Theatre Movement's 1956 national pantomime *Busha Bluebeard*, and acted with the Caribbean Thespians. In 1959 he left the Thespians to form the short-lived company of Academy Players. His ambition was to be an actor. But even before he left Jamaica in 1960 for England's Rose Bruford College, he had built on that juvenile effort at writing. Fired by the recent launching of the Jamaica Broadcasting Company, Rhone, as a clerk at the university, spent his weekends at his office typewriter, working on a radio play. He followed up with other plays, none of which achieved production. Eventually, he put his writing aside for the next seven years.

Rhone did well at Rose Bruford, where he took a three-year course in both acting and teaching. Guarding against a system that expected him to conform as the English actor he was not, he was yet quick to acquire the excellent technical skills taught, and the art of 'making do' with very little money. Both acquisitions were to prove invaluable assets in a developing nation. On graduation in 1963 Rhone returned to Jamaica full of hope, only to find himself lost in a cultural desert. Nothing was happening in theatre, and he had to take up a low-paid teaching post. After nine months he fled back to England. But there, like Errol John, he was unhappy with the kind of roles available to him as a black actor.

In 1965 Rhone made the decision to go back to Jamaica and make theatre happen. He and seven other Jamaicans, all of whom were just graduating from British drama schools, pledged to re-establish professional theatre in the island in twelve years, by 1977. Of the seven, only Yvonne Jones stayed with Rhone through the difficult early years. Years later Jones, now Yvonne Brewster, was to become one of the major forces in the promotion of black theatre in England.

Still in 1965, immediately on their return to Jamaica, Jones and Rhone founded the Barn Theatre 77. From the start they presented a varied programme of plays, both Caribbean and international. Little by little, the Barn was converted from the raw space of a garage in a private home to a comfortable, functional intimate theatre with a capacity of 150.

While the Barn was struggling to get on its feet, Rhone went back to teaching to earn his living. Fortuitously, it was the teaching that spurred him to try his hand once again at writing for the stage. He was asked to produce the pantomime for his school, St Andrew Technical, but the students were not enthused by the English scripts available. With the blessing of his headmaster, Rhone took a week off from classes, and wrote his Jamaican *Cinderella* (1966). His first performed work was so successful that for the following two years, till he left the school, he continued to write the annual pantomime.

Rhone began writing in earnest. In 1968, apart from the school pantomime, he had two works produced, the revue *I'm human . . . right?*, and a one-act play, *Yes, Mama*. In 1969, fearing that if he failed to take the plunge before he was thirty he might never find the courage to break out of the conventional pattern of job dependence, he resigned from teaching to write full time.

That year, 1969, Rhone's first full length play, *The Gadget*, won the silver medal in the Jamaica Arts Festival literary competition. Set in the luxury town house of a poor black boy who has made good, the play's essential conflict is between Len Tomlinson and his past. That past becomes his present with the arrival of the privileged schoolmate, George McFarlane, who had tormented Tomlinson as a youth.

Several productions of the play followed around the Caribbean, but Rhone was not satisfied with the work. With hindsight, he saw it as unduly cynical, and 'incomplete in terms of the psyche of the people that we're dealing with'.[8] He eventually rewrote the play in a vein superficially lighter, in a more idiomatic style and language. He introduced flashbacks to expand the time-frame, and rooted the story back in the country village where it all began. He pared down the treatment of its original Black Power element, and of other details superfluous to the primary plot, discarding even the gadget of the title, a telephone answering machine. What he retained was the central theme of the tragedy inherent in a colour caste society. He also retained all the characters except for two, Len's rebellious son Louis, and his friend Arthur. He even kept some of the original dialogue. He developed his characters more fully, but made few changes in their relationships. Rhone called the new version *Old Story Time* (1979), and it became one of his best loved works.

The Gadget was written in standard English, *Old Story Time* largely in the vernacular. Rhone had first experimented with the vernacular in 1967, in the poem *Look Two*, composed from the sounds he grew accustomed to hearing as a commuter, during his daily wait at a bus stop. The poem was well received, but for his plays Rhone had his eye on the international market, where he felt the vernacular would not be acceptable. He continued to write in standard English, winning the 1970 bronze medal for *The Blue Socks Blues*. Eventually he made a decision that, as a Jamaican playwright, he would take what he saw as a risk, the writing of a play that would be truly Jamaican, in language as in content. There followed in 1971 *Smile Orange*, Rhone's first record run (245 performances) and his most productive year as a writer.

Smile Orange has been compared to the work of Molière, a favourite writer of Rhone's, as of several other Caribbean playwrights. The script was initiated by a circular letter from the Jamaican Tourist Board, which asked playwrights to create a radio serial reflecting something to do with tourism. The Board sent Rhone around the tourist hotels of Montego Bay and Ocho Rios to gather material. Later, on an Atlantic crossing, Rhone's chance meeting with a waiter brought the work into focus. The radio serial transmuted into a screenplay, which became the stage play, which was eventually made into a film.

Set in a less than luxurious hotel on the north coast of Jamaica, the stage version of *Smile Orange*, unlike the film, never shows the guests. Yet to the audience the hotel is aswarm within and without with idiosyncratic characters such as the telephone gossip Maisie, the fat little chick making love in the cowitch patch, the one-legged tourist in soul beads who loves to dance with girls in bikinis, the irascible chef, the crab race organiser Bongo Man, and Ringo's Nemesis of a wife with her two brothers, all seen through the eyes of the five members of staff on stage. It is the 'little twis' head cocky' waiter Ringo, one of the first of the modern Anancy figures, who is the engine that powers the action, the raunchy humour, and the satirical revelations. These revelations arise partly from the conniving and cover-ups the audience sees occurring on stage, but

Fig. 3 Trevor Rhone's *Smile Orange* (PHOTO: Stanley Marshall) In this scene Mr O'Keafe (Claude Reid) attempts to exert his authority over Ringo (Wilbert Holder). This Trinidad Theatre Workshop production, directed by Rhone, was staged in 1982.

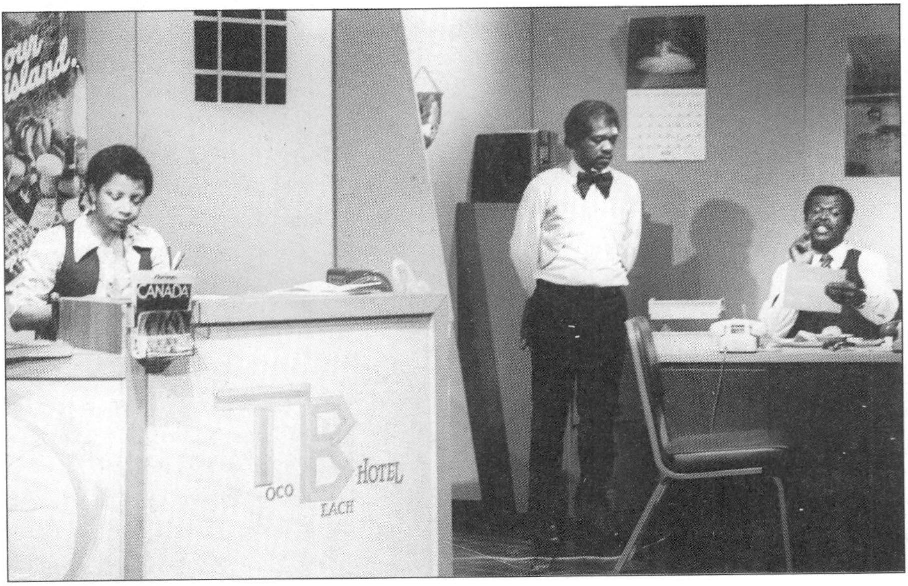

even more from what they hear in the swift, two-edged dialogue. From this aspect, one of the more memorable scenes has Ringo giving his new busboy Cyril, a simple country boy equipped with little more than a lisp and a lust, step-by-step instruction in how to reap the rewards of tourism. The key to success in life, according to Ringo's philosophy, lies with the symbolic emasculation in the play's title, a metaphor taken from a rural belief that a man risks his virility when he eats an orange. The hotel staff grow fat by eating the emasculating orange of their ingratiating smiles.

'Funny and deadly serious', writes Mervyn Morris in his introduction to the play,

> *Smile Orange* is a devastating comment on attitudes the tourist industry harbours or can breed. 'I will touch di ground,' says Joe, 'if I can find a dollar bill down dere.' 'A will go further dan dat,' says Ringo, 'A will bury my head in di san'.' Everything is put into service in pursuit of what the tourist can provide, whether money or a chance to emigrate. 'I not giving away my pearl for nutten,' says Miss Brandon. 'Is all I have. It have to work for me.' Rhone lays bare some of the sordid motivations of tourists and of the smiling workers who seem so willing to please. 'White people must pay dem way . . . Exploit di exploiter.' . . . 'If you is a black man and you can't play a part, you going starve to death.' Play-acting is a recurrent metaphor. The blacks, including Assistant Manager O'Keefe, are playing roles to which they have been assigned by the tourist industry and the realities of power. When the lifeguards have been exposed and a tragedy has occurred, the difficulties for Ringo, Joe and O'Keefe are overcome in new performances – Ringo as selfless hero, with supporting cast. A little help from the press, and they can act themselves out of trouble.

As Morris points out, writing *Smile Orange* in the vernacular was not the risk Rhone had feared. 'The way had been prepared: by – for example – Louise Bennett in her dialect writings and performance, by the LTM pantomime as it evolved, by comedians Bim and Bam in their topical stage shows, by a popular radio serial scripted by Elaine Perkins'.

Smile Orange represented Jamaica in 1972 at Guyana's inaugural Carifesta. Three years later the play was made into a film which won several awards. Rhone by then had learned some hard lessons about film-making. In 1971 he had written most of another award-winning script, that of Perry Henzell's 1972 release *The Harder They Come*. The story is of a country boy who arrives in the city with a dream of becoming a reggae star, only to fall victim to the vicious realities of the system. Henzell's is an urgent, pulsating film, whose compulsive imagery has the authenticity of documentary. Gordon Rohlehr, in his 1973 review titled *Once In A Blue Sun*, describes the work's unusual 'frank social realism and essential seriousness', and argues its importance as 'the first West Indian movie which attempts to look at the West Indian reality, with sensitivity and frankness'.[9] Rhone learned further lessons making the film of his own *Smile Orange*, but learned them too late to avoid his own dissatisfaction with the finished product, despite its rapturous reception at the regional box office.

Later in 1971 Rhone worked 'the fastest I've ever worked', when in one week he wrote his pantomime *Music Boy*, for the annual Little Theatre Movement production. His next two plays, *Comic Strip* (1972) and *Sleeper* (1974), were not among his most successful. But then in 1975 he scored with another hit, *School's Out*, based on his experiences in the teaching profession. Rhone himself created the leading role of Russ Dacres. The play ran for 278 performances, breaking his previous record.

In this unnervingly believable horror story of Jamaica's educational system, which appals even while it deftly convulses the audience with laughter, school is not 'out' in the sense of its being on holiday or after hours. The play is set in term time, but this particular church school is 'out' of all the essentials: materials, morals, manners, discipline, academic standards, an active headmaster, teachers who teach, plumbing that flushes. The audience has only a brief glimpse of one student, but offstage the directionless youngsters are running riot while the teachers largely ignore them from the shelter of the staffroom on stage. As in *Smile Orange*, Rhone presents the whole picture from the one side the public never sees, behind the scenes.

The various members of staff are too generously characterised to be stereotypes, but they are nevertheless universally familiar. Mr Josephs, the senior master and a product of outdated colonial education, is a failure who harps on the old days. Young Hopal Hendry, the ill-educated and incompetent product of the new regime, develops during the play from being the butt of his colleagues' schoolboy jokes to being, frighteningly, the one most likely to succeed in his career. Pat Campbell is an expatriate with a thin skin and pretensions to superiority. Mica MacAdam, the only female teacher, is well-intentioned but fickle. The Chaplain is unabashedly lecherous and idle. Rosco Callendar, who though little more admirable in his behaviour is the most sympathetic of this motley crew, resembles the hero of the Ti-Jean folk cycle in his swift understanding, sense of humour, private morality, and refusal to exert himself unnecessarily.

Into this abysmal collection of misfits sweeps Russ Dacres, an idealistic new broom eager to set the school to rights, but lacking the diplomacy needed to scratch up the dust without choking himself. Interestingly, the zealous teacher's name is an anagram of 'crusadress', a female crusader. But though Dacres may exhibit more than his share of the feminine principle in his active caring for the students in his charge, there is no suggestion of homosexuality. The play follows Russ's brief effort to turn the school into a genuine centre of learning, but the effort is doomed. A malfunctioning staff lavatory dominates both stage and dialogue, and in the end the triumphantly malfunctioning staff, by means of rumour and character assassination, transfer the symbolism of the stench from themselves, the staffroom, their school, and the whole educational system, to the decent and hardworking Russ.

Trinidadian critic Ken Jaikaransingh, sees Rhone's landscape as extending even beyond the school system, to the far reaches of the emerging post-colonial society, much along the lines of the metaphor in Nigerian novelist Femi Osofisan's *Kolera Kolej*, as dramatised by Trinidadian playwright Dexter Lyndersay in 1975.

> It needs little stretch of the imagination to place his (Rhone's) characters into types, and to see the staffroom as an abandoned Third World Nation, presided over, 'in absentia', by an invisible headmaster, represented now by the expatriate transient Patrick Campbell, and by the veteran Mr Josephs, whose regard for reputation and tradition has led him to adopt an alienated, uncommitted stance. The worst aspects of the colonial legacy are embodied in the chaplain, whose lechery, indolence and pettiness are masked by his clerical collar. Hopal Hendry, Rosco Callendar and Russ Dacres are the symbolic post-colonial breed. Hendry is a bastard child of the colonial experience, conspicuously under-qualified to teach, yet earning tenure by ingratiating himself with the Head and acting as house-boy for the rest of the staff. Rosco Callendar cynically rejects the hypocrisies around him, but ironically capitalises on its *(sic)* weaknesses for his own benefit. He is, in a sense, the most culpable of them all, perceptive enough to recognise the waste around him but too selfish for any reaction other than buffoonery. Russ Dacres is the '*arriviste*', full of new ideas, keen to make radical reforms, and undone eventually by his fellows, his own naivete and by the uncompromising zeal of his crusade.[10]

Though most of the staff speak the standard English of the educated Jamaican, Rhone introduces two interesting variations in his use of the vernacular. In the case of Hopal it is not the vernacular, his natural speech, which betrays Hopal's poverty of wits, but the poverty of his grasp of standard English. While Roscoe, intelligent and well-educated, speaks the vernacular as a form of protest against the system in which he finds himself enmeshed.

Rhone's next major play, *Old Story Time*, had its première in Nassau in 1979. The play went on to enjoy more productions than any other of his works, and eventually earned for Rhone one of London's most promising playwright awards in 1984.

As the title suggests, Rhone had devised a storytelling format to enable him to make a smooth transition from present to past and vice versa, as the plot developed over a period of some thirty years. Communal storytelling is an innately West Indian pastime, but the device has been seen in the region's conventional theatre only on rare occasions, most notably in Derek Walcott's *Ti-Jean and his Brothers.* In the earlier *The Gadget*, Mass Ben was an off-stage character who was Len's mother's neighbour and closest friend, and Len's own childhood confidant. Rhone took this character, retitled him the more affectionate Pa Ben, made him wise and gifted with laughter, and set him to telling the play's story to a lively audience of village children. These children are played by adult actors who, with minimal costume adjustments, then take over as the featured characters.

The story is of successful Len Tomlinson, of the degrading treatment he suffered as a poor black boy, and of his minutely planned revenge against his chief tormentor, the fairskinned bully George McFarlane, who has matured into an unrepentant villain. *Old Story Time*'s Len is a more reasonable and sympathetic character than the original of *The Gadget.* Rhone has now brought on stage some of the cruellest incidents endured by the boy, and also now shows the constant pressure that the endearing but obsessively feudal Miss Aggie put on her young son to 'advance' himself towards whiteness; 'anything black nuh good'. By forcing the audience actually to see the workings of the colour bias that not so long ago was upheld within the West Indian society even by its victims, Rhone makes more acceptable both Len's implacable enmity towards those who mistreated him in his youth, and his distancing of himself from his mother from the time he went abroad on scholarship.

The distancing, in any event, is not all one-sided. Len's behaviour is his way of saying to his mother, as Miss G says to her grandmother in Pat Cumper's *Buss Out* (1989), 'You miscalculated, you didn't bargain for change. Your world of colonial conventions imprisoned you – but it won't imprison me.' And Miss Aggie is so outraged by Len's eventual choice of a black wife that she can barely bring herself to speak to the 'tar baby'. 'Black was good enough for me. It not good enough for him'. Miss Aggie had set her heart on Len's marrying the Reverend Greaves's daughter, 'a nice brown girl with tall hair down to her back', and convinces herself that the sophisticated Lois must have worked obeah to capture Len.

Margaret Greaves is another *Gadget* off-stage character fleshed out in *Old Story Time*. In the earlier play Margaret genuinely loved Len, but took arsenic 'to bleach the colour of the baby' she carried for him. In the later play the Reverend's daughter, far from being a prospective bride for the young Len is, unbeknown to Miss Aggie, one of his principal tormentors. It is ironically fitting that she is discovered to have married her partner in crime, the crass and crooked George. The same actress plays both Margaret and the only new character in the play, Len's childhood friend Pearl. As she breeds child after child until she dies of premature old age, Pearl is a continuing dire reminder of the poverty trap from which Len has escaped. The actress can effectively play both roles straight, in the rather broad West Indian style of acting. In several productions, however, the interpretations of both Pearl and Margaret have been so burlesqued as to risk undermining the serious function of these characters.

For *Old Story Time* is, when all is said and done, an intensely serious play. It is most noticeably so in the long second half, where the laughter of the first act has suddenly evaporated, and the overall tone of the play darkens with bitterness and malice. At least one critic has suggested that the contrast between the two acts is so great that the writing seems to belong to two different plays, and that the combination lacks dramatic balance. Rhone's answer to that is the proven effectiveness of the work in touching audiences around the Caribbean, particularly as, in the final scenes, Len's family comes together in a cathartic night of repentance, forgiveness, exorcism, and love.

In all, there were four productions of *Old Story Time* around the region in 1979, in Jamaica, Grand Cayman and Trinidad as well as the Nassau première. Rhone directed the Trinidad production himself, as the first play at the new Hotel Normandie dinner theatre. He had co-founded this theatre with the hotel manager, Arthur Bentley, an English-born Equity actor. Rhone had three reasons for his interest in securing Trinidad as a second base: the oil-based economy of the most southerly Caribbean island as yet showed no signs of the downturn that was already affecting Jamaica; as a working environment Trinidad offered Rhone more seclusion than his homeland, where he was all too well known; Trinidad is also the homeland of his wife.

Old Story Time was followed at the Normandie by Derek Walcott's *Remembrance* (1977), staged by Helen Camps's All Theatre Productions. Rhone then returned to the dinner theatre with his own production of *Smile Orange*, staged in association with the Trinidad Theatre Workshop. Both of Rhone's plays were exceptionally well received by Trinidad audiences. However, Rhone did not want to be personally tied to a heavy production schedule in Trinidad. He accordingly went into partnership with theatre practitioner Judy Stone to found Studio Normandie, a company planned to run continuous dinner theatre under the immediate management of Stone. Rhone pulled out of the partnership before its first production reached the stage, but Stone's Touchstone Productions took over the Normandie project and ran Trinidad's first continuous professional theatre for three years, until the economic downturn arrived in Trinidad. Dinner theatres, running programmes of international and regional comedies, have found an audience wherever they have been established around the Caribbean. They have even on occasion engendered new plays, such as the long-running, tourist-oriented *Barbados Barbados*, by Ken Corsbie and Julia Senor.

1981 was for Rhone more notable for the publication of his first play collection, containing *Smile Orange* and *Old Story Time*, than for his ambitious musical adaptation of *Everyman*, a work which Rhone himself, after the event, considered something of a disappointment. It failed to realise the power it might have enjoyed, he thought, if he had given it a more sharply defined Jamaican identity.

The following year the playwright more than redeemed himself with the 1982 Best Jamaican Play, *Two Can Play*, Rhone's first two-actor comedy. The Jamaican production toured in the Caribbean and Canada, and other productions quickly followed, in London, New York, and in Paris as *Jeu pour Deux*. A taped version was screened in America by Kentucky Education Television.

The play is set in the late seventies, a time when Kingston was ravaged by political violence, and opens with a gun battle raging outside a down-town bedroom window. It is because of the fighting that Jim and Gloria, the occupants of that bedroom, have smuggled their three children into what they believe will be a better life in America. The parents have had to remain in Jamaica to care for Jim's dying father, Pops, one of the many off-stage characters who, as in *Smile Orange* and to a lesser extent *School's Out*, enliven the on-stage action. Jim, guarding against his offspring's possible discovery and deportation by the immigration authorities, has insisted there be no communication between the two generations until the children have managed to establish legal residence. Gloria, while apparently accepting Jim's dictate, has shrewdly worked out a code that keeps her in touch with her children at minimal risk, so that she knows where to find them when Pops's death releases the pair.

Jim, for most of the play, as he has done for the twenty years of his marriage, does a great deal of insisting. Insisting is for him proof of his status as the typical macho West Indian male. He is adept at twisting situations to suit himself, and so is unfazed by the frequency with which his decisions, often based on over-reaction, prove to have been unconsidered or simply foolish. He is unconscious of any irony in his assumption of superiority, even though his behaviour reeks of dishonesty, selfishness, cowardice, greed, laziness, prejudice and unfaithfulness. He insists that Gloria rather than he should run the gauntlet of the guns to get his father's medicine. He insists that Gloria rather than he should take the risks of their devious scheme to acquire US citizenship by one of them travelling to America and marrying there. He insists that Gloria rather than he should cook for him and clean up his three-week-old squalor the minute she walks into the house off the plane from America.

For twenty years Gloria, who of the pair has the better brains, the greater courage, common sense and resourcefulness, has accepted her role as Jim's doormat. Accustomed as she is to having continually to rescue her husband from the consequences of his bungling boorishness, yet it is not until the catalyst of the trip to America that she recognises her own self-worth, and accepts her right to life as an individual.

Gloria and Jim are two of the most acutely drawn characters Rhone has yet created. And while in the first act, leading up to the trip, the play seems to be essentially a comedy on the time-honoured theme of escape to the promised land, the second act, in which Gloria returns as the wife of an American, establishes the play as primarily a character study, with the plot being almost as incidental as the shooting. As Jamaican Prime Minister Michael Manley wrote:

> *Two Can Play* is about love, and estrangement; about domination, and liberation; about confusion, and compassion. It is about two human beings who nearly lose one another – but who eventually struggle back together through uncertainty, through quarrels, through humiliation. Ultimately, Gloria and Jim survive because they learn to communicate and, finally, to re-discover one another – not so much as they were, but as what they each can try to become.[11]

While the play itself is engagingly Jamaican in every detail, especially its humour, the subjugation of women is a subject both age-old and universal. Manley believes that Rhone's treatment, particularly in its moving resolution, elevates the writer 'above the status of a good, or even brilliant, playwright – and suggests he may indeed be a great one'.[12]

To Morris, 'Gloria and Jim can also function as metaphors for contending (political) forces in Jamaica'.[13] Many Jamaicans migrated to America in the seventies, but as Gloria says, 'America won't solve we problems, whether we go or whether we stay, until we start to look into weself an learn to help each other'. Though the American theme is secondary, it does have a particular interest, in that *Two Can Play* is one of the first plays to reverse the popular thrust to emigration for self-betterment, by suggesting, in the end, that the West Indian is better off staying in the West Indies.

A similar conclusion informs Rhone's next screenplay, *Milk and Honey*, which he had begun formulating as far back as 1979. It was to be ten years, however, before the film would be completed to win the 1989 Canadian Genie Award. Meantime Rhone's *The Game* was produced in 1985, and two collaborative works, *One Stop Driver* with Louis Marriott, and *Pepper* with Sonia Mills, were produced respectively in 1988 and 1989. The final version of *Milk and Honey* was also a collaborative work, with Glen Salzman.

The film of *Smile Orange* to some extent retains the theatrical flavour of the stage original. *Milk and Honey*, written directly for the film medium, is mercilessly realistic. The story begins and ends in Jamaica, but the main action takes place in America. In it, Rhone looks at the plight of immigrant domestic servants, and at the inhumanity of a system which encourages exploitation and personal tragedy.

Joanne, a young unmarried mother from a rural Jamaican village, leaves her nine-year-old son behind when she travels to America. There a job has been arranged for her in the household of a couple with political ambition. She has been grossly deceived about her pay, but cannot seek justice nor change her job, for she would be deported and lose her chance of achieving the coveted US resident status, with its opportunities for a better way of life for herself and her family. Without that status, she is not allowed to have her son with her, except for a holiday visit. During that visit, David's rebellious behaviour is an unspoken appeal to his mother not to desert him again. At the last minute Joanne falters in her determination not to jeopardise her case. At enormous cost, she finds a hide-away for David, and false papers to enable him to attend school. But, even abetted by David's headmaster, Joanne is fated to lose. Her employers inevitably find out her son has remained in America, David suffers starvation and beatings which draw the attention of his teacher, and a vengeful telephone call to the immigration authorities puts the pair to a flight that ends on board a plane back to Jamaica.

The fabric of the story is dense, interwoven with the lives and aspirations of other immigrants in domestic service, and with the tentative stirrings of an affair between Joanne and the white headmaster. White as well as black immigrants are trapped by the system and, even in the case of a tutor on a romantic 'tour' of women from different Caribbean islands, the unsensational treatment of the interracial relationships makes this noticeably a West Indian, rather than an American, view of life. It is, however, a marked departure from Rhone's full-bellied West Indian comedies. The lightest tone of the film is one of tender irony, as when, through a chance boast by her son as she wrestles with her cheap portable television, Joanne discovers that the money she earns with such hardship, and sends home at such a cost in personal deprivation, has been spent not on essentials, but on an outsize colour television set.

With *Milk and Honey* Rhone has entered a new mode as a writer, and tapped a new market for his audience. It is yet to be seen which of the younger generation of West Indian playwrights will follow in his footsteps. Many of them, such as Dominica's leading writer, Alwin Bully, seem content to write exclusively for the Caribbean audience.

Alwin Bully

Bully, much of whose writing has been in social realism, for stage, radio and screen, is a prime example of the many regional playwrights who are high achievers in a number of fields. At university in Barbados he was known as 'a true Renaissance man' – actor, dancer and director. He plays no musical instrument, but has composed the score for several musicals, his own and others. He designs his own sets and lighting, designs Carnival bands and Queen costumes, even designed the Dominican national flag. He has run his own television station. He is a most capable arts administrator, who for the Dominican government has been responsible for the revival of national festivals. He eventually joined UNESCO to continue his work in cultural development on a regional basis. As a playwright, his *oeuvre* cuts across most of the streams of West Indian theatre form. His plays include the ritualistic experiment of *Streak*, the melodrama of *Nite Box*, the mixed media of *The Ruler in Hiroona*, the folk musicals of *Pio-Pio* and *Folk Nativity*, his political drama *McB* drawn from Shakespeare's *Macbeth*, the evergreen popular comedy *Good Morning, Miss Millie*, and close on two hundred slice-of-life episodes in four socially oriented and closely researched radio serials. Rather than in the narrow sense of a particular style, his work is popular in the widest sense of its appeal to the people. Theatre doors have been battered in by a crowd refusing to be turned away from a sold-out Bully play.

Alwin Bully was born in Dominica in 1948, and grew up in an artistically talented family. His mother was a gifted actress, and would regularly perform for the children, playing every role in the latest film she had seen. His father was more academically inclined, and insisted that the children learn standard English, though he had no quarrel with creole. And so Bully from his youth was fluent in the three languages he was to draw on as a playwright: the English of the educated Dominican, the creole vernacular, and the patois that had been brought into the theatre by his mother's cousin, folklorist Mabel Caudeiron. More than either of his parents, it was Caudeiron who most influenced Bully in the arts. Bully's mother belonged to Caudeiron's Kairi Artistic Group, and Bully himself at an early age took part in some of Caudeiron's plays and 'calypsoperettas'.

A landmark in Bully's artistic development was 1964, when he played Antonio in a Shakespeare Quatercentenary joint schools production of *The Merchant of Venice*. As a result of this experience, Bully helped to form a Secondary Schools Drama Society, which became a Little Theatre movement when its members left school. It was for this Little Theatre group that Bully made his début as a director, with the American musical *Meet Arizona*.

The next landmark was 1967, when he left Dominica to attend the University of the West Indies in Barbados. It was a dynamic time for the Cave Hill campus, a time that saw the founding of the Cave Hill Drama Society, the Dance Society, and the Cave Hill Carnival. Excited to find himself in a society more responsive to the arts than Dominica's, Bully became a part of the Barbados theatre community. He took up directing in earnest, and began to write – short stories, poetry, and his first play, the one-act comedy *Good Morning, Miss Millie* (1970), which premièred in Barbados. Not surprisingly, the 'Renaissance man' was elected President of the Guild of Undergraduates.

Bully has acknowledged three key influences in his writing. There was the early love, nurtured by his father, of literature in general and of Dickens in particular. Then, reading English and French for his degree, he discovered the French theatre, and was particularly impressed by the structured writing, and by Molière's treatment of comedy. And thirdly, though there were no Caribbean works on the syllabus at the time, at Cave Hill he was introduced to the work of Roger Mais, which affected him intensely.

Good Morning, Miss Millie is perhaps the only work of Bully's that falls squarely into the stream of popular drama. An unpretentious rural comedy, its lasting appeal is due as much to what is, for this style of play, the exceptional craftsmanship of its fairly intricate structure, as to its mischievously romping action, easy dialogue and familiar characters. Miss Millie's father has just died, leaving her a large sum of money on condition that she marries the son of a distant friend of his. Though she has never met the family, the twice-deserted Millie is more than willing, especially when her letter to the man of her destiny brings by way of reply a personable suitor young enough to be her own son. Celsus, however, falls in love with Millie's daughter, and the determined legatee must use all her wiles to drag the unfortunate youth to the altar of her fortune. All ends unexpectedly happily, and 'cousin and cousin does make dozen'.

Bully returned to Dominica in 1971, joined the staff of the Grammar School, and began to make use of his theatre experience as a basic teaching instrument. Together with his cousin Daniel Caudeiron, Mabel's son, he took over the Little Theatre movement and renamed it the People's Action Theatre, intending it as 'a vehicle for change'. Bully directed Daniel's *Speak Brother, Speak*, which in 1972 represented Dominica at the Guyana Carifesta. However, Daniel Caudeiron's philosophy of change found little favour with the Dominican government of the time, and he emigrated to Canada. Bully continued the Action Theatre with a series of standard West Indian works such as Archibald's *The Rose Slip*, but audience response was discouraging.

It was in this climate that Bully decided he had to write a definitive piece of West Indian theatre that would draw the Dominican public, or else he would get out of theatre altogether. He wrote *Streak*.

In 1975, the year Roseau was startled from its complacency by the première of Bully's first full-length play, *Streak* had the topicality of a freshly-printed newspaper. The minuteness of contemporary detail has inevitably led to a dating, though not invalidating, of the piece. At the time, the immediacy of its events and references, together with the familiarity of its range of characters, made the play exceptionally accessible even to non-habitual theatregoers. In addition, the popular social commentary to which it gave voice, along with the excitement of an experimental form that involved mass audience participation, lent the work such extraordinary power that it had an unprecedented run of 35 performances in Dominica. In St Lucia, on the last night of the *Streak* tour, people turned away from the sold-out box office broke down the theatre doors to get in. Few West Indian playwrights can claim a similar experience.

The central plot of *Streak* is a love story, set against a troubled background of Black Power rebellion, the murder of an Englishman, and the burning of a Syrian store. The idealistic Ken, whose rumoured rebel associations and subsequent disappearances have mystified his old friends and pregnant fiancée Jan, is arrested and jailed for arson. Ken is innocent, but accepts the sentence in the belief that both his present lack of protest and his earlier secret meetings with the rebels have contributed to alleviation of the growing social unrest. He breaks out of jail to attend his baby's christening, but surrenders again, and after serving out his time he and Jan set out for a new life in the country.

The streak of the title, playing on the sense of nudity, is a metaphor as idealistic as the play's hero:

> *Ken:* What we need is a mental streak, for people to take off all their masks and pretensions and to look at themselves truthfully and openly for the first time, so that they can see all the lies and mistakes and crimes that they commit every day while they choose a few individuals to carry the blame and pay for it.

The cast of fifteen characters and as many extras comprises a representative cross-section of Dominican society, including Jan's cousin and roommate the materialistic Stella, Jan's country-bred old mother Lillian De Bique, her karate-crazy son Zen, the Rastafarian Jomo, the 'passive rebel' Stings, and Albert, the poet, who introduces the element of ritual.

A firm believer in total theatre, Bully integrated his drama with music, song, dance and drumming. He also introduced, in a rhythmic type of poetry, a ritual of call and response between actors and audience, which would build up in performance to an extraordinary theatrical experience, akin to the crowd mesmerism of political rallies and charismatic movements.

Bully followed *Streak* with a play he considers even better, the 1976 *The Ruler in Hiroona*, based on the novel by V.H. Thomas. It is a story of political corruption, but not the classic theme of innocence corrupted by power. Jerry Mole was a child spoilt by a doting mother. He matured into a self-centred trouble-maker and, by the time the play opens, as he is being persuaded to start a workers' union, he has been fired from a number of jobs. The first strike he foments wins for Mole hero status among the workers, as it wins for a wounded factoryhand Hiroona's first negotiated compensation package. Mole promptly puts the package into his own pocket. Graft follows greed. Though Mole rules Hiroona for two terms as the island's stealing, lying and conniving Prime Minister, in the end his corruption is his downfall, and his power passes to more honourable men. As in the novel, it is a nice touch and one final example of his insatiable greed that Mole, addressing the audience directly, is the deliberate agent of his own exposé, for which he has been handsomely paid.

The Ruler in Hiroona is at root as idealistic a drama as its predecessor, and may be felt to lack depth in the development of character. The play is also, in its original version, overlong for the average audience. However, Bully's mixed media approach, incorporating slides and sound effects to bring onto the conventional stage a protest march of thousands, goes far towards making his adaptation a telling piece of theatre. But a cast of twenty-eight featured characters and crowd extras, even with whatever doubling is possible, makes staging the work a major undertaking for any producer.

From the sixties on, more and more of the committed theatre production companies around the Caribbean region assumed professional or semi-professional status. For the first time actors and the entire production team were receiving pay, however minimal. But the company budgets now had to absorb this new burden of salary bills at a time when the audiences for most conventional theatre were still too sparse for a successful production to do more than break even. The consequent trend towards small-cast plays became ever more marked, echoing a similar trend in the professional theatre of England, America and Canada in periods of international recession. Only the companies drawing on voluntary group talent, such as the Jamaican Little Theatre Movement's pantomime, the Trinidad government's Best Village competition, other community theatres and church groups, could afford to stage large-scale productions. Bully continued to write plays featuring many more characters than was the norm, but he too was sensitive to the trend. In 1991, fifteen years after *The Ruler*, his new play *McB* showed a cast list of 34 roles, which could, however, be played by as few as ten actors.

Bully's first full scale musical, *Folk Nativity*, for which he wrote the lyrics and co-wrote the music, was staged in Dominica at least once each year for fifteen years after its first production in 1976. One year there were three productions around the island, and it has also toured within the region, and been produced in Trinidad.

Like Freddie Kissoon's perennial *We Crucify Him* (1967), Bully's musical is a play within a play, with the contemporary characters assuming the biblical roles. The setting is a rural village, where an eccentric hermit is on trial for the theft of a stem of bananas. In his defence, the accused tells the Christmas story. The surprise ending not only exonerates the hermit, but discovers the guilty thief to be the villager who is presiding over the trial as judge.

The following year, 1977, Bully once again branched out in a new direction, with *Nite Box*, a spoof on the Agatha Christie style of mystery. As a mystery, the plot is deliberately extreme in concept. However, it is for the most part a competently structured play. It is only in the anti-climactic final scene that the satire is carried too far and, unless rescued by inspired direction, loses dramatic tension as loose ends are tied up with a dogged meticulousness that would weary even Christie's Hercule Poirot. The spoof features a hero who is not as insane as he pretends (or is he?), enough innocents (or are they?) to provide a tidy number of victims of foul murder (to all appearances), and the requisitely confusing roster of suspects, along with assorted weapons, missing relatives, masks and disguises. There is also the vital box of the title, whose concealing device is almost worthy of Heath Robinson.

Even one of Trinidad's more demanding critics, Mark Lyndersay, described the play itself as 'a thrilling experience',[14] when seen in one of several subsequent regional productions directed, oddly, stripped of its built-in histrionics. But in

Dominica the première production, in accordance with Bully's intentions, was 'replete with creepy music and eerie lights and heavily tongue-in-cheek performances'.[15] Bully was rewarded with a new Roseau record run of 50 performances, and a sold-out tour in Antigua, Montserrat and St Kitts. In spite of the grotesquerie, *Nite Box* is strongly coloured with the idealism and social concern that were by now recognised hallmarks of a Bully play. The hero Led, leading his hermit-like existence in the family garret, has withdrawn from a less than perfect world, and passes the time painting a blank canvas with dry brushes. But in spite of himself he becomes involved in the nurses' strike that is the topical backdrop to the melodrama.

Bully's next work, staged in 1978, was a landmark piece in that it gave Dominican audiences their first experience of traditional Carnival costumes on the conventional stage. The two-act Carnival folk musical *Pio-Pio* is about a boy and a girl looking for 'It'. 'It', Bully explains, in this context symbolises the meaning of life. The search takes the pair to many different places, and it is in the forest scenes that the Carnival costumes appear, representing the wind, animals, and other entities. In the end, 'It' is found in a mirror, Bully's moral being that the meaning of life is what you make it.

Bully had now been appointed head of the Grammar School, and was already chafing at the consequent drain on his time for creative work. In 1978 he resigned, with the intention of working freelance. Instead, he found himself persuaded into creating Dominica's Cultural Department in the Ministry of Community Development. In 1982 he was seconded for a year to the Dominica Broadcasting Corporation, to run the radio station. He then returned to his position of Chief Cultural Officer. In 1987 he was seconded once again, this time as Subregional Cultural Advisor to UNESCO, a position that a year later was made permanent.

Ironically, for more than a decade after quitting the Grammar School to devote himself to writing, Bully wrote virtually nothing for the stage. He did, however, draft his 4-act drama *Pelee*, which was workshopped at the first Caribbean Playwrights Conference. He also completed two short works for schoolchildren, *The Almost Forgotten Gift* (1982) and *J.D.-D.J.* (1985). And while neglecting his writing for the stage, he managed to produce a sizeable body of work for radio, *Toto and the Town Visitors* (1982) for television, and the half-hour film *Me Too*. He also composed original lyrics and music for stage productions such as Eric Roach's *Belle Fanto*, Errol John's *Moon on a Rainbow Shawl*, and *Ti-Jean Epi Fwe-y* (1982), Bully's creole version of Derek Walcott's *Ti-Jean and His Brothers*.

The first Caribbean Playwrights Conference was held in St Thomas in 1981. It was inspired and aided by the Eugene O'Neill Foundation, which runs an annual such conference in Connecticut for both American and overseas playwrights, directors, actors and critics. The St Thomas Conference was followed in 1988 by the first Playwrights Workshop/Conference to be staged by the newly-formed Assocation of Caribbean Theatre Artists (ACTA), in Jamaica. And individual territories such as Trinidad have on occasion staged a national conference on a smaller scale.

Fig. 4 Alwin Bully's *Pio Pio* (PHOTO: People's Action Theatre) A scene from Alwin Bully's Carnival folk musical, staged in Dominica by the People's Action Theatre.

The four playwrights whose works-in-progress were the subject of intense dramaturgical treatment at the St Thomas conference were Bully with *Pelee*, Trinidad's Ronald Amoroso with *The Probe* (1980), Montserrat's David Edgecombe with *Kirnon's Kingdom* (1981), and St Thomas's own Rudolph Wallace, with *The Philosopher Limer* (1982). Actors, directors, stage managers, technical crew and others, as well as the playwrights, were drawn from all around the region. All the participants, including Amoroso, who eventually rejected the conference line of development of his work, deemed the exercise a stimulating and illuminating experience. A similar exercise was undertaken at the ACTA Workshop, where the playwrights in the spotlight were Ken Corsbie, a British Guiana-born Trinidad national living in Barbados, with *Jack and Jill* (1988), Jamaica's Pat Cumper with *Quadrille* (1988), and Barbados's Glenville Lovell, with *The Silver Web* (1989). There was also a reading of a new script by Trinidad's Ralph Campbell.

Bully wrote four radio serials in all, three of which were broadcast in Dominica. The first and most successful, the 1978 *Green Gold*, was originally commissioned by the Dominican Banana Growers Association, which supplied all the technical background. The serial ran for a total of 85 fifteen-minute episodes. It is a family soap opera, in which most of the characters are employed in banana growing. The basic plot is one of family machinations, centred around ownership of a piece of land. Week by week Bully would incorporate into each episode banana industry propaganda, and also the latest Dominican events. This topicality added considerably to the serial's popular appeal.

The following year, after Hurricane David devastated Dominica, Bully wrote a sequel serial, the 45-episode *Winds of Change*. This sequel featured the same *Green Gold* characters, and further family machinations, in a public education exercise designed to help the ordinary person cope with the aftermath of the disaster. Episodes offered such information as where repair materials were available, and such advice as how to file an insurance claim.

In 1980 the 30-episode *Secrets of La Cloche* was commissioned by the Department of Health. Again the setting was rural, but the characters and situations were new, and the thrust was towards preventive health practices. The final serial, the 1983 *Fire Go Bun*, which Bully co-wrote with Dorbrene O'Marde, and which ran for only twelve episodes, was commissioned by the Caribbean Family Planning Affiliation. It was broadcast in Montserrat.

1990 saw a staged reading, in Jamaica, of Bully's first new theatre piece in twelve years. Inspired by Shakespeare's *Macbeth*, *McB* follows the original event by event, on occasion so closely that the supernatural elements risk reviving inappropriate echoes of *Nite Box*. However, the work stands on its own feet as a monumental drama of power plays in Caribbean politics today. Bully has made one major change to the Shakespearean plot. After McBee's collapse when he sees the ghost of his murdered rival, he and his wife exchange the original roles, in a way that seems the more feasible for our own time. Fainthearted Allan McBee sleepwalks, washing his hands of bloodstains as his revealing ramblings are recorded on tape by the doctor. He then fades out of the picture, while forceful Alice McBee takes over as Prime Minister.

Alice: Woman's serving days now done;
For four centuries me did settle for second fiddle,
Watch-ya now, world – Lady McBee time a come!

The play is set on a Caribbean island, and in Miami. It opens with three Rastafarians crouched around a ganja chalice, their 'spectacular upright locks' suggestive of the traditional witch's hat. It is an appealing and effective transformation which instantly puts the audience in tune with the adaptation, and in sympathy with the sometimes uneasy blend of the familiar Shakespearian phrases with modern standard English and West Indian vernacular. The audience is also now on the alert for the parallels to come.

It is election night, and the polling results coming in show Vere Duncan's party winning. After the report of a shooting incident, Duncan decides to fire the incumbent and make McBee his next Minister of Health. This unexpected appointment is officially revealed to McBee only minutes after it has been foretold by the Rastas, who have also promised McBee that he will be Prime Minister. When Duncan takes an overnight rest at the McBee house in the hills, Alice decides to take the future into her own hands. Duncan is murdered and his guards framed. Duncan's sons flee to America, where they found a new political party to challenge the party now led by the McBees. The opposing political rallies are shown simultaneously on stage, with Alice and Junior Duncan being heard alternately, a device that Ralph Maraj used to telling effect in his 1986 political satire, *The Archbishop and the Prime Minister*. Hurricane Albert finally deals McBee his deathblow, and fulfils the Rastas' deceptive prophecy, being the agent by which Rose Hall comes to Mona. Alice McBee, crazed, whimpers as she washes in a basin of blood. The play ends with her arrest for Duncan's murder.

Two of the more memorable characters in Bully's version are Alice herself, and Peter, the modern version of the comic porter, whose role is expanded here into that of the indispensable faithful family retainer with licence to speak his mind.

When first completed *McB* was overlong for stage performance. Subsequent reworking has made the piece more manageable as theatre, but the original script, with its powerfully cinematic images, could well prove the basis for Bully's first full-length screenplay. Even on stage, much of the imagery is brought to the audience on a triptych of television screens periodically lowered from the flies.

Of several attempts to establish a film industry in the West Indies not one has to date survived the first one or two films produced in each case, largely because of the lack of support systems. Yet the region has abundant material and performing talent, optimum location conditions with long hours of light and little rain, increasing technical proficiency, and several fine realist writers to serve such an industry. The lush setting of Bully's own Dominica is an invaluable factor in the effectiveness of one rare television mini-series, *The Orchid House*, based on the novel by Phyllis Shand Allfrey. It is simply a matter of time before one of the more enlightened island governments puts together a concession package tempting enough to attract the necessary financing and administrative expertise that would give a fledgling West Indian film industry a fair chance to thrive.

Meantime, with or without film opportunities, realism remains the stream of theatre form most popular among the majority of West Indian playwrights. Majority audiences, however, by definition prefer popular theatre.

NOTES

1 March, 1954.
2 Errol Hill, 'The Emergence of a National Drama in the West Indies' *CQ*, Vol. 18, #4, 1972.
3 Entertainer Holly Betaudier in interview with Judy Stone 1990, unpublished.
4 Neil Watson, obituary of Errol John, *The Times*, 16 July, 1988.
5 *Ibid.*
6 Errol John, *People*, Vol. 2, #20, September 1977.
7 Trevor Rhone in interview with Mervyn Morris, *JJ*, Vol. 16, #1, 1983.
8 *Ibid.*
9 Gordon Rohlehr, *My Strangled City and other essays*, Longman Trinidad, 1992.
10 *DE*, 16 November, 1988.
11 Michael Manley, Introduction, in *Two Can Play*, Longman, 1986.
12 *Ibid.*
13 Mervyn Morris, Critical Introduction, in *Two Can Play*, Longman, 1986.
14 *TG*, 8 April, 1982.
15 Judy Stone, interview with Alwin Bully, *TG*, 29 January, 1985.

THEATRE OF THE PEOPLE

Reaching the masses with drama: Sistren and Pat Cumper

As the curtain draws back to reveal the opening scene of the Freddie Kissoon farce *Beauty Contest* (1975), the tightly packed audience screams with delight. The skimpily-attired 'big fat boobooloops' Beulah has been revealed, skipping – bust, buttocks, belly and bulging thighs all a-jiggle. Fresh gales of laughter and knee-slapping greet the entrance of a neighbour, as she asks Beulah in mock astonishment, 'What is it is going on here?'. Beulah's withering response causes the more excitable patrons to leap from their seats, flicking their fingers in admiration. The rest rock backwards and forwards, helpless with mirth, some of them even audibly repeating the line to milk it of extra drops of pleasure. 'I skipping. You ent see me skipping?'

Unambitious in concept, popular drama is generally most comfortable playing to the gut, the groin and the funny bone, and rarely pays more than lip-service to the head. Popular theatre exists all round the world wherever there is theatre. In his book *The Empty Space*, Peter Brook terms one extreme of popular theatre 'Rough Theatre':

> Through the ages it has taken many forms, and there is only one factor that they all have in common – a roughness. Salt, sweat, noise, smell: the theatre that's not in a theatre, the theatre on carts, on wagons, on trestles, audiences standing, drinking, sitting round tables, audiences joining in, answering back: theatre in back rooms, upstairs rooms, barns; the one-night stands, the torn sheet pinned up across the hall, the battered screen to conceal the quick changes . . . Of course, it is most of all dirt that gives the roughness its edge; filth and vulgarity are natural, obscenity is joyous: with these the spectacle takes on its socially liberating role, for by nature the popular theatre is anti-authoritarian, anti-traditional, anti-pomp, anti-pretence. This is the theatre of noise, and the theatre of noise is the theatre of applause.[1]

The rumbustiously outrageous Teat' Lari of Martinique is a rare West Indian example of this kind of rough theatre. The French islands, for better or worse, culturally as well as economically retain closer connections with the metropolitan mother country than do the former British possessions. Old mas bands and calypso plays excepted, the rough theatre of the English-speaking West Indies tends to be less abandoned than its older counterpart in England and on the European continent. It rarely takes to the streets, preferring community centres, union meeting-rooms, church and school halls, civic halls and cinemas, anywhere the swarming audience can be comfortably seated. It even occasionally appears in a conventional theatre, though the audiences for rough theatre are generally uncomfortable in a more formal atmosphere. In a conventional theatre, the production may take advantage of all the normal theatre facilities. But often the backdrop for rough theatre is merely a sheet or a drape, the lighting minimal or non-existent, the stage furniture no more than a couple of wooden chairs and a table, and the properties restricted largely to suggestion. The actors perform in an exaggerated style, and are unrelievedly loud of mouth. The directors are seldom concerned with more than a few rudiments of stagecraft, if so much. The companies that travel have a popular repertoire of farces that their audiences see so frequently, they can sing out a favourite line before it is spoken by the actor. Usually one-acters, the pieces are simply written and devoid of subtlety. The dialogue is in a broad vernacular, and the humour depends heavily on an earthy vulgarity which is, however, less challenging than that of the late twentieth century calypso tent. All the plays are closely identified with the unpretentious lives of the people who flock to see them. Literature, in the sense of the craftsmanship of the writing, is not a concern of the playwrights.

However, no overview of West Indian theatre can afford to ignore the region's popular drama, or 'roots theatre' as it is known in Jamaica, with its uniquely intimate view of West Indian life. By numbers, the audience for rough theatre alone far surpasses that for the more sophisticated theatres. Even these latter, in many cases, tend to place more emphasis on performance aspects of a production, and less on textual refinements, than can be found in other western cultures. In addition to the rough and roots theatres, for the purposes of this study the stream termed 'Theatre of the People' also carries such diverse modern bedfellows as Jamaica's self-styled 'crotch' theatre and the Gun Court theatre, political and African-oriented people's theatre, a range of community theatres including church theatre and the theatres of group therapy and social education, storytelling and the specialist children's theatre. The musical or total theatre, which is the most popular of all West Indian theatre forms, is treated as a separate stream in the following chapter, *Total Theatre.*

Among the region's popular drama playwrights in the later half of the twentieth century are Tobago's Bernadette Allum; Montserrat's Vincent Browne; Guyana's prolific Francis Quamina Farrier, and also Harold Bascom, Bertrand Charles, Victor Forsythe, William Harris, Frank Pilgrim and Sheik Sadeek; Barbados's Anthony Hinkson; Grand Cayman's Frank McField; Grenada's Wilfred Redhead; and Jamaica's Michael Denton, Hall Anthony Ellis and Easton Lee. Lee, it may be noted, along with Trinidad's Willi Chen, enjoys the rare distinction of being a West Indian playwright of Chinese descent.

By far the most productive, active and regionally well-known of such playwrights is Trinidad's Freddie Kissoon. Kissoon's introduction to the theatre was in the early fifties, when he joined the Nelsonians, the popular theatre group founded by Arthur Roberts. Today, many of his older fans see Kissoon as having taken on the mantle of Roberts. However, one pronounced difference between the two writers is that Roberts had a puritanical aversion to vulgarity.

After appearing with the Nelsonians, Kissoon was invited to join the Whitehall Players, for whom in 1954, at the age of twenty-four, under the direction of Errol Hill, he gave an 'excellent characterisation'[2] of old Hounakin, in Derek Walcott's *The Sea at Dauphin*. Four years later, in 1958, after several other stage appearances in productions such as the John Ainsworth *Macbeth* and *Hamlet*, Kissoon created the role of the boy Ti-Jean in Walcott's own première production of *Ti-Jean and his Brothers*.

The previous year, 1957, Kissoon had won a recitation contest as the representative of a mythical theatre company invented to meet the contest rules. The Strolling Players refused to remain mythical. Despite Kissoon's initial reluctance to lead it, the company staged its first performance in 1961, at the St Ann's Mental Hospital. The programme included Kissoon's first two plays, the one-acters *Zingay* and *Mamaguy*.

By this time the novice playwright, having struggled as an actor with the foreign speech patterns and rarefied intellectual content of plays by Shakespeare, Ibsen and Shaw, had become convinced that the most urgent need in West Indian theatre was for plays that ordinary people could comfortably enjoy – short, undemanding comedies about themselves and their ordinary concerns, written in their own everyday language, and buoyant with their own unobscure humour. *Zingay* is a vernacular comedy featuring an errant schoolboy, his gullible mother, and the role played by Kissoon, an obeah 'doctor' as crooked as Hill's Diable Papa. Kissoon also squeezed in a fat Barbadian neighbour, knowing that in Trinidad she would be a guaranteed popular rib-tickler for any one of her triple combination of characteristics: the generous feminine attributes, the skimpy dress, and the droll Barbadian accent. Five years later *Zingay* became the first Trinidadian drama production to be screened, live, by the four-year-old national television station. *Mamaguy* is another vernacular comedy, in which several conspirators, attempting to milk money from a rich relative by a scam which includes dressing a man as a woman, find themselves hoist with their own petard.

Kissoon and his company overcame early difficulties to grow from strength to strength. In 1962 Kissoon won a British Council Scholarship to study at London's Central School of Speech and Drama. He returned to Trinidad in 1963. Over the next three decades the Strolling Players toured indefatigably within the nation, around the Caribbean, and as far north as Toronto. They performed with frequency on radio, television, and in feature films and advertising commercials. Most of the work presented by the company was written and directed by Kissoon. And, atypically for a popular drama director, he conducted regular acting workshops with the company. Increasingly in later years, the playwright also encouraged individual Players, and others, to develop their talents as both writers and directors.

Kissoon's own output has been considerable, encompassing more than 60 plays of varying lengths, a 78-episode radio serial, two television serials, and some screenplays, as well as a pocket handbook of drama exercises for beginners.

Several of his plays have been produced around the world, in the United States, Canada, England and Nigeria. Not all his work is as slight as *Beauty Contest* (1975), and though he will long be affectionately remembered by his public for his creation of the Beulah character, through the ample medium of actress Shirley King, he will also be remembered for the evergreen *Calabash Alley*, which began life in 1970 as a radio serial; for the three-act historical drama *God and Uriah Butler* (1967), commissioned by the Oilfield Workers' Trade Union; for his award-winning three-act drama *King Cobo* (1965), in which the murderous blackmailing cripple Cobo and his prostitute daughter appear like a stark negative of Errol John's *The Tout*; for the frequently produced *Zingay* and *Mamaguy*; and for the passion play *We Crucify Him* (1967).

Besides Kissoon, Trinidad enjoys another popular drama playwright in a class by himself. Ralph Maraj is the resident playwright-director of the San Fernando Drama Guild, which is based in southern Trinidad, an area where the majority of the population is of East Indian extraction, as is Maraj himself. Since 1976, the year Maraj took over the company, the Guild has been staging only Maraj's works. The Guild's membership has become almost exclusively Indo-Trinidadian, and the company has built up an exceptional following comprising almost exclusively Indo-Trinidadian patrons. Yet Maraj's work is not overtly East Indian in character. The playwright does not draw on the classical Indian drama and, except in those of his plays that focus on race relations, the majority of his roles could be played by any West Indian actor of whatever ethnic origin.

Maraj himself is a powerfully charismatic actor, as capable of a finely tuned interpretation of Macbeth as of a heart-wrenching Pariag in Earl Lovelace's *The Dragon Can't Dance*. He first made his mark on stage as a student, in two consecutive years winning a Best Actor award in the Secondary Schools Drama Festival, and in 1974 played the leading role in the film *Bim*. However, with the Guild actors he has developed a broad popular acting style that is part melodrama and part music hall, with a ranting delivery. The style is complemented by Maraj's deft direction at a whip-cracking pace, and is to a certain extent integral to the later plays.

Maraj's first play was the 1973 award-winning *The Last Competition*; he continued to win awards with frequency. His plays fall loosely into three categories: farces, romances and political satires. He has also written an award-winning musical, the 1979 *Wake it Up*, for which he modelled the dialogue on the calypso verse of Errol Hill's *Man Better Man*. Soon afterwards he repeated the experiment in one of his better plays, *Under the Sapodilla Tree* (1980).

A teacher of English, Maraj writes with a concern for craftsmanship matched by few other West Indian playwrights working in this style of theatre. His themes are familiar, topical, uncomplex and of the people. His treatment combines an element of juvenile vulgarity with a tendency to undisguised moralising that is often described as 'preachy', and that strikes some critics as naïve, but that Maraj himself calls 'content'.[3] As a teacher, Maraj is in close touch with young people, and several of his plays, such as the romance *Cynthia Sweetness* (1981) and the farce *The Flowers of the Nation* (1987), are written for actors still in or fresh out of secondary school.

His most widely-admired work has been three political satires, *The Missing File* (1982), *The Broken Bridge* (1989) and in particular *The Archbishop and the Prime Minister* (1986). The latter, a shrewdly funny send-up of the day's political scene, was staged just before the general elections that brought to an end the thirty-year dynasty of the People's National Movement, the party founded by Eric Williams, independent Trinidad's first Prime Minister. In 1991, five years and two increasingly bitter political satires later, Maraj won his San Fernando seat for the PNM's return to power. He joined the Cabinet as Foreign Minister, bringing his theatre career to at least a temporary halt. He had followed a trail blazed around the world by several illustrious politician-playwrights, such as Martinique's Aimé Cezaire and Czechoslovakia's Vaclav Havel.

Trinidad's third popular drama writer of note, working in this case in church theatre, is Hal Greaves. Greaves and his exceptional group of dedicated young churchgoers, My People Incorporated, have developed a style of morality theatre that is engagingly entertaining, and draws packed houses of loyal patrons who are much inclined to cap their laughter with loud interjections such as 'Praise the Lord' and 'Amen, amen!' Working with such a large volunteer group, Greaves writes scripts with casts of as many as twenty or thirty featured characters. In his earlier plays, such as *Victims* (1985), he tended to cram in references to virtually every sin known under the sun. His later work has taken a closer focus. One of his best plays, the 1989 *Others*, in which actors pose as the dummies in a clothing store, deals exclusively with the community responsibility for the prevention of incest and child abuse.

Sistren

There are several vibrant community theatre organisations in the Caribbean. One such is the Eastern Caribbean Popular Theatre Organisation. Founded in St Vincent in 1983, ECPTO has now drawn in under its umbrella community theatre groups of Antigua, Barbados, Dominica, St Lucia, Grenada and the Grenadines. Regionally and internationally, however, the most widely-known community theatre in the Caribbean is that of the Jamaican Sistren. This women's theatre collective developed in 1977 out of a community drama presentation for a Worker's Week Festival. All thirteen founder members were grass-roots women from the Kingston ghetto, and all thirteen were at the time casual labourers in a temporary national employment programme. Ill educated, ill paid, and exploited by the system, from the outset the Sistren saw the playmaking process as an opportunity for self-improvement. With the help of an experienced dramatist, Honor Ford-Smith, they collectively created *Downpression Get a Blow*, based on their personal experiences of maltreatment of factory workers. One result of the production was the group's discovery, from as far afield as Sri Lanka and Korea, of the universality of what they had thought their problems alone.

After the Festival, ten of the Sistren remained together. Before a decade had passed they had developed Sistren into a professional theatre company that won award after award while working in popular education. At the same time Sistren had developed a research unit that, amongst its other achievements, had filmed a compelling documentary, *Sweet Sugar Rage* (1984). The company also produced Sistren's own quarterly magazine, and other publications such as the autobiographical *Lionheart Woman* and several playscripts.

'We have gone on', writes Ford-Smith in a 1986 *Jamaica Journal* (Vol. 19 #1), 'to discuss the experiences of go-go dancers and prostitutes, of domestic workers, of rural children, of migrant men and women, of higglers, housewives and secretaries. This discussion, this naming of experience, has brought out in public, after years of whispering, the specific problems of many women in our community. Through dialogue, through encounter with others, we have discovered that the possibility of our power can shape forces which at present still shape us.'

Sistren's second play, *Bellywoman Bangarang* (1978), was built around four pregnant women, and their various experiences as mothers and as girl children. It showed the causative effect of unemployment and urban poverty in such matters as rape and domestic violence. In all Sistren's work, most of the characters speak in a down-town vernacular so raw, much of it is incomprehensible to an ear untuned to the Jamaican accent. Yet the company has successfully toured around the Caribbean, to Canada, England, Holland and New York. The Sistren's ability to communicate across the dialect barrier stems from the powerful performance orientation of their work, which incorporates elements such as children's games, songs, ritual and storytelling. All the roles, men and children included, are played by the Sistren, amongst whom are several fine interpretive actresses.

The technique of collective creation from actual experiences has been used by other Caribbean companies, such as Stage One of Barbados in *Lights* (1985), the Trinidad Theatre Studio in *Testimony* (1990), and ECPTO. However, Sistren pioneered in the field and, with a record of at least one new play each year, shows the most comprehensive body of such work. Sistren's plays include *Nana Yah* (1980) on the role of women in the liberation of the West Indian colonies, *QPH* (1981) on society's neglect of the elderly and infirm, *Domestick* (1982) on the abuse of domestic servants, *Muffet Inna All A We* (1985) on sexual violence, the musical *Sistren Song* (1985) and the Jonkunnu-inspired *Ida Revolt Inna Jonkunnu Stylee* (1985).

Pat Cumper

Though Ford-Smith remained with Sistren, other playwrights and directors have worked with different productions by the company. The widely-praised *Buss Out* of 1989, for instance, which is based on *Lionheart Gal* and improvisation by the actors, was finally scripted by Pat Cumper. Cumper is one of Jamaica's more significant young playwrights, and the most important of the few female playwrights currently working in the region. She is the latest in a notable tradition, Jamaica being the only West Indian territory with a relatively continuous history of serious female playwrights, dating back to Una Marson in the thirties.

Buss Out, which draws on the nine night ritual of the Jamaican wake, opens in a yard in Chiggerfoot Lane. A child has just been killed during the squatters' resistance to an attempt to force them off land they have occupied for years. The play opposes two strong women from contrasting backgrounds, the community Warrior Auntie Bev, mother of the dead boy, and the crusading television interviewer Miss G. The Warrior demands a violent revenge, while the up-town woman believes in the power of the media to force the resolution of the squatters' problems through legal process. The women are jailed together. Through flashbacks that show the individual paths these two central characters followed from childhood to become the social rebels they are today, they journey towards an understanding of each other. Eventually they come to realise that each has a part to play if women are to 'buss out' of the constraints of class, race, sex and circumstance to new possibilities.

Patricia Cumper grew up in a family whose social awareness was exceptionally active. Born in Jamaica in 1954, the playwright was the second of three children whose English father and Jamaican mother had met in England at Cambridge University. On the newly-wed couple's setting up house in Jamaica, where Cumper *père* held a chair in economics at Mona, Cumper *mère* forsook a possible career in the legal profession and turned to the social services. She was, writes her daughter, 'tremendously active in a number of organizations and committees which shaped social services in this country: this culminated in her setting up the Family Court and redrafting the Bastardy Act so that there are no longer illegitimate children in Jamaica'.[4]

Cumper's parents, her father in particular, were also responsible for her interest in the arts:

> I had always been exposed to theatre and literature. My family went to see plays, recitals, ballet and any kind of dance; my father collected everything from Sparrow and Kitch to Rachmaninov and Beethoven, from T.S.Eliot to Dossie Carberry. I remember seeing productions of *Sea At Dauphin*, *Malcochon*, *The Rose Slip*, *Man Better Man* and many others including Shakespeare, Wilde, Ibsen, even *The Duchess of Malfi* at Stratford in Canada. Revues like *Eight O'Clock Jamaica Time* never missed us. I was usher for *Smile Orange* when it played at the Ward Theatre, and was one of the actresses (at seventeen) involved in the creation and first performances of Rhone's *Comic Strip*. I never had any formal training in drama but I would drive my mother mad hanging around drama groups at school where people like Greta Lyons and Dennis Scott, Keith Noel and Trevor Rhone would come and work with us. I was always discouraged from the theatre as a career; my parents feared I would come to a bad end![5]

Cumper cruised through the school years more interested in drama and swimming than in books. She had, however, inherited her share of the family's academic aptitude. She won the 1972 Jamaica Scholarship, and read archaeology and anthropology at Girton College in her parents' alma mater, Cambridge University. On her return to Jamaica, Cumper found herself on her own, her family having emigrated after the Black Power upheavals of the early seventies. She worked in several different jobs and, after a relatively sheltered childhood, began to learn first-hand about her own country.

Within a year of her return home Cumper had, at the urging of theatre producer Ed Wallace, expanded an original skit into her first full-length work, a vernacular drama. *The Rapist* was staged in December 1977. It was an immediate success, winning an award for the Best New Play of 1978, and continues to be produced around the Caribbean.

In view of Cumper's background, it is hardly surprising that her first play is one of social realism. Less predictable are the young playwright's original perspective and a quiet but keen sense of humour, both of which are structured into this examination of the far from humorous subject of rape. The two central characters are the rapist, Errol, and his prospective victim, Sharon. However, even though events inevitably progress towards an act of rape, the play is more about the causes of rape than about the act itself. In contrast to those of Rhone's contemporaneous *Old Story Time*, the class distinctions that motivate some of Cumper's characters are economic rather than ethnic. And for the creation of a victim as for the creation of an aggressor, Cumper suggests, the family environment may be largely to blame.

Like Rhone's Miss Aggie, Errol's working-class mother claims to want to better her son's position in life. A self-righteous virago, she never lets pass an opportunity of reminding her family how she has laboured to this effect, though the family is well aware that much of the labour has been in the arms of her employer. Errol despises his weak father, who has been unemployed since his wife had him fired from a job she considered beneath *her* husband. Errol wants to be a mechanic, but when the opportunity came his way his mother had him fired from a job she considered beneath *her* son. Father and son idle their days away, exorcising their emasculation, the one through drink, the other through rape.

Sharon's middle-class parents, though genuinely loving, are too busy, making money and spending it, to appreciate that their once malleable little daughters are now young adults with their own needs. The parents' materialism is taken to further lengths by Sharon's cynical and sensual sister, Rosa, who is determined to sell her body to the highest bidder. The more sensitive Sharon wants something better of life, but her need for understanding companionship, coupled with her unworldliness, have made her vulnerable to playboy Wilson, her supposed boyfriend. When, largely for the sake of her relationship with Wilson, Sharon escapes the pressures of her home by moving into her own apartment, she finds herself virtually abandoned, and even more vulnerable.

A key character in the play is Munchie, a likeable, peanut-chewing, plain-clothes police rookie who happens to be Errol's friend. Since the audience is soon cued in to the fact that Errol is the rapist, the play's suspense depends not on who, but on whether: whether Errol will go through with the rape of the girl who has befriended him; whether Munchie will tumble in time to Errol's increasingly daring hints as to the rapist's identity. As Munchie says, when Errol first brings up the subject of the rapist, 'Any man who commit dem breed a crime deh wan' fi get ketch'.

'Eventually the play is about rape in a wider, more pervasive sense than sexual violence,' writes James Lee Wah, who directed *The Rapist* in Trinidad in 1988.

'It asks us to consider the values of the society (our values, for we are the society) which breed conditions which harbour rape. Consider the rape parents commit on their children's sensibilities or the rape that parasites like Winston or Rosa commit. The play asks us to consider our relationship one to the other, parent to children, man to woman and vice versa. In the final analysis we are all responsible. We reap what we sow.'[6]

Fired by the success of *The Rapist*, Cumper turned producer for her next play, *Rufus*. Dennis Scott directed, the cast was exceptional, the production was a financial disaster. Cumper gritted her teeth in the determination that not only would she continue writing, she would be the best writer she could be.

In 1983 Cumper's grit was rewarded with the Prime Minister's Award for the best play in a competition celebrating Jamaica's twenty-one years of independence. *Coming of Age* was read in 1984 at the Jamaica School of Drama, but has never been produced. For the time being, it was the last of her wholly original works for the stage, except for 1988's unproduced *Quadrille*. Apart from her output over the next decade as the writer-producer of popular radio serials, such as *Mortimer Simmonds*, *Aloysius*, and *Malvina's Revenge*, all Cumper's subsequent writing was either collaborative or based on the work of another writer. In 1984 she co-wrote with Lloyd Reckord, from a scenario by Scott, the book for that year's national pantomime. *Sipplesilver* was her second experience with pantomime; in 1979 her adaptation of a fairy tale had become the basis of Michael Reckord's *The Hon. Allpurpus and the Dancing Princess*.

Cumper's next major work for the stage was commissioned by the Groundwork Theatre Company. *The Fallen Angel and the Devil Concubine*, like *Buss Out*, was scripted after improvisation by the actresses, in this case Sistren's Ford-Smith and Carol Lawes. There was also input from other artists, notably Hertencer Lindsay and Eugene Williams. The première was eventually staged in Jamaica in 1987. The production has since been performed around the Caribbean, in England, America and Canada, to universal acclaim. Much of the credit for the play's success is due to the exceptional performances by the original cast, but the script is in itself a compelling piece of theatre. Its two roles are amongst the most searching and challenging ever written for specifically West Indian actresses.

The two women, as with the leading characters in *Buss Out*, come from contrasting social and ethnic backgrounds. Unlike *Buss Out*, however, this is not a case of privilege and oppression, book learning and street sense, rich and poor. Both women are destitute, elderly, and to some extent deranged. Judy Stone's *Guardian* review (4 June, 1990) of a Trinidad performance opens:

> 'Thwack!' thunders Lettie's aggressive stick again and again, punishing floor, wall, table, memories, life.
>
> 'Crack! Crack!' explode on the walls of the derelict house the missiles pelted by prowling boys in search of victims.
>
> 'Clack-clock, clack-clock,' echo Katie's heels, one high one low, as she hunches along on her painful, lying, selfish, greedy, pitiful, crazy search for crumbs of food, of comfort, company, love, and the way of life she threw away.

> There is a startling violence to the abrupt sounds that punctuate *The Fallen Angel and the Devil Concubine* . . . Far more destructive, however, is the slow, stealthy, life-long violence done to the two women of this play, by the West Indian society that has bred and raised them and made them what they are.
>
> Born at opposite ends of the social scale, they meet on the common ground of stark poverty. One black, one white, they meet in the common experience of oppressed and abandoned women. Both have borne a child to a man of a different race, have loved the child, and have lost it. Both have been rejected by their families.
>
> And though Katie sometimes attempts to restore the old order and lord it over Lettie, and though the two are fighting over possession of the filthy ruin that has become their home, they come to realise that they are all each other has, and it is the two of them against the outside world.

The Fallen Angel is Katie, the spoilt daughter of a planter, who had her own way once too often, when she ran away from an arranged marriage with a rum-sodden, lecherous old friend of her father's, and set up house instead on the beach with the black companion of her childhood, the fisherman Altamont. Her family disowned her, Altamont was lost at sea, and as she had no money to pay a doctor her idiot child died of a fever. Lettie, the Devil's Concubine, had her own times of grandeur, travelling with her employer to Italy, but both her employer and her family turned against her when she became pregnant after being raped, and the distraught Lettie was never able to trace the baby that her own mother gave away.

The language of the play is mainly in the vernacular, but is remarkable for Katie's versatility. She is as adept at parodying a Bishop's wife – 'I see you've got my favourite little Bourgeoislais wine to have with dinner tonight . . .' – as she is at letting loose a rangotang tirade that has Lettie gasping, 'Yu no know seh white people no fi gwon so!'

In 1988 *Quadrille* was workshopped at the ACTA Playwrights' Conference. Cumper wrote this stylised and heavily symbolic play to celebrate the 150th anniversary of Jamaica's 'full free', as Emancipation is known. Even in its structure the play is unusually free, being measured in 22 short scenes which, within the freedom of an abstract set, take place in a variety of locations around an estate. The language is spare, with an economy of lines of almost lyrical simplicity, in both standard English and the vernacular. The cast of four comprises two blacks and two whites. Cumper suggests that the latter may be played by black actors in half-masks, a significant reversal of the previous centuries' black-face of white actors. Ever since Genet's *The Blacks* introduced the device of the white half-mask to the Caribbean in the sixties it has regionally, as in other countries, become increasingly popular with writers and directors as a means of underscoring the metaphysical aspects of plays that explore questions of race and colonialism.

Both the play, *Quadrille*, and the estate where it is set, are held together by the slaves Peter and Belle. They are the rocks against which is dashed, as Emancipation looms, the increasing madness of their masters. In the opening scene the two have just arrived as a gift from Antoine's uncle. Antoine himself is also a recent arrival, reluctantly returned from the pleasures of England to oversee the estate following his father's illness. In view of his comparatively liberal attitude and ignorance of planters' ways, his incompetence is an advantage to Peter and Belle. They realise they can easily manipulate both Antoine and his crazed mother. Instead of running away from the strange household, the slaves determine to stay and work out their time until Emancipation. Step by step Peter and Belle improve their lot, in spite of the flood of negrophobic edicts brought from the father's sickroom by Antoine's mother, who is the only person allowed contact with the old man. Belle even craftily succeeds in having herself taught to read. Meanwhile Antoine's innocence is corrupted when he mixes with his fellow planters. Peter and Belle are now apprentices, but Antoine begins to treat them worse than slaves. Even so, when there is a rebellion, Peter saves Antoine's life. Goaded by unanswered questions, Antoine storms his father's sickroom, only to find the colonial slaver a withered mummy, long dead, but still clung to by the woman who cannot give him up. The son burns down the estate house, and all its horrors. A new life is to begin.

In 1989 *Buss Out* was written. Then in 1990 came one of Cumper's most highly-praised works, an adaptation of the extraordinary Erna Brodber novel, *Jane and Louisa Will Soon Come Home.* The same year saw the première of *Flameheart*, a docudrama on the life of Claude McKay, which Cumper wrote with Maureen Warner Lewis. Her major work in 1991, *Benny's Song*, is an adaptation of Shakespeare's *Romeo and Juliet.*

Storytelling

Like that of Alwin Bully, Cumper's *oeuvre* bridges several streams of theatre. Squarely within that of theatre of the people is the oral tradition of communal storytelling. Universal as that ancient tradition is, West Indian storytelling draws most deeply on African culture. The best-known example is the Anancy cycle of stories, which is discussed in further detail in the following chapter.

The Caribbean's two favourite storytellers are Trinidad's Paul Keens-Douglas and Jamaica's Louise Bennett-Coverly, better known as the inimitable Miss Lou. More than any other single person in the region Louise Bennett, as she was billed for most of her career, is credited with the legitimising of the vernacular on stage. In 1991, at an occasion honouring the 72-year-old Miss Lou in Toronto, Prime Minister Michael Manley's message of tribute described how 'she took the rich language of the people of Jamaica, embroidered it with wit and wisdom, and made it even more beautiful'.[7] Apart from their genial vernacular verse-stories, with which either performer can, on their own, hold a theatre audience for a full evening's programme, both Bennett-Coverley and Keens-Douglas have experience in writing more conventional theatre scripts. Bennett-Coverly has contributed in no small measure to the development of the Jamaican national pantomime in which she starred over a span of 32 years. Among the panto scripts she has written or co-written are the 1949 *Bluebeard and Brer Anancy*, *Anancy and Pandora* (1955), *Anancy and Beeny Bud* (1956), *Busha Bluebeard* (1957) and *Queenie's Daughter* (1963). The pantomime is itself popular theatre, and perhaps the most popular form of all. Being musical theatre it is treated in the following chapter, *Total Theatre.*

NOTES

1 Peter Brook, *The Empty Space, Avon Books*, 1968.
2 Trudy Konwalina, review, *EN*, 16 August, 1954.
3 Ralph Maraj in interview with Judy Stone, *TG*, 25 October, 1983.
4 Pat Cumper, letter to Judy Stone, 2 September, 1991.
5 *Ibid.*
6 James Lee Wah, programme note, *The Rapist*, San Fernando Theatre Workshop, 1988.
7 *TG*, 8 October, 1991.

5

TOTAL THEATRE

The mass appeal of the musical: Roderick Walcott, Earl Lovelace

Hanuman, the monkey god, in his search for Lord Rama's stolen bride Sita, crosses the mighty Indian Ocean in one jingling, somersaulting, acrobatic bound. Acrobatics, drumming, mime, music, dance, martial arts, animal masks and elaborate make-up, helmets and draped costumes of brilliant colour, fire-light and burning incense, with a narrator to tell the story, and audience participation in the thousands, are all part of the Ram Leela Festival. This annual re-enactment of the love story of Rama, and his great battle with the Demon King Ravan, takes place in a single performance that stretches over a period of from seven to fourteen days and nights.

Ram Leela was brought to the West Indies in the mid-nineteenth century by the indentured labourers from India. Today, in Trinidad in particular, the festival is more popular than ever. Though the majority of the celebrants are of East Indian ancestry, increasingly there may be seen on the Ram Leela grounds representatives of every race to be found in the multicultural population of the region.

Other ethnic folk celebrations brought from the various motherlands have also survived to the present. Still others, such as the flower festivals of St Lucia, have evolved out of the particular circumstances of the West Indies. Most West Indians at one time or another have 'jumped up' or 'wined' or 'chipped' along the streets of Trinidad's Carnival or Jamaica's Jonkunnu or Barbados's Cropover or Guyana's Mashramani. Many have danced to the tassa drums of the Hosay parades with their magnificent glittering tadjahs. Some have felt their pulses quicken to the drumming of pocomania or cumfa or shango, as a worshipper 'catches the spirit' and begins to shake and gyrate in the palais. Others have seen the descendants of slaves bring a vital exuberance to the demure dances of the former French colonists, such as the bele and the pique, or to the Spanish joropo.

Dance and drumming, music and the masquerade, are so much a part of everyday West Indian life that many hold these elements to be essential to any theatre claiming to be West Indian. From this point of view, the only truly West Indian theatre is total theatre, the often lavishly costumed theatre which incorporates the major performing arts, and sometimes others, into what is loosely termed a 'musical'. Errol Hill propounds his theory of a form of total theatre based on the region's carnivals. Derek Walcott has also defined the West Indian character latent in the musical, with such works as *The Charlatan*, *Ti-Jean and His Brothers*, *Dream on Monkey Mountain*, *The Joker of Seville*, *O Babylon* (1976), *Marie Laveau* (1979), and *Steel*. However, Walcott's total theatre is atypical of the region in that its prime element is the minutely crafted language.

Walcott calls his musical works variously musical plays, musical comedies, plays with music. The West Indian musical has taken many other forms, the best known being Jamaica's national pantomime, Trinidad's Carnival theatre, folk musicals, and what Nigerian writer Wole Soyinka has termed the 'calabash' theatre, which is a regimented form of folk musical under the control of governments around the region. The scores of these various musicals have drawn on a wide range of musical forms, including West Indian ones such as reggae, parang, folk and calypso.

Calypso, and subsequently the calypso theatre discussed in Chapter 2, developed as an art of political and social comment. The calypso-oriented Carnival theatre developed in the early eighties by the Trinidad Theatre Workshop actress Helen Camps and her Trinidad Tent Theatre (originally All Theatre Productions) was also a vehicle for social comment. The Carnival musicals were peopled by satirical characters such as the Baby Doll, Clown, Dame Lorraine, Jab Molassi, King Jab Jab, Midnight Robber and Pierrot Grenade. These characters, with their topical 'picong', or barbed wit, were rather more entertaining than the plots they presented, which year after year played bland variations on the simple basic theme of the universal struggle between good and evil.

Among Camps's writers were Paul Keens-Douglas, Mark Lyndersay, and the Irish-born Camps herself, but her principal playwright was Felix Edinborough. As well as scriptwriting, Edinborough specialises in performing as the loquacious Pierrot Grenade. Before joining Camps, Edinborough, a secondary school teacher, had been working with the Best Village Competition. After the demise of the Tent Theatre in the mid-eighties, he returned to his original platform and continued to write for Best Village. Among Edinborough's most successful works are such Carnival musicals as *Go To Hell* (1984), *King Arthur and His Merry Men* (1987), and *J'Ouvert*, of which the latter toured England and Europe in 1982.

Carnival theatre and its content of social commentary took a markedly different form in 1989, in the hands of controversial masman Peter Minshall. Minshall was born in British Guiana but has spent most of his life in Trinidad, where he has developed something akin to a cult following for his extraordinarily visionary Carnival band themes. He is also an internationally acclaimed designer who has worked in London, Barcelona and São Paolo. His gigantic kinetic puppets, developed out of Carnival, have danced in Toronto, Miami and Japan, at the Bastille Day celebrations in Paris and at the Barcelona Olympics.

In 1989 Minshall hired Trinidad's national stadium for the staging of a single performance, on the Carnival Monday night, of his pageant-like presentation, *Santimanitay*. It was theatre on a vast scale, in which the rise and fall of mas, or Carnival, became an allegory of the rise and fall of man. Simultaneously around the arena various scenes, some aswarm with masqueraders and some focused on a single performer, were mimed by members of Minshall's Carnival band. This minutely choreographed cast numbered more than a thousand, and was supported by actors, dancers and a large choir. All were elaborately costumed, the obscenely grotesque mingling with the soaringly beautiful. A commentator introduced the scenes, which were accompanied by the recorded music of the French composer Jean-Michel Jarre and live narration by Papa Mas, the sole speaking character. Only the two opening actors in this multitude wore traditional costume, that of the Pierrot.

Turning from Carnival to Jonkunnu, we find that several West Indian writers have written Jonkunnu plays. Among them is Edgar White, whose *Redemption Song* (1984) recreates a modern version of an old Jonkunnu tragedy. Sylvia Wynter's *Maskarade* (1973) embodies the Jonkunnu experience to a greater degree than does White's play. Wynter has puppets performing the ritual mummery to the traditional music of fife, drums, conch shell and cow horn. The actors play the mummers of 1841 who don the costumes of Pitchie-Patchie, the Queen, the Actor Boys, the Executioner and Jack of the Green, to play out a love quadrangle to the death. Jonkunnu theatre has not generally produced the kind of topical social commentary typical of its Carnival counterpart. One exception is Sistren's *Ida Revolt Inna Jonkunnu Stylee.*

Topical social commentary is the essence of Tony Gambrill's popular *Jamaica Time* revues, the first of which was staged in 1965. Similar revues have been produced from time to time in most of the territories. In Guyana, for instance, also in the sixties, Frank Pilgrim engineered a series of *Brink* shows such as *On the Brink* and *Brinkmanship.*

However, the principal musical vehicle for social comment in Jamaica is the annual national pantomime. Traditional English pantomime had been popular entertainment in the island during the late eighteenth and early nineteenth century. It then disappeared from the stage until naval and military officers at Port Royal revived the tradition in 1898. The 1899 Christmas pantomime of *Dick Whittington and His Cat* was to some extent localised to a Kingston setting. The development of the Jamaican pantomime to the national institution that it is today, however, is credited entirely to the Little Theatre Movement founded by Greta Bourke Fowler and her husband Henry.

The LTM staged its first pantomime, *Jack and the Beanstalk*, in 1941. The script came from England, but the LTM's familiar satirical treatment was apparent from the start. Ingeniously the Giant, who sentenced his captives to prison without trial, had been turned into a recognisable caricature of the current Colonial Governor, Sir Arthur Richards. At the time Richards had just, without trial, interred Jamaican political leaders, including Alexander Bustamante, who twenty years later would become the first Prime Minister of independent Jamaica.

The LTM has staged a pantomime without fail every Christmas since that inaugural year. In 1943 the company staged its first original Jamaican pantomime, Vera Bell's *Soliday and the Wicked Bird.* Despite the outstanding success of the indigenous piece, the next few pantomimes reverted to English scripts, adapted where possible to the Jamaican scene. Then in 1949, Louise Bennett and Noel Vaz collaborated on the original script, *Bluebeard and Brer Anancy.*

The response confirmed that locally-written pantomimes were what the public wanted. The next few English scripts were drastically adapted, by Michael Wickers and Ranny Williams among others. And from the time Greta Fowler's *Anancy and the Magic Mirror* arrived on stage in 1954, the pantomime has never looked back. Every year since then has seen an original Jamaican pantomime, with few revivals. The roster of leading playwrights who have helped to shape the annual panto to its present form includes Balfour Anderson, Louise Bennett, Pat Cumper, Ted Dwyer, Greta and Henry Fowler, Barbara Gloudon, Samuel Hillary, Lois Kelly, Gloria Lannaman, Sonia and Don Mills, Lloyd Reckord, Michael Reckord, Verena Reckord, Trevor Rhone, Dennis Scott, Carmen Tipling, Noel Vaz, Ranny Williams and Sylvia Wynter.

Today's Jamaican pantomime is almost totally severed from its roots, and might conceivably be seen as owing more to the operettas of Gilbert and Sullivan than to the traditional British panto. It has become essentially a Caribbean folk musical comedy, characterised by a strong flavour of political satire, and by a panache and polish not often seen on the folk stage. It is the biggest theatrical event of the year. Fifty years after its inception, each panto costs close on two million Jamaican dollars to mount, employs about a hundred performers and crew, and plays to a total audience of some seventy thousand, over a run of three months.

Many of the pantomimes are based on the Anancy (or Anansi) cycle of stories which came originally from Africa. These stories are popular throughout the West Indies. Anancy the spiderman is a trickster. The weakest creature in the forest, he survives by nimbleness of wit. Wholly amoral, he steals and lies shamelessly, and sometimes goes to greater lengths. Even though the other animals throughout the cycle are also described with anthropomorphic qualities of speech and habit, several of the stories have Anancy not only killing but eating his victims. West Indians empathise with and admire the imaginative guile with which the small spider outwits those more powerful than he. They enjoy the innate comedy in the tales. And since the spider is morally in the wrong, the finest joke is the rare occasion when he himself is finally outwitted and brought to book, as is Don Juan in Derek Walcott's *The Joker of Seville*.

Heroes, or anti-heroes, with Anancy characteristics, such as Ringo in Trevor Rhone's *Smile Orange*, or the picaroon Jerry Mole in Alwin Bully's *The Ruler in Hiroona*, appear frequently in West Indian theatre, not in pantomime alone. Even a British playwright, Michael Hastings, in creating the West Indian immigrant Meadowlark in his *Gloo Joo* (1978), made this leading character a quintessential Anancy figure. And Anancy as the original spiderman appears in such works as Elliot Bastien's musical *A Nancy Story* (1971), Zeno Constance's *The Agouti's Tale* (1987), and *Riding Haas* (1969) and *Tiger Dead* (1991) by Colville Young of Belize. In Stafford Ashani Harrison's Rastafarian musical, *Anansi and Unsung Heroes Out West* (1978), Anansi is the spider God of Babylon, who takes on human form as the violent gunman Baddest.

The triumph of the spirit of creativity over the disabilities of nature is a universal tradition. It can be found throughout myth and legend, in works of Shakespeare and many other sources, including a second West Indian cycle of stories, less well known than the Anancy cycle, that of the amiable young man, Ti-Jean. Apart from Derek Walcott's *Ti-Jean and his Brothers*, the only other plays of any note representing this second cycle are Roderick Walcott's *The Prowess of Ti-Jean, or, The Sound of a Wild Flute* (1973) and Eintou Springer's *Ti-Jean and Mariquite* (1987). Roderick also used a Ti-Jean story in a dance-mime sequence in *Chanson Marianne* (1974). Ti-Jean is another folk hero who uses wit and common sense to triumph over those more powerful than he. However, the imaginative resourcefulness that he displays, like that of Anancy, is channelled by an innate disinclination to work, and a lack of responsibility, that in other cultures may be seen as less admirable.

Folk traditions and experiences, some of ancient and some of more recent vintage, have also found their way into musicals. *Kanima at Sun Mountain*, by Guyana's lone Arawak playwright-composer Basil Rodrigues, is a story of the clash between cultures when a tribesman's life is threatened by malaria. A decision must be made whether to take him to the paiai (pronounced 'pea-eye'), as the Arawak medicine-man is called, or to the nearest practitioner of orthodox western medicine.

Guyana has produced a number of musicals, the earliest on a Guyanese theme being *Stabroek Fantasy* (1956) by Helen Taitt and Cecile Nobrega. Particularly successful among more recent writers of Guyanese musicals have been the Tradewinds musician Dave Martin with *Raise Up* (1989), and Paloma Mohamed with *Reggae Marley* (1989), based on the life of Bob Marley.

Roderick Walcott

Of all the playwrights who have created musicals out of the tradition of West Indian folk festivals, one of the most highly regarded is Roderick Walcott of St Lucia. Roderick Aldon Walcott, while not achieving the international eminence of his twin brother Derek, is by many considered to be, of the two playwrights, the more genuinely representative of West Indian theatre as a genre. Whereas the elder Walcott, Derek, is devoted to classical form and fine detail, the younger works in broader strokes, taking the approach favoured by Hill as he draws on the simple basic rhythms of the region's folk forms. Roderick Walcott broke new ground with his folk musicals, based on the flower festivals of St Lucia. Several of his short plays continue to be produced, and the places of *The Harrowing of Benjy* (1956) and *Malfinis* (1960) appear assured in the region's permanent repertoire.

It may seem a quibble to refer to the elder and younger brothers, when the one followed into the world only minutes after the other, but Roderick himself felt keenly, particularly in his boyhood days, that he 'has been behind ever since', as he wrote in 1956 in the manuscript of his first plays. At school, Roderick was a year behind his twin. He adopted George Orwell's phrase for his own ironical use, as when he began to write for the stage: his 'Big Brother' was watching him. But it was Big Brother who brought him to the stage, with the *Henri Christophe* première that launched the St Lucia Arts Guild into theatre when the twins were twenty. With that production, Roderick knew he had found the outlet for his own talents, in arts administration. He was to run the Guild for the best part of the next two decades, until in 1968 he left for Canada, where he took a B.A. degree in Fine Arts at York University.

In 1951, six months after *Christophe*, Roderick directed his first production. It was a double bill of *Paolo and Francesca* and *Three Assassins*, two new one-act plays by his brother. He soon became, and remained for many years, Derek's most trusted interpreter of his plays, other than the playwright himself.

Like his twin, Roderick Walcott is gifted in several aspects of the arts. He is an exhibited artist, with a style not dissimilar to his brother's. Like Derek, he is a designer. Unlike Derek, he acts. He has played pan. He has choreographed. He has directed a wide variety of plays, not only Caribbean but also world classics and contemporary international works. And he writes.

He wrote his first three plays, he claimed, 'to try to scare his Big Brother'.[1] More to the point, he wrote them as his first contribution to 'a National West Indian Theatre'.[2] From the outset he established his own vision in this regard. The three one-act plays are each set in a different Caribbean island: *The Harrowing of Benjy* in Jamaica, *Shrove Tuesday March* in Trinidad, and *The One-Eye is King* in St Lucia. All three are written in the vernacular. But Walcott deliberately avoided an accurate rendering of the parochial dialect of each island. He worked instead with a linguistic compromise, that had a ring of the West Indian region without any particular local identity. This compromise, he felt, was what was required for a regional theatre.

It is the language that is the greatest strength of *Shrove Tuesday March*, the first of the younger Walcott's works to go before the St Lucian public. The piece was aired as a radio play in 1956, with original music for the ping pong and tenor pan by Eric Branford, who also played two of the characters. Later the same year, the Guild presented the three plays as a triple bill directed by the author.

At the time, Walcott was a member of a steelband that had its home in his own backyard. Stanley French, another leading St Lucian playwright, who played a steelbandsman in that 1956 première, was also briefly a member of this band. It was through this association with Roderick Walcott that French joined the St Lucia Arts Guild, where he was first inspired to write for the stage.

Just as Errol Hill's participation in a steelband had flowered into *The Ping Pong*, so Walcott's like participation produced *Shrove Tuesday March*. The Trinidadian setting is a steelband hideout on Carnival Monday. Though marred by speeches that are overlong for its realistic style, the language of this first play is urgent, vivid and unpretentious. For the rest, the piece is something of a disappointment, slight in plot and unpersuasive in treatment. The Serenaders Steelband has been in a J'Ouvert fight with the rival Marauders, and a Marauder has been killed. Both bands believe that Serenader Sharkey, the dog with a bad name for making trouble, is the murderer. Not until it is too late to save Sharkey does the truth come to light, that the murder was committed by Sharkey's closest friend, the mute Bones Williamson. The six Serenaders of the cast are sketched so lightly that their motivations are invisible, which makes it difficult for an audience to understand why Bones killed Honey Price in the first place, or to credit that Sharkey would have sacrificed his own life to save his friend's.

Walcott called the other two of his earliest plays 'character studies', but the term sits uneasily on *The One-Eye is King*. In this gentle comedy a petty crook washed up from the, comparatively, big city of Port of Spain, fleeces in entirety the 'elementary people', as Derek Walcott has described them, of a St Lucian fishing village. Despite his theory of a regional language, in this play Roderick Walcott has made a careful and effective differentiation between the language of the St Lucian, which is flavoured with patois, and that of the 'Trickidadian'. However, as the playwright writes, 'there is still no attempt to make the play only acceptable in the two islands concerned. There has been, therefore, no prolonged effort at research into the particular dialects of these islands to capture entirely the mood and settings of these plays'.[3]

The One-Eye is King is a more satisfyingly worked piece of theatre than the pan piece, and there is more depth to the characters. But it is not a study of the calibre of Roderick Walcott's most frequently produced play, *The Harrowing of Benjy*. In the 1957 Jamaica Drama Festival *Benjy*, directed by Hill, won an unprecedented five awards, including best West Indian comedy.

Benjy is a vagrant preacher, a figure familiar throughout the Caribbean, whether Baptist or, as Walcott perhaps less appropriately suggests, Rastafarian. Benjy's morning has begun badly, with his being rousted by a new and officious constable from his bed under a lorry. There is a latent violence in the preacher which surfaces only under provocation, but provocation is only too ready to heap up on Benjy's head. Passing college boys provoke him, his sniggering congregation provokes him, his runaway woman Agnes provokes him. And when young Constable Horner returns to provoke him further, it is the last straw that kindles the smouldering Benjy to flame. Benjy has a long record of assault and even murder, but the older hands in the police force consider him harmless if left alone. Yet there is something in Benjy that revels in the challenge of the provocation he half-deliberately attracts. It is not until the Sergeant in the police station, in a symbolic emasculation, confiscates the arrested preacher's precious razor, that Benjy's spirit is genuinely harrowed along with his manhood. The cocksure rioter who had swaggered exhilarated into the station departs a broken man.

The Harrowing of Benjy is a boisterous, gripping and sympathetic play, which closely involves the audience as part of the crowd, and offers actors and director considerable potential for humorous elaboration. Part of its fascination lies with the ritualistic elements in the preparation and delivery of Benjy's streetcorner sermon on the Scarlet Woman, in the preacher's baiting by the lookers-on and by the errant Agnes, and in the police routine.

This first Benjy play proved so successful that Walcott wrote two more to form a trilogy. *A Flight of Sparrows* had its première performance in 1958 during the Guild's first tour of Dominica, and won the 1959 Jamaican Festival award for the best West Indian drama. But neither this second play nor the 1960 *The Education of Alfie* achieved the lasting popularity of the original.

Roderick Walcott's next work, the musical *The Banjo Man* (1971), was to prove a milestone for several reasons. It was the first St Lucian play, and one of the earliest West Indian plays, to bring into the theatre a folk festival of the region. It is also believed to have been the first and still the only regional play to have been banned by the Catholic Church. Both Carnival and calypso, however, have a long history of attempted bans by governments of Trinidad, and to a lesser extent elsewhere, such as Barbados.

The Banjo Man, along with Derek Walcott's *Sea at Dauphin*, had been selected as the St Lucian entry for the 1958 Federal Arts Festival in Trinidad. This first production of *The Banjo Man* had been in rehearsal for ten weeks when the Vicar-General imposed the ban, on the grounds that the theme of Roderick's musical was 'contrary to the doctrine of the Church'.[4] During the fierce public controversy that ensued, the playwright was accused of profanity and blasphemy, and the play of glorifying 'drunkenness, fornication, seduction and general lechery'.[5] In the opposite camp were those who saw the play as 'an appealing tale of love and mating',[6] as a valuable documentation of a fading tradition, or as the long-awaited genuine mirror of the West Indian society. The playwright himself eventually stepped in to point out that the theme of the play clearly, for 'those who could see further than the ecclesiastical nose',[7] supported morality. Even so, the Guild withdrew the piece, St Lucia sent no entry to the Festival, and it was thirteen years before *The Banjo Man* eventually trod the boards in St Lucia's 1971 Development Day celebrations. Ironically, with the swing of the social pendulum over little more than a decade, attitudes in St Lucia had broadened to such an extent that the musical was now praised even beyond its due, and acclaimed an unqualified triumph. The government, grown more sensitive to its responsibility for the preservation of the island's folk heritage, brought Walcott back from his studies in Canada to redirect the production as the St Lucian entry in the 1972 Carifesta, where it won further ovations.

The 'Lawoz' festival of *The Banjo Man* is celebrated by Sosete Lawoz, one of two rival St Lucian societies. Each society is named for a saint, the Lawoz after St Rose of Lima, the first saint born in the New World, and the Lamagrit after St Marguerite. The societies were in existence before Emancipation. At their peak, early in the twentieth century, the two societies could claim that the majority of St Lucians were allied with one or the other, either as active participants or, in the case of more prominent citizens, as affiliated patrons. Membership was declared by the wearing of the appropriate flower, and each festival was held on its saint's day. The festivals combined visual splendour, prayer and thanksgiving, refreshments, music, dance and general merriment, the latter mainly at the expense of the rival society.

Dan Crowley in an issue of *Caribbean Quarterly* describes the Lawoz festival beginning with 'the King, Queen and other dignitaries parading through the streets to and from Mass wearing magnificent robes and carrying gold-emblazoned flags. In the evenings there is a ceremony of homage to the "royalty", a grand march, a dance, and plenty of cakes and drinks. The special dance form is called Mapa, danced in a circle and sung by a chantwel and the dancers.' Walcott, for years an outstanding Carnival band leader, himself designed the elaborate festival costumes for the Carifesta production.

The chantwel who is the banjo man of Walcott's title, Estephan, first surfaced in earlier works of the playwright. Cobra's Trinidad accent sounds to the villagers of *The One-Eye is King* 'like is singing. Comme cuatro Estefan', the cuatro being a common West Indian term for the ukulele, or guitar banjo. And the man for whom Agnes left Benjy is 'a licentious banjo-player', an intimation of the sexual symbolism of the banjo as Walcott uses it in his musical. Sexual innuendo is richly enjoyed in the West Indies, both in the theatre and in daily life.

The play opens on the morning of the Lawoz festival. The itinerant musician Estephan, the traditional chantwel of Belle Maison, still has not arrived. The conversation of the villagers discussing his exploits sketches a picture of a joyous Pied Piper of the banjo, whose advancing age has impaired neither the exceptional musicianship that has him in demand all over the island, nor his ability to attract women wherever he goes. With Estephan's eventual appearance the Festival begins and virtually becomes the musical. What little dramatic tension the plot offers lies in a burgeoning affair between Estephan and the new Queen, wife of the jealous Son Son. Before the first carefully contrived step in the *pas de deux* is completed, however, Estephan overhears a conversation that opens his eyes to the pain he has caused by his habit of singing about his conquests. Conscience-stricken at having made a woman cry, he leaves the Queen and Belle Maison, never to return.

As a piece of theatre, *The Banjo Man* is by today's standards quite inoffensive, and indeed charmingly entertaining, but it lacks balance. Its slender plot is so overweighted with songs that impede rather than power the action, that at times the effect is more that of an elaborately staged concert than a musical play. However, as a record of the St Lucian heritage, and an early experiment in line with Hill's thesis of a West Indian theatre drawn from the region's festivals, it is a work of historical importance, even to its glossary of the St Lucian patois scattered through the dialogue.

Walcott later wrote a companion musical on the Sosete Lamagrit, *Chanson Marianne* (1974), and a third, *Romiel ec Violette* (1979), in which a Romeo and Juliet love story brings the two societies together. These two musicals, and his *Papa Diable* (1977), which is based on the St Lucian Carnival, were produced for the St Lucia government on national occasions. Walcott has also written several Carnival shows, such as the 1959 *Carnival Revisited*. More recent musicals include *The Wonderful World of Brother Rabbit*, and *The Guitar Man's Song*, which had its première in St Lucia in 1989.

It is the character of Estephan that makes the original musical the most memorable. Identifiably West Indian, Estephan has his contemporary counterpart in the calypsos of Trinidad's Mighty Sparrow, and in any number of footloose 'sweetmen' up and down the islands. Living his life openly as he likes, 'full as I can make it . . . no belt to tie me, no tie to hang me, no braces to support me', as a character of West Indian lore, Estephan is closer to the open-hearted Ti-Jean than to the devious Anancy. Yet he descends too from the bloodline of the Don Juan who also sired Derek Walcott's *Joker of Seville*. And Juan himself goes back to Dionysus, while Lawoz and Lamagrit can also trace back their sources to the fertility festivals of the ancient world.

Estephan's friends refer to him affectionately as 'malfinis', or the chicken hawk, for his ability to raid other men's yards and capture the hearts of their 'chickens'. Walcott was to return to the malfinis, but first he tried another character study. *The Trouble with Albino Joe* features a barely plausible Caribbean gangster and his blind side-kick. The playwright's intention was to show the influence of Hollywood cinema on a raving psychopath. The one-act melodrama had its première in St Lucia just prior to the Guild's 1959 Trinidad tour.

After this less successful effort, Walcott then wrote a longer one-act play that he called *Malfinis*. This play was inspired by the film *Roshomon*, and based on a famous murder case in St Lucia. Staged for the first time in 1960, when it won the award for the best 'Long Serious Play', it is the only work of the younger Walcott's which experiments with classical form. And this malfinis has nothing to do with affection. The hawk takes the heart of its captured chicken in reality, and in a most gruesome manner.

There are in fact three chicken hawks in *Malfinis* – the three murderers of a 13-year-old boy deliberately brought from Barbados to St Lucia for the purpose of sacrifice. At the opening of the play Montoute Edmond, St Luce Leon and Edgar St Hill have all paid for their crime under earthly justice. Now their souls are once again on trial, in purgatory.

The purpose of the present trial, before a Chorus of four and their Leader, is to clarify certain mysteries left unanswered at the earthly trial. As each soul testifies, a different tale of the murder is played, protesting the speaker's innocence, blaming the evil on the others. Out of the web of lies emerges a murky but constant picture of a satanic book, a gardeur who believes prosperity can be conjured through the head and heart and hands of a dead child, a sick man willing to murder for health and money. Eventually an eye-witness arrives, the soul of a blind man who had been too afraid to testify in life. His account apportions the guilt of murder equally to all three of the accused. Unexpectedly, the Chorus Leader first argues against the new witness, then against further examination of the case. It is only when he fulfils an earlier vengeful threat to condemn the blind soul to eternal damnation, and then unmasks, that we discover the 'mighty judge' is none other than the ghost of the satanic gardeur and murderer, Montoute.

It would have been possible for the playwright to achieve a sufficiently dramatic study of the psyche of the murderers without showing the actual murder even once, and there are those who find excessively distasteful his repeated replay of the deed. Such considerations aside, *Malfinis* is Roderick Walcott's most powerful work and, in its own grim way, his most poetic, with its patois rhythms and imagery. It is one of his most frequently produced plays.

Walcott left for Canada in 1968. He continued to write, and in 1973 a Guild programme of excerpts from his unstaged plays listed scenes from *The Legend of Tom Fool*, *The Image of Canga Brown*, *The Prowess of Ti-Jean* and *Make a Joyful Sound*, along with *Papa Diable*.

In 1977 Walcott was appointed Director of Culture for St Lucia, a position he held until 1980, when he returned to Canada. He continued to write, and his *The Guitar Man's Song* had its première on the tenth anniversary of St Lucia's independence.

Calabash theatre

Nigerian writer Wole Soyinka coined the term 'calabash theatre' after the regulation of an African government that decreed any play not incorporating a calabash (a dried gourd shell, commonly used as a storage or drinking vessel) could not be considered indigenous theatre.

Both the calabash tree and the calabash theatre are familiar sights in the Caribbean. Several of the West Indian islands run or have run government-sponsored folk festivals of performing arts which place similar arbitrary artistic straitjackets on their amateur participants. In the sixties and seventies most playwrights, serious theatre practitioners, and other professional performing artists, decried the work produced in these festivals as substandard, fake and shallow. The region's intellectuals saw the festivals as political sops to the masses, and a tourist-oriented threat to the genuine culture of the West Indies, in Michael Gilkes's phrase, a 'masquerade of belonging'.[8]

Derek Walcott in *What the Twilight Says* writes:

> Every state sees its image in those forms which have the mass appeal of sport, seasonal and amateurish. Stamped on that image is the old colonial grimace of the laughing nigger, steelbandsman, carnival masker, calypsonian and limbo dancer. These popular artists are trapped in the State's concept of the folk form, for they preserve the colonial demeanour and threaten nothing. The folk arts have become the symbol of a carefree, accommodating culture, an adjunct to tourism, since the State is impatient with anything which it cannot trade.

However, even within the restraints of the calabash theatre, some genuine progress has been made in the development of West Indian folk musicals. In Trinidad, the current Prime Minister's Best Village Competition was begun by Eric Williams in 1963 with a handicraft competition under the banner of Better Village. In 1964 it expanded into the Festival of Folklore, the first in an annual series of amateur folk concerts. In 1971 the competition was upgraded from Better to Best. For many years the rules of this competition required each village to include in its entry set items of specific length, such as various ethnic folk dances and folk songs, a traditional Carnival piece, a stickfight, and a skit.

As early as 1974 the Petit Valley Village pioneered the experiment of incorporating the concert elements into the skit, to achieve a full-scale dramatic folk musical. By the turn of the decade, all the leading villages were following suit. Both young and established writers sympathetic to the folk movement, such as Ronald Amoroso, Felix Edinborough, Norvan Fullerton, Reginald Griffith, Earl Lovelace, Godfrey Sealy and Efebo Wilkinson, became interested in the potential of the form, and began to work closely with the villages. Subsequently, during the eighties, there emerged out of that scorned village competition several folk musicals that transferred to the conventional stage, where they played to considerable acclaim, in some cases winning top national and even international awards. The more successful folk companies were now rehearsing and performing year round, instead of coming together purely for the weeks of the competition. By the start of the nineties, the competition regulations had been relaxed to allow for fuller development of the folk musical.

Earl Lovelace

The most widely esteemed playwright to have worked with Trinidad's Best Village competition is novelist Earl Lovelace. Although Lovelace did not come to prominence as a playwright until more than a decade after his first novel was published, his first play was in fact staged even before he became established as a writer. Lovelace is unusual in several respects. He is the only major Trinidadian novelist of his generation who has not, as have most internationally published West Indians, emigrated from his homeland. Few Caribbean writers of his calibre have worked so intensively in the realm of folk. Few have seen their novels adapted to the stage, let alone undertaken the scripting themselves, as Lovelace has done with *The Dragon Can't Dance* and *The Wine of Astonishment* (1988). In addition Lovelace has written several original plays. All his work resonates with his deep sympathy for the disadvantaged in his society. One of his primary concerns is to establish a historically 'truer representation'[9] of the quality of the cultural struggle fought by black West Indians. However, being an artist rather than a sociologist, he is also concerned with 'the affirming of the human spirit, and the questions that, as human beings, we [all] face all the time'.[10]

Born in 1935, in Trinidad's relatively remote coastal village of Toco, Lovelace spent his childhood in Tobago, but was resettled in Port of Spain for his secondary education. The sudden plunge from the slow rhythms of country life into the city hustle proved to be an unsettling change. The teenaged Lovelace failed the Exhibition twice, 'in those days a devastating failure', as journalist Judy Raymond writes (*SE*, 4 August, 1991). After leaving the Ideal High School, he worked briefly as proof-reader for the *Trinidad Guardian*, and then became a forest ranger. In the isolation of the Valencia forests, he decided that he wanted to be a writer. Over the next few years he read voraciously, began to write poems and short stories, attended meetings of a small literary group, and took to watching rehearsals of the Trinidad Theatre Workshop (Derek Walcott managed to lose the poems the shy young apprentice proffered for comment).

Lovelace's first play was written for the independence celebrations of 1962. *The New Boss* symbolised the island's independence as an estate that had been left to its workers, and explored the new responsibilities of the people. The medium-length play was staged outdoors on the Rio Claro savannah, with a cast composed largely of members of the Rio Claro football team. A second production of the play was staged in Tobago in 1965, while Lovelace was working there as an agricultural extension officer.

Meanwhile, in 1964 Lovelace's first book, *While Gods are Falling*, won the

BP Independence Literary Award. The young writer used the prize money to further his studies at Howard University, Washington. By the time his second novel, *The Schoolmaster*, was published, in 1968, he had married. Novel painstakingly followed novel, and then in 1976 there appeared on the Best Village stage Lovelace's second play, *My Name is Village*. Lovelace had written this piece especially for the villagers of Matura, where he then lived with his family. Other villages have subsequently staged this folk musical, and it has also appeared in the Secondary Schools Drama Festival, for which, also in 1976, Lovelace was commissioned to write *The Seekers*, a short play which he describes as 'religious'.[11]

My Name is Village was one of the earliest works to incorporate the requirements of the Best Village competition into a single piece of theatre. The basic plot, set in a village, is one of adolescent romance. The themes touch on youth and age, unemployment and survival, manhood and self-betterment, but the principal theme is one recurrent in Lovelace's work, the search for individual identity. The treatment contrasts town and country life, with town portrayed as the place of opportunity, but also as a frenzy of materialism and immorality.

The play's seams may be thought to show a measure of strain over such obligatory inclusions as the Jab Molassi dance. But for the most part the various competition requirements are woven into the fabric of the musical in such a way as to lend it both strength and character. And the novelist in Lovelace draws out some unexpectedly delicate nuances in moments of pathos and gentle humour, in contrast to the razzamatazz vaudeville act of the devilish Town Test and his two Yes Men.

Perhaps inspired by the Best Village competition itself, perhaps inspired by Hill's recently published thesis on Carnival theatre, perhaps inspired by his own intense respect for Trinidad's Carnival as a creative expression of his people's freedom, Lovelace was already experimenting with the metaphor of masquerade that he was to use to considerable and surrealistic effect in later plays, such as *The New Hardware Store* (1980).

In 1977 Lovelace again wrote the Best Village entry for Matura. *Pierrot Grenade* once more opposes town and country life, but this time in a town setting. Again, the musical was constrained to meet the competition regulations of the time, but the later relaxation of those regulations eventually allowed Lovelace to rework the piece.

Lovelace's next work for the stage treated an unusual aspect of the search for identity. *Jestina's Calypso* (1978) is an examination of the concept of ugliness, and of the power of appearance to affect evaluation of worth.

With her fortieth birthday approaching, Jestina is suffering a mid-life crisis. She is pilloried by her fellow villagers for her phenomenal ugliness. All her life, men have used her body without affection. All her life, she has worked hard to make a living, 'weeding and toting water and cutlassing like a man'. She is now the owner of a village 'parlour', a tiny shop. It is not enough. Jestina dreams dreams. And now a dream is on the verge of realisation. In her heart Jestina dreads that reality will destroy the dream.

Jestina's penfriend is coming home to marry her. The two have never met, but have fallen in love through their letters. He, who is never named, has sent Jestina his photograph, the picture of a warrior. She too has sent him a photograph. But, as a blaring taxi waits to take her to the airport, Jestina, alternating between courageous determination and terrified refusal to meet her destiny, confesses that the snap she sent was not of herself, but of her pretty friend and role model, Laura. The ugly woman has learned too well that 'this world judges by surfaces'.

Eventually Jestina, the bravest of warriors, throws away wig and warpaint and, with Laura, travels to the airport to present herself to her fiancé in total honesty. The heckling villagers play out the rest of the tale, as Jestina is cast aside, and the returning hero chooses 'empty beauty'.

The script shows Lovelace the novelist in ascendance over Lovelace the dramatist. *Jestina's Calypso* is essentially a play of ideas, and as such it is in some respects more effective in the reading than in the performance. Ostensibly a realistic play, the treatment adopts an element of surrealism in what on stage can prove an uncomfortable blend. The requirement for a split stage, showing simultaneously the interior and exterior of Jestina's house, has the potential for heightened drama and humour, but occasionally its use hampers the action. In performance the first act, in particular, seems over long and lacking adequate dynamics, while characterisation is incomplete; the villagers often speak with the voice and intellect of the playwright. The language itself occasionally flows less easily than in his later works. But the tone of Lovelace's plays has always been as important to him as that of his novels, in particular the capturing of a genuine West Indian rhythm in the dialogue.

Whatever its theatrical shortcomings, *Jestina's Calypso* is bold in form, and makes its points with a disturbing power. On a deeper level it is symbolic of the historical rape of the West Indies by colonialism, and of the modern seduction of West Indians by metropolitan materialism. Jestina describes herself in terms of her island:

> What an island! My heart broken by lovers, their names I do not even remember. My breasts dragged down by centuries of bearing cane and coffee and cocoa, sag now like landslides. Oh, what an island! The marrow of my bones drained out like oil, pumped out, syphoned to infuse another's heart.

Jestina's Calypso had its première in a student production on the St Augustine campus of the University of the West Indies in 1978. It has enjoyed several subsequent productions, including a revival by the original players.

1978 also saw the earliest stage in the dramatisation of Lovelace's major novel, *The Dragon Can't Dance. A Dramatic Reading of Excerpts from The Dragon Can't Dance (A New Novel)* was the first production to be staged by the Trinidad Theatre Workshop following the traumatic 1976 resignation of its founder-director, Derek Walcott. The story is set in the fifties, and is driven by the extraordinary power of Carnival over the lives of the underprivileged but resilient residents of an actual Port of Spain ghetto, Laventille. The Workshop presented the première performance in the Laventille panyard of the Desperadoes Steelband. The dramatised readings were accompanied by original music composed and played by André Tanker, an exceptional Caribbean musician who is a descendant of Trinidad's most renowned nineteenth-century painter, Jean Michel Cazabon.

In 1980 similar readings of *The Dragon Can't Dance* were held in New York, and in 1981 the Theatre Workshop readings were staged in Barbados, representing Trinidad for Carifesta. Meanwhile, Lovelace was working on a full stage adaptation. An early script was workshopped at the Eugene O'Neill 1984 Playwrights' Conference in Connecticut, with a cast drawn from around the Caribbean. The full musical, with a complete score by Tanker, had its première in Trinidad for the 1986 Carnival, but was found to be over long. After further tightening the text was finally published in a 1989 collection, *Black Plays: Two.*

In an interview with Hugh Lynch, just prior to the 1990 London production of *The Dragon Can't Dance*, Lovelace spoke on the difficulties inherent in translating creative work from one art form to another. In this particular translation, the playwright explained, some events had been interpreted 'in a theatrical rather than a novelistic sense . . . The differences might be in emphasis and scale. But I would like to think that the central theme of the novel runs through the play.'[12] Lovelace also felt he had managed to keep on stage the community sense of the novel.

He does not see dramatic adaptation as detracting from the importance of the novel: 'The novel remains the novel. What the play does is bring it to another audience',[13] and the play should be seen as a work in its own right.

Yet another of Lovelace's works dealing with the search for identity, *The Dragon Can't Dance* is essentially a yard play in the mould of Errol John's *Moon on a Rainbow Shawl.* The latter, however, is not a musical, though a version incorporating an original score was staged in Dominica by Alwin Bully. The music of *The Dragon* – calypso, rapso, road march, parang – is fully integrated with the drama, making Lovelace's adapted novel, rather than *Moon*, or any precursors from the calabash folk theatre, the first authentic yard musical. Stylised in form, the work advances in 'movements', rather than scenes. These movements reflect the lunge and retreat pattern of the traditional Dragon dance, performed by the shackled Beast as goading imps guide it through the streets.

The Dragon is one of Trinidad's old-time individual Carnival masquerades that today, with the development of the professionally designed 'pretty mas' costume bands several thousand members strong, has been driven to the edge of extinction. For unemployed Aldrick, who builds his costume anew each year, the Dragon is his life, his identity, his manhood. Each scale he sews has its singular history. Meantime, in the flowering of her womanhood, young Sylvia has captured Aldrick's heart, as she has the hearts of all the men on Calvary Hill. But Aldrick feels he has nothing to offer save his Dragon. Sylvia, her love for Aldrick meeting no encouragement, reluctantly turns to the elderly landlord, Mr Guy, for her own Carnival costume. Aldrick is spurred to break out of the comfortable cocoon of his costume into open rebellion against the social shackles of his colonial heritage. With the notorious Fisheye he steals a police jeep and drives around town, shooting air. The escapade is just another masquerade. It is during his five years in jail that Aldrick finally learns self-respect. He returns to Calvary Hill, not to dance the Dragon, but to look for Sylvia.

Several subplots are interwoven with the love story of Aldrick and Sylvia. There is the story of Fisheye, who became somebody when he joined the steelband, and nobody when the new sponsors had him thrown out. There is the story of the calypsonian Philo, who is forced to betray his artistic vision in order to win the calypso crown and the right to climb Miss Cleo's stairs. There is the story of the outsiders, the East Indians Pariag and Dolly, and the communal hatred provoked by their difference, and even by their pathetically ill-advised attempts to win acceptance.

The Dragon Can't Dance is more bitter than sweet in its exploration of human relationships, but it is potentially a dynamic piece of theatre, swift with the excitement of its celebration of Carnival. Lovelace's adaptation from page to stage is not always totally successful, particularly in the incident of Aldrick's shooting escapade, which is a highlight of the novel but fails to make sufficient impact in the play. No novel, however, can convey the pulsating force of Carnival with the immediacy of theatre.

Lovelace's next original work for the stage, *The New Hardware Store*, again incorporates Carnival, in a more metaphysical manner. Dramatically, it is the most tightly crafted of Lovelace's plays. First performed in Trinidad in 1980, the piece won the playwright a particularly warm reception in London's 1985 Black Theatre Season, and subsequently moved across from the Arts Theatre to the Albany, for a second West End run.

On the surface, the play is about an ordinary day in an ordinary store, in which ordinary sorts of arguments break out between the boss and his workers on levels of pay, job description and time off. But there are no customers and no sales clerks in this store, only philosophers. The New Hardware Store is a metaphor for the Third World in general, for the Caribbean and Trinidad in particular. Set soon after the latter's 1970 abortive Black Power revolution, the play questions the appropriateness of certain life-styles in a newly-independent state. Five representative characters argue the cases: the businessman, pragmatically sticky-fingered A.A. Ablack, first local owner of the Store; the artist, Rooso the sandwich-man-cum-nightwatchman; the ordinary honest citizen, bookkeeper Miss Calliste; youth, in the person of the teenaged typist Miss Prime; and Dillon, the dead revolutionary with Che Guevara overtones.

'We will import a life for you, and assemble it locally', is Ablack's preferred solution. Like his name, Ablack's philosophy is a denial of his race. All his ambition is to stand in the shoes of those who have left, to wield the same power, enjoy the same privileges, rake in the same profits. His only soul brothers are his own pockets. Miss Prime, the latest product of the enlightened educational system and years of American television programming, at first sides with Ablack. But by the play's end she agrees with Rooso that people's lives should develop out of their own experience even if, as Ablack warns, they risk making a mess of things.

'There is no bias', writes reviewer Julian Keeling (*Plays and Players*, May,

1985), 'only compassion and humour to make the figures sympathetic. Though their ideals are diametrically opposed it is apparent that they are opposite sides of the same coin. They are linked together by a common understanding of their mutual victimisation. Tension is sprung from the subtle tipping of the scales as the edge of power slips from one faction to the other.'

The first act is in a realistic mode. It fills in the background to the characters and sets out the basic premises of the arguments while Rooso (whose performance begins in the theatre lobby as the audience arrives) and Ablack do some preliminary, time-honoured skirmishing. The second act takes on mythic dimensions as it 'breaks into a play within a play, or rather two plays within a play,' writes novelist Lawrence Scott (*SE*, 28 April, 1985), 'the first taking off into a demonic encounter between Ablack as the Midnight Robber and Rooso (who is dressed as a clown at the beginning of the play) as the other Carnival speechifier, Pierrot. The Midnight Robber, with his bombast and acquisitiveness, heightens the character of Ablack as well as taking the play on to a quite other level of humour, with Rooso seeking to win the battle of words with lyric philosophy and calypso'. In the second play within the play, Rooso takes on the role of the martyred freedom fighter Dillon, former lover of Marva Calliste.

Keeling was not the only critic to feel that in the second act the characters 'seemed to be merely vehicles for Mr Lovelace's internal dialogue', but he added, 'Though the audience was deprived of a dramatic climax, the rich exploration of both sides of the main theme of conflict made the realism of its lack of conclusion strangely satisfying'. Of all his plays, *The New Hardware Store* is Lovelace's most inventive in his development of the Carnival masquerade.

The theme of the necessity for the identity of a people to mature out of that people's own experience, rather than from a borrowed culture, reappears in Lovelace's next and last theatrical piece of the decade. *The Wine of Astonishment*, its title taken from Psalm 60, is Lovelace's musical adaptation of his novel based on the early twentieth century persecution of Trinidad's Spiritual Baptist movement, whose members were popularly known as 'Shouters'. An outstanding Best Village company, Malick Folk Performers, staged the première in 1988. Like Lovelace's earlier adaptation, the musical had been workshopped at a playwrights conference, in this case Trinidad's first, in 1985. It also underwent an intense ten-day dramaturgical exercise under Barbadian director Earl Warner, and was further reworked in rehearsal. The script that emerged was a piece of ritual theatre, structured on a framework of certain Baptist rites of passage – Separation, Building, Baptism and Mourning, Transition, Pre-Incorporation and Incorporation.

The Wine of Astonishment opens with a masquerade of piracy, as the skull-masked, hook-handed, sword-bearing Governor of Trinidad reads the 1917 Shouters' Prohibition Ordinance that robs the people of their freedom of worship, their freedom to be themselves. The Ordinance is seen in action as a Baptist meeting is attacked by the police, the screaming worshippers forced to flee, the flowers and candles overturned, the bell silenced. After this prologue, the time reverts to the present, long after the 1951 repeal of the hated Ordinance, to a Baptist ceremony conducted freely in the heart of Port of Spain. It is

Fig. 5 Earl Lovelace's *The Wine of Astonishment* (PHOTO: Bruce Paddington) In this scene, Bolo (Garvin Lemessy) confronts Corporal Prince (Claude Reid) under the disapproving gaze of Leader Bee (Errol Jones). The 1988 production staged in Trinidad by the Malick Folk Performers was directed and designed by Earl Warner, choreographed by Shelford Trotman, with Roland Gordon as musical director.

from this ceremony that Mother Eva carries the thread of narration throughout the play. She begins to tell the story of three decades of the Shouters' fight against oppression. As the action once again moves back in time, the free worshippers begin to impersonate the various characters, much in the way of the ragtag masquers of Rawle Gibbons's *I Lawah*, or the masquers of Derek Walcott's *The Joker of Seville*. There follow several further time shifts, allowing the playwright the occasional ironic juxtaposition of words with deeds.

There are numerous subsidiary characters, such as Eva's children and the pro-American hustler Mitchell, who influence the events, but the prime movers in the story are three men: Eva's husband, the Baptist Leader Bee, and two lost sheep from his flock, Ivan Morton and Bolo. Bolo, once a champion stickfighter, believes that the community must defend its rights with physical force, even to the extent of killing the sadistic Corporal Prince who hounds the Shouters in the name of the law. Seeing the futility of such violence, Bee prefers to rely on Morton, the community's best educated son, whom the Baptists have voted on to the Council specifically to free their Church.

But while Bee waits for Morton to act, years pass. Bolo is imprisoned for fighting the arrest of the faithful. Children of the faith mature and have to marry outside their Church. Congregations are eroded as worshippers lose confidence in the eviscerated ceremonies. Eventually Morton frankly admits that he would view the restoration of the Church as a backward step. He sees his role in the community as one of promoting colonial education. Not until Bolo forces the community to face up to itself, with the tragic outcome of the deaths of Bolo and Mitchell's daughter, does Morton too experience a change of heart, leading to the eventual repeal of the infamous Ordinance.

The final scene has something of the *Deus ex machina* stretch of credibility. The first free Baptist ceremony fails to catch the spirit until Taffy, the son whose career as a steelbandsman has hitherto deeply disappointed Bee, unexpectedly arrives at the church with his band, playing music that ignites the worshippers and wins Taffy back his father's respect.

The reference to the steelband movement, though little more than glossed over in this treatment, is another important aspect of Lovelace's main theme. 'Where colonialism has been oppressive, it has inaugurated resistance from the oppressed; where it had sought to destroy old institutions, the people have struggled to create new ones; where its objective was to deny the personhood of people under its rule, it drew forth from these same people the affirmation of self. It is these contradictions that I have sought to underline in the play', wrote Lovelace in his première programme note. 'Hopefully, we come away cleansed of the sense of victimhood that our historians, educators and media propaganda have imposed upon us, and with a much more appropriate respect and reverence for the adventure that has been our Caribbean experience.'

The première of *The Wine of Astonishment* revealed a work of exceptional power and grace, that stirred a sense of national pride and won the national award for the year's best original play. However, it was a work that was not without its dramatic weaknesses. The original script is overlong, and is over-dependent on the director, both to clarify changes in time and role-playing, and to create dynamics in a play that is otherwise monotonously even in rhythm. It is also dependent on a musical director capable of arranging a theatrically effective score from a number of repetitive, rhythmically unvaried Baptist songs. Audiences as well as critics have found the representations of actual Baptist ritual excessive, and detrimental to the tension of the drama. At the same time, the play's historical background of the Baptist struggle has been for many theatregoers an awesome revelation.

'Perhaps the most bitter taste left in the cup of *The Wine of Astonishment*', wrote Lovelace in his programme note, 'is that the Spiritual Baptist community whose own struggles symbolise those of the Caribbean people in their confrontation with colonialism, have not been elevated in the national consciousness to the status of heroes of Caribbean civilisation that befits their contribution.'

There are fruitful comparisons to be made between *The Wine of Astonishment* and Derek Walcott's musical *O Babylon!* on another persecuted religious movement, Jamaica's Rastafarians. Like the Rastafarian, the Baptist movement has been seen only rarely on the stage, and then principally in burlesque in the calabash theatre. The few sympathetic works include Louis Marriott's *The Shepherd* (1960), on Jamaica's nineteenth-century revivalist preacher Alexander Bedward, and Rawle Gibbons's *Shepherd* (1981). *The Wine of Astonishment*, both as a novel and as a play, did, as the author hoped, evoke a greater national consciousness of, and respect for, the Baptist movement. For Lovelace, it was an outcome that fully vindicated his decision to remain based in the West Indies.

NOTES

1 Roderick Walcott, author's note to MS *Three One-Act Plays*, JSJS collection.
2 Roderick Walcott, 'A Question of Dialect', introduction to MS *Three One-Act Plays*.
3 *Ibid.*
4 *History of Roderick Walcott's 'The Banjo Man'*, programme *The Banjo Man*, St Lucia Government, Carifesta, 1972.
5 *Ibid.*
6 Errol Hill, introduction, in *A Time and a Season*, Extramural Studies Unit, UWI, 1976.
7 *History of Roderick Walcott's 'The Banjo Man'.*
8 Director's note, programme Derek Walcott's *Franklin*, WWB, 1990.
9 Earl Lovelace in interview with Hugh Lynch, *SE*, 22 July, 1990.
10 *Ibid.*
11 Earl Lovelace, personal communication to Judy Stone (1992).
12 Earl Lovelace in interview with Hugh Lynch.
13 *Ibid.*

6

CLASSICAL THEATRE

The legacy of Europe: Derek Walcott

. . . Sirs, make a white mist
In the mind; make that mist hang like cloth
From the dress of a woman, on prickles, on branches,
Make it rise from the earth, like the breath of the dead
On resurrection morning, and I walking through it
On my way to my charcoal pit on the mountain.
Make the web of the spider heavy with diamonds
And when my hand brush it, let the chain break.
I remember, in my mind, the cigale sawing,
Sawing, sawing wood before the woodcutter,
The drum of the bull-frog, the blackbird flute,
And this old man walking, ugly as sin,
In a confusion of vapour,
Till I feel I was God self, walking through cloud,
In the heaven of my mind.

(Makak in *Dream on Monkey Mountain*, by Derek Walcott)

The previous three chapters have discussed three streams of theatre: realistic drama, popular drama and the musical. Between them, in quantity, these three streams account for all but a modest percentage of theatrical writing in the Caribbean region. Within these streams, the playwright's role is the more honoured for its invisibility, in one sense or another. In all three streams, the audience must be wooed into total involvement, if not actual participation. The playwright strives for representational credibility within the conventionally accepted artifice of his dramatic structure. In controlling his material he must be truthful to his context, in speaking through his characters he must be truthful to their individual voices. When the playwright's presence becomes jarringly obtrusive through loss of these truths, whether by undercrafting or overcrafting, it detracts from the persuasiveness of his drama. Only in the musical theatre is form overt, and that is with few exceptions a form of unremarkable simplicity. Only in the theatre of realism is content likely to be intellectually stimulating. Freddie Kissoon speaks for most popular writers when he expresses the belief that a 'well-made' play, one that is consciously crafted and challenging in content, would frighten away his popular audience.

Against such a background, the dramatic achievements of the poet Derek Walcott appear all the more isolated, and all the more extraordinary.

Derek Walcott

Walcott's writing for the theatre has passed through several phases in its development from the verse play through a lyrical dialect to a dialogue akin to realism, but his work remains rooted in the ancient classical drama of Europe. Walcott's theatre is a unique creation, woven out of the stuff of the West Indies, but since it draws much of its strength from the ancient values, it is here termed classical theatre. Time has muted the poet's use of heightened language, but the hallmarks of his work have not changed: an exceptional ability with words and love of word play, inspired imagery, and the flung gauntlet of his intellect. Unlike the above performance-oriented streams of theatre, Walcott's theatre is primarily a theatre of speech. As in the theatre of Sophocles and Aristophanes, the playwright's presence is paramount. The immediate effect is of a distancing between the audience and the performance, a space demanded for critical appreciation of the playwright's craft, a space in which the audience has the opportunity to become mentally active in its own upliftment. It is a form of alienation that can greatly enrich moments of emotional involvement.

The range of Walcott's work is wide. The five of his plays which, in terms of reaching audiences, have proved to be most successful, are markedly different each from the other: the anguished African parable *Dream on Monkey Mountain*; the ribald Don Juan adaptation *The Joker of Seville*; the two-actor Robinson Crusoe comedy *Pantomime*; the existentialist *The Sea at Dauphin*; and the folk musical *Ti-Jean and his Brothers.* All five of these plays, however, as with the majority of Walcott's work, are essentially West Indian.

Walcott's early vision was of the creation of an heroic West Indian theatre in which language held pride of place, accompanied by the music, dance and visual appeal inherent in West Indian life. In later years he came to see himself less as a West Indian, more as a universal playwright. His themes are for the most part universal. One that recurs with frequency concerns aspects of the dichotomy between two cultures, the classical and the creole, which is the colonial legacy of the West Indies. Walcott's ongoing exploration, brought to a peak in *Steel*, of the possibility, even the desirability, of harmony between the two, is in effect an exploration of his own role as a classical writer in his native region.

EARLY PLAYS: *Flight and Sanctuary*, *Harry Dernier*

Derek Alton Walcott was born in St Lucia in 1930. He wrote his first surviving play in 1946, when he was 16 years old. Although he was testing his metal in a different medium, for the adolescent Walcott drama was essentially an extension of his already exceptional ability as a poet. The small, pastoral, banana-dependent island of St Lucia at that time offered little in the way of conventional theatre production. Walcott's childhood theatrical memories are of the living theatre around him: the street theatre of the Salvation Army recruiting patrol, the

Christmas devils with their street-corner black masses, familiar town characters among the poor and deranged. He also recalls lamplit folktales croaked 'at the creaking hour',[1] a toy theatre of twig actors created with his twin brother Roderick, and his own marathon poems on Greek heroes, which he used to declaim on his home verandah with his back to the street. His acquaintance with the formal stage owed more to printed texts than to performance, and he brought to drama the same influences and classical values that helped to shape his early poetry. He wrote *Flight and Sanctuary* as a verse play, with a Chorus.[2]

The story is of a hermit who has renounced life in the nearby city, but whose solitude is invaded by city dwellers fleeing plague. To preserve his way of life, the hermit eventually kills his first visitor. Later, however, he finds himself so affected by the sight of a subsequent visitor, a young boy dying of the plague, that he voluntarily returns to the city to help the sick. In expiation for his denial of life, he is embracing almost certain death.

Despite the uplifting conversion of its hero, *Flight and Sanctuary* is in the main a somewhat desolate play. It presents a harsh analogy of the dilemma of the artist who must isolate himself from the world in order to create, but who must not lose touch with the world which is his source of creative inspiration. As theatre, this early work is not a particularly successful piece of writing. It is nevertheless remarkable for the scope and maturity of its vision. It is not a West Indian play in any sense, and its themes such as the role of the individual in society and of society in the life of man, of the existence of God and the inevitability of death, are universal. 'Whereas most other playwrights begin with a locale cluttered with images of temporal value', wrote Errol Hill in 1971, 'Walcott begins with a vision of man. It is this vision that gives his plays a dimension lacking in many playwrights of the region, it is this that makes him not only a major poet but the major dramatist of the West Indies.'[3]

Also in 1946 Walcott wrote his second play, *Harry Dernier*, a verse duologue for radio. Another essentially bleak piece, questioning the meaning of life, it was not broadcast until 1952, in London. In the same year it was printed in Barbados and staged in Jamaica, directed by Walcott. The BBC radio production featured Hill in the title role of the last man left alive in the world, a pot-bellied 'whiskey priest', who in his tormented self-questioning might have emerged from a Graham Greene novel. Raised in the strict mores of the Methodists, a minority faith in an island virtually ruled by Catholicism, Walcott learnt unusually early in life to question the infallibility of the Church. He was only fourteen when a Catholic priest accused him in print of heresy. He had published in *The Voice of St Lucia* a Wordsworthian poem that spoke innocently of finding God through communion with nature. Walcott has written of the incident as causing him painful shock and horror. Subsequently, though the tenets of his childhood faith powerfully inform many of his plays, such as *Dream on Monkey Mountain* and *The Isle is Full of Noises* (1982), throughout his *oeuvre* his treatment of churchmen is at least as unceremonious as is his treatment of all men.

From the outset, Walcott's love of words was infected by his delight in word play:

Dernier: Each day the sunset swears under its breath
that it will not commit the daylight any more,
But curl its will into the womb of dark,
And leave the stars to shift for themselves . . . God, God, my God. . .
GOD . . .
The Echo (sounds distantly): Od.
Dernier: MY GOD.
Echo: I-GOD.
Dernier: Why hast thou forsaken. . .
Echo: Shaken. . . .
Dernier (frantically): Ha! The alter echo.

Walcott was reared in the Elizabethan tradition that used the *double entendre* for both comic and dramatic effect. It is a tradition that continues to flourish in the Caribbean today, through the art of the calypsonian. From his youth, Walcott's sense of humour was so beguiled by the flexibility of the English language that for many years he was more likely to risk mood, character, or the dynamics of a scene, than to sacrifice an ingenious pun.

In 1947, now aged seventeen, Walcott wrote a further three one-act verse plays: *Another World for the Lost*, *The Matadors*, and *A Simple Cornada*. As with *Flight and Sanctuary*, none of these was staged. For the next two years he devoted much of his energy to his first teaching job, but continued to write for the theatre.

PLAYS OF THE FIFTIES: *Henri Christophe*, *The Charlatan*, *The Sea at Dauphin*, *Malcochon*, *Ione*, *Ti-Jean and His Brothers*, *Drums and Colours*

1950 was a particularly significant year for Walcott. He and Maurice Mason co-founded the St Lucia Arts Guild, 'to promote and encourage in St Lucia the arts of music, painting, drama and literature'.[4] Walcott became the Guild's first president. Also that year he won a scholarship to university in Jamaica. And he had by then generated four new scripts, including the earliest version of one of his major plays, *Henri Christophe*. He was rewarded the same year with his first stage productions at home, his first radio production abroad, and his first sight of his own dialogue in print.

Robin and Andrea was never completed, but an extract was published in *Bim* (Vol. 4, No. 13, December 1950), and Walcott later developed the plot into his first musical, *The Charlatan*. He was still writing his plays in verse. The one-act verse play *Senza Alcun Sospetto*, which the St Lucia Arts Guild was to stage in 1951 under the title *Paolo and Francesca*, was in 1950 broadcast in London on the BBC programme, *Caribbean Voices*. The one-act verse play *Cry for a Leader*, a political debate between nationalism and colonialism, was staged in late 1950 by the Guild. But the play that launched the Guild's theatrical programme was the full-length verse chronicle, *Henri Christophe*, directed by Walcott.

The eighteenth century Haitian revolution and subsequent independence marked the region's first effective seizure of power by black slaves from their colonial masters. The historic events have inspired a number of playwrights, among them two great Caribbean philosophers, Aimé Cezaire and C.L.R. James. Walcott was to return repeatedly to this period: *Henri Christophe*, *Drums and Colours*, *The Haytian Earth*. Whatever the flaws in the characters of these Haitian revolutionaries, there is a magnificence in their achievement so rare in West Indian history that their story inevitably attracts an artist searching for an heroic model for West Indian nationhood. The revolution was led by the visionary Toussaint L'Ouverture, a chief's son who believed in democracy. While he controlled Haiti, L'Ouverture built roads and schools around the country. His genuine love for his people was reciprocated to such an extent that his rule could have lasted his natural life had he not been betrayed by his generals and captured by the French. After Toussaint three of his generals ruled Haiti in succession. The vainglorious Jacques Dessalines first seized his chance to be crowned; he built twelve palaces. Then came Henri Christophe, an enigmatic leader who combined the vision of the one predecessor with the fanaticism of the other; he also wore the crown, and built a citadel. Lastly, the well-intentioned mulatto Jacques Petion became president, and built up the Haitian Republic.

When Walcott turned to Haiti for his hero in the classical mould, James had already treated the obvious in *Toussaint L'Ouverture*. Walcott chose for his Hamlet the enigma, the lesser man but more complex mortal. In the 'two-sided mirror' of Henri Christophe, he reveals a character as merciless in his unceasing self-examination as in his material ambition and lust to avenge the years of slavery.

The play opens as news reaches Haiti of Toussaint's death in France. Dessalines successfully schemes to be made king. Christophe is stripped of his army and is turned into a bureaucrat, illiterate as he is. Years pass, and Christophe bides his time. Eventually Dessalines, in his murderous excesses, succumbs to madness. Christophe and Petion arrange his assassination. The people are coerced into crowning Christophe. A wise soldier, well-taught by Toussaint, Henri I proves leader enough to secure Haiti's safety from the French. But he is at last overwhelmed by his own excesses, and duped by those around him. The play closes to the drums of Petion's approaching army as Christophe executes his own assassination.

This tale of men's ambition to be king has its own individual colour in the theme of liberation from slavery, but throughout it is stitched with threads from the classics: Marlowe's *Tamburlaine*, Eliot's *Becket*, O'Neill's *Emperor Jones*, and diverse works of Shakespeare. The widely praised scene, in which a man teaches his young assistant the gentle art of murder, owes more to *Richard III* than simply a scene between two assassins. Like the Bard, Walcott uses the scene for comic relief, and for that purpose he also reverts from verse to the more immediate vehicle of prose. Not only is this the first instance of Walcott's prose dialogue, it is the first instance of his using dialect, and the occasional passage of patois:

1st M: Well, you shaming your father. I remember how he was always saying you would make such a good apprentice. What is the matter, you are scared of

> a little blood? You never kill a crab, or a chicken, or an old woman? You all are funny, yes. . . . Murder? *Eux tue un homme, Bon dieu, bon dieu, qui cote, nous cai courir*? We must, quiet, ladies, quiet, gentlemen, we must apprehend the killer. *Chembez lui*, apprehend him.

The murderers' scene was not performed in the première production in St Lucia. The omission was made at the behest of the nuns of St Joseph's Convent, in the hall of which the production was staged. The scene was restored for Errol Hill's 1952 London production at Hans Crescent. And in the 1954 production in Trinidad, this scene came as welcome relief not only to the audiences, but to the disconcerted critics. Accustomed to the modern movement into a theatre of realism, the West Indian critics of the fifties hardly knew how to react to this apparent Elizabethan throwback. The play failed to conform to their most basic theatrical requirements, and yet in the calibre of its writing and intellectual challenge it contained a power and a grandeur never before achieved in the indigenous West Indian theatre. On the printed page, the play drew admiration for its poetry. On radio, the poetic cadences lulled the listener to sleep. On stage, several early productions in London and around the Caribbean met with mixed reception, but on balance there was more ennui than enthralment. The play had no dramatic form, the critics complained. The action was slow to start. There was no difference between the characters. The audience was left emotionally uninvolved. There were too many soliloquies. There was altogether too much talking. And there was no justification for the poet's putting his elevated language, his sonorous cascades of rhymed couplets and triplets, into the mouths of rough, uneducated slaves, who had not even the rudiments of formal education.

But Walcott was not trying to photograph these self-made men, he was trying to paint them, in a style as epic as their achievements. He shared Naipaul's ambition, to attach the Caribbean 'to great names and great events . . . Seeing (it) as part of the globe, seeing it sharing in the antiquity of the earth'.[5] He was trying to create a West Indian theatre that would win international recognition as one of cultured sensibility, and he was doing it the way he knew best, with heroically poetic language.

> *Christophe:* I shall build chateaux
> That shall obstruct the strongest season,
> So high the hawk shall giddy in its gyre
> Before it settles on the carved turrets.
> My floors shall reflect the faces that pass over them,
> And foreign trees spread out the shade of government;
> On emerald lawns I will hold councils.
> I'll pave a room with golden coins, so rich,
> The old archbishop will smile indulgently at heaven from
> The authenticity of my chateaux.
> I will have Arabian horses, yellow haired serving boys,
> And in the night the chateaux will be lit
> With lanterns bewildering as fireflies,

Over the lawns at night, like mobile candelabra.
I who was slave am now a king; after my strength
Not England, Jamaica, or Napoleon
Shall send ships to disgorge invasions, but search for
Trade and quiet. Hayti will flourish,
When I am king.

The most scathing critic of *Henri Christophe* admitted his belief that Walcott might one day write a great play.[6]

Walcott continued writing and rewriting in that quest, learning the mechanics of theatre by the trials and errors of production, honing his skills as a poet, determined to reconcile his marriage of the two art forms, poetry and drama. He was to become equally determined to marry two voices, the poetic and the vernacular, to create an authentic voice for his heroic West Indian theatre.

In September of 1950, on a Colonial Development and Welfare Scholarship, Walcott flew to Jamaica to become one of a class of twenty students accepted for the first Liberal Arts course offered on the Mona Campus of the University of the West Indies. He was to become president of the Mona Dramatic Society, for which he directed, and editor of the student publication *The Barb*, later *The Pelican*. He would also, while in Kingston, publish his third collection of poems. The present study is not concerned with the literature of West Indian poetry, but the reader of this chapter should not lose sight of the extraordinary circumstance that, all the while Walcott was assiduously working in theatre, he was simultaneously writing and publishing a body of poetry that would eventually win him the Nobel Prize for Literature.

In 1951 two further Walcott plays were staged by the St Lucia Arts Guild, the verse play *Three Assassins*, and what appears to have been Walcott's first play in prose dialogue, *The Price of Mercy*. Then came *Soso's Wake*, a comedy about fishermen which was soon to develop into *The Sea at Dauphin*. Walcott's tenacious hold on his scripts, many of which were to surface again and again rewritten in different forms and under new titles, was particularly apparent in 1954. That year saw the première productions of *The Sea at Dauphin*, *The Charlatan* (from *Robin and Andrea*), and *Crossroads*, which latter eventually developed into *Malcochon*. The same year Walcott, while returning from a brief teaching stint in Grenada to his teaching post in St Lucia, and marrying for the first time, wrote the full-length play *A Georgian House*, and rewrote it as *A Sound of Hunting*. His 1976 television play *The Snow Queen* is based on the latter.

Nearly forty years after its première, *The Charlatan*, alone of all Walcott's lasting works of this period, still had not been published, other than in a UCWI mimeograph, which suggests that the musical was still undergoing revision. Not infrequently, when he came to work with his own theatre company, Walcott would continue revising a script even during a production run. Actors in the 1973 Trinidad Theatre Workshop production of *The Charlatan* would regularly arrive at the theatre an hour before curtainrise to find themselves presented with a fresh page of dialogue, a new speech, a revised speech, or a speech with the original lines juggled into a new sequence, which they were to incorporate into that night's performance.

'My attitude is that whatever happens to plays in terms of reviews or box office, they can always be improved,' Walcott argues. 'I don't consider that you're doing anything different to what a painter may do. A painter may show a painting and then take it back and work on it.'[7]

Subtitled sometimes *A Carnival comedy*, and sometimes *The Little Carnival*, *The Charlatan* is both Walcott's first full-length comedy, and his first musical. It is the only work in which he successfully explores the integration of traditional Carnival characters into a conventional stage piece, though he has used Carnival in other ways in works such as *Drums and Colours*, *Batai* (1965) and *In a Fine Castle* (1970). He also later drafted a musical, *Birdie*, about calypsonian Mighty Sparrow, the flamboyant and often-crowned Carnival King of Calypso. The piece has never been staged, but *Steel* celebrates the calypso as well as the steelband pioneers.

Set in Trinidad on the eve of Carnival, the plot of *The Charlatan* is essentially a romance, between the daughter of a voodoo priestess and a young painter suffering from a fraudulent heart condition. Plot and sub-plots take a wild romp through house-breaking, eviction, dead bodies, a seance and a host of scams perpetrated by nearly every member of the engagingly amoral cast. The overt Carnival characters include two calypsonians and a bat, with lagniappe of a police and thief chase in which the thief is himself an ex-policeman, and the chase is for love, not law. Then there is the deadly Dame Lorraine of Clarissa Upshot, and the Baby Doll of her stepdaughter Heloise. But the most memorable character, and the most original, is the eccentric quack of the title, the frank Midday Robber Dr Theodore Holley, a white, silver-tongued obeah man whose black magic works by luck, and whose only real talent is for joy. Walcott took his own ferocious joy in this opportunity for some dense punning in musical numbers such as *The Song of India*.

Corpie: Kamasutra, Kashimir,
is my raga, I.M. Singh,
any Kashankari deal
under madras hyderabad
golden bangla, kash galore
uttar useless, mon soon die,
every prophet del hi dat
na matta macha karash i ghat
warda high or barrack pore
canna carri kash wit tim
it is written 'Mon soon die'.

Most of *The Charlatan* is written in free verse, but for this musical comedy Walcott abandoned the heightened language of his dramas for a faster-paced, more colloquial dialogue, the occasional genial extravagance of which has an operatic rather than a Shakespearian flavour. A few characters, such as the policeman-turned-vendor Corpie, speak mainly in a form of vernacular prose.

In just one version of the play, performed in Los Angeles in 1974, the cast was expanded to include Clarissa's husband, 'Brigadeer John Calthorpe Upshott'. But the Brigadier had been banished offstage again for the 1977 version, which also reshaped the musical from three to two acts. For the 1974 production, *The Charlatan* emerged clad in a new score by the composer Galt MacDermot. In the same year MacDermot wrote the classic score for Walcott's most popular musical, *The Joker of Seville*. MacDermot was a scion of the Jamaican family that had produced the early writer Tom Redcam. He had earned a certain notoriety internationally for his work on the nude musical hit of the sixties, *Hair*. His other theatrical compositions include *Two Gentlemen of Verona*, *Hamlet*, and a rock opera based on *Troilus and Cressida*. His partnership with Walcott continued to flourish through such works as *O Babylon*, *Marie Laveau* and *Steel*.

The Sea at Dauphin is one of the trio of Walcott's one-act St Lucian plays that has survived from the fifties. Each touches on the lives of small-islanders who scrape their meagre living on the brink of existence: the fishermen of Dauphin, the estate labourers of *Malcochon*, the urban vagrants of *Jourmard*.

Steeped as it is in patois, there is about this first play of the trio a quality as rolling and timeless as the sea itself. Drawing its initial inspiration from Synge's *Riders to the Sea*, it is a tale of death, rather than life. The sea is at its most violent, recalling drowned fishermen of the past. Old Hounakin, half-starved and heartsick since the loss of his wife, is dissuaded from accompanying to almost certain death the only boat going to sea. Afa and Augustin return with a portion of their slender catch put aside for the old man. Too late, they discover he has thrown himself down a cliff, and died. Afa curses God and the priest, but life washes relentlessly on. At the close of the play a young boy is permitted to join the two fishermen as crew. An existentialist essay, one early critic termed it, on the inscrutability of God's ways with his creatures, the inevitability of tomorrow, and the vanity of a man's rebellion against his existence.

The 1954 world première of *The Sea at Dauphin* was directed by Hill in Trinidad shortly before the St Lucian premières on radio and stage. The production met with considerable acclaim. The audiences understood 'two words in seven'[8] of the patois, but there is no record of denouncements of the fine language in the mouths of uneducated fishermen. Walcott had achieved his first satisfying blend of poetic imagery with folk idiom, and of noble sentiment with folk wisdom. The play won the 1956 Jamaican Drama Festival award for the best West Indian drama.

Walcott took account of his audiences' difficulty with the patois, and never again used so rich a mixture. In *Malcochon*, a strangely gentle, balletic tale of hacking and stabbing, murder and hanging, adultery, theft and terror, the patois is seldom more than incidental. Part prose, part verse, part song, this second play in the trio is subtitled *The Six in the Rain*. As *Malcauchon*, it had its première performance in 1959 in St Lucia. Reminiscent of Jean-Paul Sartre's *Huis Clos* (1943), it brings to judgement six people trapped in a hut by a thunderstorm. A notorious, misanthropic one-time convict, the woodcutter Chantal, is the drunken judge. Against the backdrop of violent confessions, those who survive learn to value the humane virtues of responsibility, friendship, forgiveness. They learn to see with the Conteur that 'Man's beauty is sharing his brother's pain'.

The last, and least compelling, play of the trio is *Journard*, which Walcott wrote for the St Lucia Arts Guild tour to Trinidad in 1959. Having more in common with the popular Benjy trilogy by his brother Roderick, it is a comedy of wily destitutes attempting to raise drinking money on Easter Sunday by preaching around a spurious corpse.

In 1956 Walcott took up a teaching post in Jamaica. That year Jamaica saw the world premières of *The Golden Lions* and *The Wine of the Country* – a *Wine* that was to mature into *Franklin* (1968). Then, in 1957, Jamaica's Federal Theatre Company staged the première of a remarkable play, *Ione*. Fired by the successful merging of patois and poetry in *The Sea at Dauphin*, Walcott had conceived a full-length classical tragedy, in the folk setting of rural St Lucia.

Walcott is not the only playwright to have seen the possibilities of transposing the Aegean myth to the isles of the Caribbean. In his musical *Pecong* Steve Carter, an American playwright of West Indian descent, weaves the story of Medea through Carnival in Tranky Island, 'A Caribbean Island of the Mind'. Stephen Landrigan's *The Pan Beaters* (1987) sets the legend of Phaedra in Trinidad. Dennis Scott wrote a contemporary version of the Clytemnestra tragedy in *The Crime of Anabel Campbell* (1970). Walcott himself, fifteen years later, began writing *The Isle is Full of Noises* based on the story of Philoctetes. But for *Ione* Walcott did more than transpose. He created an original myth of classical dimensions, using classical themes and classical characters, constructing his drama true to the classical unities of time, place and action, and couching his dialogue in the classical language at which he excelled, made the more musical by its recasting in a patois mould. In this play Walcott developed a technique of balancing the patois lines with their English complement, for more certain comprehension.

Theresine:	*La fumée ka aler au nore . . .* *I sorti en choeur du feu-a . . .* *Ni choeur un ti mamaille . . .* *Jeté parmi ces cendres-la . . .*
Washerwoman I:	*Ave Maria, beni nous, beni nous . . .* Bless us . . . . .
Theresine:	The blackbird is hunting the hawk, The smoke writhes to the south, A hole in the ground is hungry.
Man's Voice:	Helene! Helene! Helena ooooy.
Washerwoman II:	That is Diogene Alexandre.
Washerwoman III:	He will dead for a woman.
Man's Voice:	Helene!
Washerwoman III:	*A nous payer il sous.* Drunk, I betting you.
Theresine:	Disaster is here. It always begin, With the act of an idiot.

In their French form, the heroic names of old sing through the text a burden of great deeds and great passions: Helene, Achille, Alexandre, Diogene, Mercure. The story is of two hill tribes, headed by the half-brothers Alexandre and Victorin, which for two generations have feuded over land. Victorin's younger daughter Helene hates Achille, the husband her father forced her to marry. More beautiful than her sister Ione, and caring nothing for the feud, Helene has become the bridge between the two tribes that 'barefoot men must walk across'. The widowed Ione, contemptuous of Helene's licentiousness, is herself pregnant by a visiting American, and only awaiting his summons to leave the island. Theresine, Walcott's Cassandra, foretells the imminent destruction of both tribes. The destruction begins when Achille returns early from the fields to find his wife naked in bed with a man from the rival tribe. Achille slaughters Diogene and his own baby son. The tribe of Alexandre demands vengeance for Diogene's death, Helene is stoned, Victorin collapses into senility, Ione on discovering herself abandoned kills herself and her unborn child, and the two homesteads rage into flame as blood follows blood.

To modern audiences, all this Sturm and Drang may seem excessive, lacking as it does the seal of the bureau of antiquity. But *Ione* does have the genuine terrible beauty of the archetypal tragedies, and the potential to generate an adrenalin excitement rare in West Indian theatre. More rare still are roles that so challenge the West Indian actor. It is to be regretted that, apart from a student presentation in Edinburgh, and an excerpt staged in St Lucia, there seem to have been no further performances after the Jamaica and Trinidad productions of 1957. This may be in part because the critics, while lauding the performances, slaughtered the play. Again, Walcott's proclaimed fault was that his work was not realistic. No one seemed to realise that the very magnificence of the performances could not have been achieved with realistic material. Indeed, it may be that the performances did not fully achieve the quality demanded by the play. If they had, the audiences should have been able to appreciate *Ione* for what it is. Years later, in *A Branch of the Blue Nile*, Walcott was to explore the dilemma of the West Indian artist and the conflict of classical with creole forms in terms of theatre, whether it is possible for a Caribbean actor to achieve greatness in classical terms. As he writes of his Trinidad Theatre Workshop actors, in his exploration of the same theme in *What the Twilight Says: an Overture*, 'their genius is not violent, it is comic'.

Walcott was now commissioned by the Extramural Department of the University College of the West Indies to write an epic drama, for the opening of the First Federal Parliament of the West Indies in Trinidad in 1958. In preparation Walcott, funded by a Rockefeller Foundation grant, made his first trip to the United States and to Stratford, Ontario. In the five days he stayed in New York, 'out of sheer terror of the place and a fierce but illuminating nostalgia for the untheatrical simplicities of St Lucia,'[9] he wrote the initial version not of the epic, but of one of his most unassuming and best loved works, *Ti-Jean and His Brothers*. In the stress of his unfamiliar environment, inadequately prepared for the size and sophistication of the metropolis, 'under the pressure of sudden loneliness and exile',[10] the 27-year-old Walcott's creative spirit sought encouragement from a St Lucian folk tale. It was one of the Ti-Jean cycle he knew as a child, in which common sense or 'manwit', of which Walcott had more than his share, always triumphed over more obvious powers.

In the version published in 1972, *Ti-Jean and His Brothers* is a tale told by a chorus of animals, of a mother with three sons, who live in a hut in the forest. The Devil sends the Bolom (an unborn foetus) to deliver his challenge to the family. If one of the brothers makes the Devil feel human emotion, he will be given great wealth. If he tries and fails, the Devil will eat him. The eldest brother, Gros Jean, leaves home to pit his brute strength against the Devil, and fails. The middle brother, Mi-Jean, follows to fight the Devil with his half-witted scholarship, and also fails. It is the little brother, Ti-Jean, who with his intuitive wit and practical view of life succeeds in aggravating the Devil to anger, and then to the miracle of a tear.

Simple as the surface story is, *Ti-Jean*, like most of Walcott's works, went through several transformations. As its own bolom, a ballet, it was staged in 1957 by the St Lucia Arts Guild. As a play, with incidental folk music, it first saw the light of stage in Trinidad in 1958. Twelve years of revision later, in 1970, it was restaged by Walcott's Trinidad Theatre Workshop with a haunting original score by André Tanker. After several further productions on stage, radio and television in the Caribbean, Canada and America, it was finally rewritten for Joe Papp's 1972 Central Park production for the New York Shakespeare Festival. It is this latter which is the published version, which continues to be produced with some frequency in the Caribbean and elsewhere. Papp, who died in 1991, was a producer of rare vision and courage, to whom America's minority theatre owes an incalculable debt. He also introduced to America the work of writers from around the world; his West Indian protégés included, along with Walcott, Edgar White from Montserrat, and others.

A team from the Canadian Broadcasting Corporation flew to Trinidad in 1970 to record a radio version of *Ti-Jean and His Brothers*. The following year another team, from the American NET Black Journal, flew to Trinidad to film extracts. The play was videotaped in Barbados in 1970 and again in 1979. A creole version, *Ti-Jean Epi Fwe-y*, was written by Alwin Bully for staging in Dominica in 1982. The play has also received the unusual accolade of being issued as a picture book, adapted to prose, hand-lettered and illustrated by art nouveau artist Stuart Hahn.

Walcott has called *Ti-Jean and His Brothers* his most West Indian play, 'the least forced, the most spontaneous, the least laboured of my plays so far, both in rhythm and concept'.[11] He explains his choice of form. The basic structure is 'as universal as the skeleton',[12] with its digital rhythm of three movements, three acts, three moral revelations. He wanted to flesh out this skeleton with 'a softly measured metre whose breathing was formally articulated yet held the lyrical stresses of dialect speech'.[13] He found that when he broke the iambic line in half it became more lilting, 'with the innocence of a child's recitation'.[14]

Frog: One time it had a mother,
That mother had three sons.
The first son was Gros Jean,
That son he was the biggest,
His arm was hard as iron,
But he was very stupid.

Walcott was trying to recreate the country atmosphere of his youth, of firelit storytelling accompanied by flute, cuatro and drum. Other St Lucian memories and rituals influenced this play too, such as the Christmas black mass dances of Papa Diable, his Jabs and the Bolom, with their traditional chants and music. With hindsight, Walcott also later acknowledged such influences as the African griot, the language of Lorca, Brecht in the distancing of characters, and the No Theatre in the use of masks, musicians, and the mimetic indications of scenery. Even deeper lies the source of the world's peasant mythology, where Papa Bois is the goat-footed god Pan.

In Walcott's version, Papa Bois is one face of the only complex character in the play, the Devil, who also appears as himself, and as a white planter. In his introduction to *Ti-Jean* in *Plays for Today*, Hill discusses the several interpretations of the play that hinge on this triple role, such as the metaphysical and the militant black interpretations, and others which see the play as a metaphor for the overthrow of colonialism, or for the movement of generations through West Indian history.

On his return home from North America, Walcott returned also to writing the commissioned epic drama for the opening of the Federal Parliament. His brief was to encapsule in a single piece of theatre, of standard length, four and a half centuries of West Indian history, measuring the evolution of West Indian consciousness. At college in St Lucia, he had never learned the history of his own region. As was the practice in those colonial days, he had been taught a history of the British Empire, 'in which the most memorable things for me were the exploits and *bon mots* of heroes such as Clive of India, Wolfe on the plains of Quebec, Drake singeing, and Spaniards cringing'.[15] He had now to read up Caribbean history 'first as a schoolboy, then rather quickly as a research scholar, all the while marking incidents and issues which would be of dramatic interest'.[16] He had already determined that the epic should have a theatrical form, and not be 'merely a succession of cold slices of history'.[17]

The form of the play would be influenced by the architect-designed stage to be specially built for the production, outdoors in the Royal Botanical Gardens of Port of Spain. To accommodate the anticipated audiences of up to 1500 a night, the technical advisers from Stratford Theatre in Ontario had suggested a return to the apron shape of the Elizabethan era. There would be three acting levels, backed by the arc of a sounding board, and the audience would surround the stage on three sides. In addition, the players would use areas of the vast arena forming the auditorium. It was a staging that would shake actors out of the complacency of proscenium performance into direct contact with the audience. Working in such a large area, and unable to be facing all the audience all the time, the players would have to perform in a more than usually vigorous style. Noel Vaz, who directed most of the scenes, called it a 'three-dimensional' style of acting. As in Shakespeare's time, there would be no backdrops, no scenery, none but indispensable props.

For the playwright, the stage and the style meant the impossibility of intimate scenes, and of subtle or leisurely action. To gain insight into the use of this unaccustomed medium, Walcott delved deeply into the mysteries of Elizabethan drama. 'One of the things that impress me, particularly in Shakespeare's plays', he is quoted as saying in a *Sunday Guardian* interview of November 1957, 'is that nobody sits down . . . except it is a king, and then he would sit, splendidly gowned, on a high level, with other actors grouped around and below him, in which case the visual impact of such an apex is of itself dramatic . . . '

Walcott continues to write with a painter's eye for tableaux, which is most apparent when he directs his plays himself. He is in fact a water-colourist of some considerable talent, who has been exhibiting since 1950. It is his habit to illustrate his own texts, particularly when he is directing, in preparation for which he will draw in the margins of his copy details of sets and characters. 'Even the atmosphere, mood and lighting were indicated', notes director-playwright Ken Corsbie, 'also the actual actor.'[18] On occasion he has produced a comprehensive portfolio of sketches to illustrate one of his works, usually a film scenario. Walcott may also add into his directing script appropriate pictures, such as a hat, a dress, a face, snipped from magazines and other sources.

But for *Drums and Colours* movement took priority over the picture. Walcott accordingly allowed for the incorporation of much folk dancing and singing, including calypso, both for atmosphere and actually to promote the action. It was possibly the first time the indigenous music of the West Indies was used in this way. He also brought directly on stage intensely dramatic incidents such as hanging and flogging that would normally be reported as having happened out of sight of the audience.

The form Walcott finally evolved was that of a play within a play. In the prologue, several masqueraders agree to 'organise into a serious mas' ',[19] acting out the history of their own origins with the help of their Carnival costumes. The actors in this scene, wrote reviewer Adrian Espinet (*SG*, 27 April, 1958), 'not only represent the racial diversity of the region, but, by appearing under various guises at various points in the body of the play, and again in their original character as masqueraders in the epilogue, serve to tie together and round off the entire action'.[20]

Walcott presented his history in twelve scenes structured around the personal tragedies of five heroes of the region: Columbus, Raleigh, Toussaint L'Ouverture, George William Gordon, and what reviewer Veronica Jenkin described as 'a little squingy shoemaker called Pompey',[21] one of Jamaica's rebellious Maroons, who represented the grass-roots of the West Indies. 'In one or two instances,' wrote Walcott, 'for purposes of cohesion, I have rearranged dates and incidents, but the general pattern of discovery, conquest, exploitation, rebellion and constitutional advancement has been followed.'[22] It was, praised Espinet, a 'really intelligent selection', with a chorus 'to fill in the gaps in some fine 'Queen's English''.[23] Jenkin particularly admired the characterisation of minor as well as major roles, the haunting verse, and the comedy, tragedy and pathos of the prose scenes. Her only reservations in an otherwise glowing review were a sense of imbalance in the first half of the play, and the universal criticism, shared by directors Vaz, Hill and Dagmar Butt, of the première's three-and-a-half-hour duration. Jenkin saw two principal themes emerging, 'the corrupting and destructive power of greed for gold and the fact that men learn tolerance –

to dwell together in unity – through strife and suffering'.[24] Dubbing the work one of vigour, perception, wisdom and humanity, an exciting and fitting centre-piece for the Festival, Jenkin gave the following description of the action:

> There is no danger of monotony. Mood and pace are varied by different devices, all quite naturally introduced. In the Columbus scene, besides the baffled, disappointed hero on his way home to Spain in chains, there are some vigorous crude sailors, a conscience-stricken Spanish officer, a half-caste ship's boy; in the next scene, in Spain, merchants bargain, Spanish whores and soldiers sing to the guitar, a Jew comes seeking release from 'this charnel house' of Europe, a cargo of slaves is loaded on to a ship bound for the West Indies. Then, in a desolate grey winter, an old derelict who was the ship's boy, tells the young Raleigh and Gilbert of the 'fabled city of Manoa, El Dorado'. The grown up Raleigh off Guiana, sends his son to his death and abandons the search, going home to die. Short effective scenes are interspersed: a moving scene on board a slave ship, a comic interlude between a Barbadian steward and a drunken English sailor.
>
> The second half opens with the mannered elegance and cynicism of French generals and their wives in Haiti on the eve of the slave rebellion. Violence and savagery erupt in an exciting voodoo episode and we are introduced to the victorious rebel generals, desperate and blood-drunk, except for the tortured Toussaint. The scene thereafter shifts to Jamaica: George William Gordon sets out to make his final speech in Kingston and is hanged; a Baptist preacher begs his flock of slaves to 'dwell together in unity' and one of his flock is forced to run away to a ragged little army in the hills: this is the last hero, Pompey, who is shot in a fight with the British. His friends gather round him, and after his death bury him, and the Carnival people return to end the play with a jump-up in which all the characters join.[25]

Not all the critics were as enchanted by *Drums and Colours* as Jenkin, whose intimate involvement with the work as a member of the production team, and a close friend of the playwright, would have lent her valuable insight but possibly impaired objectivity. Espinet described the work as a clever but not really successful experiment, and claimed that Walcott 'ploughs a barren field of imagery',[26] though he quoted lines he thought especially fine, such as this description by a young Haitian mulatto of his father's part in his parentage:

> He recognised my mother only after dark,
> In that republic where complexions do not matter.

Espinet's is a more vigorous version of the lines Walcott eventually published:

> *Anton*: He recognised her in darkness, in that republic
> And that act, in which complexions do not matter.

But to the majority, *Drums and Colours* was a resounding success, even though the vagaries of the weather during the run caused the production to be known backstage as 'Drums and Water-colours'. Walcott's epic kindled in both participants and spectators a lasting pride in their West Indianness. Of all its remarkable aspects, *Drums and Colours* made its most indelible impression by being the first production, and decades later still the only production, to bring together such an extraordinary array of some two hundred of the foremost talents from all around the Caribbean and further afield. Carifesta features not one common production, but individual productions from each territory – as had in fact been the original proposal for the 1958 Federal presentation. The Jamaican-based Pan Caribbean Theatre Company, which in 1986 took Rawle Gibbons's *I Lawah* and Dennis Scott's *Dog* to London for the festival Caribbean Focus, drew on the region's talents on a smaller scale, and survived as briefly as the Federal Theatre Movement. Other companies, such as Sistren with the Caribbean Popular Theatre Exchange, Barbados's Stage One and WWB, and Walcott's own Trinidad Theatre Workshop after his departure, have occasionally employed actors and directors from around the Caribbean. But there has been nothing to compare with Walcott's epic. *Drums and Colours* proved that an integrated regional theatre company creating West Indian theatre is not only possible, but capable of outstanding accomplishment.

It was the experience of *Drums and Colours* which decided Walcott that, at the age of twenty-eight, the time had come for him to retire from teaching so that he might write full time. He planned to make his base in what he had found to be theatrically the most vibrant of the Caribbean islands, Trinidad. It was Trinidad, he felt, that offered him the most propitious circumstances for the development of his work. It was in Trinidad that he would build a theatre company of the calibre demanded by his plays. Before settling in his new home, however, he went back to the United States on a Rockefeller Foundation Fellowship. He studied theatre under José Quintero at The Circle in the Square, and production with Stuart Vaughan at the Phoenix Theatre. On his return to Trinidad in 1959, he founded what is now the Trinidad Theatre Workshop.

The doyenne of Trinidad dance, Beryl McBurnie, had transformed her family residence in Port of Spain into a small theatre called the Little Carib Theatre. This theatre was the home of McBurnie's Little Carib Dance Company. Walcott joined forces with McBurnie, thereby gaining a home for his own fledgling company, which he called the Little Carib Theatre Workshop. Before the year was out the Workshop staged a private *Showcase* to an invited audience. The six scenes staged included two from *Moon on a Rainbow Shawl*, an adaptation of Sam Selvon's *Basement Lullaby*, and extracts from works by Arthur Miller, George Bernard Shaw and Tennessee Williams. The programme established from the outset that Walcott's vision for the model West Indian Theatre company was far from parochial. He planned to stretch his actors and his audiences with the best of international as well as Caribbean works.

PLAYS OF THE SIXTIES: *Franklin*, *Dream on Monkey Mountain*

There was to be no public performance by the new theatre company until 1962, only intensive training. Meanwhile, during 1960, Walcott joined the staff of the *Trinidad Guardian* as a feature writer, married for the second time, and wrestled with his most naturalistic play up to that time, *Franklin*.

Walcott is himself 'divided to the vein';[27] his grandfathers were both white, while his grandmothers were of predominantly African origin. From his boyhood, Walcott was exercised by the question of the rightful place in the West Indies of the minority whites and mulattos, the descendants of the colonists, and of their European culture. *The Wine of the Country*, which was the early roughcast for *Franklin*, *In a Fine Castle*, and the latter's later development *The Last Carnival* (1982), examine the role of the French creole in the West Indies. *Pantomime* and *Franklin* itself look at the British expatriate. *Dream on Monkey Mountain*, *Drums and Colours*, *Henri Christophe*, and also that *Franklin* roughcast, touch on the dilemma of the West Indian mulatto.

There are at least five distinct versions of *Franklin*, which is still unpublished. A study of the five exemplifies the playwright's progression over the years from heightened language towards ever greater naturalism. The earliest version to be staged, the 1956 *The Wine of the Country*, is written in blank verse. A full length play, it is Chekhovian in spirit. The outsider on the point of reluctant departure from his pleasant seat of power in the island is the mulatto Bemminger, District Commissioner of Dauphin. The conflicts between the characters are rooted in racial discrimination. At one point the mulatto speaks to a French creole woman with the voice of Walcott:

> I have been spurned and booted by two peoples,
> Bewildered between two cultures and two tongues,
> Between desire and despair, between death and hope,
> My people mock me as I am not black,
> Your people mock me as I am not white,
> And yet I am divisible to both, what has my skin
> To do with my desires, is my death different,
> Don't I bend when I age, can't I talk English . . .
> Is it so strange, because I am a mongrel sort of man
> To think that my true purpose is nobility?

As in *Franklin*, the outsider, Bemminger, for all his apparent impassivity, has pledged his heart to this country, not his own. He has, in the metaphor of the play's title, drunk deeply of its heady wine. Even so, he is aware that the islanders who pay him respect do not respect him. To them, he is 'the garbage of government'.

Among the parallels with *Franklin*, there is the small clique of men, ageing expatriates and one greenhorn, who drink and philosophise in the colonial twilight. There is the favoured local man undergoing grooming to take the outsider's place. There is a love affair with a local girl who consequently dies. In this initial version, however, the girl is not an East Indian innocent but a French creole with an unsavoury reputation. And it is not the father who refuses to countenance Marguerite's union with Bemminger, but the harpy of a mother, after the rebuff of her own attempted dalliance with her daughter's lover.

The Wine of the Country is in structure both simpler and rather more tightly knit than its later versions, but it is also one of Walcott's less subtle and more cynical plays. The French creoles living at Versailles estate are exhausted from decadence and inbreeding. Even the best among them, sensitive François Soubirous, the elderly sybarite with 'the touch of Africa', who represents all that is fine in the heritage of European culture that Walcott himself treasures, is killed in the end, along with the callous Marguerite.

The second version of the play, completed by 1961, has been compressed to one act; it is the first to be titled *Franklin, a Tale of the Islands*. The third version is expanded back to three acts, and was a prizewinner in the Barbados Arts Council playwriting competition of 1968; it was produced in Guyana in 1969. Walcott revised the play yet again for his own 1973 production in Trinidad, and virtually rewrote it for a Barbados production in 1990. Both the 1969 and 1990 productions were directed by the Guyanese playwright-director Michael Gilkes. Gilkes reads in *Franklin* a message similar to that of his own *Couvade*, 'that a whole, authentic Caribbean society can emerge only if it takes into full account *all* of its parts, especially its three main surviving cultures: Europe, Africa and Asia'.[28]

Gilkes met the play halfway through its metamorphosis, when characters and plot had already been reworked to a more fully representative symbolism of the West Indian society on the verge of independence. The most essential change between *The Wine of the Country* and *Franklin* is that the lead character is no longer mulatto but white. Bemminger has become the retired English schooner captain Luther Franklin. Even in his new choice of name Walcott is making a telling comment on the colonial position; franklin is the old English term for a freeholder.

In the 1990 version of the play Walcott has the liberal Franklin flanked, philosophically, by two other whites. On the right is Willoughby, a former army major turned planter. On the far left is a naïve young English preacher. The play no longer presents any French creoles, nor any native whites. Blacks are represented by four contrasting characters. Charbon is a fisherman, obeah man and leader of the estate workers union; it is he, the grass-roots labourer, not the better educated Clive, who challenges Franklin over possession of the Great House, and he who ignites the workers' rebellion against Willoughby. Clive Morris, Franklin's adopted son, is to be the next captain of the schooner, but he lacks in loyalty and betrays Franklin in love. Clive's mother, who is Franklin's cook, and Fagette from the schooner's crew, who is the play's endearing Feste, have a greater sincerity and more lucid vision than the others.

Of key importance to the revised plot are the characters representing the East Indians, a major sector of the West Indian population which the theatre has largely neglected. Kole Omotoso comments, 'Even *Drums and Colours* had no place for Indians',[29] and Walcott has written few plays with roles specifically for Indo-Trinidadians. One major exception is *To Die For Grenada* (1986).

Luther brings Maria Ramsingh into his house intending to ask her father's blessing on their marriage. The traditionalist pundit is mortified by his daughter's independent behaviour, and embittered by the inevitable process of West Indianisation which he sees as a vitiation of Hindu religious and cultural values. Behind Luther's back he turns his blessing to a curse, and disowns Maria. The young girl, uprooted and out of her depth with the elderly foreigner, has sought consolation with her own generation, in the person of Clive. The resultant pregnancy exacerbates her distress, making her father's rejection more than she can bear, and she takes her own life.

The tragedy of Maria and Clive is the tragedy of the small society, for in that union lay the promise of the future. Shocked into self-reappraisal, the antagonists avoid further confrontation. The play ends with Willoughby's departure, the mutual reconciliation of Franklin and Charbon, and Franklin's own decision to leave the island. 'What makes a genuine Caribbean person?' asks Gilkes. 'Who should inhabit the Great House of the Caribbean?'[30] All the peoples of the West Indies came from somewhere else, and in the end the only deed of possession is love, love as commitment, love as the comprehending heart. 'Islands', writes Walcott in his poem of that name, 'can only exist / if we have loved in them.'[31]

In early 1962 the Little Carib Theatre Workshop opened its doors to the public and general acclaim with a double bill. Samuel Beckett's *Krapp's Last Tape* featured the most accomplished West Indian actor of the time, Slade Hopkinson, directed by Walcott. Dennis Scott's *The Caged* was directed by Hopkinson. Before the year was out, the Workshop had presented its second production and first Walcott work, *The Charlatan*. Then Walcott again withdrew his company from the public eye, to undergo another year of intensive training. In 1964 the Workshop returned to the public with another double bill, consisting this time of *Malcochon* and Ionesco's *The Lesson*, both directed by Walcott.

The following year, 1965, Walcott was commissioned to write a script for the Dimanche Gras show. This was the annual national show that incorporated the judging of finalists in several Carnival competitions. For the previous two years, Errol Hill had been attempting to develop the show from its traditional revue style to an integrated folk musical. Walcott followed suit, and attempted to raise his musical to a higher level of artistic achievement. *Batai* had a cast of two hundred, including actors from the Theatre Workshop, dance troupes, a choir, steelband and orchestra. The playwright directed this unwieldy mammoth himself. The outcome was not a success and Hill, freshly smarting from Walcott's unsympathetic critique of *Man Better Man*, with undisguised glee and six half-columns of merciless chastisement, described it as 'an unmitigated calamity'.[32] In essence, the failure of *Batai* seems to have lain with the unsuitability of Walcott's classically constrained approach to an innately folk occasion celebrating liberation.

1965 was to prove an unsettling year for Walcott and his Workshop; first came *Batai*, and then the Basement. Walcott broke away from McBurnie and the Little Carib, and relocated in the most promising space he could find, a former bar in the basement of the Bretton Hall Hotel. With a stage along one side and benches along the other, the Workshop's new home could squeeze in some sixty-odd patrons per performance. Mere months after its opening in 1966, the Basement Theatre had established itself as a cultural centre, staging repertory seasons by what was now known simply as the Theatre Workshop, and readings by poets and novelists from around the Caribbean. The Workshop was awarded a three-year grant by the Rockefeller Foundation.

1967 was the year the Workshop first left Trinidad on tour, and consequently became identified as the Trinidad Theatre Workshop. It was also the year that the Company performed, at the Caribana Festival in Toronto, the world première of the most challenging and arguably the greatest of all Walcott's works, *Dream on Monkey Mountain*.

If *Henri Christophe* is Walcott's *Hamlet*, the majestic *Dream on Monkey Mountain* is theatrically his *Lear*. It is also a Caribbean *Tempest*, in which Caliban takes the role of Prospero. And poet Wayne Brown has traced back the

Fig. 6 Derek Walcott's *Dream on Monkey Mountain* (PHOTO: Hollister Chong) Makak (Errol Jones) describes his dream to Moustique (Stanley Marshall) in this scene from *Dream on Monkey Mountain*. This Trinidad Theatre Workshop production, directed by Walcott, presented the world première of the play in Toronto in 1967.

wrote Walcott, '. . . is in a sense a play about the problem of emigration, visionary or nostalgic . . . we do not accept the reality of where we are'.[38] Journalist Owen Baptiste, writing in 1970 as Benedict Wight, applied the metaphor to Walcott himself. 'His is the sympathy and conflict behind Makak; his is the contempt and the arrogance behind Corporal Lestrade; his is the dedication and determination behind the small theatre company.'[39]

Walcott would not deny that running his theatre company in a climate of scant public support for serious theatre, and in the face of the continuing indifference of Trinidad's government in the sixties and seventies, was a crucifying experience. It is no coincidence that this play, which ostensibly rejects the colonial legacy lock stock and barrel, draws much of its power from the colonisers' Christian tradition. There are, for example, the night of the visitation, the miracle of healing and the resurrection of the dead, the Judas betrayal by Moustique, the humiliation of Makak, the two neighbouring thieves – Souris who repents, Tigre who does not – the mauling of the stab-wound in the side, the pieta of Makak and the dead Moustique, the sanitised Heaven of Makak's perfect Africa, the call and response of Lestrade's invocation of the law. (The ritual of call and response, it should be noted, is also intrinsic to much traditional African singing.) In productions that end the dream with the Apparition lying upstage on a sacrificial altar, her body forms a cross with Makak at the climactic instant of the beheading, in an image that recalls Lear's final entrance with the dead Cordelia in his arms. But such a staging of the beheading is not in accordance with Walcott's directions.

In his 1985 article, Brown suggests that, though there remains in the depths of the play the essence of the theme of passing time drawn from the earlier poem, because of that very passage of time, at the surface level the play has dated. With the progression of world events, Brown believes, no one any longer dreams of being a king in Africa. He writes of an 'odd, sad-making mutedness about [the play], of the depths calling without echo from the surface, and the viewer, in consequence, threatened with falling through the latter into the painful, muffled realm of "pure" poetry. It was a most curious feeling, that reversal of the imprecision with which a metaphor sometimes calls up its meaning. Instead one had the meaning, calling half-in-vain for its metaphor'.[40] Even in 1970, a letterwriter to the *Trinidad Guardian* (20 February 1970) described *Dream on Monkey Mountain* as 'a fossilised social structure of a forgotten age in a contemporary setting'. From such a viewpoint, Walcott's irony seems, ironically, lost in the persuasiveness of its metaphor.

But outside Trinidad the play evoked powerful audience response and enthusiastic reviews. As a result of a 1969 run of the Trinidad Theatre Workshop production at the outdoor amphitheatre of the Eugene O'Neill Foundation in Waterford, Connecticut, the play was staged by the Negro Ensemble Company at the Mark Taper Forum in Los Angeles. It then moved to New York, where it won the 1971 Obie Award for a Distinguished Foreign Play. The following year the Negro Ensemble performed the play for the Olympic arts programme in Munich, where the company received a standing ovation at the end of each performance. The largest broadcasting network in the United States, the National Broadcasting Corporation, shot a one-hour version of the play on location in Trinidad, with a 'huge supporting cast of villagers, dancers, musicians and African warriors'.[41] The colour print was screened in Trinidad for an invited audience the night before its world première showing, in black and white, on Trinidad and Tobago Television in February 1970. The shortened version did not do the play full justice, and viewers found it difficult to follow. Of the exceptional number of letters to the press that resulted, the majority were only too ready to classify Walcott's *Dream* as a nightmare. But there were also letters of enthusiastic appreciation, supported by further letters from abroad, after the NBC broadcast.

As the play continued to tour and to appear in fresh productions, an early criticism of Walcott's work revived from time to time: Makak was too eloquent, his language over fine. But for the literary critic the language of *Dream on Monkey Mountain* is, in its magnificent fusion of poetic imagery with the rhythms of dialect, the pinnacle of Walcott's theatrical craft to date.

A Munich critic touched on another aspect of the language: 'The Negro Ensemble Company has had difficulties making this work contemporary. Walcott's English is not the English spoken in North America and the creole dialect corresponds but poorly with the jargon of Harlem'.[42] The actors of the Trinidad Theatre Workshop, however, appeared to relish the language, fine as it might be, and whether or not they were fully in command of its nuances. They had, of course, refined their appreciation of the art of language, the English language, whether standard conversational or poetic or vernacular, from the years spent working with Walcott. 'Acting in a Walcott play under Derek's directorship was a literary education in itself',[43] recalled Albert Laveau, the current Artistic Director of the Workshop, in a 1992 interview.

Walcott, as both playwright and director, was jealous for every word in each of his plays. Even where the production in question was not his own he easily became incensed by any apparent lack of respect for his script, as when the actor playing Jackson in a 1978 Trinidad production of *Pantomime* took some licence with the lines, or when a Guyanese actor performing in a 1987 *Joker of Seville* failed to articulate to Walcott's satisfaction.

Some playwrights invite actors' contributions to their scripts. And in recent times there has been a growing trend towards collective creation. But though Walcott encouraged improvisational exercises as part of the training of his Theatre Workshop, in rehearsal or during a run he rarely countenanced any such conscious input by the actors. He did, however, often create a character with a particular actor in mind, most notably, the role of Jackson for Wilbert Holder. And there were other ways in which actors sometimes inadvertently affected a script. One night during the 1971 run of *In a Fine Castle*, for instance, the actress playing Shelley failed to respond to her entrance cue for the final scene. The actress was an American brought to Trinidad by Walcott specifically to play this Black Power role. She lacked the discipline of the Workshop actors and, as it transpired, was not averse to substance abuse. Whether his reasons were artistic or otherwise, for the remainder of the run Walcott deliberately cut those closing pages of dialogue.

Walcott had previously invited American directors to work with his company. *In a Fine Castle* was his first in several ventures that brought into his Trinidad productions performing talent from overseas. He cast other American actors in *The Joker of Seville*, *O Babylon* and *The Last Carnival*. He brought several actors from St Thomas for *Marie Laveau*. He also invited a Barbadian director, Earl Warner, to direct his Trinidad production of *A Branch of the Blue Nile*, Warner having earlier directed the world première in Barbados. In addition, Walcott never ceased to promote assiduously the casting of his leading Trinidad actors in American productions, though many such opportunities were lost through Equity rulings.

The Theatre Workshop actors were accustomed to changing roles, even at short notice, in any Walcott production. In *Dream on Monkey Mountain* in particular, despite Walcott's minutely detailed direction, a change of actor could make a marked difference in the interpretation of a character, particularly in the case of Lestrade. Later, Walcott took to touring this play, and others, with a smaller company. He would fill in the lesser roles with local actors, as happened in St Croix in 1974, lending a pan-Caribbean aspect to the production. Some time after Walcott's 1976 departure from the Workshop and Trinidad, several of the Workshop's leading actors, in particular Errol Jones, the creator of Makak, were to find themselves much in demand overseas, accepting work around the region and further abroad, in Walcott's plays and in others.

In 1968, the year following the première of *Dream on Monkey Mountain*, Walcott began an extraordinary meditative essay in commemoration of his first decade with the Trinidad Theatre Workshop. *What the Twilight Says: an Overture* became the prologue to his first published collection of plays, the 1970 *Dream on Monkey Mountain and other plays.*

PLAYS OF THE SEVENTIES: *In a Fine Castle* and *The Last Carnival*, *The Joker of Seville*, *O Babylon*, *The Snow Queen*, *Remembrance*, *Pantomime*, *Marie Laveau*

More than three years passed between *Dream on Monkey Mountain* and Walcott's next new work for the stage. In February 1970 Trinidad was shaken by a brief Black Power revolution. Walcott was inspired by the event to a fresh perspective on a subject that had long preoccupied him: the validity in the West Indies of European culture, and the rightful place there, if any, of the colonial descendants. Walcott spent his curfew hours working on a play in which, by alternating his scenes between the black and the white milieux, he contrasted the militant extremism of the Black Power movement with the gentle decadence of a French creole enclave. The Trinidad Theatre Workshop premièred *In a Fine Castle* that same year, 1970, but in Jamaica.

The action takes place during the two days of Carnival prior to the revolution. The castle of the title is the town house of the De La Fontaines. There actually is such a castle in Trinidad, known as Stollmeyers' Castle. It is reputed to be a replica of a wing of Britain's Balmoral Castle, and is one of 'the curve of fantastical mansions in various styles . . . on the rim of the Grand Savannah of Port of Spain'.[44] To the play's French creole family, beleaguered by the changing times, the castle is their home is their castle. There, under the vast, second-rate copy of Watteau's *The Embarkation for Cythera* left unfinished by the death of François De La Fontaine (in actuality painted by Walcott for his production), the older generation clings to a dying way of life. There, the younger generation looks out through the railings to the green 'pastyah'[45] where the masses deny them the right to play their own Carnival, and where the marching revolutionaries deny them the right to exist. But when Clodia, the De La Fontaine daughter, gives up her Carnival Queen crown, the castle is invaded, and the family loses its privacy. A reporter, Brown, comes to interview Clodia. He creates a bridge between the black and the white camps when he becomes the second black ever to be invited to dine at the castle.

Brown, as his name implies, represents another of Walcott's preoccupations, the mulatto. It has been suggested that he in fact personifies Walcott's own frustrations as a journalist. Played by a black actor, he is nevertheless the familiar Walcott mulatto in his sensitivity to two cultures. He is an accepted brother of the revolutionaries, though he leaves their meeting in disgust when the leader's wife is ejected from the movement because she is white. A poet, he is better educated in the European arts than are the De La Fontaines. It is through Brown that Walcott makes his most explicit claim to date for European art to be accepted as a universal heritage, not Europe's alone, and specifically a Caribbean heritage.

But Brown's role in the play is more symbolic than realist. Rational and worldly as he appears to be, he yet allows himself to be drawn into an affair with Clodia, the representative white goddess, and then into an extraordinary charade, over dinner, in which he assumes the role of the family's Uncle Tom retainer, George. Much to Walcott's justified irritation, the minor role of the taciturn George, by dint of the actor's irrepressible upstaging during the 1971 Trinidad run, became the most popular character in the play. There were also nightly ovations for the Carnival robber speech by the most complex of the De La Fontaines, Clodia's suffering brother Antoine, a young Soubirous. For most of the play, however, *In a Fine Castle* performed to peculiarly unresponsive audiences. This may have been in part because, in spite of the element of the revolution in what was Walcott's most naturalistic drama since *Franklin*, there is a dearth of action on stage. The dynamics of the play are ripples rather than rollers. The speeches, both prose and free verse, are long-winded. Humour is uncharacteristically spare. The overall effect is of little more than a philosophical debate in some half dozen languorous or abrasive voices: those of the narrator Brown, of the younger De La Fontaines, of their bluff planter uncle Oswald, of the outsider Agatha Willett, of the revolutionaries such as leader Sydney Prince and Brown's girl Shelley, and of George, when played as written.

The first Trinidadian reviews attacked *In a Fine Castle* with the critics' own revolutionary zeal. The play was 'garrulous', 'boring', 'monotonous', 'inconclusive', 'totally pessimistic', 'deliberately rolled weed to sell to the gullible', in sum, unreal. 'The French Creoles will damn him for portraying them in this Tennessee Williams twilight of rotting decadence,' wrote poet-playwright Eric Roach (*TG*, 1 November, 1971), '. . . The blacks will abuse him for mocking their new movement, their new awareness, their new identity.' The adjective 'Negro-Saxon', applied with a pejorative connotation, appears no fewer than fifteen times in the *Sunday Express* review by Earl Augustus.

But, in the months that followed, two critics, Syl Lowhar and Denis Solomon, wrote more considered analyses of the play, suggesting that an important work had been misjudged through the preconceptions of its detractors. Lowhar (*Tapia*, 26 December, 1971) drew a reference to *Henri Christophe* when he commented 'the poet is wary of black leaders whose motive force is an intense hatred of the whites. They often end up enslaving the very people in whose name they shouted power'. 'What the white characters of his [Walcott's] play represent', wrote Solomon (*DE*, 4 and 5 January, 1972), 'is different depending on whether one considers them as representations of threatened privileged classes (drinkers of brandy and champagne and shelterers of refined and indigent governesses), symbols of metropolitan exploitation (coconut planters), whites threatened by black revolution, or West Indians who happen to be white.'

In a Fine Castle went on to a Los Angeles production in 1972. The Canadian Broadcasting Corporation sent a team to Trinidad to record a shortened version, for broadcast in 1973. Walcott also adapted the play for television, under the title *Un Voyage à Cythere*, but this version was not produced. In 1982, more than a decade after the world première of *In a Fine Castle*, the play reappeared as *The Last Carnival*.

The new version is virtually a completely new play. Walcott had 'unthreaded the characters and themes of one play, and rewoven them into a wonderfully different, richer, far more effective dramatic tapestry'.[46] He had also largely abandoned the Black Power cause, in the cause of better understanding of his French creole plantocracy. By transforming the Black Power leader Sydney Prince into George's nephew Sydney, and making him the sole representative of the Black Power movement, Walcott was able to compress the events of *In a Fine Castle* into the second act of the rewritten work. The new, delicately evocative first act, set on the De La Fontaines' Santa Rosa estate and spanning the period 1948 to Trinidad's independence in 1962, is given to exploration of the influences and incidents that have made the family what they are in 1970. In the overall play, the arguments are much as before, but in the new version the voices have an enthusiasm, a humanity, a poignancy, that demand the concern of the audience. The language, though still holding the elegance of verse, has a greater immediacy and naturalism than that of the earlier play.

After the Trinidad production, Walcott did some further reworking. He expanded the new role of the maid, Jean. He introduced the Black Power character, George's nephew Sydney, as a boy on the Santa Rosa estate. He created an additional minor character, the Major. The published version of *The Last Carnival* opens with the arrival from England of Agatha Willett, a 25-year-old Londoner, hired by Victor De La Fontaine to raise his two motherless children. Victor, the Watteau painter who does not appear in person in the first play (in which he is referred to as François, another echo of Soubirous) selected his governess less for her credentials than because she 'looked like a Watteau shepherdess. All the other applicants had faces like prams!' The play, like the life of the De La Fontaines, is soon revolving around the influence of Agatha. In spite of her fresh and innocent air, the inexperienced governess has a worldly wisdom and a finely honed sense of justice. She also has the advantage of an outsider's viewpoint. Inevitably she becomes Victor's mistress, and after his suicide the mistress of his brother Oswald. Equally inevitably, the class barriers of the time ensure that neither brother marries her. Yet Aggie wastes no tears on her own treatment as socially inferior. She devotes herself to Victor's children, Clodia and Tony (Antoine). At the same time, she sets out to teach the younger black workers on the estate how to read, write, and take control of their own, and eventually their island's, future. It is because of Aggie that in 1970 Jean, the Santa Rosa maid, has become a government minister. It is because of Aggie that Sidney, George's nephew, is a Black Power guerrilla on the run. It is because of Aggie that Clodia, the abdicating Carnival queen, will eventually leave the island.

Yet, as Earl Lovelace points out, in a review (*DE*, 25 July, 1982) that recognises the play as powerfully significant in essence, but deplores what the critic sees as elements of superficiality in its treatment, of all the De La Fontaines it is Clodia who belongs to the island, 'by birth, by culture, by all that makes a native native of a place. Where, as a member of a new generation, she is an advance on the old, is in her acceptance and understanding of a truth that others have been blind to: that France, the home of her forefathers, is not her home; Trinidad is, and she cannot ignore it and pretend herself the possessor of a superior culture like her father Victor, nor exist with her heart a silent cry of pain, like uncle Oswald.'

Walcott has written *The Last Carnival* in such a way that the leading actress plays the young Agatha in the first act, and Clodia in the second, in which the older Agatha is played by a supporting actress. In the same way, the leading actor plays Victor in the first act, and in the second Victor's son, Tony. However, just as all the characters of the first act, even the now loquacious George, have been expanded from their original treatment in *In a Fine Castle*, so the characters of the second have to some extent suffered diminution. This diminution is particularly noticeable in the cases of Clodia and Brown, and results in the loss of a measure of persuasiveness in their already unlikely relationship. But that relationship itself is less important in this version, the seminal black-white relationship now being between Clodia and Sidney, long before Black Power burned down Santa Rosa.

After *In a Fine Castle*, another three years passed before the première of a new Walcott piece. In late 1973 Walcott found the Theatre Workshop actors less than enthusiastic about his current work in progress, the musical *Heavenly Peace*. It was Walcott's first American play. Through his work with the Eugene O'Neill Foundation, through the first few American productions of his plays, and through his 1971 Obie Award for *Dream on Monkey Mountain*, Walcott had already established an association with the United States that had carried him across the threshold of international theatre. This association was now beginning to extend his artistic references, and would eventually encourage him to move his base from the Caribbean to America.

Heavenly Peace is about the Vietnam war. It was inspired by the poems of Daniel Berrigan, one of two Irish-American brothers, both Catholic priests, who had been jailed in the United States for preaching pacifism. Walcott used some of Berrigan's poems as lyrics. The score had been composed by Gary M. Friedman, who also assisted with the authentication of the Hebrew content of the musical. Walcott took as his central theme the impossibility of serving a cause in which one does not believe. In what one of the Workshop actors has described as a rather 'mannered' script, the cast of characters includes among others an Inquisitor, Dante, a street poet named Moondog, Berrigan himself, and a chorus that appeared in a range of roles such as Vietnamese peasants, soldiers, and communicants.

An American production of *Heavenly Peace* reached a fairly advanced stage of planning. Eventually, however, due perhaps in part to certain developments in connection with the Berrigan brothers, the project was abandoned. Perhaps on account of the Workshop's lack of empathy with the play, perhaps because of other demands on his Trinidad company, Walcott for once did not attempt to push through a Caribbean production. His Vietnam musical has never been staged or published.

Meantime, Walcott had been commissioned by England's Royal Shakespeare Company to recreate the Don Juan legend in an adaptation of Tirso de Molina's sixteenth century masterpiece, *El Burlador de Sevilla.* Walcott speaks no Spanish, and had to make his acquaintance with de Molina's text through Roy Campbell's mainly blank verse translation. 'Yet without knowing Tirso's speech,' writes the poet in his introduction to *The Joker of Seville*, 'I felt a contemporary, provincial, and immediate enthusiasm for his play because of Trinidad. The wit, panache, the swift or boisterous elan of his period, or of the people in his play, are as alive to me as the flair and flourishes of Trinidad music and its public character.'

The 1986 *Carib* (No. 4) carries a partial transcript of a seminar held at the College of the Virgin Islands, St Thomas, in which Walcott discusses the purpose behind the modern rewriting of a classical text, reveals something of the process he followed in making his adaptation, and describes his approach to the elements of the plot. He also touches on his contention that verse dialogue develops as naturally in the West Indian culture of today, with its living oral tradition, as it did in the Europe of Shakespeare's time. Walcott holds that it is because it has developed itself beyond the oral tradition that the metropolitan western society now perceives artifice in the pentameter. To Walcott, recreating de Molina's verse form for his adaptation was the most vital factor in the overall challenge of retaining the essential exuberance, pace and popular vulgarity of the original.

He began his task laboriously by trying to reproduce exactly in his English translation the old Spanish form comprising eight-foot lines of alternating rhymes. He soon gave up. The form was unsuited to modern English. And if a word-for-word adaptation was what was required, he concluded, 'they should have got someone who knew Spanish'. It occurred to him that the validity of this project of rewriting an established classic lay in what he, without pretensions to superiority, could bring to it of his own identity, the fresh perspective of a poet from the West Indies. Accordingly, he now felt a far greater freedom of interpretation. This freedom is most noticeable in his transportation of de Molina's parody of a pastoral shepherdess, Tisbea, to the West Indies. There she symbolises the rape of the New World, and so gives the work an added dimension. Influenced by the Spanish guitar poet and playwright Federigo Garcia Lorca, Walcott found that he could remain true to the tempo and rhyme scheme of *El Burlador* by working in the clipped lines of a form which he drew from the parang, an urgently rhythmic West Indian folk music of Spanish origin. Galt MacDermot then composed his hauntingly poignant score from several musical forms common to the West Indies, including calypso and the revivalist spiritual.

Perhaps the most markedly West Indian aspect of *The Joker of Seville*, however, is that the drama's warriors lunge and parry not as sixteenth century swordsmen, but as Caribbean stickfighters. It is a transformation which allows Walcott free rein for some ribald word play, from the opening introduction of Don Juan as 'the greatest stickman' of them all. Though most of the action ostensibly takes place, as in *El Burlador*, in Europe, between Naples and Seville, Walcott has in essence transferred the entire play to the New World. His prologue introduces the performance as an annual tradition on a Caribbean estate. The resulting festival atmosphere of masquerade has in it something of Carnival theatre, favouring a broader style of performance as the actors play the villagers who then assume roles in the play. For the première production, Walcott transformed the Little Carib auditorium to a stickfighting gayelle, with the audience seated on bleachers round all four sides of the arena stage.

Due to unexpected cutbacks in its funding, the Royal Shakespeare Company had found itself unable, during the period it held the rights to its own commissioned work, to undertake the production of a musical of such magnitude. Walcott was given permission to stage the première of *The Joker of Seville* in Trinidad, which he did with his Theatre Workshop in 1974. It was to be another two decades before the RSC was able to première a commissioned work by Walcott, when in 1992 the Company staged Walcott's musical adaptation of Homer's *Odyssey.*

For all its length, the *Joker* première was an unprecedented success, with rapturous patrons nightly packing the bleachers shoulder to shoulder. This magnificent popular reception led to the issue of Walcott's first record, later followed by a cassette tape, and several further productions, including Joe Papp's 1977 New York showcase, of what is probably still Walcott's most universally admired work for the stage.

The Joker of Seville is a great deal more than a catalogue of deflorations. In its revelations of the subjection of women, one of its principal themes is of women's liberation, epitomised in the role of Isabella, Duchess of Naples. It is with Juan's seduction of Isabella that the play proper opens, followed by the Duchess's banishment to the Convent of the Barefoot Nuns. In the Convent Isabella learns that, ironically, Juan has taught her freedom – the freedom of self-realisation as a woman. Walcott deliberately focuses on the ironies of the text. 'The joke that Juan plays in each case is that he reinforces the flaw that exists in the people he plays his tricks on . . . When Octavio decides that he is going to get past that citadel where his love is and get into the palace, he himself is breaching a code . . .' Walcott sees in Juan's jokes a satirical morality that holds up to ridicule the pretensions of his society. De Moto's embracing of a last night with the whores before going to his true love, allows Juan the double joke of a last night with that true love, Juan's own once intended bride, Ana. The farm girl Aminta's vision of herself as a duchess allows Juan the joke of making her one. The final joke, however, is played against Juan, by the vengeful Octavio and strolling actor Rafael, with a living statue that is the lover's death.

Walcott followed close on the heels of *The Joker of Seville* with another musical scored by Galt MacDermot, *O Babylon!*, an original work set in Jamaica's Rastafarian community. The many-layered story is poignantly in sympathy with the Rastafarians as it contrasts their peaceable and devout existence, in the face of poverty and persecution, with the glitz and greed of materialistic Babylon, as the cult terms the non-Rastafarian world. Walcott had drawn several elements of his new musical from another script in progress, *The Isle is Full of Noises.* Among these borrowed elements were the displacing of the dispossessed by a Mafia hotel; the singer and his back-up group; the names Aaron and Priscilla; and a vision of horsemen that became Aaron's dream of the horsemen of the Apocalypse.

As with many of Walcott's works, the published text of *O Babylon!* shows extensive revisions from the script of the première performance, staged in Trinidad in 1976. As with *In a Fine Castle* and its later version *The Last Carnival* in particular, a fundamental difference between the first and the final versions of *O Babylon!* is that Walcott eventually elected to move his play back in time, and to open the action with incidents that previously were merely reported from the past. Initially, the play opened in Trench Town, a small Rastafarian beach settlement, in 1966, two years after Brother Aaron had converted from a life of crime to fulfil his dream of becoming a woodcarver, days before the momentous visit to Jamaica of the then Ethiopian Emperor Haile Selassie, who is worshipped by the Rastafarians as the Living God. The published play opens outside Babylon's Club Number One, with the gangland shooting of the criminal who will become Aaron. The latter opening has the cinematic drama of a police thriller of the period, with gun shots, running figures, police sirens and flashing lights, a rising half moon and heavy rhythm, and a flock of dancers in their nightclub feathers.

All through the musical, Walcott creates the necessary dramatic energy by using the frenzy that is Babylon to punctuate the slow pace, underlying melancholy and dreamlike quality of the Rastafarians' secluded life, wreathed in the smoke of the holy weed. The original opening also featured nightclub dancers, in this case the Rudettes backing one-time peanut-cum-marijuana vendor, now a 'big black reggae star', Rude Bwoy Dawson. Rude Bwoy moves freely between the worlds of Jah and of Babylon, and when necessary explains mysteries of the one to the other – on occasion wickedly untruthfully. In the première version Rude Bwoy is the narrator, addressing the audience directly as he tells the story of *O Babylon!*, which is both the love story of Aaron and Electric Gyal, and the story of the Trench Town community's struggle for survival against the encroachment of Babylon, in the form of a new luxury hotel. In the published text Rude Bwoy's narration is confined to the second act, but he remains the most endearing character in a roster of memorable individuals that includes General Sufferer and his Virgie, and the deadly Deacon Doxy and his Dolly. Other characters in the original production, two Mafia gangsters and stuttering Edwin the astronaut, have been almost wholly eliminated. The result is a tighter play, and Walcott has also eliminated elements of humour that at times rang somewhat discordantly with the essential realism of his theme.

Walcott discusses his approach to the language of *O Babylon!* in his note to the text:

> Jamaican is a highly melodic language. Rhetorical negatives appear for the music's sake. 'The proof of the pudding is in the eating' might become 'De proof of the pudding nat ina da eating, den?' So, in trying to seek a combination of the authentic and the universally comprehensible, I found myself at the centre of a language poised between defiance and translation, for pure Jamaican is comprehensible only to Jamaicans. But the promulgation of a national language is as much a part of education now as it is of politics. When I considered that, within that language itself, the Rastafari have created still another for their own nation, I faced another conflict: if the language of the play remained true to the sect, it would have to use the sect's methods of self-protection and total withdrawal. This would require of the playwright not merely a linguistic but a spiritual conversion, a kind of talking in tongues that is, by its hermeticism and its self-possession, defiantly evasive of Babylonian reason.
>
> The Rastafari have invented a grammar and a syntax which immure them from the seductions of Babylon, an oral poetry which requires translation into the language of the oppressor. To translate is to betray. My theatre language is, in effect, an adaptation and, for clarity's sake, filtered.

Trinidad audiences received *O Babylon!* with enthusiasm, but the critics were rather more reserved in their praise. Later in 1976, for Carifesta, the Workshop's Rastafarian musical travelled to Jamaica to represent Trinidad, a tour of coals-to-Newcastle irony for Caribbean separatists, but a milestone in terms of Caribbean integration. *O Babylon!* was also eventually staged both in America and in England. It appears, however, in spite of Walcott's extensive and theatrically satisfying reworking of the script, not to have achieved the lasting universality of appeal of its predecessor, *The Joker of Seville*.

Walcott's second play of 1976 was his first piece written specifically for television, *The Snow Queen*, based on his stage plays *A Georgian House* and *A Sound of Hunting*. Even though intended for the more naturalistic medium, *The Snow Queen* is written in free verse. The play went into rehearsal for Trinidad and Tobago Television, but was never screened. However, extracts and rehearsal photographs were published in Trinidad's *People* magazine of April 1977.

The Snow Queen of the title is a middle-aged Englishwoman who lives in 'a decaying old estate house in high forest on a West Indian island'.[47] Lady Anne

Palmer spends her days peacefully playing the piano through a haze of cocaine, interlaced with screaming bouts when her sole, elderly companion thinks it time to withdraw her 'medicine' and bury it in the garden. Into this eccentric *ménage* stumble two armed fugitives escaping to Venezuela. The two are on the run from a bungled bank robbery turned murder, and on the run from their former brother guerillas as well as from the police and the army. As the arms of the law close ever more tightly about their sanctuary, the fugitives indulge themselves in a pathetic travesty of gracious living, 'playing aristocrat', tasting tenth-rate 'Colonial happiness'. The younger, Vittorio, who has something of a Don Juan reputation, rather than rape Lady Anne sets out to seduce her. The only resistance he meets stems from her distaste for her own ageing appearance. The 'lover boy' finds his routine patter affected by the haunting atmosphere of the wild and desolate place, as well as by the strangeness of the woman herself. A genuine relationship begins to blossom between the two, and in the end it is Vittorio who is seduced, into the arms of cocaine, until the army takes him.

The Snow Queen's combination of decayed gentility and artistry with criminal violence was to surface again in *The Rig* (1983). The combination is also present to varying extents in *The Wine of the Country*, *In a Fine Castle* and *The Last Carnival*. Walcott's absorption with the subject of the changes wrought by time dates back to his very earliest plays. In *Flight and Sanctuary* and *Harry Dernier* the teenaged Walcott treated ageing and death from the theoretical viewpoint of an observer. But even as a teenager he had a strong sense, perhaps honed by his Methodist upbringing, of the rarity value of time, of the importance of making the most productive use of each minute, as of each experience, and of the impossibility of reliving wasted time. With the passage of years, the poet-playwright became ever more acutely aware of his own time passing, ever more intimately involved in his ongoing discussion of life and death. His fortieth birthday was a landmark event in his own mind, and was heralded a couple of years in advance by *Dream on Monkey Mountain*, the play in which Wayne Brown sees a theme of rebellion against the inevitable passage of time, the play in which death is a key character. Age and death inhabit works as diverse as *The Sea at Dauphin* and *The Joker of Seville*, *Remembrance* and *Marie Laveau*, but *The Snow Queen* was the first of Walcott's plays in which ageing was given so personal a face.

More than for either *The Snow Queen* or *O Babylon!*, 1976 is remembered in West Indian theatre as the year that Walcott left the Trinidad Theatre Workshop. He simultaneously withdrew the Workshop's right to stage his plays. It was not the first occasion on which Walcott had handed in his resignation to the company. In his middle years a man of powerful charisma, as demanding of perfection in others as in himself, staunchly loyal, caustic in tongue, quick to jest but slow to forgive, and capable of implacable rage, Walcott, by force of personality, by the genius of his artistry, by mutual affection and admiration, had welded together the finest theatre ensemble in the Caribbean. He brooked little deviation from his dictates, or from the precise path he charted for his company. But past differences between Walcott and Workshop members had always eventually been resolved sufficiently amicably for Walcott to agree to return.

This time, dealing a crippling blow from which the Trinidad Theatre Workshop has never entirely recovered, Walcott's decision was final. Perhaps it was simply that his time had come to move on beyond the Caribbean.

As a result of the parting, two of Walcott's next three works, *Remembrance* and the musical *Marie Laveau*, had their premières not in Trinidad, but in the US Virgin Islands. Ostensibly Trinidad remained Walcott's base until the early eighties, but for much of the time he was out of the island, involved in productions of his plays, or teaching semesters at universities such as Columbia and Yale. Even so, for a number of years Walcott's work continued to show evidence of the Workshop's influence. And two or three times annually Walcott returned to Trinidad, where for some years he continued to undertake productions. Initially, in these post-Workshop Trinidad productions, Walcott avoided casting core Workshop actors. His first such production was the 1977 *Charlatan* which introduced MacDermott's score to Trinidad. The 1982 *Last Carnival* was his first Trinidad production as Warwick Productions, named in tribute to his father.

Remembrance was commissioned by the St Croix theatre company which staged its 1977 première, and which had previously worked with touring productions of the Trinidad Theatre Workshop. The Courtyard Players brought Walcott to St Croix as soon as he became available to work with the company, and to direct his new play. The Players also brought from Trinidad Wilbert Holder, to create the demanding leading character, Albert Perez Jordan. Holder was an exceptionally gifted self-styled 'Walcottian' actor originally from Guyana.

'There was a generation of West Indian teachers', Walcott wrote in his 1979 programme note to *Remembrance*,

> to whom radicals and revolutionaries now pay grudging or ironic tribute. Believers in 'the strap', in 'the old values', venerators of Latin, men who sweated in tweed suits in the fierce sun on their way to school, men ultimately bewildered and frightened of change and the new politics. Between their day and ours there is 'a great gulf fixed', and the tides of change have left them beached on their pensions, exaggerating lost glories. They laid foundations for those who went on to colleges and universities. They have become as anachronistic as their clothes. But they were not mere imitators, they believed in the Caribbean. They were honest. They were gentlemen. Their contribution is immeasurable, their example Roman. *Remembrance* is a sincere and painful tribute to such a teacher. If this play appears to praise convention it may be more radical than it seems, in a time when nothing is more conventional than revolution. But it was not written in a spirit of reaction. It was written in honour of great teachers I had the privilege of knowing in my boyhood, whose encouragement and love have made it possible for me, a generation later, to write a play for them.

Remembrance is one of Walcott's most poetically structured works, with its 'rhythmic recurrence of the Remembrance motif within an elegant frame – a motif of echoed lines, echoed movement, echoed characters'.[48] Through the device of an interview, the action moves easily between past and present as One Jacket Jordan, retired schoolmaster and acknowledged literary lion of the island, is forced into an uneasy examination of his life, and to the conclusion that, rather than a lion, he had been no more than 'a mouse with a fountain pen'. Nor had he been any more successful in reconciling his now unfashionable love of British culture with the evolution of his family and community in independent Trinidad. The violence of his elder son's rebellion against Jordan's way of life led to the boy's death in the Black Power revolution of 1970.

As part of his interview, Jordan records his two most successful stories, *Barrley and the Roof*, and *My War Effort*. The first is a satirical comedy with undertones of colonial patriotism and independence, in which an American visitor attempts to buy the Stars and Stripes which Jordan's younger son, Frederick, has painted on the roof of the family home. The second story is 'a love story that is to repeat itself, straddling Jordan's life like a jeweller's pincers, holding up the man's flaws for inspection.'[49] As a young man, although he considered himself English, Jordan hadn't the courage to marry England, in the person of his adored Esther Trout, and 'cross over'. It was, he believes in later life, a mortal error. Unknown to Jordan, his exorcism of his own pain in the thinly disguised fiction of his alter ego, Padmore, has deeply wounded his wife.

The role of Mabel Jordan was the most fully rounded and realistic that Walcott had written to date for a woman. The most challenging roles in his work are for male actors, a reflection of the male orientation of the Trinidad Theatre Workshop. With few exceptions – *The Last Carnival* offers one – Walcott's female roles are secondary and often superficially drawn, or even unpersuasive. Quick-tongued, pragmatic Mabel, however, has the stature and earthy credibility of the classic West Indian mother figure, Errol John's Sophie Adams. Mabel is Jordan's 'monument', loving and quarrelling with her two surviving men as she holds her family together, burying her heartache in her bawling hymns.

Remembrance is as much about the family as it is about Jordan, and as much about the island nation as it is about the family. Dwight Arthur, director of a 1989 production in Trinidad, writes,

> For me *Remembrance* goes beyond the glorification of teachers. It touches on the psyche of Caribbean people and in particular on their allegiance to the trappings and values of foreign lands which many have only visited via the media. It reiterates the plight which many Caribbean artists endure – to remain unheralded within the environment which has nurtured their creativity or to flee to alien lands in search of recognition and remuneration.[50]

Remembrance was the first of Walcott's new-style prose plays. It introduced the more naturalistic dialogue that would characterise much of his future work. Even so, Marilyn Stasio of the *New York Post* commented after the 1979 production at the New York Shakespeare Festival Public Theatre, 'Walcott writes beautifully, in a rich poetic idiom which he clearly loathes to cut and shape into a clean dramatic style.' As he moved into greater realism, Walcott perhaps inevitably began to withdraw from the symbolic mode that had formed an intrinsic part of his plays up to that time, and that had, together with his heightened language, infused his theatre with its exceptional power. But he did not abandon metaphor altogether, as *The Isle is Full of Noises* was to show.

Walcott had parted from his Theatre Workshop, but Trinidad and its actors were still an inseparable part of his creative process. He wrote the initial version of his next play, *Pantomime*, literally overnight while he was in Tobago, the Robinson Crusoe island where it is set. He wrote the two-hander for two specific Trinidad actors, both gifted in comedy. Wilbert Holder, to whom the play is dedicated, was one of the two. Holder created the character of Jackson for the 1978 world première in Trinidad, and until his death in 1987 continued to play the role in subsequent productions, both in the Caribbean and in the United States. The comedy continues to be produced around the world, and seems certain to survive on record as Walcott's most frequently staged play, with only *Ti-Jean and His Brothers* also in the running.

As a work by Walcott, *Pantomime* is remarkable not only for its frequency of production, but also for the speed with which it was written, for the wholly naturalistic flow of the two-edged dialogue, and for its being the playwright's first to feature a cast of only two actors. One actor is black, the other white. In his programme note for the première, Walcott wrote:

> While the trend in contemporary theatre of having as few characters as possible with a single setting is dominated by economic necessity, and may continue for some time, I was not influenced by any such idea, the play suddenly emerged whole, after hearing its two characters arguing in my head. The two virtually dictated the play to me, and I simply found myself to be a witness-stenographer to a debate that sprung its own tensions. It is basically, I suppose, about two actors, and their different racial and cultural origins creating whatever conflicts exist from their approach to theatre, its ritual, its meaning, its style. It may also be saying that the self-torturing schizophrenia that precedes the resolution of an identity can achieve a resolution with dignity. It may be a political play, with its subject, independence, but that process first has to be human before it can become political.

Even with this play which had 'emerged whole', Walcott, subsequent to the première, revised the work, though less drastically than usual. At the same time he expanded the original short script to full length. The essential part of the work remains the play, or rather the improvised rehearsal, within the play.

The published version of *Pantomime* begins with a ludicrous music-hall performance by Harry Trewe. Trewe is an Englishman and one-time actor who has run away from his failures – as a husband, as a father, as an artist – to become owner-manager of the failing Castaways Guest House in Tobago. Castaways is deserted, closed for repairs, and Trewe is occupying his empty days by trying to work up a Robinson Crusoe pantomime as entertainment for the guests expected when he reopens. To this end he has been attempting to co-opt the talents of the sole member of staff to have stayed on during the closure. The waiter Jackson is also a runaway from the entertainment industry, being a former calypsonian from Trinidad, but he has no intention of allowing Trewe to disturb the tranquillity of his present existence. Each attempts to outmanipulate the other, Trewe by a heavy-handed mix of cajolery and unselfconscious colonial condescension ('I can bring it all down to your level'), and the more practical, farsighted and nimbler-witted Jackson by sleight-of-tongue, as he adroitly side-steps all threats to the balance of the existing master-servant relationship.

Trewe is suddenly inspired to suggest a role reversal, with Jackson as a black Crusoe, and Trewe as a white Friday. It is an inspiration he quickly regrets. Trewe had seen no further than a token reversal but, once embarked on the project, Jackson is unstoppable. His ensuing shrewd burlesque exposes the fallacies in the relationships of master-servant, coloniser-colonised, white-black. And with his seizure of independence the relationship of Jackson to Trewe becomes a drama of man to man.

Jackson the calypsonian has turned Trewe's pantomime into a santimanitay, an extemporaneous battle of words '*sans d'humanite*'. As actress-director Sonya Moze describes it in an unpublished BA essay, the victory goes to the calypso tent over the music-hall. Before the rehearsal ends, the unhappy Trewe finds himself disconcertingly on the receiving end of the colonial experience. He is forced, to the point of pathos, to reassess himself, his life, his prejudices, his liberal philosophy. Trewe's reward is his own freedom of spirit as he cuts from his neck the albatross of his failed life. And the catharsis is not one-sided. Jackson too has had to examine himself, with the result that he returns to his true vocation in calypso. The relationship between the two men has meanwhile developed into one of mutual respect.

In the late twentieth century, Daniel Defoe's nearly three hundred years old paean to white supremacy is increasingly seen as 'a beautiful, unconscious image of the colonial process, bringing out its *naïveté* as well as its arrogance and cruelty.'[51] Walcott is one of several writers, such as the poet Adrian Mitchell in his 1975 novel *Man Friday*, who have brought new light to the story by reversing the theme. In *Pantomime*, the outcome of the reversal is an objective comparison of two strikingly different cultures, which points to the futility of judging the one by the values of the other.

Once again, as he had done as recently as *Remembrance*, and was later to do in *A Branch of the Blue Nile* and *Steel*, Walcott was raising the question of compatibility between the classical and the creole. Included in that question is a comparison of cultural approaches to art. 'If you take this thing seriously', Trewe warns Jackson, 'we might commit Art, which is a kind of crime in this society.' As with much of the swift and sometimes ribald wit in this play, the sting in the tail of this witticism draws its potency from Walcott's years of experience as a playwright-producer in Trinidad.

But, interestingly, Walcott neither produced nor directed the first, or any, Trinidad production of *Pantomime*. The 1978 première was staged by the Trinidad Theatre Workshop offshoot company All Theatre Productions, and directed by Trinidad Theatre Workshop actor-director Albert Laveau. With the arguable exception of Michael Gilkes's 1969 *Franklin* in Guyana (Walcott directed the première of the original version, *The Wine of the Country*), it was the first time in nearly twenty years, since his brother Roderick had directed the first *Malcochon* and *Jourmard* in 1959, that the world première of a Derek Walcott play had been staged without the official involvement of the playwright.

Over the years, devotees of Walcott's dialogue had learned to expect the unexpected in more ways than one. The poet relished the vibrant language of the street just as he relished more classical writing. On occasion, for dramatic effect, he would lace his imagery with expletives and epithets considered unacceptable in Trinidad's middle-class society. *Pantomime*'s naturalistic dialogue between two men is alive with unselfconsciously ripe language to such an extent that the first production came under police scrutiny. The comedy was allowed to continue its run unbowdlerised, however. It was not until 1991, and not in a Walcott play, that an actor was arrested for the use of obscene language on the Trinidad stage.

Walcott followed *Pantomime* with his first original work to be staged that had a setting established as outside the West Indies. Its voodoo subject has strong associations with Haiti and the whole Caribbean region, but *Marie Laveau* is set in the American city of New Orleans. By now Walcott had developed stronger associations with America, through his lecturing, his publications, his awards, the widening international recognition of his work as both poet and playwright, the increasing incidence of metropolitan productions of his plays, and his recent familiarity with the US Virgin Islands. The new musical, scored by Galt MacDermot, had its première in St Thomas, in 1979.

The mulatto priestess Marie Laveau is an historical figure, of such enduring interest that her life is the subject of a permanent museum exhibition in the Mississipi River city that she ruled as, Walcott suggests, Cleopatra ruled the Nile. And on one level the musical is a continuation of Walcott's longstanding debate on the classical and creole cultures. *Marie Laveau*, though less intense, also has something in common with earlier works such as *Dream on Monkey Mountain*; both these plays, for instance, incorporate voodoo, a resurrection scene, and African degradation as well as African supremacy. But *Marie Laveau* has comparatively little affinity with Walcott's other voodoo musical, *The Charlatan*. The later work takes itself and its powers far more seriously than does the Carnival romp.

The action of *Marie Laveau* takes place in 1825, and introduces Marie at the moment of her vanquishing of Papa Sam, her only rival to the voodoo throne of black New Orleans. Now the Queen of queens, Marie is obsessed with her vision of the palace she claims, one particular house she coveted as a child:

On 1900 Rampart Street there's a white house
With gingerbread arches and a long balcony
With white arching steps leading up to white windows
That open onto an astonishing sea
You see, as you stroll down its mile-long verandah
Its garden-walls foaming with white Queen Anne's lace,
Lemon trees, jasmine and blue jacaranda,
I think I could manage in such a place.

Each sunset its windows would blaze to the night skies
Like a paddle-boat floating on a river of green,
And high on the tide of the on-rushing sunrise
It rode on the light like the barge of a queen;
I see a small black girl whispering with wonder,
Her eyes fever-bright in that innocent face,
Lemon trees, jasmine, and blue jacaranda,
Some day, Marie, you will have such a place,
You will have such a place. . . .

Among the obstacles to the realisation of Marie's dream are the facts that the present owner of the 'palace' is in excellent health, that Rampart Street is a residential area for whites, and that the law does not allow blacks to own property.

Marie Laveau lays her plans with exquisite cunning. Through her hairdressing salon she learns the secrets of society. She has discovered that the Rampart Street house is mortgaged to the Cotton Exchange. She has approached the directors of the Exchange 'soft-mannered as a moth' with a proposal: if they will supply her with a suitable house, she will keep it as their house of love. The directors are enamoured of the scheme. They select three beautiful 'nieces' to attend Marie's 'school of etiquette', and call in a mortgage on a well-furnished house for their purpose. Unfortunately, it is the wrong house.

Marie is unfazed by the temporary setback. When her arguments fail to persuade the Exchange directors to exchange the house for the one she wants, she moves into their 'matchbox' with the girls, whom she promptly trains in the tactics of Lysistrata. When sexual frustration proves too slow a form of persuasion, the cotton market begins to fail, owing to rumours of a curse on the crop. When economic pressure still does not bring in the Rampart Street mortgage, the owner of the coveted house becomes the next in a mysterious series of deaths of prominent citizens who have crossed the path of Marie Laveau. The house reverts to the Exchange, but is reserved for the imminent state visit of General Lafayette. Marie sends a letter of blackmail to the board of directors. The directors are by now in a desperate situation, and terrified of Marie's ever-increasing power as 'she waits, black and venomous at the centre / of a network of streets, mortgages, spirits!' The board hires the Reverend Bythunder to exorcise the priestess. Marie Laveau sabotages the ceremony with a plague of frogs, and Papa Sam is moved to kill the preacher.

A subplot introduces a new factor into the equation when Felice, director Blondin's 'niece', runs away with her true love Luke. For the lovers' safety, Felice takes with her Marie's little black box of power. The loss means that Marie Laveau cannot summon her gods to save Papa Sam from the gallows. Yet she is far from powerless, and her ingenuity triumphs at every call upon it. In a second, charmingly comic subplot, an engineered love affair allows Marie access to the Exchange's cooked accounts books, and consequently victory over the scruples of Blondin, the one relatively incorruptible director who still stood in her way. Through this victory, and through the priestess's influence with General Lafayette, by the end of the play Papa Sam has been pardoned, the little black box has been returned, Felice has been raised from the dead, and Marie has moved into her palace.

The poet-playwright Edward Brathwaite has suggested that a significant value of Walcott's *oeuvre* is his 'mediation' between North and South, between America and the Caribbean. It may seem surprising, then, that a widespread reaction in Trinidad to the 1980 production of *Marie Laveau* was that Walcott had sold out to Broadway and white America. The Afro-Trinidadian painter-poet LeRoy Clarke, for instance, having lived for many years in New York, savaged the musical with epithets such as 'sham and decoration . . . blasphemous and exploitative . . . an "artificial resurrection" which giddies in the void and courtship of spectacle for tourists . . . shimsham con and popular gloss . . . mediocrity and trash'.[52]

Most of the critics agreed that, as a musical in the Broadway mould, *Marie Laveau* was Walcott's most successful to date. It fully integrated the songs with the action, whereas his earlier musical works were more accurately described as plays with music, the songs appearing to have been added into a finished text. Victor Questel, rowing against the tide, and in spite of his disappointment over the unevenness of the production and weaknesses in the writing of the title role, praised Walcott's treatment of his material, and argued that it demonstrated significant spiritual growth in the playwright. In the Governor Plum 1980 *Trinidad and Tobago Review*, Questel cites a passage from *What the Twilight Says*, in which Walcott suggests that 'for us, Afro-Christians, the naming of the god estranged him. Ogun was an exotic for us, not a force'. 'If Walcott still believed that "we had lost both gods, and only blasphemy was left",' wrote Questel, 'he could not have attempted a play such as *Marie Laveau*. Walcott's intention is very positive and marks a crucial reversal of his 1970 position . . . . it now appears as if Walcott realises that he cannot deny the African gods nor can he deny the syncretism that has taken place . . . . in a scene of resurrection . . . all the loa work together in one circle or cycle of strength . . . . Walcott's instinct to go for psychic wholeness rather than self-knowledge is correct, but in the theatre to go for the former without completely exploring the latter is to make the resolution seem too easy . . . . Walcott is saying home is where our loa are at. He is saying home is where Christ circles with Damballah and Erzulie turns with Mary.'

PLAYS OF THE EIGHTIES: *Beef, No Chicken*, *The Isle is Full of Noises*, *The Rig*, *A Branch of the Blue Nile*, *The Haytian Earth*

The decade of the eighties, and in particular two events of 1981 – his appointment to the faculty of Boston University, and his receipt of one of the first MacArthur Fellowships recognising genius – made several material changes in Walcott's life and work. The momentum of his inspirational years with the Trinidad Theatre Workshop was slackening, but his third marriage, in 1982, was to a Workshop actress, and the Workshop continued to imbue his work with a nostalgia most evident in *A Branch of the Blue Nile*. One of the notable developments in his writing was his increasing interest in the medium of film, resulting in scripts such as *Hart Crane* (1986), a documentary, and the screenplays *The Haytian Earth*, *To Die For Grenada*, *Steel* and *The Rig*.

'Theatre is so expensive, the West Indian future may be in film,' he told journalist-critic Kathlyn Russell (*SE*, 4 September, 1983). He drew a parallel with the explosion of a vibrant film industry in Australia, created by a new generation that grew up with 'no theatre of quality. It's almost simpler to do a film and spend the money there instead of putting it into a production to which nobody comes.'

Several new plays springing from this decade, such as *Solo on the Hudson* and *Viva Detroit* (1990), were read or went into rehearsal, but were not to reach the stage until the nineties, if at all. Walcott's only new piece to be staged in 1980, a children's play, was not even his, other than in concept. The father of a son by his first marriage, and of two daughters by his second, Walcott has devoted little of his genius to children's theatre. *Ti-Jean and His Brothers*, which is dedicated to his son, appeals to children, but it is not purely or even essentially a children's play. Walcott once drafted a musical based on Antoine de Saint-Exupery's *The Little Prince*, but it never reached the stage. He is given partial credit by the Lilliput Children's Theatre of Trinidad for the company's 1980 children's play, *Mammy Mammy Look Snow*, but his contribution was no more than a one-page outline.

In 1981, the première production of *Beef, No Chicken*, a play set in Trinidad and clearly written with Trinidad Theatre Workshop actors in mind, was staged in Trinidad by the Workshop. The company had by now achieved a measure of reconciliation with Walcott. The playwright, however, was not there to direct this initial version of his comedy about the victims of progress. The Workshop production was directed with emphasis on the farcical aspects of the script, at the expense of its inherent tragedy, provoking audiences to an automatic laughter that left a sense of profound dissatisfaction they did not quite understand. The critics blamed the play.

'Walcott's new play is a bit of a sitcom', wrote Mark Lyndersay (*TG*, 12 May, 1981), 'with lots of jokes and witticisms, but no direction and purpose at the core, the result is awfully funny, but terribly flat, nothing ever seems to happen . . . I felt rather cheated by it. The themes and characters in the play are dealt with half-heartedly and with a basic kind of weariness'. Raoul Pantin (*DE*, 3 May, 1981) described the play as 'surprisingly flaccid'.

'That first Workshop production', wrote Judy Stone several years later (*CC*, June, 1985) '. . . left me convinced that the playwright had tried an experiment that hadn't worked. The plot meandered without point, the situation was so ludicrously far-fetched as to be beyond credibility, the humour so forced it fell flat.'

Walcott rewrote the play for its American première in 1982. By 1985, when the play was staged in Barbados, it had been yet again reworked, and director Earl Warner fully appreciated the role of the tragedy underpinning the comedy.

'It is a delicate process to take a tragic situation and shape from it a hilarious comedy without crudity and insensitivity to the subject matter,' Warner writes in his programme note. 'The success of this comedy as literature and theatre testifies to the power of Walcott's acute and masterful craft. The play is a Kaiso, a seriocomic ballad on a real social experience. Yet, finally, the pathos within the given situations is never lost, and the ambivalence of progress is illuminated.'

The Barbados production was indeed an unqualified success. 'The result', Stone wrote, 'revealed one of Derek's most accessible works, genuinely a "hilarious comedy" as advertised, but layered with the small personal tragedies that are concomitant with progress. Far from being pointless, the production drove home a clear statement to every one of us in these developing societies; and what had seemed ludicrous was now presented with its own inner logic so consistently intact as to be entirely credible on its own terms.'[53]

Beef, No Chicken is set in Couva, a small country town that actually exists, in central Trinidad. At the time of the play, progress is making its way through Couva in the form of a new highway under construction.

'You ask one of these same governments for, say, six scholarships for six actors, they tell you that they have to build a road somewhere,' Walcott complained bitterly in an interview just prior to the 1976 Carifesta (*People*, July, 1976). 'My policy is roads before writers, sewers before surrealism', announces the philistine Deacon Doxy in the early *O Babylon!*

In *Beef, No Chicken*, the policy of progress is roads before roti vendors, or any other small business. Roti is a peculiarly Trinidadian delicacy of East Indian antecedents, comprising a skin of split-peas dough wrapped around a curried filling, of which the most popular varieties are beef, chicken, shrimp, goat and potato. 'Beef, no chicken' ostensibly refers to the rotis sold by Otto's Auto Repair and Authentic Roti. But the title is a punster's delight, offering a variety of interpretations, such as on the one hand a complaint (beef) against the progress of time (no chicken) and the timing of progress, and on the other a reference to the vigour (beef) and courage (no chicken) with which Otto fights his doomed battle against the road that threatens his home and livelihood. While on the subject of puns (of which this comedy is a never-ending cornucopia), it should be noted that, in the Trinidad vernacular, 'Otto' and 'Auto' are pronounced identically, while 'Authentic' has the assonant ring of 'Ottentic'.

Among the intricately plaited strands of the plot are Otto's campaign to scare away the highway workmen by his midnight prowls disguised as the avenging (female) spirit of a slaughtered silk cotton tree; the hostilities between Sumintra, the Authentic maker of roti (married), and Otto's recently arrived sister Euphony (unmarried); the wooing of Euphony by the schoolmaster Eldridge Franco, in the face of her betrothal to a man who left her ten years previously to make his fortune in the Welsh mines; Otto's relationship with his bank, and that with the scatter-brained florist Mitzi Almandoz; the accident that catapults television idol Cedric Hart into Otto's affairs, and Otto's niece Drusilla onto the television screen; the determination of the Limer, or loafer, to become a calypsonian; a minor robbery that turns into a major heist; and the machinations of businessman Mongroo and the Borough Council.

'The story is true for any developing society where choices are made in the name of progress and development at the cost of human life, leaving the pain of loss, the broken circle,' writes Warner. Indeed, the theme's application is universal, for nowhere on earth is spared the alterations made by the progress of time. And Walcott's riotously funny yet tenderly affectionate treatment might well have made this one of his most frequently produced works, were it not for its comparatively large cast. It is a cast, however, that includes some memorable characters, among them Sumintra, Euphony, Franco and Mitzi.

The one unforgettable character in Walcott's next play to première, a hermit whose suppurating leg emits a stench that makes strong men blanch, is drawn from the ancient Greek legend of Philoctetes. Walcott began writing *The Isle is Full of Noises* in the early seventies. He took his title from Caliban's line in *The Tempest*, and there are several ironic parallels to be found between the two plays. A Trinidad Theatre Workshop production was planned for 1975 but, following the exceptional success of *The Joker of Seville*, Walcott cancelled that plan and instead diverted elements of the current *Isle* script to his new musical, *O Babylon!* In the late seventies, a drastically revised and refined version of *The Isle is Full of Noises* was showcased in New York by the Negro Ensemble Company. The world première was eventually staged in Hartford, Connecticut, in 1982.

The Isle is Full of Noises is set in the fictitious island of Santa Marta. Through Walcott's relentless arc of references, Santa Marta represents the entire chain of Caribbean islands. The play presents an argument for a new Federation of the West Indies. At a deeper level, the argument is for the federation of mankind. Like *Dream on Monkey Mountain*, it is a play of metaphor, in this case a metaphor of political corruption. Walcott extends the metaphor to the political corruption of the Christian church, which he contemptuously embodies in a drunkenly subservient archbishop, and the 'bishop-headed vultures' on a village midden. Yet, as in *Dream*, the play's metaphor is fuelled by powerful images from the life of Christ: the symbolism of the rock; the baptist doing penance in the wilderness; the Judas Prime Minister betraying the cause; the Pontius Pilate of the British Ambassador; the martyrdom of the crusader. The Christian parallels are intertwined with others from Greek and African mythology, and given a peculiarly Caribbean application. It was Walcott's most intense exploration to date of the colonial cultural conundrum that had vexed him since childhood.

In its development through various drafts, from two acts to four and back to two, *The Isle is Full of Noises* has shown elements in common with several early works, such as *Flight and Sanctuary*, and *Ione*. As with *Beef, No Chicken* and *O Babylon!*, the catalyst in the plot is progress, in the form of construction development that threatens the lives of the already dispossessed. (*O Babylon!*, it will be remembered, is the half-brother with which, even at maturity, the new play still bears a marked resemblance in feature, though not in character.) The events are seen through the journal of the Ambassador, Sir Geoffrey Thwaite, who is ostensibly addressing a London convention on the day Santa Marta becomes a republic.

The island's Prime Minister, Papa (alias Doc, as in Haiti), is determined by fair means or foul to remove the foul-smelling hermit, Robinson, from his cave on an offshore islet. American wheeler-dealers are lining Papa's pockets for the right to exploit the islet's potential in their development, but their destructive project cannot begin until the hermit leaves, which he adamantly refuses to do. The Americans have lost patience, and demand the use of force. Though Papa controls the press, he is reluctant to precipitate an incident in this election season, particularly as the hermit is no less of a personage than Papa's predecessor, and the one-time Prime Minister of the former West Indies Federation. Such considerations, however, are less of a deterrent than the fact that 'Crusoe' is armed with a speargun. In Walcott's surrealistic treatment this speargun, on which the plot hinges, symbolises the bow of Philoctetes, the rod of Aaron, the weapon of an African warrior, the standard of the Caribbean crusader, and both the Aegean and Antillean archipelagos.

The hermit proves immune to bribery. Eventually, as a last effort at a diplomatic resolution before sending in the troops, Papa attempts to engineer a betrayal of Crusoe by his godson, James. Like Brown of *In a Fine Castle*, James is a poet-journalist. He is also Papa's nephew and has been, up to the present time, the party hack. The contretemps, however, has sensitised James to the government's betrayal of the federal vision with which Robinson had baptised him as a boy. As the editor of the party paper, he has made his first stand against corruption by printing an edition of blank pages. While subplots of sexual licence and intrigue revolve around him, James feels himself in the throes of an identity crisis, 'a sundered man' who must 'fuse his halves'. He becomes Ajamu, the Yoruba warrior, 'He who fights for what he wants'. Sent by Papa to seize the hermit's weapon, Ajamu seizes it like a baton, taking Crusoe's place in the race to save his people from the rule of corruption and mediocrity. He returns with the speargun, determined to eradicate the source of the evil and save the people by shooting Papa. Instead, his grand purpose is diverted from the general to the particular, as he wounds a mere Minister to save the innocence of the girl he loves. But it is Ajamu, and not Robinson, who becomes the martyr of Santa Marta. And it is as a consequence of Ajamu's death that riots are incited which cleanse the island of its corruption, and return a cured, herb-scented Robinson to his visionary leadership.

On the surface, *The Isle is Full of Noises* might appear to be one of Walcott's more entertaining musicals. Just as in *O Babylon!*, this play has its brash singer, Papa's personal calypsonian Vox Populi and his three Unities. And there is even a court jester, in the person of the Minister of Security. But the jests are more acid than amusing, the gaiety is forced, the songs are of vacuous praise, and the overall atmosphere is as dourly overpowering as the gangrenous stench which, in Walcott's stage directions, 'floats through the theatre'. The script is full of unlovely noises: sirens, obscenities and screams of agony. It is a gripping and provocative but, as Walcott no doubt fully intends, also a joltingly uncomfortable play.

Consequent on the unexpectedly brief première run of *The Last Carnival* on his mid-year visit to Trinidad in 1982, Walcott found himself with time on his hands. Impetuously he offered to script and direct a new television series then being planned by Banyan Productions. Banyan was a young video house whose directors' innovative commitment to local programming the playwright admired. It was not his first attempt at writing for the screen. In the early seventies, for instance, he had written and illustrated for film-maker Dino De Laurentiis *Angelo Nero*, a still unproduced treatment on the theme of a black Christ. Nor was it the first of his work to appear on the screen. Over the years, versions of several of his stage plays had been filmed. But *The Rig* was Walcott's first original screenplay to complete production. His 1976 television play, *The Snow Queen*, was based on earlier stage plays and did not progress beyond rehearsal.

Commentator Jeremy Taylor describes the collaboration (*DE*, 1 August, 1982). The Banyan producer briefed Walcott on the team's ideas for the series. 'Apparently Walcott started writing at five o'clock next morning and by lunch-time had seventeen pages of lively script ready'. Shooting began almost immediately, on the south Trinidad beach of Mayaro, with Walcott simultaneously writing, directing, and re-writing. Eventually the projected series became a single feature film.

The theme of *The Rig* is the dilemma of the artist in the developing society: whether to remain at home, true to the source of inspiration, struggling for survival, or whether to give in to the temptations of emigration, opportunity, glamour, an easier life. The artist in this case is Laurie, a dedicated folk dancer. Laurie is depressed by the failure of her efforts to keep her village dance group together, and horrified by the manipulations of her petty crook boyfriend to get her onto the nightclub circuit. She is on the verge of giving in and flying out, when she meets a genuine failure in life, the drifting owner of a mortgaged coconut estate.

The title refers to a marine oil rig which lours on the sea's horizon, representing the oil boom and its effect on the island culture. The plot is interwoven with crime and violence, the workings of the power network in a small society, the vulnerability of rural life. For most viewers, when *The Rig* eventually had its première screening in 1984, these various threads of plot and sub-plot appeared tangled without a clue to unravel their relationship. A more experienced team of film-makers would probably, for the medium of television, have simplified the linear progression of the primary plot. For all its layers of meaning, with a little less subtlety in the presentation the story would then have been revealed as essentially no more mystifying than that of the average adventure film. As it was, *The Rig* met at best a luke-warm reception, in spite of its relevance, evocative scenes and some excellent characterisation.

Hardly had *The Rig* completed shooting and editing than Walcott found himself, 'quite startlingly',[54] shaping the first draft of another, vastly different, film script, newly commissioned for America's Public Broadcasting System. In its sensitively directed and edited realisation, this film was to prove both flawless and enthralling. A docudrama on the life of the early twentieth-century American poet, *Hart Crane* is essentially an exploration of the creative process. Walcott not only wrote the script, he makes several appearances in the film, as himself, discussing Crane's work and his use of language. Certain scenes were shot in St Lucia, and interestingly, in a casting particularly pleasing to Walcott, the title role is played by Nigel Scott, a Trinidad Theatre Workshop actor with a pronounced resemblance to Crane. The film took some three years to complete, and was eventually screened, in both America and in Trinidad, in 1986.

Meantime, in 1983, the world première of *A Branch of the Blue Nile*, Walcott's play about the Trinidad Theatre Workshop, was staged not in Trinidad, but in Barbados. Walcott's relations with his former company were once again at a low ebb, due to production disagreements the previous year. It was not until 1985 that this play was staged in the island of its inspiration, and even then it was produced not by the Workshop but by Walcott's Warwick Productions.

A Branch of the Blue Nile is, as director Earl Warner describes it in his programme note, 'a play-within-a-play-within-a-play'. Even the opening scene of the play turns out to be an improvisation, by actors creolising Shakespeare as part of their rehearsal process for two contrasting plays, *Anthony and Cleopatra*, and a vernacular comedy by one of the company, Chris. Towards the end of the play it becomes apparent that Chris, accused of 'ducking' his talent by writing creole, has been inspired to write a serious play based on the experiences of the small theatre company, and that this play is *A Branch of the Blue Nile.*

The basic theme of this play explores Walcott's lifelong concern with the conflict between the classic and the creole, which here becomes a conflict between tragedy and comedy, grace and vulgarity, the great and the petty. The thrust of the argument is not primarily whether the Caribbean is capable of classical form, for in the first scene Sheila gives a mesmerising performance as Cleopatra. (Walcott takes a great risk with this scene; if the actress playing Sheila does not in fact, while still dramatically 'cold', achieve a sufficiently powerful performance, her failure undermines the whole play.) The key question is whether the classical form has a place in the Caribbean. The play is, in effect, an examination of the validity of Walcott's own role in his native region.

Sheila, having been touched by greatness, at first rejoices, and then, afraid, rejects her gift, even more roundly than Chris, her married lover, had rejected his. Without warning she deserts theatre and friends to join the Adventist church. Her place in the production is taken by Marilyn, an actress of limited talent, whose performance as Cleopatra is exalted to stardom by a critic of limited perception. Chris eventually seeks Sheila out and brings her to the realisation that she has simply exchanged stages and roles. But Marilyn, clinging grittily to her newfound fame, refuses to stand down for Sheila to reclaim her place. In the end, though, as the youngest members of the theatre take over from those who have left the island, to die or to seek their future elsewhere, Sheila does return, to bring the new company together.

This play about theatre has its Chorus in the person of Phil, an unforgettable Walcott portrait of a derelict, who represents the artist destroyed by his society. It is Phil, rather than Sheila or any of the company, who has his finger on the pulse of the artistic spirit of the Caribbean. The fragile nurturing of that spirit, the struggle for honesty of expression, the pressures on the artist to leave his homeland – 'If you so good, Harvey, what you doing here?' – are a reworking of themes of *The Rig*.

When it eventually reached Trinidad, *A Branch of the Blue Nile* stirred a measure of controversy. At least one critic – Trinidad and Tobago Television's Mark Lyndersay – took offence at what he considered its insulting inferences. Most, however, agreed with Raoul Pantin when he wrote that Walcott 'strikes at truth like an anvil' (*SE*, 18 August, 1985).

To celebrate the 150th anniversary of Emancipation, the St Lucian government in 1984 voted an unprecedented allocation, not only for the commission and staging of an appropriate new work by Walcott, but for the conversion of former barracks on the Morne to a new outdoor theatre for the occasion. Walcott had for several years been working on a screenplay that treated the Haitian revolution not from the point of view of the revolutionaries, as in *Henri Christophe*, but from the point of view of the peasant, represented by Pompey, a character borrowed from *Drums and Colours.* For the St Lucian assignment Walcott converted the work from film to a new stage epic, *The Haytian Earth*, with original music by St Lucian Luther François.

Artist Kennedy Samuel reported in the St Lucia *Weekend Voice* (18 August 1984) on one of the four three-hour long performances:

> Walcott looks again at these so-called heroes and recognises instead betrayers, abusers and oppressors of the simple Haitian people . . . too ignorant and uneducated to rule a country, too weak to face their own weaknesses and too inexperienced in power to use it wisely . . . driven and blinded by egoism and ambition at the expense of the people. . . .
>
> Walcott looks generally at revolutions and sees noble ideals turning corrupt when small men touch power . . . . The play raises many other issues. These include a sustained criticism of war and its subsequent useless destruction and human tragedy. . . . In all this, Walcott's hero remains the same as in many of his other important plays. He is the common man, the peasant, the charcoal burner, the fisherman, the country boy, the folk. . . .
>
> '. . . the real generals are those who fight the seasons . . . Men without guns but scythes.'
>
> . . . when one understands the symbol of the country as a woman, a wife and a whore, one can appreciate the significance of Yette, the whore, being raped by Dessalines, hanged by Christophe, paid for and abused by the white man, but loved so deeply by Pompey who represents the simple, uneducated, hard-working, spiritually rich, Haytian Folk. There is also the frequent use of the pig image to describe the leaders . . . .
>
> For the student of literature, the script is littered with examples of puns, double meanings, alliteration, delightful sentence construction, sarcasm, manipulation of different language groups and levels to assist in characterisation and atmosphere, folk rhythms, and many other devices.

Just as the Haitian generals had, in their shining, made shadows of their people, so, Samuel suggests acerbically in his closing paragraphs, the circumstances of the staging of Walcott's 'highly significant' epic made shadows of the ordinary St Lucians, few of whom could afford the ticket prices. The production was sparsely attended. A performance of *The Haytian Earth* was recorded on videotape and later shown on television, but the small screen hardly did the grandeur of the work justice.

Walcott's last two new plays of the decade were *To Die For Grenada* and *The Ghost Dance*. The former is set in Trinidad at the time of the assassination of Grenada's Prime Minister, Maurice Bishop, and the consequent invasion of Grenada by American forces. The issue of Trinidad's neutrality is argued between an Indo-Trinidadian and his white American lover, against a backdrop of the Hosay festival and a peaceful offshore island retreat. *To Die For Grenada* had its première in Ohio in 1986. The same year pre-production work began for the filming of the play in Trinidad, but the project fell through.

The Ghost Dance, which had its première at Oneonta in 1989, is based on the story of the American Indian Chief Sitting Bull and the last days of the Sioux tribe. Walcott worked simultaneously on the play and on an epic poem, in both of which he used the same incident to draw a parallel between the genocidal aspects of colonialism in America, and in the Caribbean.

' . . . But it doesn't centre so much around the Indian as it does a woman,' Walcott explained in a 1989 interview (*Voices of the African Diaspora*, Vol. VII, No. 2, Spring, 1991) while the work was still in progress,

> a white woman named Catherine Weldon, who is very concerned about the treatment of the Sioux. You see the conscience, the mental conscience of a country does not reside in a man, it resides in a woman. A man treats it politically and that is not sufficient. Conscience is feeling. It is not that men are incapable of feeling, but that women don't make war. They don't justify war. . . . I'm not just choosing this hero because it's fashionable to have a woman as a centre. . . . The play changes from me as the narrator to her. So it's trying to enter into her – I'm working on that – to become her.
>
> The history of this part of the world is a history of genocide. It's a history of colonialism – we know that. Look at what's gone – the Caribs and the Arawaks, God knows how many million Africans thrown overboard, the decimation of the tribes in America. That is the epic – it is immoral. The idea of conquest and empire and exploration and development – the aboriginal Indian in the Caribbean died for these. Disease brought by the Europeans killed them off as much as the murder and labour. Same thing that alcohol did to the American Indian. It massacred them. It emasculated them. Whether you have alcohol, syphilis or forced labour, it's all the same thing. So it's not an artificial connection between what happened in the Caribbean and the United States during slavery . . .

PLAYS OF THE NINETIES: *Viva Detroit*, *Steel*, *The Odyssey*

In his sixties, Walcott was still rising at five in the morning to begin his working day. He continued to produce major scripts, in particular his musical, *Steel*, a fictionalised documentary of the history of the steelband movement. He was also still actively directing. In 1992, he directed a Swedish-language production of *The Last Carnival* for the Royal Dramatic Theatre in Stockholm.

Shortly after that production he returned to Stockholm to receive the world's supreme accolade, the Nobel Prize for Literature. Walcott's response to the award was typically generous and visionary. He donated a large share of the prize money to the development of the arts, through scholarships for young artists, a contribution to the Trinidad Theatre Workshop, and the establishment of an artists' retreat on St Lucia's Rat Island.

Walcott's first play to première in the nineties had originally surfaced in the eighties. *Viva Detroit* is a melancholy little comedy set in the gazebo beach bar of a St Lucian hotel, where the barman oversees a love affair between a beach bum and an American girl. This particular intercultural relationship has been the subject of several West Indian plays, such as Ken Corsbie's *Jack and Jill* and, peripherally, Mustapha Matura's *Rum an' Coca Cola*. In Walcott's treatment each of the three characters comes to terms with life through a form of role-playing, and none more so than the bum. Sonny has the chameleon gift of Ram in Matura's *As Time Goes By* (1971), adapting himself and his story according to the nationality and circumstances of each tourist he scams. He is, as the American girl Pat understands, afraid of being himself. Yet, as a genuine relationship develops between the two, Sonny finds himself beginning to take reality more seriously. In the end, however, at the crucial moment he is unable to face the truth.

Viva Detroit had its world première in Los Angeles in 1990, and then underwent considerable revision before its London première in 1992. Meantime, 1991 saw the première of *Steel*.

A masterly blend of fact and fiction, with a cast of characters that includes several historical figures in calypso and the steelband movement, *Steel*, like *The Haytian Earth*, began in the eighties as a screenplay. Sadly, no backing was forthcoming for a film of vital significance to the Caribbean. Eventually Walcott scaled down the screenplay to a stage version which, with a score by Galt MacDermot, had its world première in Boston. The reviews were less than glowing. 'Walcott's *Steel* hammered in US' headlined one Trinidad commentator, in a tongue-in-cheek pun worthy of Walcott himself (*SG*, 28 April, 1991).

In translating his lengthy screenplay to the stage, Walcott had to sacrifice the encompassing sweep of his original vision. The play was restricted to a single set. Even so, the playwright still tried to retain more of the film than was perhaps suited to the new medium. Added to which, the première production featured only four pans, too few to make a convincing representation of a full steelband. It seems probable, too, that the unfamiliarity of the Boston audiences with the Caribbean cultural experience made it difficult, and often impossible, for them to understand Walcott's references. Whatever the reason, the Boston critics panned *Steel* for incoherence, melodramatic plotting, stylistic afflatus, and characters that lacked credibility. One reviewer, discounting Walcott's 45 years of writing for and working in theatre, went so far as to accuse the distinguished playwright of theatrical *naïveté*.

There were also, the critics claimed, too many songs. This latter was probably a fair comment on the dramatic structure of the play, though again there was that element of subjectivity in comparing a work from one culture with the norms of another. At its première, *Steel* had 36 compositions in all, certainly more than would be expected in your average Broadway musical comedy. In the Caribbean, familiar with four-hour Indian films in which the action stops every few minutes for a new song, and accustomed to street festivals and calypso tents and calabash theatre and musical competitions all of which can run most of the night, audiences for musical shows are made of tougher stuff. It took Rawle Gibbons's acclaimed calypso musicals to make these audiences echo the cry of 'too many songs'. *Sing De Chorus* (1991) has 41 calypsos, *Ah Wanna Fall* (1992) 54, and *Ten to One* (1993) 57 calypsos.

The reaction to the stage version of *Steel* makes it all the more regrettable that Walcott's finest and most important screenplay to date was not realised on film. In its original medium, *Steel* is a drivingly exciting adventure of the artist's personal development and achievement in the face of society's early condemnation, and later exploitation.

The screenplay begins in 1945, as Trinidad celebrates the end of the war. The effect of the American presence is established through Joyce, a young East Indian woman whose baby is half white. When her American lieutenant is posted home he abandons Joyce, who eventually turns to prostitution for the sake of her daughter, Zora. Parallel with Zora's story, on lines that eventually meet in the love affair at the heart of the film, is that of the orphan Winston, reared in the Salvation Army by his aunt and uncle. Winston is a natural musician, who is instinctively drawn to the newly-evolving music of the steelband. He also has a fine mind, and the potential to win a scholarship to London. His guardians have strictly forbidden him to waste time on steel. However, as a reward for his scholastic efforts, they sacrifice so that he may take piano lessons with a former concert pianist. The pianist derides the steelband – 'a garbage can cover produces garbage'. But, in an odyssey that takes him from his guardians' home to abysmal poverty when he rejects the potential scholarship for the sake of pan, then through steelband wars, Syrian sponsorship and sexual liaison to America, and finally back home to the finals of the steelband competition, Winston is able to pass on to his band the classical musicianship of his formal training, culminating in a final soaring performance that draws tears from the pianist's eyes, and the admission that steel can indeed produce music.

It is Walcott's familiar argument once again, of the respective roles in West Indian society of the classical and the creole. Expressed in the musical terms so peculiarly appropriate to the region, this is perhaps Walcott's most moving and most accessible exploration of the subject. It is also a rare tribute to past musical artists of Trinidad, including the calypsonians, who are represented principally by the character of Growler, a father-figure to Winston.

Following on his award-winning poem, *Omeros*, which pays a uniquely Caribbean homage to Homer, Walcott's latest play is the 1992 adaptation of Homer's *Odyssey*, commissioned by the Royal Shakespeare Company. Walcott's version, like his poem, emphasises the sense of exile that the West Indian poet shares with Homer, and the urgency of homecoming. Prior to its London première, *The Odyssey* was workshopped at Stratford Upon Avon to mildly favourable reviews.

'Down the road in *The Other Place*', wrote critic Michael Coveney in the London *Observer*, 'the sound of the sea washes through *The Odyssey*, an imperfect but enjoyable workshop production . . . . 'Derek Walcott's 1990 epic poem

Omeros . . . ingeniously transplanted Homer's heroes to his native Caribbean. That idiom is employed here in the figure of a blind blues man . . . and in the keening wail of Odysseus' nurse Eurycleia. . . .

Whatever Walcott writes, is splendoured by the particular light of his Caribbean heritage. And whether Walcott's dramatic work is considered West Indian theatre, or theatre by a West Indian writer, as works such as *Steel* demonstrate unarguably, there is no other playwright, past or living, whose work is more deeply rooted in the historical circumstances of the Caribbean.

NOTES:

1 Derek Walcott, *What the Twilight Says: An Overture,* in *Dream on Monkey Mountain and Other Plays,* Jonathan Cape, 1972.
2 The entire discussion of *Flight and Sanctuary* is based on Errol Hill's description of the play in 'The Emergence of a National Drama in the West Indies', *CQ*, Vol. 18, #4, 1972.
3 *Ibid.*
4 Programme note, St Lucia Arts Guild 1959 tour of Trinidad.
5 V.S. Naipaul, *The Enigma of Arrival,* Viking, 1987.
6 'Having said which, I must add that enough remains to persuade me that one day Mr Walcott is going to write a very good – possibly, even, a great – play.' J.S. Barker, 'A Canvas Too Large For Walcott's Brush', *TG*, 30 November, 1954.
7 Anna Walcott, 'Walcott on Walcott', *SG*, 19 July, 1992.
8 J.S. Barker, 'Not The Stuff For A W.I. National Theatre', *TG*, 18 August, 1954.
9 Derek Walcott, 'Derek's "most West Indian play" ', *SG Magazine*, 21 June, 1970.
10 *Ibid.*
11 *Ibid.*
12 Derek Walcott, *What the Twilight Says: An Overture.*
13 Derek Walcott, 'Derek's "most West Indian play" '.
14 *Ibid.*
15 Derek Walcott, quoted '500 years of W.I. history', *Trinidad Chronicle*, April, 1958.
16 *Ibid.*
17 *Ibid.*
18 Ken Corsbie, marginal note to Judy Stone (1992).
19 Quoted by Adrian Espinet, inferred source script of *Drums and Colours*, *SG*, 27 April, 1958.
20 Adrian Espinet, ' "Drums And Colours" Seeks To Trace WI Consciousness', *SG*, 27 April, 1958.
21 Veronica Jenkin, 'Drums and Colours', *Bim*, Vol. 7, #27, Jul–Dec, 1958.
22 Derek Walcott, author's note, 'Drums and Colours', *CQ*, Vol. 7, #1–2, Mar–Jun, 1961.
23 Both quotations taken from Adrian Espinet, *op. cit.*
24 Veronica Jenkin, *op. cit.*
25 *Ibid.*
26 Adrian Espinet, *op. cit.*
27 Derek Walcott, 'A Far Cry from Africa', in Walcott, *In a Green Night: Poems 1948–1960*, Jonathan Cape, 1962.
28 Programme note, *Franklin*, WWB, 1990.
29 Kole Omotoso, *The Theatrical into Theatre*, New Beacon Books, 1982, p. 72.
30 Director's Note, programme *Franklin*, WWB, 1990.
31 Derek Walcott, 'Islands' in Walcott, *In a Green Night: Poems* 1948–1960.
32 Errol Hill, 'No Tears for Narcissus', *TG*, 7 March, 1965.
33 Wayne Brown, 'Chow time, King Kong', *DE*, 21 March, 1985. The poem 'Goats and Monkeys' appears in Walcott's collection *The Castaway and Other Poems*, Jonathan Cape, 1965.
34 Derek Walcott in 'Makak symbolises Workshop', *TG*, 1 August, 1974.

35 *Ibid.*
36 Gordon Rohlehr, *My Strangled City and other essays*, Longman Trinidad, 1992.
37 Derek Walcott, 'A Note on Production', in *Dream On Monkey Mountain and other plays.*
38 Derek Walcott in 'Makak symbolises Workshop'.
39 Benedict Wight, 'The success of Derek Walcott', *DE*, 16 February, 1970.
40 Wayne Brown, *op. cit.*
41 'Walcott's "Dream" for ttt', *TG*, 12 February, 1970.
42 Quotation from *The German Tribune*, *DE*, 4 September, 1972.
43 'Derek Walcott, poet and playwright', Wayne Brown talks with Albert Laveau, *SG Magazine*, 18 October, 1992.
44 'On the rim of the Grand Savannah of Port of Spain there is a curve of fantastical mansions in various styles, and while these actually exist, the Castle in this fantasy is itself a composite, nor is its family meant to represent any of its previous or present owners, living or dead.' Playwright's note, 1970 MS *In a Fine Castle.*
45 The term 'pastyah' as the creole pronunciation of 'pasture', meaning in this instance Port of Spain's Queen's Park Savannah, the major Carnival venue, is introduced in the later version of the play, *The Last Carnival*, Farrar, Straus and Giroux, 1986.
46 Judy Stone, 'Death of our dodos in "The Last Carnival" ', *TG*, 15 July, 1982.
47 'The main action takes place on the grounds and in two interiors of a decaying old estate house in high forest on a West Indian island. Also, a beach. Forest paths. Night.' 1976 MS, *The Snow Queen.*
48 Judy Stone, 'At last, masterpiece on the middle class', *TG*, 13 July, 1979.
49 *Ibid.*
50 Director's Note, programme *Remembrance*, Central Bank of Trinidad and Tobago, 1989.
51 Jeremy Taylor, quoted in programme *Pantomime*, All Theatre Productions, 1981.
52 LeRoy Clarke, ' "Marie La Veau" – an artificial resurrection', *DE*, 18 June, 1980.
53 Judy Stone, 'Warner's "Beef, No Chicken" an inspired Production', *CC*, June, 1985.
54 Derek Walcott quoted by Kathlyn Russell in 'Give me film, says Derek Walcott', *SE*, 4 September, 1983.

THEATRE OF RITUAL

Caribbean Lab and other experimental theatre: Dennis Scott, Rawle Gibbons, Michael Gilkes

'The very genesis of theatre, whether you go to the Greeks, or Africa, or Asia, is really located within the rituals of people's lives,' said Barbadian director Earl Warner, in an interview (*TG*, 11 October, 22 and 29 November, 1983) during which he discussed, among other aspects of his work, his involvement with the Caribbean Lab.

In the last couple of decades, principally in Jamaica, a small corps of theatre activists and playwrights has been conducting intensely intellectualised experiments in the creation of a mentally stimulating theatre peculiarly West Indian not only in form, but in every aspect of its genesis and presentation. The larger body of work coming out of these experiments is based in West Indian ritual, in a tangential development from Errol Hill's more performance-oriented Carnival theatre which, as discussed in earlier chapters, is based in the ritual of festivals around the region.

The most formal approach to this experimental groundwork in serious West Indian theatre has been undertaken by the Caribbean Lab established by the Jamaica School of Drama. Warner ran the Lab for nearly three years. His research into the unique ethnology of Caribbean society resulted in the development of indigenous theatrical techniques that were as applicable to Shakespeare's plays as to the newly emerging ritual plays that were the Lab's prime interest. One of the major undertakings of the Lab was the creation of *Sufferer's Song* (1983), a reworking of two plays – *Sufferer* (as *Improv*, 1981) and *Two Choices* (1982) – by the Trinidadian poet Victor Questel, who assisted with the project until his sudden death at the age of thirty-three.

At the time, in the early eighties, the Director of the School of Drama was Dennis Scott, himself an experimental playwright, generally considered one of the most important Jamaican playwrights of his time, who also died comparatively young.

Dennis Scott

Undoubtedly, Scott's death in 1991, at the age of fifty-one, was an incalculable loss to the development of West Indian theatre. Scott's was an exceptionally incisive intelligence. His gift for perceptive analysis was matched by his skill in lucid exposition, both of which talents he dedicated to the definition of Jamaican form in several spheres of the arts. He was an award-winning and widely anthologised poet, an award-winning published playwright, a visionary director, a powerfully expressive dancer and choreographer, and an actor who at the time of his death was playing a featured role in a top-rated American television series. Dance and theatre critic for press and radio, he was one of his country's few commentators sensitive to the search for cultural identity. As Director of the Jamaica School of Drama he was, possibly at the expense of his own artistic output, guide and mentor to a number of playwrights, such as Pat Cumper, Stanley French, Rawle Gibbons and Trevor Rhone. To Gibbons, who at the School of Drama worked closely with him for several years, Scott is the only West Indian playwright to have completely mastered the craft of translating ritual into terms of theatre. Scott could take any ritual, as formally structured as the Afro-Caribbean nine night or as informally as western tea drinking, and extract its theatrical essence while retaining the integrity of the ritual. This mastery is particularly evident in *Echo in the Bone* (1974); his other major play is *Dog* (1978), and both are as West Indian in particular as they are universal in theme.

Scott was born into a fairly well-to-do Jamaican family in 1939. He went to boarding school in Kingston, and from there to the Mona campus of the University of the West Indies. Perhaps unsettled in his own view of his future, he interrupted his studies and left Jamaica for Trinidad, to take up a post teaching English at the prestigious boys' secondary school, Presentation College, in San Fernando. He became involved with the thriving theatre community there and directed several plays, including early work of his own. His *Terminus* and *Ritual* were staged at the College in 1962.

He was already making a name for himself as a poet and avant-garde playwright. Scott's first play was an adaptation of the story *Cold Equation* by Tom Godwin, which was staged in Jamaica in 1959, when he was twenty. He was to undertake further adaptations, in *The Crime of Anabel Campbell*, based on the ancient Greek tragedy of Clytemnestra, and *Sir Gawain and the Green Knight* (1977), based on the medieval English poem from the Arthurian cycle of the Round Table. Both these adaptations, and several other original experimental works written during the sixties, have little overt West Indian character. This lack of regional identity is the more remarkable in the face of Scott's influence, even in the early years of his own artistic development, in the definition of the region's culture. In his early dramas the playwright was working towards universality of treatment as well as theme. He later came to believe that his work could both gain and lend strength if it had cultural identity. In a *Gleaner* article of 1970, Scott wrote that 'an essential part of our freedom in the West Indies is the freedom to adapt any device from anywhere, and use it to make statements which define our situation.'

The best known of Scott's early work is the one-act *Terminus*, which brings to judgement five self-serving souls, whose bodies lie at death's door after a car crash. The play is closer to Sartre's *Huis Clos* than to Derek Walcott's *Malcochon* or even Roderick Walcott's *Malfinis*, in that it takes place entirely in limbo, in this case a nameless terminus to which the unsuspecting souls have been brought by bus. The dialogue is in standard English. Like *Malcochon*, the play teaches that the value of life lies in man's love for his fellow man:

> *Judge:* You've hurt each other, twisted each other's lives, wasted everything good you ever had. Hatred and hurt and waste. . . . Don't you see that's sin? That's all sin is. That's why you cannot live, like men. That's why you will not be allowed to live.

Unlike the elder Walcott, though his theme is one of humanity, Scott himself shows no mercy. In this beggar-my-neighbour of evil capping evil, not one of his five defendants at the bus stop is allowed the least redeeming feature, and not one escapes the judge's sentence of termination. As a result the play lacks a telling dimension that could have touched the audience, and it remains a work of alienating bleakness.

Scott returned to Jamaica, but not immediately to Mona. Instead, he joined the staff of Kingston College. He continued writing, and in 1963 enjoyed a lighter-hearted stage experience, when he contributed dialogue and lyrics to the most successful ever of the Little Theatre Movement's national pantomimes. The collectively created *Queenie's Daughter* was revived in 1966, and again in 1973. For the creative process, the 23-year-old Scott had joined forces with such long-established luminaries as Louise Bennett-Coverly, the Fowlers, Noel Vaz and Ranny Williams.

In 1965 Scott joined the recently founded National Dance Theatre Company of Jamaica. The same year he began writing reviews on the performing arts. In *Dance Jamaica*, the renowned artistic director of the national dance company, Rex Nettleford, writes:

> Dennis Scott achieved distinction through the strength and intelligence he brought not only to lead roles but also to ensemble work. . . . Scott's discipline, analytical powers, and dramatic sense served the Company well until postgraduate work in the fine arts caused him to leave Jamaica. His early dance training is reflected in the choreographic sense of design he always brings to his productions of plays . . .

Nettleford also gives valuable insight into Scott's thinking on the emergence of a Jamaican cultural identity. More important for the development of the Dance Theatre Company than the national controversies over European aesthetic, political manipulation, and pure technique without content, Nettleford writes,

> was the appreciation on the part of the members themselves of the problems involved in discovering form through the spiritual energies of the Jamaican people and re-creating it with technical authority and aesthetic logic. Such a task demanded of the Company dancers, choreographers, and other creative personnel not only technical facility but also insight and a genuine curiosity about their own cultural history and social dynamics. Not all of the members were responsive, but those who were found it possible to fulfil their specific artistic needs within the framework of the Company's commitments. One dancer who understood the

> challenge was Dennis Scott, whose insight as a poet and playwright may have lent him an advantage. In 1970 Scott made the crucial observation that in order to create at all in the Caribbean society one must deny the verdict that the past deprived the artist of everything. He felt that when a former slave society like Jamaica 'imposes discipline on itself from within, it begins to wipe out a tradition of submission . . . . It is the beginning of freedom to choose.' Rank imitation is never discipline from within, and indiscriminate use of other artists' creativity passed off as one's own never reveals the freedom to choose.

Scott's earliest literary awards were for his dramatic writing; the poetry awards came later. In the Jamaica Festival literary competition of 1966 he won the gold medal, for *Chariots of Wrath*. In 1969 he received the Festival bronze medal, for *The Passionate Cabbage*. Meantime, in 1968, he had picked up his studies again at Mona, and had been appointed editor of the prestigious UWI magazine, *Caribbean Quarterly*. In 1970 he was awarded a first class honours degree. That same year Scott left Jamaica again, for the United States, where he attended the University of Georgia on a Schubert Playwriting Fellowship.

Scott's one-act play, *The Crime of Anabel Campbell* was also premièred in 1970. In Greek legend, when the ruler of Argos, Agamemnon, returned home after the Trojan War, he was accompanied by his newly-won concubine, the prophetess Cassandra. Argos's wife Clytemnestra, who bore an implacable hatred towards her husband for the blood sacrifice of their daughter Iphigenia, then conspired with her lover, Aegisthus, to butcher the king. Clytemnestra's own son, Orestes, eventually avenged the murder of his father, by killing his mother. The story has been dramatised by numerous playwrights and, some two and a half millennia after Aeschylus wrote his *Oresteia* trilogy, the first play of the three, *Agamemnon*, which is usually considered the greatest of all the surviving Greek plays, is still performed around the world. The version by Scott retains the tensions of the original tale, but changes certain particulars for a shift in emphasis and a more subtle interplay of emotions. A study of the psychology of this revenge murder, the play casts new light on an old story.

In *The Crime of Anabel Campbell* the action abandons the unities to shift in time and place between the police station where the murderess is held awaiting trial, the later testimony of Sergeant Moses in court, and the actual events that took place in the Campbell house the day John Campbell came home.

The opening passages of the play share something of the confusion of the imprisoned Anabel's overwrought mind, as she wanders between past and present, and seems to recognise husband and son in the same person. Gradually the picture is clarified. We learn, among other things, that the returning husband indeed represents the son even in a physical, as well as emotional, sense, having brought home with him the dead boy's ashes. Scott's treatment is economical, and several factors contributing to Anabel's murder of her husband John are merely hinted at in passing, rather than spelled out in detail. We learn early of her fierce possessiveness towards her son Johnny, and that she was 'never good at forgiving'. We can appreciate why Johnny, having made the decision to fly overseas to join his mistress, Dimity, fled from home under cover of darkness without a word to his mother. We glean that John Campbell's jealousy of his son led him to conceal letters that Anabel eventually found. She sent John to bring Johnny home, but was not to see her husband again for three years. He had found the boy dying, and stayed on to comfort Dimity. Anabel could have forgiven all else, she claims after the murder, but she could not forgive John for returning to her house with his and his son's concubine on his arm.

Yet, though she had not expected Dimity, Anabel had prepared a house of death, emptied of furniture, scrubbed and polished, with a new, blood red carpet on the floor and newly sharp knives in the kitchen. The knives, in an ironic twist to the legend, had been sharpened by Bernie Moses, the police sergeant whose feelings for Anabel remained unrequited, and who was fated both to discover the bodies, and to make the arrest of the woman he loved. In an even closer parallel with the legend, Dimity senses the blood-letting to come and, just as Anabel has begged John to send the girl away, the girl begs her lover to let her go. But John takes no more notice of Dimity's forebodings than did Agamemnon of Cassandra's.

Perhaps the most harrowing aspect of the carefully prepared execution is Anabel's deliberate seduction of her husband on the red carpet, like some terrible ritual of a temple priestess, just before she stabs him to death with the same blade that has killed his lover.

Scott returned home in 1971, without having completed his MFA, and took up a post as Senior Teacher at Jamaica College. In 1972 he left Jamaica once more, this time for a year in England, where he took his Diploma in Drama in Education at the University of Newcastle-upon-Tyne. In 1973 he returned to Jamaica College where he remained, teaching English, until 1976.

Also in 1973, Scott had his first experience as one of the directors at the Eugene O'Neill Center's National Playwrights Conference in Waterford, Connecticut. He was to return repeatedly, and through this connection was enabled several years later to realise a longstanding ambition to dramatise *Sir Gawain and the Green Knight*.

Before that, however, 1974 saw the Jamaican première of what is generally considered Scott's most important theatrical work, *Echo in the Bone*. A psychological study of oppression and rebellion, the play spans a sweep of the Afro-Caribbean slavery experience, from 1792 to the mid-twentieth century, from the slave ship and the auction block to the post-Emancipation Great House and the peasant holding.

This intensely intricate play of relationships is based on the nine night ritual common throughout the Caribbean, a rite of passage for the dead. The spirit possession associated with such rituals is a key element of the play, not only in the plot, but in the role of each actor. Members of the all-black cast wear half-masks when playing white roles. The surface story is a simple one, in which a wake is held for the spirit of Crew, who has drowned himself in the river after killing estate owner Mr Charles (the stock Mas' Charlie). However, during the ceremony, Crew's wife Rachel, his two sons, and his friends, plumb the sources of the murder as they become possessed and re-enact ancestral experiences that still echo in the bones of the descendants of slavery.

In his programme note to his 1976 production of the play, Rawle Gibbons writes:

> The play reflects and retains important moments in our history. Its truth is presented with a nakedness found in few other plays of the Caribbean theatre . . . Beyond the situation of the dead wake, the play is itself ritual. It is envisioned as a healing ceremony for its principal characters, who are catapulted into the enactment of their fears, secrets, resentments; it is a vast purgative experience for all its enactants because of the forces it invokes. In its final statement, it is a celebration of 'communitas', the recognition of an essential wholeness.

Echo in the Bone represented Jamaica in Lagos at the Festival of Black Arts in 1976, the same year that Scott directed Edgar White's *The Defense* in New York, and won a national medal as Best Director. In 1977 Scott was appointed Director of the Jamaica School of Drama, an institution that had been in existence since 1969, but was now newly-adopted and funded by the government. 1977 also saw the première staging, at Washington's Kennedy Center, of Scott's adaptation commissioned by America's National Theatre of the Deaf, *Sir Gawain and the Green Knight.*

The supreme English example of the chivalric romance, the original medieval poem was inspired by the seasonal decay and renewal of vegetative life. Part of the alliterative work's particular appeal for Scott must have had to do with its innate richness of ritual – the rituals of nature, of knighthood, of the court and courtship, of Christianity and morality, of folk beliefs and the supernatural. The story grows from a stranger's Christmas challenge to any one knight of King Arthur's Round Table, to exchange a blow for a blow. Sir Gawain accepts, and his single stroke cuts off the Green Knight's head. The immortal knight, however, simply picks up his head and rides away, holding Gawain to his agreement to meet a year later to receive the return blow. When Gawain nears the place and time when he must keep his vow and lose his life, he is persuaded to spend his last three days in Bercilak's castle. Each day, while Bercilak hunts game, Bercilak's wife Alison hunts Gawain's virtue.

In his introduction to the printed text, Scott describes the creation of the script out of the particular circumstances of working with speech-impaired actors:

> We developed the play together: director, actors, and myself. I brought them a draft, and what could have been a point of contention was instantly agreed. We would create a play not just for children, nor merely for a deaf company, but for all people, young or old. We would attempt to include some of the wit, the elegance, and the psychological perceptiveness of the original. We would include the marvels, the adventure, the magic, and the sense of mystery that all men cherish.
>
> We decided, as well, that in this particular production, for deaf and hearing actors together, the actors who were to speak the lines being performed by deaf actors would not be mere convenient mouth-pieces. They, themselves, would become characters in the story. So they, too, have roles in the play, and transform

> into a variety of creatures: courtiers, wild animals, and above all, the Conteur. It is he who tells the story, and who focuses our attention, like an old friend, on the things in it that matter most of all . . . .
>
> Our constant aim was to find the words that would translate accurately and gracefully the sign-mime of the performers – that dance-like combination of sign language, mime, and finger spelling with which the National Theatre of the Deaf create their theatrical images. I had chosen to adapt the Middle English of the original into a light, loose, and freely alliterated form of Standard English; it seemed the best way of retaining the narrative tone . . . .
>
> What seemed central was the testing of Gawain. That we tried to retain in all its rich and ritual form. We wanted very much to keep the comedy of the seduction game, and the splendid cruelty of the hunts outside which parallel the pursuit of Gawain by the Lady.

Apart from his choices in selecting and presenting the material, Scott made two key changes to the original tale. To underscore the parallel between the two hunts – one within and one without the castle – he interlaced the action. And, in what he saw as a logical extension of the meaning of the poem, he made Bercilak's wife a shape-shifter, like her husband, the Green Knight. She became a small red bird.

> Gawain, a mortal, embarks on a quest for the Green Knight, the perennial life force. Like any other comic hero, the knight is purified of his pride and folly. But something curious happens in the process. The Christian ethic and the courtly, less than Christian values that Gawain espouses are shown to be in conflict. He is caught between them. And though he survives, the winner is neither of the two value systems he lives by. Instead the victor is life itself, and instinct – the free and darting thing that has tempted him, tested him, and that survives him. On stage the image of that force unhesitatingly became that of a magic bird, gorgeous and dangerous, that Gawain is wooed by and must beware of.

In addition to his perceptive appreciation of this early classic of the world canon, Scott had brought to the adaptation his years of experience in developing Caribbean ritual theatre. The combination proved inspired, resulting in a richly layered, timeless and captivating theatrical experience of universal appeal.

Premièred in 1978 was Scott's most original and provocative work, *Dog*, in which the vicious contempt of the privileged rich for the dispossessed poor is blazoned by portraying the former as people, the latter as a pack of wild dogs. 'If it had been a straightforward allegory', wrote Judy Stone (*TG*, 28 October, 1987), 'set squarely in the world of dogs, as Victor Questel's *Two Choices* is set squarely in the society of vagrants, I feel sure that the audience would have watched the play with comfortable comprehension, with a little patronising enjoyment of the actors' doggy antics, and would have left intellectually stimulated but spiritually untouched. What confounded and confused this audience, and left it feeling very uncomfortable indeed, was the way Scott juxtaposed people and dogs, and grades in between the two.'

In a time 'quite soon',[1] in a place that is any inner city, every person's hand is against the pack. The wild dogs are, after all, a source of fear. It's quite all right for real people, nice people like you and me, to form vigilante groups against dogs, to kill them brutally on sight, to try to trap them and poison the starving creatures with doctored food. 'Murder is a perfectly natural act.' Good dogs are domesticated or adopted, become more or less human, but it's still socially acceptable to desex them, or to get rid of them if they become inconvenient.

In his foreword to the play, Scott writes, 'Throughout the dogs are naked, except for scraps of material which cover the genitals. It should be obvious that the play has nothing to do with sexual titillation.'

The play is shaped in a series of vignettes, linked by the central character of Dog, a young pup who, when his mother is killed, is adopted by Daddy and Mummy, a couple of suburbanites with a tame dog gardener named Finger. A more subliminal link is the multiple role-playing by the actor who takes the part of the Narrator.

Willys Marshall describes (*People*, October, 1981) the climax of *Dog*, as performed in the 1981 Carifesta:

> Finger, hurt that Mummy should discard him as her lover, tells Dog to go and dig up the rose bed. He is fully aware of the fact that Dog's mother, Bitch, lies buried there. As Dog digs and digs, deeper and deeper, the suspense builds up and then . . . the lights go out and the Narrator asks the audience, 'What is your appetite for pain?' He personalises the entire experience even more when he asks, already knowing the answer, 'Would you stop him if you could?' The lights go on and he bellows, 'I will show you nothing,' knowing full well that the audience is in search of a conclusion to the play, but denying us that gratification . . . .

In 1982 Scott was invited to direct at the Yale Repertory Theatre. The following year, 1983, he returned to Yale University as Visiting Professor of Directing. He had resigned from the School of Drama and left Jamaica for the last time. The last of his plays to première in Jamaica, at the School, was the not particularly successful 1983 political satire, *Live and Direct from Babylon*. With the Jamaican Prime Minister's 1983 Medal for Service to the Arts in his pocket, he emigrated to America, frustrated by West Indian bureaucracy, and by his realisation that, for all his insight and strength of purpose, he could not carry the School further. Indeed, he could see the institution slipping back from lack of finance. In 1984 Scott joined the permanent staff of the Yale School of Drama as Assistant Professor (Adjunct) of Playwriting.

One of Scott's last great theatre experiments was in 1989 when, as part of a student exchange scheme, he staged in the USSR, with Russian actors, the American play *Sodbusters*, by drama student Craig Volk. At the time of his death Scott was appearing on American television as Lester, the father-in-law, in the Cosby show, and was working on a playscript titled *Quartet*.

Rawle Gibbons

Of all those playwrights influenced by Dennis Scott, the one who could probably claim the greatest dedication to the theatre of ritual is Rawle Gibbons.

Gibbons's *oeuvre* is comparatively small, but he has a particularly finely constructed ritual play in the stickfighting *I Lawah*. Scott has praised Gibbons for his exceptional understanding of the 'primary function'[2] of theatre, which, in Scott's definition, is 'the simultaneous excitement of eye, ear and mind through the enactment of a story'.[3]

Gibbons was born in Trinidad in 1950 and grew up in Belmont, a Port of Spain suburb originally developed by the island's early free blacks, which today is still a predominantly black, lower middle-class residential area. Gibbons attended Trinity College, a prestigious Anglican secondary school for boys. At the age of fourteen he joined the Catholic church. He practised his new faith with perhaps even more than the traditional zeal of the recent convert. Five years later, he was to bring a similar intensity of passion to his adoption of theatre, which he discovered as an undergraduate in Jamaica.

His initiation to the stage was as an actor, playing a small role in a student production of Roderick Walcott's *The Harrowing of Benjy*. He soon advanced to leading roles, and then tried his hand at directing in the Tallawah, the Mona campus inter-hall Festival. He was elected President of the University Drama Society. In 1973, with Jamaican Tony Smith, Gibbons founded the Caribbean Theatre Workshop, and began to write plays. Amongst his earliest works are *Games* (1982), which Gibbons co-wrote with Michael Reckord and Dennis Scott, and his first full length play, *Shepherd*, the première production of which became the Jamaica School of Drama 1981 Carifesta entry in Barbados.

Shepherd is set on a beach, on the holy mourning ground of Spiritual Baptists, and is based on the Baptists' mourning ritual. There are parallels with Dennis Scott's *Echo in the Bone* in the replaying of scenes from the past. However, the strongest thread throughout this play is not the ritual, but the struggle over the unborn child whose life is threatened by the ritual. In his programme note for *Shepherd*, Dennis Scott writes:

> The Company of actors announces a story to be told. They show us fourteen days in the life of a flock of worshippers. During that time a novice, a 'Pilgrim', undertakes a perilous journey through his own darkness, and the darkness of his people. Eyes banded, lying on the sacred ground, he encounters in the spirit the Powers that crush human hope. Only one man before him, the 'Shepherd', has ever endured those deaths of the soul and won through to leadership. The purpose of that rite of passage is to renew hope in the flock, and kindle life where there was none. It is the purpose of all our leaders.
>
> Rawle Gibbons has written an important Caribbean play. Its metaphors are wonderfully strange – images of convulsed sleep, of painful vision, of ecstasy, of the collective unconscious that operates in each man to create moments of historical choice. They weave a complex dramatic poetry. And these images are rooted in the rituals and folk customs of many ordinary people. They are familiar, and hidden, as our earliest memories.
>
> Through those images this play proposes that failure is a habit that must and can be broken. That despair is an offence against self. That irrationally, instinctively, we must choose Life, and make our own sacrifices for it, or it will elude us.

Shepherd is a challenging, densely layered play – over dense, over layered, and 'very subjective', according to Gibbons himself ten years later, when he termed it 'the most esoteric play in the Caribbean'.[4] It is also, Walcott aside, one of the finest examples by any playwright of the lyrical potential of the West Indian vernacular.

After graduating, Gibbons continued to move back and forth between Trinidad and Jamaica. He spent a year teaching in Trinidad, during which time, in 1974, he directed a cast of Point Fortin schoolchildren in what those who saw it describe as one of the most unforgettable productions of Derek Walcott's *Ti-Jean and his Brothers.* He spent the following year in Jamaica, doing post-graduate work for his drama oriented M. Phil. He returned to Trinidad to work on the St Augustine campus. There he founded Group 15 to stage Scott's *An Echo in the Bone*, which he directed. Subsequently he founded the Yard Theatre, which staged *Agamemnon* and Trinidad's première production of C.L.R. James's *The Black Jacobins.* Gibbons directed both pieces. He then went back to Jamaica, first working with a summer workshop for the School of Drama, then taking up a full-time position with the School, teaching directing. In 1985, towards the end of his tenure there, the School presented *I Lawah* as an experimental piece.

The play is intended to be performed, like Derek Walcott's *The Joker of Seville*, in a stickfighting gayelle. It is set in the Port of Spain of 1881, at the time of the Canboulay riots. 'Lawah' is the patois term for 'the king'. Gibbons's Lawah is the stickfighting king of a 'jamet' (anti-establishment) band called Helles Enfants. The raggedy gang forms a dramatic chorus, led by a shantwell, the historical antecedent of the calypsonian. As an entity, the chorus takes a drivingly active and versatile part in the performance, while individual members dressed, sketchily, as appropriate Carnival characters, play out the various roles in the story.

It is a story of abject poverty, oppression and revolt. Lawah brutally wrests from Sophie Bella the last cents she has earned working with the Le Blancs. He buys rum, and their child dies for want of medicine. In an act of irreversible defiance, Sophie leaves the yard to live in with the Le Blancs. She finds herself at the mercy of the unwanted attentions of M. Le Blanc, but she cannot return to her own people for Lawah will kill her. Meantime, the newly-arrived Chief of Police, the infamous Inspector Baker, as a result of an injudicious visit to 'jamet' town, has had the worst of an encounter with Helles Enfants and Lawah. This encounter is in effect the 'karray', the challenge and presentation of sticks before the fight proper begins. Baker's first blow is to ban Carnival's traditional Canboulay torches. He follows up quickly with the arrest of Lawah, who is beaten into submission. The Canboulay fires are quenched. At the Le Blancs', however, the daughter of the house, Therese, fascinated by her idealised vision of black life and culture, desperate to escape an arranged marriage with an older man she does not love, turns herself into a Canboulay torch. Sophie Bella, in trying to save Therese, herself catches the fire, and it is Sophie who, on her return to a subdued and silent jamet town, lights the Canboulay fires as the crowning blow against Baker.

'Gibbons's play', writes Ken Ramchand (*TG*, 10 June, 1987), ' . . . is about the interpenetration of cultures and about the role-playing endemic in such contact situations. It is also about the search for the true self. . . . It focuses on the jamet bands but it is really concerned with a sense of dissolution and reconstruction at all levels in the society.'

Ramchand sees a powerful dramatic link between Therese and the dead child:

> Therese, drawn by the spirit of Carnival and Canboulay, seeing song and dance even in the labours of the Blacks, this white child longing for another life, comes to blazing fulfilment as an incarnation of the dead child of Sophie Bella, absconding queen of the Lawah. I'm not sure that Gibbons . . . (sees) the child motif working out in this way but it is the logic to which the actors are groping. It flows back to give motivation to Sophie's concern over the child who dies; it puts an emphasis on the quality of possession in Therese's dancing; and it helps to make Sophie's return to Helles Enfants much more clearly a self-discovery and self-confirmation.

There are many West Indian plays about stickfighting, most memorably Derek Walcott's *Joker of Seville*, and also Errol Hill's *Man Better Man*, Dennis Noel's *Tears in the Gayelle* (1972) and Ronald Amoroso's *Warrior Bois* (1982). In fact most of the plays coming out of the Best Village competition incorporate an obligatory stickfighting sequence. Few if any of these plays are so closely researched as *I Lawah*. None other so embodies the ritual of the stickfight in its very structure.

It was to be six years before the première of the next new work by Gibbons. In the meantime, he returned to work on the St Augustine campus, as Director of the Calypso Research Project of the Institute of Social and Economic Research. In 1986 he was appointed the first Co-Ordinator of the campus's Creative Arts Centre, inaugurated in early 1987. He continued to direct, mainly for the Centre. His *Sing De Chorus* was planned for staging in 1990. In the end it did not première until the Carnival season of 1991, when it drew probably more, and more laudatory, letters in the Trinidad press than any previous production by any playwright. *Sing De Chorus* won five of the national Cacique awards for the year, including Best Original Script. For Trinidad audiences, not having had the privilege of seeing Derek Walcott's *Steel*, Gibbons's calypso musical was the first of its kind, a unique celebration of their own achievement. In its lively wit and brawling relationships, in its passion, courage, tenderness, terror, heartache and determination, it created a dizzying excitement.

Gibbons paints with a broader brush than Walcott, splashing a series of vivid historical events onto his main storyline. His conflict is a bold confrontation between 'us' and 'them', between the people and the colonial powers, whereas *Steel* shows the more subtle conflict within the society, between 'us' and 'us'. *Sing De Chorus* showcases 41 authentic kaisos of the period, several of which the audience sings with the cast. These kaisos themselves constitute the engine that drives the play, and the wheel that steers the storyline. Walcott's kaisos, in contrast, are empowered by the storyline of his original screenplay.

Set in the 1930s, *Sing De Chorus* is a period docudrama on the development of calypso in its Golden Age, the dynamic decade that saw, as recorded by historian Gordon Rohlehr, 'the paradox of a formalisation of State censorship of the performance of Calypso, in a year (1934) when opportunities for its recording had just begun to unfold'.[5] The history of calypso is a history of the Trinidad society. *Sing De Chorus* is a history of colonial suppression, labour riots, the burning of the policeman Charlie King, the outbreak of the Second World War and the arrival of the American forces. Against this social background, the play follows the lives of several calypsonians, in particular King Radio, at the peak of his career, and the Siparia Kid, at the start of his.

Ironically, it was in the year of the première production of *Sing De Chorus* that the artistic suppression which is a major theme of the play, and the very 1934 Theatres and Dance Halls Act introduced to muzzle the calypsonians, were revived to clamp down on Godfrey Sealy's *Home Sweet Home*.[6] Under the same act, and despite public outcry, police harassment continued the following year, 1992, during a re-run of Sealy's 1988 popular and internationally-performed AIDS-education play, *One of Our Sons is Missing*.

Planned as the first play in a trilogy, *Sing De Chorus* was followed in 1992 by *Ah Wanna Fall*, based on the life of the Mighty Spoiler, and featuring calypsos of the 1940s and 1950s. The third play, *Ten To One*, follows the career of the internationally successful calypsonian, the Mighty Sparrow.

Fig. 7 Rawle Gibbons's *Ah Wanna Fall* (PHOTO: Jeffrey Chock) Rhoma Spencer plays Ma Popo in this scene from the calypso musical. The Canboulay Production was staged in Trinidad in 1992, directed by Louis McWilliams, with musical direction by Desmond Waithe, choreography by Felix Harrington, sets by Ken Crichlow and costumes by Henry Muttoo.

Other playwrights, other rituals, other experiments

Rawle Gibbons has taken a minutely structured approach to the presentation of ritual in the theatre. Among other West Indian playwrights who have taken individual, but intensely intellectualised, approaches to the theatre of ritual is Marina Omowale Maxwell, whose *Play Mas* (1968) is based on Trinidad's Carnival, and *Hounsi Kanzo* (1973) on a Haitian ordeal ritual of consciousness. Trinidadian Lennox Brown, the winner of a record number of international playwriting awards in Canada, England and the United States, draws primarily on Afro-Caribbean culture in his unique development of ritual in theatre.

One other notable Caribbean experiment in theatre of ritual is exceptional in its abandonment of language and conventional structure. Henk Tjon, of the Doe Theatre in Surinam, has developed and toured the West Indies with an improvisational theatre on the lives of primitive peoples, in which communication depends on gestures, facial expressions, body language and sounds, rather than words.

Zeno Constance is rare among West Indian writers in having virtually invented his own ritual for theatre, evolving a formulaic construction that has now been adopted by other writers. Constance's work is also unusual in that every play was originally written for student actors, and received its première performance in Trinidad's annual Secondary Schools Drama Festival. Yet his subjects – incest, murder, rape, death, pupil-teacher seduction – and treatment appear more suitable for mature audiences. He does not condescend or write 'down' to any adult concept of an adolescent 'level'. Adult companies have produced his work with mixed success. A Constance play usually consists of a succession of arguments from various perspectives, and requires inspired direction to breathe theatrical life into what is essentially a physically static exercise in mental conflict. However, his plays continue to be exceptionally popular with the schools. He began writing in the mid-seventies, and since his first entry, in 1978, every Festival has showcased one or more of his plays. One year five schools entered Constance plays. He is a prolific writer, producing from one to three new plays each Festival. He almost invariably wins the award for the best new play, even from adjudicators who protest the unsuitability of his material for young people.

Constance's first Festival play aroused national controversy in 1979 when, on its screening by Trinidad and Tobago Television as the best play of the 1978 Secondary Schools Drama Festival, it was blanked from the screens after twenty minutes' viewing and several irate calls to the station from shocked members of the public. The 'unsuitable' subject of this play, *The Ritual*, was teenage pregnancy. Constance is a secondary school teacher whose subject is the practical world of physical education, rather than the academic world of most teacher-playwrights. He believes that not only are the actual life experiences of his students 'suitable' material for their peers, seen through the role-playing of his treatment these experiences can be a source of assistance to adolescents adrift on adult seas. Yet, his plays do not offer solutions, they simply open up the different aspects of a problem. It makes an interesting rider to the controversy that in 1983, only four years after its original censorship, *The Ritual* was screened in full by the same television station, unabridged, and without protest from the public.

Constance's plays are notable not only for their blunt candour, but also for their craftsmanship. Their architecture is powerfully rhythmic. Several, such as *Duelling Voices* (1984), are based on rituals of children's games, the ritual of the game informing the structure of the play more extensively than do games in the works of other West Indian writers from Walcott to Sistren. Constance's language, while relatively spare and devoid of poetic imagery, in its very brevity often takes on the mesmeric rhythm of a chant, with echoing phrases or recurring passages that serve the reinforcing purpose of a chorus. His use of a basic core of actors, who with rhythmic precision assume and discard a variety of characters, also reinforces the sense of ritual. His characters may be virtual ciphers, with no names, each representative of a single point of view. Or he may use several actors to play different aspects of one role. His plays require no set. A few boxes may serve as furniture, a hand prop or costume accessory, such as a scarf, suffices to indicate a change of character.

Some of the later plays are disappointing, too obviously following the Constance formula by rote, lacking in fresh insight. All in all, though, Constance has a body of work whose potential has barely been tapped. In 1989 one company suggested the range of that potential by presenting *Patricia, a love story* (1986) as a folk musical, incorporating traditional song and dance.

Aside from the work in theatre of ritual, other playwrights have experimented with surrealism. Trinidad's Lennox Raphael, another political playwright, has written several surrealistic works, among them *Waiting for Mick Jagger* (1980) and *The Politicians* (1981). He is most widely known for his *Che* (1968), which was banned off Broadway. Raoul Pantin writes plays of realism, such as *Sanctuary*, but he also blends surrealism into realistic works such as *Radio 555* and his most important work, *Hatuey*, a study of an Amerindian tribe under Spanish occupation.

Michael Gilkes

Another playwright whose most important play achieves a blend of realism and surrealism drawing principally on the Amerindian culture, but also on the multiplicity of cultures from which the West Indian peoples have originated, is Michael Gilkes, whose *Couvade* represented Guyana at the first Carifesta. An academic, Gilkes has written comparatively little for the stage, but from his youth he has been involved with the theatre, mainly as director and actor.

Michael Arthur Gilkes was born in British Guiana in 1933. His parents were middle class, Methodist, and between them endowed their son with nearly every ethnic variety of gene known to the region. Gilkes's father, a self-educated pharmacist, was of East Indian, African, Amerindian and European extraction. Gilkes's mother blended in her veins the bloods of Portugal, England and Africa.

Contemporaries remember the young Michael as a natural comic, with an irresistibly infectious laugh. As a teenager in Georgetown, he was a member of the Taitt Yard, an informal association of family and friends that nurtured several leading Caribbean sportsmen, and artists such as the London-based poet Marc Matthews and ceramicist Lawrence Taitt, the St Lucia-based painter Ron Savory, the Amsterdam-based dancer Helen Taitt, the Barbados-based actor Clairmonte Taitt and theatre activist Ken Corsbie, and the 'Walcottian' actor Wilbert Holder, who became a dominant figure on Trinidad's stage.

The political and economic pressures under the Forbes Burnham socialist regime forced the emigration of these artists in the sixties and seventies. Eventually Gilkes was to follow suit and settle in Barbados. As a young man, however, he spent the years 1962 to 1967 in London, emerging with a first class honours degree. He returned to Guyana and spent a year teaching Spanish and English at St Stanislaus College. He then took up an appointment as Assistant Lecturer in the Department of English at the University of Guyana.

Since his Yard days Gilkes had been committed to theatre. He was a member of the leading Georgetown theatre company, the Theatre Guild, and it was the Guild that premièred his first full length play, *In Transit*, in 1968. His only previous work for the stage, *Young Aesop*, was a children's play presented by St Gabriel's School in 1967.

A voyage of discovery of selfhood, *In Transit* boldly experiments with mixed media, dance, free verse, a chorus, and multiple black and white role playing. Unexpectedly, it is in his own country that the young protagonist Stanley is physically in transit, between university training in England and greater opportunities in Canada. But the play is about spiritual, rather than physical, transition.

Chorus: . . . in this journey all the ports
And stations are the same
And we return from where we came
It is the traveller who must change.

Stanley meets prejudice wherever he is, with his White Goddess in England or within his own family in Guyana. To find himself as he is, and not as others see him, he has to stop looking at himself alone, and to make the transition from the self-centredness of youth to a maturer appreciation of those around him, most of all the girl he will choose as his life-partner.

Like Stanley, Gilkes was at this time pursuing his own search for selfhood. Like Dominica's Alwin Bully, he was multi-talented. Apart from his academic achievements, he was a qualified pharmacist. He also studied economics. He was a pianist of considerable ability. He played an 'excellent first pan'[7] in Guyana's first steelband, the Symphonia, which won a major award on its maiden appearance in the annual national music festival. Whatever Gilkes did he did well. But to his friends he seemed unable to settle to any one direction in life, and somewhere along the way the laughing child stepped into the shoes of an unexpectedly serious and driven man. It is tempting to speculate that Gilkes may have drawn his compulsion to excel from a sense of responsibility stemming from a perception of himself as representative of the multi-racial Caribbean man he was to idealise in *Couvade*.

In 1970 Gilkes returned to England on a three-year Commonwealth Scholarship, for postgraduate studies in English and American Literature at the University of Kent. After obtaining his Ph.D. in 1973, he returned to the University of Guyana for a year, as Lecturer in the Department of English. Meantime, while he was still in England, a deputation from Theatre 70's (a splinter group from the Guyana Theatre Guild) flew across the Atlantic to commission Gilkes to write a play for the new company. He wrote *Couvade*, a strikingly unusual play inspired by Wilson Harris's *The Sleepers of Roraima*.

The Theatre 70's production was chosen to represent Guyana, the host country, in its pioneering staging of the first Caribbean Festival of Creative Arts in 1972. This national tribute to his work, however, did not deter Gilkes from his decision to emigrate. In 1974 he moved with his family to Barbados, registered as a British/Barbadian citizen, and was appointed Lecturer in the Department of English on the Cave Hill campus of the University of the West Indies. In 1976 he returned to the University of Kent for a year, on academic exchange. In 1980 he became Senior Lecturer at Cave Hill, and in the same year was awarded a Fulbright Fellowship at the University of Indiana. A Leverhulme Fellowship followed in 1986, at the University of Warwick, after which Gilkes spent a year at Warwick on academic exchange, and then in 1988 returned to Cave Hill as Reader of Caribbean Literature and Head of the Department of English.

Once settled in his adopted home of Barbados, Gilkes was soon once again active in the theatre. In 1979 he became both founder and first Artistic Director of what was swiftly recognised as the new leading theatre company in Barbados, Stage One. Gilkes continued to direct and act with Stage One until 1992, when he resigned from Cave Hill and returned to Guyana. Even so, fifteen years passed between the première of *Couvade*, and Stage One's 1987 première of his next play. *This Island Now* is a dramatised history of Barbados, and again uses mixed media. The following year, 1988, saw a staged reading at London's Royal Court Theatre of a script commissioned from Gilkes, *A Pleasant Career*, on 'the life and fictions of Edgar Mittelholzer'. Mittelholzer is one of the West Indian writers of whom Gilkes the academic has made a particular study.

Gilkes has also translated onto videotape the works of other West Indian writers, such as Derek Walcott and Jean Rhys. But, as with Raoul Pantin, it is Gilkes's Amerindian play that marks his own place in the history of West Indian theatre. *Couvade* is a complex, intricately woven work that can be interpreted on several levels. Intellectually intense, it is not in every respect dramatically satisfying, but with imaginative direction and acting, as it had in the première production, it is a powerful and provocative piece of theatre. In Gilkes's handling of the supernatural, as well as in the theme, there are constant echoes from the writing of Wilson Harris. Mark McWatt, in *A Comparative Study of the Language of the Imagination in Contemporary Commonwealth Literature*, might justifiably have included *Couvade* when he wrote of the exploration in all Harris's works of 'the familiar theme of re-discovery of origins in the face of a run-down of the present world, and in visualising the tribal origins of the Amerindian consciousness. Harris – and in turn Gilkes – 'displays a surprising originality of imaginative perception in an area that has always been conscripted into a murky, irredeemable picture of a past ruined by sub-human atrocities and a chronic incapacity to survive.'

Unlike Pantin's play, *Couvade* is set in modern times. The plot is slender. Pat is pregnant with her first child. The child's father, Lionel, who is a painter, begins to experience a sequence of strange dreams. He feels compelled to paint these dreams, to the exclusion of normal life. When not painting, he retires to the couvade hammock which, in the original production, dominated the stage (in pre-production plans for a 1992 Guyana Theatre Guild production which failed to materialise, Gilkes adjusted the staging so that it was the painting that dominated). Lionel becomes so reclusive, hiding behind his dark glasses, that his wife and friends fear for his health and sanity. At the end he interprets the dreams as symbolising the birth of the child as the new Caribbean man.

In structure, *Couvade* has similarities with Gilkes's earlier play, *In Transit*. The action is frequently interrupted for commentary directly to the audience by the chorus or one of the characters, and the thread of the plot is regularly interrupted by the interspersed dreams. Music is intrinsic to the text, and for the première production was written by Gilkes's wife Joan, based on authentic Carib Indian themes.

Two aspects of this play give it lasting importance. One is the use of Amerindian ritual, the other is the theme of Caribbean integration. The couvade ritual is widespread, taking different forms around the world. The common factor is that the father of an unborn child undergoes withdrawal, usually to his bed, and hardship, such as fasting or wounding or near-drowning, which create

Fig. 8 Michael Gilkes's *Couvade* (PHOTO: Pat Pierre) The rain forest set for the 1993 Guyana government production was designed by Ken Corsbie. Gilkes directed the production, which included in the cast 16 native Amerindians and 11 chowtal singers.

a bond between the male parent and his child. This male bond has a strength equivalent to the natural maternal bonding, and so ensures the child's future welfare.

Gilkes establishes that the child of Lionel and Pat melds in his veins the blood of many different races. He then, through the mystical dreams of the couvade sleeper, draws on these ancestral races (Carib, Ashanti, Indian), and on a cross-section of Guyanese folk figures such as the pork-knocker, preacher and politician, to weave a whole cloth of Caribbean society. Significantly, all the roles are played by the actors of the central plot.

On the given level, the integration is seen as producing a homogeneous Caribbean man, drawn from all the cultural strands present in the West Indies. The play can also be seen as symbolic of racial integration, and of integration of the nations of the Caribbean region.

In his introduction to *Couvade*, Errol Hill has written:

> There may be those who will question the author's apparent advocacy of an integrated Caribbean culture as an absolute priority, giving the argument that it is necessary first to forge stronger links with one or other of the major non-Western ancestral cultures that have historically been ignored, despised and suppressed. They would argue that only when these cultures, from which most of our people came, are re-established to a place of esteem in our consciousness, will the Caribbean man and woman be psychologically ready to fulfil the dream of *Couvade*.

NOTES

1 The Playwright's Foreword, programme *Dog*, Central Bank of Trinidad and Tobago, 1987.

2 Dennis Scott, personal inscription in Rawle Gibbons's copy of *Sir Gawain and The Green Knight.*

3 Dennis Scott, 'Introduction', *Sir Gawain and The Green Knight*, Anchorage Press in association with National Theatre of the Deaf, 1978.

4 Rawle Gibbons, in interview with Judy Stone, unpublished, 1991.

5 Gordon Rohlehr, *Calypso and Society in Pre-Independence Trinidad*, Rohlehr, 1991.

6 See Prologue.

7 Clairmonte Taitt, in interview with Judy Stone, unpublished, 1992.

BLACK BRITISH THEATRE

The theatre of exile: Edgar White, Mustapha Matura, Caryl Phillips

'You get use to exile, don't you?' says the gentle, scholarly Ferret in Edgar White's *The Nine Night* (1983). 'I mean West Indian means exile.'

Edgar White

Of the many playwrights living, in Britain and elsewhere, in exile from the West Indies, it is Edgar White who in his works shows the most concern with the theme of exile. Yet, of them all, he seems the least constrained by his own exile. He has turned his homelessness to advantage, becoming a citizen of the world. He spends more time in the Caribbean than do most of the exiled writers. He has been domiciled on both sides of the Atlantic. He resides in no country to the exclusion of others. The largeness of his personal life reflects the largeness of vision that is a marked characteristic of his plays. His sweeping treatments, even to his panoramic stage directions, often read like film scripts, yet they are innately theatrical. White's playwriting career – he is also a novelist – has from the outset been one of exceptional achievement. Of a younger generation than Derek Walcott, by the mid-eighties White already boasted as many published play collections as did the older poet – who has, however, a far greater published *oeuvre* in toto. For many observers White shows promise of becoming the most important playwright since Walcott to emerge from the West Indies.

Edgar Monk White was born in 1947, in Montserrat, the smallest Caribbean island to have produced a playwright of international stature. White credits his early education in the island as being of such excellence that when he emigrated to America he was already a voracious reader, although he was only eight years old. He remained in the States for the next quarter-century, growing up bilingual in Spanish-speaking Harlem. His reading fed his innate bent for introspection, and as a teenager he joined a seminary to study for the priesthood. At the same time, feeling that he had read all there was to read, he began writing copiously. He grew disillusioned with the church. As he pondered his next step, a friend suggested he turn to the theatre, and dared him to write a play for Joe Papp.

The first play White had ever seen had been a Joe Papp Shakespeare production in modern dress. He took up the challenge with extraordinary success. He was only eighteen when Papp produced *The Mummer's Play* (1965), in which two frustrated black artists confront St Peter. Even at this début, the young writer's instinctive feeling for theatre was as marked as his erudition, his soaring imagination, his sense of irony, and the leanness of his language. The production went so well that Papp subsequently staged the next four of White's plays, one of which was bilingual, Spanish-English.

White had left the church, and yet he kept the church with him in his writing, recognising the parallels between the rituals of religion and the rituals of theatre. To these he would bring from his half-forgotten childhood the rituals of the West Indies, in particular those originating from Africa.

In 1968 he graduated from New York University. By the mid-seventies 14 of his plays, many of them short pieces, had been produced in New York. Six of his plays had been published in two collections, and also three novels. He had taken up a writing fellowship at the Yale University School of Drama, and become artistic director of the Yardbird Theatre Company of Harlem.

One of White's most striking plays of the period is the 1975 *Lament for Rastafari*. It is a vast historical and geographical panorama of the trials of Rastafarian life, presented in an unsentimental treatment that has none of the playfulness of Walcott's Rastafarian musical, *O Babylon!*, and is the more deeply disturbing. The first act, set in Jamaica, reaches back into the inhumanity of slavery, then forward to the mid-twentieth century, following the Rastafarian experience through poverty and hardship, discrimination and prostitution, to flight from the island. The second act is set in England, the third in America. Each act is a series of brief scenes, some realistic, others with surrealistic elements, several simply monologues played directly to the audience. Each scene represents, like links in a chain, some aspect of the overall tribal experience. The chain is welded together through the central character of Lindsay, a writer, who travels a difficult path to reach the realisation that 'everybody own us but ourselves'.

In 1981 White flew across the Atlantic to see his first British première, *Les Femmes Noirs*, a play that was originally produced by Papp in 1976. On the spur of the moment White decided to make London his new base. And for the next five years most of his world premières were staged in London.

As much as *Les Femmes Noirs* is about the tribulations of black women, it is about the ineffable sadness and loneliness of the human condition. 'I'm beginning to think if nobody is watching, then no one is really kind,' says Mary Alice. Even more devastating is Pee Wee's comment, 'You know, in all my life I ain't never met a woman really liked herself.'

In a sequence of short scenes, characters disappear and reappear as various women are shown in the isolation of different relationships, the unconnected mother and daughter, the voices in the catacombs, Roberta waiting for Sharkey. The one constant presence in the play is the television set which is the focal point of each home, of each life. Television is the real world for these women, in a way that their own lives are not.

'She don't even see you, nigger,' says the crippled King Alfa. 'You don't look like nothing she's seen on TV, figure she must of had 'bout 20,000 hours by now in front of that set. So you ain't real to her.'

King Alfa and the weak-spined Mary Alice are two of a number of characters in White's plays whose spiritually crippling lives are manifested in the physical impairment of their bodies. For the most part, his paraplegics have learned the art of accommodating their afflictions, just as his fitter protagonists have to learn to triumph over the less tangible but no less cruel psychological blows inflicted by society.

Among White's works receiving a London world première in the eighties *Masada*, a play on South Africa, received the accolade of a transfer to the West End, with the original Kiskidee Theatre black cast. The South African question is one of White's major concerns, explored in several of his plays, such as *Like Them That Dream* (1983). He also, in plays such as *Man and Soul* (1982), set in a British jail, and *The Boot Dance*, set in a British mental asylum, explores the relationship between Africans and West Indians. His primary theme, though, is that of exile, in particular the black West Indian exile. White examines the way the exile relates to others in the country to which he has emigrated, how he has dealt with the changes in his own life, how he reconciles his children to their uprooting. He sees West Indians as the new Diaspora. 'West Indians are the most in exile,' he has said. 'You find them everywhere in the world.'[1]

The great exodus of the fifties, after the Second World War had opened West Indian eyes to another, presumed better, way of life, diminished but never ended. Yet the exile from poverty, ignorance and lack of opportunity always longs to come back home. In *Redemption Song* the recently returned exile tells his father:

> *Legion:* I wish you never send me away, America, England. You never did me any favour, you know.
> *Bramble:* It was a chance.
> *Legion:* It was a sentence.

It is the exile from wealth, ignorance and lack of opportunity who, in the 1982 *That Generation*, clings to his poverty and anonymity in the big city.

In *The Nine Night*, which premièred in London in 1983, Hamon Williams, who lives in England, is an exile of twenty years. The nine night ritual for the dead is performed to help the troubled soul cross into Paradise. It has been explored by a number of West Indian playwrights, such as Glenville Lovell, in *When the Eagle Screams*, and Dennis Scott, in *Echo in the Bone*. Hamon's nine night is a cathartic experience of challenge, self-examination and release, that succeeds in giving him the impetus to cross the Atlantic back to Jamaica. England has 'come in a the house' and divided the family. And Hamon's own past, surfacing in the person of an illegitimate daughter, has alienated his favourite child, Sabina. Hamon calls a family gathering to propose that the family can regain its unity by returning to Jamaica. But his eldest child, Eulet, is engaged to a white girl, and as a successful footballer has a chance to make 'some real money' if he stays in England. Sabina is also dating a white companion, and sees no future for herself in 'some island in the sun'. Hamon's wife has no wish to leave the metropolitan comforts of her home. Though the play opens with a potentially violent confrontation between Hamon and his shiftless, thieving younger son Izak, a confrontation which barely abates before the end of the play, it is Izak, the child most like him, that Hamon manages to 'save', by persuading him to make the trip home with his father.

This 'ambitious, savagely funny and sad play', as *The Standard* described it, was considered the best production of the Black Theatre Co-operative to date, and subsequently toured extensively. White's greatest strength, wrote *The Guardian* critic, 'lies in the force and humour with which he dives headfirst into the domestic battlefield. His dialogue is economical and biting.'

Ritual by Water (1983) had its première in London a month after *The Nine Night*. This is the story of an immigrant younger than Hamon, and unmarried. The intellectual small-islander Barzey has kept the ideals of his youth in spite of approaching middle age. Having begun working at a Hackney Youth Centre 'as a lark', he has become increasingly committed to the youths in his charge. At a deeper level the play examines the universal relationship of father to child. Deeper yet, it explores the value of life itself, independent of the past.

'The best way to kill your father is *not* to become like him,' Barzey says to Silence, a West Indian teenager whose father drove the boy's mother to attempted suicide. Only two genuine fathers appear on stage, but *Ritual by Water* is peopled with the results of disastrous parenting. All too often, these offspring seem trapped in a cycle, as they answer the outrage of their upbringing with their own version of their parents' behaviour. Silence wants to 'take a razor' to his bullying father. The white East Ender, Nutter, whose father beat him and taught him hate, sees war as his only possible future. Barzey's woman, Yvonne, and her sister Sybil, never lacked the material necessities of childhood, but their father drank, fornicated, and eventually married a woman not their mother. Sybil's response to this rejection has been an implacable hatred that cuts out of her life not only her father but all black men, and admits her hard-drinking Jewish husband no rights in their child.

White shows the other side of parenting in the West Indian youth Juda, whose instinctive bonding to his 'seed' is so great that it leads to a chilling scene in which the young father is arrested and beaten by the police. But the two most successful fathers in the play, Barzey and Uncle Charles, are childless. Barzey, having been abandoned by his father as an infant, cares as intensely for the Centre's disadvantaged youngsters as if they were his own. He has broken his own cycle of abuse, and idealistically attempts to help those in his care do the same, to take their lives into their own hands, and to refuse to accept their symbolic emasculation by an alien society. Against all the odds stacked up by the suffocating system, he manages to gain the youths' trust and make progress with the education essential for their survival, whereat he is promptly fired.

Barzey has been supported and guided through this baptism of life by a father-figure visible only to himself, one-legged Uncle Charles, an earthy guardian spirit who combines the Shakespearian characteristics of chorus and comic relief, and who, though dead, is one of White's most lively, original and unforgettable creations. In the end, Uncle Charles has brought Barzey to a closer understanding of his own father, of his isolation, and of what life is all about.

Barzey:	And what about love?
Uncle Charles:	Is too much book you a book. To live, man, that is the love. The white man put us in the sea to drown us, and instead of drown we just came bapitised. That is the ritual by water. Who can swim, swim. Who drown, drown, and we can't look back to weep. Never. You father give you his seed which they try to take. That is the love.

To a purist such as Rawle Gibbons, White's use of ritual in his plays is incomplete. The ritual of the title is the baptism of experience, but *Ritual by Water* does not follow the West Indian baptist ritual either in representation, as Earl Lovelace does in *The Wine of Astonishment*, or in linear structure, as Rawle Gibbons does with the stickfighting ritual in *I Lawah*. What the playwright has drawn directly from the Baptist ceremony can be found in certain surrealistic elements such as the working of the spirits, the uneasy welding of cultures in the child wearing the black and white voodoo mask of death, and the motif of the bells. But the rhythm that powers the play is not the lilting rhythm of Baptist music, it is the driving heartbeat of life itself, intensifying at moments of pressure, as it pulses through the tolling of the Antigua bell for the death of a slave, the BBC pips and the martial signature tune of the News, the urgency of reggae music, the steady slapping of cards on a table, the tapping of Uncle Charles's crutches on the floor.

The ritual of *Redemption Song*, which had its world première in London in 1984, is drawn from Jamaica's Jonkunnu festival. The plot, which is more a play of action than is characteristic of most of White's work, is a modern version of a traditional Jonkunnu love triangle and murder. The play opens in Redemption village with the mummers dancing. Among them is Fowler, a rich man and former undertaker, wearing the horse's head costume that is a symbol of his coming cuckolding. Also in the crowd is a stranger from England, the poet Legion, who has just arrived 'out of exile' to claim his relatives and his inheritance. His plan is to settle in this village where he was born. He is devastated to discover that his newfound father, Bad Bush Bramble, a half-paralysed drunkard, has sold the house that had been left to Legion by his grandmother.

Ironically, it is Fowler who has bought the house, and it is Fowler who has married Verity, Legion's childhood sweetheart. Fowler is a boorish philistine who judges the value of a book of poetry by weighing it against a mango. He has little respect for other people and less for ethics. Knowing that for Legion to claim his house through the courts could take years, Fowler with feigned generosity offers to sell the disputed property back to the poet. He adds insult to injury by setting a price inflated far above the property's worth, further above what the 'grave man' paid Bad Bush for it in the first place. While Legion attempts to lay hands on documents that will prove his claim to his inheritance, romance slowly rekindles between himself and Verity. Fowler is apprised of the affair. Incensed, in the middle of the Jonkunnu festivities he forces a stickfight on the reluctant Legion. Fowler falls, but he is not beaten. Legion fails to heed his father's warning that with Fowler's wealth, 'What him can't do, him can buy'. At night, by torchlight outside the house where he was born, three men stone Legion to death.

In the materialistic society of Redemption, Legion had been seen, even by his family and his lover, as an unwanted threat to the status quo. With the threat removed, Fowler expected the status quo to return to normal. But Legion's brief sojourn had touched each life permanently, for the most part with a touch of redemption. Miss Bea's heart had softened towards her delinquent brother Bramble. The crippled albino, Sores, had been kissed by a beautiful girl and found a father in Bad Bush. Verity had thrown off the shackles of servitude to her family. Many home truths had been spoken, and even Fowler had been affected for the better. Only Simon, Fowler's downtrodden illegitimate son, a policeman, and the poet's friend, had moved into a deeper personal hell as a result of Legion's passing.

It took a trip home to Montserrat before White was able to draw directly on his West Indian roots for his writing. In the mid-eighties he began to shift his base over to the Caribbean, travelling from island to island, seeing his latest plays première in Jamaica, Cuba, Antigua. His most powerful work, *I, Marcus Garvey (and the captivity of Babylon)*, examines the life of the Jamaican leader of the thirties, and had its première in Barbados in 1987.

It is a work of monumental scope, encompassing in two hours on stage Garvey's active political life from 1912 to his death in 1940. In 34 episodes, three prologues and an epilogue, White accomplishes a remarkably comprehensive distillation of the historical facts. The brief scenes flash back and forth highly charged with events, with memorably sketched characters, with the playwright's sympathetic insights into the forces that drove Garvey. White uses several theatrical devices to make this potential chaos of material easily accessible to his audience. He also ensures accessibility by keeping his language simple, though in style it ranges widely; but whether West Indian dialect or standard English, there is a poetry in its clean and rhythmic structure.

Three of the devices White uses in this play are pre-recorded dialogue, a chorus and slides. The introduction of the slides offers a director valuable opportunities for the setting of atmosphere, by the quick recall of familiar images of social history. But essentially their purpose is to establish the location of each scene, as Garvey is harassed back and forth between Jamaica, America, London, Canada, Antigua. The chorus allows a relatively small cast to present the necessarily large roll of characters, even to the working class crowds at Garvey's rallies. The pre-recorded dialogue draws on the Garvey persona for comment on and clarification of his motives, his life. The director of the première production, Earl Warner, chose to replace the recording with a live actor as the Old Garvey, whose compelling presence remained on stage thoughout the performance, set above the action as though Garvey's spirit were sitting in benign judgement on himself.

Between the two aspects of Garvey, the one living the life, the other looking at it, White has disclosed a human being of infinite depth, flawed but majestic, tender but implacable, of universal vision, whose tragedy, as novelist John Wickham writes, is 'the world's'.[2] In paying tribute to one of his heroes, White has created a work of heroic stature.

Black British theatre

'The migratory West Indian feels rootless on his own earth, chafing at its beaches,' writes Derek Walcott in *What the Twilight Says.* West Indian playwrights have worked in many of the major areas of the world: Dexter Lyndersay in Nigeria and Holland; Errol Sitahal and Lennox Brown in Canada; Brown, Glenville Lovell and Lennox Raphael in the USA; Devindra Dookie in India. But by far the most significant body of West Indian playwrights in exile is for historical reasons to be found in England, where even Edgar White moved eventually. White, Brown, Michael Abbensetts, Jan Carew, Felix Cross, Alfred Fagon, C.L.R. James, Errol John, Evan Jones, Mustapha Matura, Caryl Phillips, Jimi Rand, Barry Reckord, Samuel Selvon, have all settled or sojourned in England, along with the first generation of West Indian-descended playwrights such as Winsome Pinnock.

Mustapha Matura

More than one London critic has referred to Mustapha Matura as England's finest dramatist of West Indian origin. Reviewers repeatedly mention his humanity and warmth of feeling, his clarity of vision, and his knack for observing human oddity. Of the comparatively small body of West Indian playwrights of East Indian descent, Matura is the only one to achieve international status, and to see his work staged at England's National Theatre. Yet when he left Trinidad at the age of twenty-one, he had no thoughts of becoming a playwright.

Born in 1939, Matura was not raised in a traditional Hindu household as was his countryman, novelist Vidia Naipaul. Although his father claimed Brahmin ancestry Matura, who as a child was called Noel, grew up as a Christian, a member of the Anglican church. The only ethnic influence that Matura himself acknowledges from his East Indian heritage is a certain reflective quality which informs his attitude to life.

Life in the Trinidad of Matura's childhood was a time of acute political awareness. His early years were coloured by the distant world war, and the consequent disruptive invasion of the island by friendly American forces. As a teenager, he lived through the heady days of the island's internal struggle for independence. After leaving school, Matura worked as a solicitor's clerk.

'He relished the formal, arcane language of the law,' writes Heather Neill in *The Times* (10 July, 1991), 'and the way that young blacks in similar positions ("qualified, but not qualified: they didn't have a piece of paper") would quote Hartley Shawcross's speeches to each other for sheer pleasure. "We would take care how we used words, to suggest mood or attitude, or tempo or time. We would say mundane things, but in an intellectual way, an entertaining way, to show how clever we were, to show what we thought of the person we were talking to. There was an element of competition." '

But Matura's inclinations were artistic, and the small island society offered too little opportunity for him to explore his talents. During the fifties he had seen the mass emigration of Trinidadians seeking greener pastures in London. Now it was his turn to go. It was a hard decision. All through his writing career, Matura's work has resonated with his love for his island home and his abiding interest in its development since independence. Most of his best work, though written for London audiences, is set in Trinidad.

He arrived in London in 1960 having never seen a play about Trinidad, never seen a play by a West Indian, never seen a play with a black cast. His sole acquaintance with theatre had been as a member of the audiences for a couple of the productions of British comedies staged by a competent resident company of white, largely British expatriate amateurs. He began his self-imposed exile with no job, no more than a temporary place to stay, and no clear idea of his future as an artist. He rather thought he wanted to be a painter.

In London, Matura began seeing a great many plays and films. But it was not until a chance experience in Rome, where he found himself at the Theatre Goldoni, working as assistant stage manager to a company of black American actors performing the Langston Hughes *Shakespeare in Harlem*, that he felt fired to create his own play. He returned to London and wrote *Dialogue* (1970), a pithy 4-page exercise that pits the lures of the consumer society against the ideals of Black Power. Matura's deceptively casual dialogue, his sharp eye for character, and his particular brand of seemingly innocuous humour, with its sting in the tail, are all there in embryo in this first one-acter. Along with two further short *Black Pieces* by Matura, *Dialogue* was staged in 1970 at London's ICA, with an all-West Indian cast. From the beginning, Matura set out to create opportunities for black actors. Among his more memorable characters are the scheming Ram of *As Time Goes By*, the colonial barman Drakes of *Independence* (1979), the failed calypsonian Creator in *Rum an' Coca Cola*, and several of the cast of *The Coup* (1991). He has never created a female role to equal these.

In itself too brief to be listed among his major works, *Dialogue* heralded several full length plays Matura was to write on the particular pressures met by the West Indian living in Britain. The first of these, *As Time Goes By*, had its première in Edinburgh, and later was staged on the London fringe, winning critical acclaim and two prestigious awards, the George Devine and the John Whiting, for most promising playwright of 1971. This early comedy is set in London, but except for a couple of weed-happy flower children the cast is West Indian. The central character, Ram, is an East Indian Anancy smartman, an amiable confidence trickster something akin to Ganesh of Naipaul's *The Mystic Masseur*, in his knack of achieving success virtually in spite of himself.

A recurring theme in Matura's work is the necessity for a comparatively powerless entity – whether a black immigrant or a third world country, as in *The Coup* – to appear to adapt to the surrounding stronger forces, if the weakling is to retain any choice of opportunities and control over its own destiny. Ram has a chameleon's aptitude for adapting to his immediate environment, even to shifts in the language he uses. His wife, Batee, one of the few women Matura has created with some substance, and the source of the liveliest conflict and comedy in the play, has no such aptitude. She heartily despises her surroundings, and is consequently miserable. It is Batee who speaks Matura's home-sickness:

Batee: Look, child, is five years I here and every night a go ter bed a pray dat when a open me eyes in de morning a go see de sun shining, home. An' every morning a pray dat dis is me last day here, a pray dat something would come an' pick me up and take me.

Thelma: But you'd be surprised yer know, Trinidad's changed a lot, de Government.

Batee: A don't care how much it a change a don't care if as soon as a land der de shoot me. I'd die happy, really happy. Not happy fer a minute because yer see something funny on de telly but happy all de time, here in yer heart even when yer en happy yer still happy in yer heart, a carn't describe it but is a feeling yer have inside.

Benedict Nightingale, in a review (*The Times*, 16 March, 1991) of *Meetings* (1981), comments on the fundamental seriousness with which Matura writes of people who, like himself, have in some sense become severed from their roots.

Over the next two years Matura saw his first televised play, *Bakerloo Line* (1972) on BBC 2, he saw his first published collection of plays, and he saw more of his work staged on the London fringe, including the neatly crafted *Nice* (1973). This beguilingly funny monologue creates a collection of tenderly recognised individuals, most of them lonely hearts. The characters are created with an economy of description, and yet without dependence on impersonations by the actor. The story line contrasts the opposing attitudes and consequent fortunes of two West Indians in London. One is an apparently ingenuous new arrival with an ever open palm of friendship, the other an old hand hostile as a scarred fist. The credibility with which, in the final few lines, the polarity of these two main characters is virtually reversed, gives this resolution a completeness which is deliberately avoided in most of Matura's plays.

In 1974 *Play Mas*, the first and one of the two more important of Matura's Trinidad plays, opened at London's Royal Court Theatre with a West Indian cast and costumes by Carnival designer Peter Minshall. It won Matura the *Evening Standard*'s award for the year's most promising playwright. The Carnival of the title is woven into the fabric of the play, sometimes to an unnerving extent, as when the doctor summoned to a deathbed appears in grass skirt and body paint, and the undertakers are mistaken for revellers. And though his costume is soldier, the mas that Samuel plays in life has much akin with the Midnight Robber.

Play Mas, though on one level a comedy, is Matura's first serious examination of the relationship between the races in West Indian society. It is also a study of the effects of independence in a small island. The leading characters are Ramjohn, an Indo-Trinidadian running the family tailoring business, and his Afro-Trinidadian assistant, Samuel. Each is a cultural curiosity to the other, but they co-exist fairly amiably given their different stations in life. Ramjohn lives a self-contained existence, follows traditional Hindu practices, works hard, ignores Carnival and politics, and has an uneasy time of it trying to adjust to independence. Samuel plays his mas to the full, and is open to every opportunity. He throws up his job to join the new political party, greases his own palm from the party subscriptions, and with independence rises to the position of Chief of Police, able to summon and good-naturedly play mas with his old employer at will.

By the end of the play, though, too much mas has been played. Samuel's good nature has been corrupted to brutality and armed suppression. As with *The Coup* to come, Matura seems to be tackling the question as to whether independence for the small nations of the world is really possible. *Play Mas* looks at the interior forces which work against successful self-rule, *The Coup* examines both the interior and exterior forces.

Play Mas opens with a set-piece of a scene in which Ramjohn vividly describes the pinnacle of his ambition, the making of a double-breasted eight-buttoned three-piece suit.

> Witout de linings yer en' have no suit, so yer have ter make sure dat wen yer put in a lining it stay, but de lining have ter do everyting de suit do, it must follow, but it mustn't lead, an when de suit say stop, de linings must stop, an wen de suit say go, de linings must go, dey must be like brodder and sister, yer see wat a mean.

Even in the Trinidad of the fifties, only an East Indian could have made that last analogy.

Matura's works contain several such set-pieces, where the busy traffic of the plot momentarily pulls aside for a passage of beguiling imagery, like a voluptuous Carnival float sailing sedately through the down-town rush hour. In *Meetings*, the passage describes creole food. In *The Coup*, it describes the making of a soldier, as Black Lightning attempts to escape the firing squad by the stalling tactics of Scheherazade. Matura excels at colloquial dialogue that while apparently banal is rich in idiosyncratic metaphors, and carries the play along with a naturally lilting rhythm, sometimes punctuated by one or two phrases repeated like a refrain. British critics have found his dialogue 'quirky' and 'unpredictable', but to the West Indian, and to Matura himself, the language is part of his inheritance, the peculiarly colourful and everchanging amalgam of the Trinidad vocabulary and syntax. Matura has also drawn attention to another aspect of the language which he uses.

'There is no such thing as an ordinary conversation in Trinidad, there's always a story behind the words, always the person is saying something other than what they seem to be saying.'[3] This aspect of Matura's writing was apparent from his first play, and continues throughout his work, being at its most evident in Samuel's role in *Play Mas*. Much of Matura's humour depends on a similar principle.

With the success of *Play Mas*, Matura's direction was firmly pointed. He liked, he has said, the 'immediacy'[4] of theatre. The plays came quickly and with an assurance. The more important works of this period are three Trinidad plays – *Rum an' Coca Cola* (1976), *Independence* (1979) and *Meetings* (1981) – and *Welcome Home Jacko* (1979), set in a British youth club. All four of these plays follow the now recognisable Matura form of a play which opens and runs for most of its length ostensibly as comedy, but which at the end makes an abrupt turn into darker, often almost surrealistic and perhaps less plausible territory.

In each of the first three plays, the essential conflict is between the old ways and the new. In *Rum an' Coca Cola*, an ageing calypsonian is driven to murder to stop his apprentice leaving for a better life in America. There is another pupil-teacher duo in *Independence*, which is set in a shabby colonial hotel very far removed from that of Trevor Rhone's *Smile Orange*. At the end, the hotel is destroyed, and will never rise again while Drakes the barman haunts its ruins, but the young waiter Allen has his chance at a more rewarding life. *Meetings* is an unadulterated paean of praise for the old ways, folk wisdom and home food of the West Indian past, compared with the destructive new culture of the modern middle-class consumer society. *Welcome Home Jacko* runs in a darker vein from the start, looking at the aimless lives of deprived West Indian teenagers in Britain, and those who try to help them without resources.

Apart from a 1972 shortened radio version of *As Time Goes By* recorded by the Trinidad Theatre Workshop, *Rum an' Coca Cola* and *Independence* were the first of Matura's plays to be staged in his homeland, in 1980 and 1981 respectively. *Meetings* was his first play to première in New York. In Trinidad Matura's writing about his own people, while earning critical acclaim, is widely consid-

Fig. 9 Mustapha Matura's *Rum an' Coca Cola* (PHOTO: Kenneth Sue Wing) Creator (Horace James) and Birdie (Learie Joseph) play for Miss Tourist in this 1980 Touchstone Production staged in Trinidad, directed by Judy Stone.

ered to be from the perspective of an outsider, and his humour to have a distinctly British quality.

By now Matura had, in 1978, co-founded the Black Theatre Co-operative. He had done stints as writer-in-residence at Kingston Polytechnic and the Factory Community Arts Centre, and he was beginning to flex his muscles as a director. In 1981 he directed the production of *Independence* in Trinidad, in 1982 in Hampstead he directed the première production of *Meetings.*

Matura's highly successful television series, *No Problem*, which started in 1983, ran on the London Weekend Television Channel into 1985. Matura also later created the television series *Black Silk*, for which he wrote the first episode.

In 1984, London's innovative Tricycle Theatre, which was eventually to appoint Matura to its board, staged the first of his West Indian adaptations, *The Playboy of the West Indies.* Based on the John Millington Synge *Playboy of the Western World*, Matura's unexpectedly popular version transposed the Irish plot to Trinidad soil, or sand. Trinidadians have long claimed an affinity with the Irish – a kinship of spirit rather than anything to do with the multiplicity of Irish priests who have educated the population. Works by several Irish playwrights have been successfully adapted for Trinidad audiences, but this was the first time an Irish play had been reworked on such a scale. Trinidadians also claim a particular affection for the works of Chekhov, which again have often been produced in the island, even Derek Walcott having staged *The Seagull.* Matura next tried his hand at an adaptation of *Three Sisters.* Artistically, *Trinidad Sisters* was less successful than *Playboy.* The transition of characters was less complete, and Vershinin, instead of taking his place in the plot as a West Indian character with West Indian concerns, remained compromisingly European.

Having strolled down the side street of adaptation, Matura returned to his own creation with renewed force, in his best work to date, on his most prestigious platform. *The Coup*, a surrealistic farce, opened at London's National Theatre in 1991, establishing the playwright once and for all on an international level. It is another of his Trinidad plays. And though the coup on which it is based is the 1970 Black Power uprising with its army mutiny, and though the play was written before the 1990 attempted overthrow of Trinidad's government by a cadre of fanatical Muslims, several of the plot elements eerily presage actual occurrences of the later coup attempt.

The same 1990 coup inspired an exceptionally swift response from an unusual number of Trinidad's playwrights, with plays such as Ronald Amoroso's *Man Overboard* (1991), Valerie Belgrave's *The Night of the Wolves* (1991), Shane Bickram's *Land of Soap and Story* (1990), Azard Daniel's *Dinner Time* (1992), Hal Greaves's *Gaps: Let the Fires Burn Again* (1991), Dorothy Jolly's *Will All The Looters Please Stand Up!* (1991), Judy Stone's *The Three Wives of Mahmoud the Saviour* (1992), and *The Estates Within* (1992) by Eden Shand, who at the time of the coup was a government minister, and one of the hostages held for five days in the parliament chamber of the Red House. Apart from *The Coup*, which has come more than twenty years later, the only works of any note to emerge from the 1970 uprising were Ronald Amoroso's *The Dry Season* (1975) and Walcott's two versions of one play, *In a Fine Castle* and *The Last*

Carnival. This neglect of such current events has been the more typical of playwrights throughout the region. The fact that, other than in Jamaica, violence on a national scale is relatively rare in today's West Indies, makes only the more surprising the scant theatrical response to these dramas when they do occur. A few plays are set against a background of violence, as Trevor Rhone's *Two Can Play* and Ginger Knight's *Whiplash* are set against Jamaica's gang warfare. In the decade since the assassination of Grenada's Prime Minister Maurice Bishop, and the subsequent American invasion, only two plays have drawn on the events: Glenville Lovell's *When the Eagle Screams* and Walcott's *To Die for Grenada*.

In Matura's *The Coup*, the President, a character based on Trinidad's charismatic father of the island's independence, Eric Williams, is being held hostage. He is wounded. The rebel soldier who guards him is young, naïve and religious. The President declares himself impressed by his guard's discipline, and painstakingly develops with him a relationship of trust, through which the captive hopes to gain his freedom.

At the same time this worldly-wise President draws on his experience in manipulating opposing international forces abroad, and his own squabbling ministers at home, in an attempt to regain control of the situation by playing his ingenuous Marxist captors off against each other. It is a process made the more simple by the dissension and distrust between these cheerfully corrupt, drug-dealing, power-hungry, ludicrously incompetent rebel officers, one of whom manages to shoot himself while aiming at the President.

The play's première director, Roger Michell, describes the main concern of the play as how a small independent nation can retain its integrity, while performing the post-colonial dance between the powers of East and West. Independence is a shallow word, an easy word, says Matura, but no country is really independent, and Marxism will not work in Trinidad. The only man who can maintain a small island nation in comparative harmony and stability of economy, is one experienced in the game of international wheeling and dealing.

Though the critics felt obliged to criticise certain aspects of Matura's 'untidy'[5] script, both they and the audiences clearly immensely enjoyed the chaotically bumbling farce. The notices also betrayed a strong undertone of awe at the length of the licence taken by the playwright in holding his mother-land's military up to ridicule. 'Were Matura himself not a distinguished son of Trinidad,' wrote Sheridan Morley in *The Herald Tribune* (24 July, 1991), 'his comedy would be branded as both patronising and racist.'

'Always irresponsibly funny,' wrote Robert Cushman in *The Independent* (21 July, 91), 'Mustapha is not getting any Matura, which is extremely good news.'

Caryl Phillips

Caryl Phillips belongs to the new generation of black British writers, though, following in Naipaul's footsteps, he is bitingly articulate in his rejection of the confines of such a label. He prefers not to be pigeonholed. Yet, though he left the West Indies when he was still too young to retain any memories of his native island, most of this writer's works, whether novels or plays or screenplays, are either set in the West Indies or retain an active West Indian connection. His immigrants in Britain are forever toying with the idea of returning home, and on occasion the idea bears its own bitter fruit, when the return becomes reality.

The first child in his family, Phillips was born in St Kitts in 1958. Later the same year his young parents emigrated with the infant Caryl to England, in search of a better life, and education for their son. As with so many West Indian arrivals at that time, Phillips's father found employment with British Rail. The family eventually settled in Leeds, in an area with a significant West Indian population. Over the next few years, three more boys were born.

Perhaps if his parents had talked to him about St Kitts, Phillips might have satiated his curiosity, lost interest in the West Indies, and settled down to being as British as his brothers. To the best of his memory, even his mother never mentioned her homeland. From the time that he became aware that he had not, like his brothers, been born in England, that his native land was a sub-tropical island he knew nothing about, Caryl Phillips developed a powerful sense of individuality. It was a sense without values of superiority or inferiority, a sense simply of being 'different'.[6] That sense became an ace up his sleeve in the difficult years ahead.

Phillips was not quite a teenager when his parents divorced. Taking the boys with her, his mother moved into a predominantly white, working-class district of Leeds. Outside the protection of the West Indian community, the family was faced with continual, overt racial hostility. At school Phillips and his brothers were the only black students. In self-defence he became a rebel and a trouble-maker. In 1973 he was sent to live with his father in Birmingham, where he stayed for nearly three years. The area in which he lived there was a little more middle class, a little less crudely hostile, but again he attended an all-white school. It was not a happy experience, and the harried boy found it a relief to return to Leeds for the holidays. 'I still come out in a rash when I think of Birmingham! I could live the rest of my life quite happily, and never go back!'[7]

These abrasive years of his adolescence are almost certainly the principal source of the undisguised anger in the writer's treatment of the gulf between the black West Indian and the white British cultures. His greater concern, however, is the gulf between individuals – between those who share the same culture, between members of the same family. The widest of these gulfs, to which he returns repeatedly, is that between the young black West Indian male and the girls, black or white, with whom he has a sexual relationship.

Against all the odds, the teenaged Phillips's natural intelligence won through. In 1976, reading English Literature on a government grant, he entered the world of privilege at Queen's College, Oxford. Rubbing shoulders with the elite was an enlightening experience for Phillips, and effectively dispelled any mystique which the ruling classes may have held for a youth reared in working-class Yorkshire. The experience, as Phillips describes it, 'demythologised British society, which made it easier to be confrontational.'[8] By inclination as much as by environmental influence, Phillips is an iconoclast, particularly where the establishment is concerned.

At Oxford Phillips discovered theatre. He directed several student productions, and joined the executive of the university's Experimental Theatre Club. In 1978 he both founded and chaired the *Observer* Oxford Festival of Theatre. The following year he became the Artistic Director for the Festival. He was also a regular contributor to *World Student Drama News*, and founded and edited the University drama magazine.

Having graduated with an honours degree, Phillips went to Edinburgh for three weeks to work with the Festival. He stayed on for a year and a half, living on the dole and writing *Strange Fruit*. This first play, which had its genesis in the Eddy Grant song, *Living on the Front Line*, had its première in Sheffield in 1980. Its success enabled Phillips to make his first pilgrimage home to St Kitt's.

In *Strange Fruit*, Phillips introduces what seems to be a comfortably familiar matriarchal West Indian family, comprising a widow with two sons in early manhood. Layer upon layer of the comfortable illusion is ripped off before our eyes, until in the end the bewildered mother loses both her sons and swallows a lethal dose of tablets. Vivien had worked herself mercilessly to ensure a reasonable middle-class life and education for her family. But both her sons accuse her of 'playing white', resent their upbringing according to Anglo-Saxon mores, and are psychologically disturbed by the consequent suppression of their roots. The younger, Errol, a character who surfaces again in *Playing Away* (1986), expresses his rebellion by 'playing black'. He has become a strike agitator for the Black Front, talks of going back to Africa, has a cache of guns for a planned bank robbery, and takes sadistic pleasure in abusing the simple-minded white schoolgirl who carries his child. More realistic, and innately more stable than Errol, it is Alvin who deals the deathblow to the family, on his return from his grandfather's funeral in the West Indies. His first trip back to his homeland had been a shattering revelation. His knowledge of himself has been founded on deception. His relatives spurn him as a traitor, he despises the island 'full of all the diseases of decolonisation'. Worse, the dead father he had been taught to respect all these years had been alive, an alcoholic failure and, like Charlie in *Moon on a Rainbow Shawl*, a cricketer who had been smartly bowled out of the West Indies team when he made a stand against racist practices.

The racial prejudice encountered by the family in England simmers under the text throughout, breaking through in several harrowing, if not altogether persuasive, passages.

Mother: 'Get off the bus, nigger and walk. I'm not taking any of you liver-lipped lot, whether you've got the money or not. Well, move on or there'll be another Notting Hill riot right here.' Did his grandfather own my grandfather? I began to walk but the houses all looked so big, they all looked the same and all the streets even seemed to have the same cars parked on them. The same little dogs played in the garden and the same hands pulled the children back from the gate as I passed. I'd walked in a circle. I was lost. I opened a gate and knocked at a door. I saw the

> curtain move but I had to ask. A woman of my age opened the door except she was white. 'Excuse me please, but which is the way back to town, please?' No answer. 'Excuse me please, but . . .' She spat in my face and my stomach rushed into my mouth as I was sick. She screamed and a man ran out and punched me in the face. He dragged me out of the gate, onto the pavement, and threw me onto the grass verge. I continued to be sick. No food, just bile. Green and white slime. Then it began to snow. I'd never seen snow before but I'd always thought that when it did snow – when I did get to England and see snow – it would be the happiest moment of my life. Nature's most beautiful costume and I'd never seen it. I wet my pants and shivered.

The language of *Strange Fruit* for the most part moves with a brisk fluency. It is a careful mixture of the standard English spoken by Vivien and Alvin, the riper version spoken by Errol, the working-class dialect of his girlfriend, and the unaffected creole of Vernice, the neighbour who brings a welcome touch of humour to this otherwise oppressive tragedy. It is Vernice who reminds us of the importance of the Baptist church in giving new immigrants communal encouragement and strength for survival, a phenomenon explored in surprisingly few West Indian dramas.

Given Vivien's personal strength over the years, the final climax of her sudden collapse and suicide may seem a little too patly on cue, even allowing for the catalyst of Alvin's rejection. But for a first play *Strange Fruit* is a remarkably shrewdly constructed, intense and provocative work.

Unlike Alvin, Phillips was not disappointed in the West Indian heritage he discovered on his first visit to St Kitts. He recognised the futility of judging the one culture by the values of the other, and realised that his native island had much to offer him by way of affirmation and inspiration. He determined that, in time, he would make himself a second home there.

In 1981 Phillips was appointed Resident Dramatist at the Factory in London, and saw his first play published. His second play, *Where There is Darkness* (1982), opened a year later at the Lyric, Hammersmith. Again it shows a generation gap, and again the gulf between individuals of the same and of different races. The younger generation, represented by Remi Williams and his orphanage-bred girlfriend Sonja, is the more sure of itself, in spite of Remi's subservience to his father, Albert. It is Albert who, on the eve of his return to the West Indies after a quarter-century in England, finds himself anguished and resentful as he looks back over his life. The juxtaposition of flashbacks with the present weaves an ironic commentary, heightened by the device of using the same actress to play both Sonja and Remi's mother as a young woman, much as Derek Walcott in *Remembrance* uses one actress to play two key characters in the life of Albert Jordan.

The 1983 première of *The Shelter* also opened at the Lyric. Phillips's third piece is his most original to date, a pairing of two complementary short two-actor plays. In several respects it is a departure from his previous work, though his premises have not essentially changed. A shelter, Phillips reminds us by a quotation from a public service poster used in St Kitts, is a temporary place of

Fig. 10 Caryl Phillips's *The Shelter* (PHOTO: Ray Abbott) Irene (Kathryn Pogson) and Louis (Rudolph Walker) in a scene from the 1983 production staged at the Lyric Studio, London, directed by Jules Wright and designed by Tim Bickerton.

refuge in a disaster. It cannot be like home. The temporary refuge of *The Shelter* is the relationship between a black man and a white woman. Whatever comfort or spiritual sustenance the two may draw from each other, Phillips suggests, depends on a deviation from the norm, and rightfully has no permanent place in lives which by heredity are at too great a remove for essential understanding. In both plays it is the man who is in control of the relationship. However, in contrast with the earlier works, he is a man whose strength is gentle, and whose search is introspective. Reaching out of this quietness is a violence that makes this a more jolting piece of theatre than the earlier diatribes of Phillips's conventionally angry young blacks.

The play of the first act takes place perhaps half a century before Emancipation, at the start of the relationship. A woman from Wessex finds herself shipwrecked on a desert island, with a free black man the only other survivor. She assumes all the clichés of his inferiority, only to find that her survival depends on his superior skills. The deeper resonances in the male character, and in the conflict between the two, save this piece from all but the most superficial resemblance to James Barrie's *The Admirable Crichton* (1902). The second play looks, two hundred years later, at the end of the relationship. The woman is no longer blinkered and understands her partner better, but the pressures of society against them are still great, and for all her willingness she is unable to meet his spiritual needs.

Also in 1983 Phillips began documentary writing for television. In 1984 his *The Hope and Glory* was the BBC Play for Today, and his *The Record* appeared on Channel 4. The same year his radio play, *The Wasted Years*, which drew much of its inspiration from his teenage experiences, won the Giles Cooper Award, and was published the following year in a collection. Phillips had by now turned to the novel, winning the Malcolm X Prize with his first, the 1985 *The Final Passage*. He continued to write quite an abundance of scripts for radio and television, often on commission. Among his more noteworthy pieces for radio are the 1985 *Crossing the River*, the 1987 *Prince of Africa*, and the 1991 *Writing Fiction*. His television pieces include the 1985 *Lost in Music* and the 1986 *Playing Away*.

Ostensibly a comedy, *Playing Away* as filmed describes the experiences of a scratch West Indian team, the Brixton Conquistadors, playing a 'friendly' cricket match for Third World Week in the fictional rural English village of Sneddington. In the hands of a writer such as Sam Selvon, the promising basic concept would have flowered in gentle laughter, making its race relations commentary with good humour and telling subtlety. In the hands of Phillips and his director, Trinidadian Horace Ove, what little humour there is in *Playing Away* appears forced, and in the filmmakers' attempt to stuff too many threads of plot through the eye of a single film, the audience is bludgeoned with a shorthand of clichés and white stereotypes, of upper-class twits and lower-class rowdies, of young white women of both classes panting for sex with black men, and of young white men panting to rape a black woman. Caricature belongs to comedy, but these stereotypes are too aggressive to be funny, and they undermine the more serious purpose of this essentially bitter film. *Playing Away* comes as a disappointment after the limpidly intelligent and perceptive writing in Phillips's earlier plays and novels. It is a disappointment, too, from the director who was later responsible for the brilliantly evocative Dominican mini-series *The Orchid House*.

Following the sale of the film rights to his 1986 novel, *A State of Independence*, Phillips spent some time in Hollywood, working on the screenplay. Time lapsed on the contract, which he did not renew, but in the meantime the project had paid enough for him to build his own home in his native island, St Kitts, where he now spends what time he can. Perhaps not surprisingly, in view of his rebellious history, this film is not the only project from which Phillips has withdrawn. In 1988, for instance, he demanded the removal of his name from a production of *All Or Nothing At All*, a stage play based on the life of Billie Holliday.

Apart from this rejected effort, Phillips had no further new plays staged in the eighties, though he continues to write for the theatre. In 1991 he completed work on *Hotel Cristobel*, a play for three actors, set in a rundown old colonial hotel in the West Indies. Meantime *The Shelter* has received a number of productions, in countries as diverse as Ghana, Poland and Canada, and in New York.

When not writing, Phillips lectures and gives readings. He has taught at universities in Britain, India, Sweden, the United States and the West Indies. He is an Honorary Senior Member of the University of Kent. He has also served on the Drama Panel of the Arts Council of Great Britain, as a member of the Production Board of the British Film Institute, and as a board member of the Bush Theatre, London.

Although he avoids the label of 'Black British writer', Phillips readily acknowledges the influence in his life of such writers as, in particular, Edgar White and Mustapha Matura. Matura's *Welcome Home Jacko* opened up new ground for Phillips, as the first play to legitimise and articulate some of the dilemmas of Britain's youth of West Indian descent. He wishes Matura had continued to explore in this direction, instead of returning to, as Phillips sees it, a nostalgic view of the Caribbean. Phillips also speaks of his admiration for the mystical quality and diasporan sensibility of White's *Lament for Rastafari*, for the way the play breaks out of the restrictions of conventional naturalistic form. White's work, he feels, in its global sensibility of the connections between the survivors of black slavery – in the Caribbean, in America, in Britain, in Africa – and its use of black ritual and mythology, forms the 'prologue'[9] to a theatre that is to come.

NOTES

1 Edgar White in interview with Judy Stone, *TG*, 31 July, 1987.
2 John Wickham, 'Marcus Garvey at Frank Collymore', *S. Sun*, 12 April, 1987.
3 Mustapha Matura in interview with Judy Stone, unpublished, 1991.
4 *Ibid.*
5 Sheridan Morley, *Herald Tribune*, 24 July, 1991.
6 Caryl Phillips in interview with Judy Stone, unpublished, 1991.
7 *Ibid.*
8 *Ibid.*
9 *Ibid.*

CURTAIN CALL

The epilogue

Caryl Phillips anticipates the development of a new theatre of the black diaspora, which would incorporate the Afro-Caribbean experience. Such a theatre, however, would be geographically too wide and ethnically perhaps too narrow in scope to be termed a West Indian theatre.

But what should we, then, consider as the essential West Indian theatre? As this chapter draws back the curtains one last time, for the curtain call on this brief historical representation, and as the region's leading playwrights stand on stage before us for our review and applause, out of which currently active stream of theatre do we anticipate the development of the West Indian theatre of the future?

Can a regional theatre be comprised of the work of one man alone? Derek Walcott, as both poet and playwright, has achieved an international stature greater than that of any other writer born in the West Indies. His plays, if occasionally dramatically unwieldy, are of an intellectual and literary calibre unrivalled within the region. But for many his work is not truly representative of the region's culture; even Shakespeare's writing was not so isolated in form from that of his contemporaries. As for the playwright's own view of the matter, in his 1989 interview for *Voices of the African Diaspora* Walcott admitted that he had still not 'connected' with Boston and that his soul remained in the Caribbean. But in 1991, 13 years after he moved his base to America, Walcott had no compunction about his mature preference for recognition as a global rather than as a West Indian artist, and expressed his concern that contemporary West Indian education had excluded the world in its emphasis on regional identity. 'Real West Indian achievement will be not to have an identity,' he told a press conference in Trinidad (*TG*, 27 July, 1991).

Walcott cannot avoid a West Indian identity, and it is doubtful that he would ever really want to. Nor are national and global identities necessarily mutually exclusive. But if, for argument's sake, we agree to disqualify Walcott's classical theatre as a contender in the West Indian theatre stakes, reserving his entry for the world event, the runners that remain are the streams of realism, theatre of the people, total theatre, and theatre of ritual.

At this point it is interesting to look at the development of national theatres elsewhere, and specifically Japan. The Japanese have for centuries enjoyed three distinctive forms of national theatre, two of which – the No and the Kabuki –

are internationally recognised today. The Kabuki, like the less widely known doll theatre, is a popular theatre, and has evolved according to the demands of the box office. Stylistically fluid, often racy, violent and sensational, the Kabuki theatre represents aspects of Japanese culture that are untouched by the formal and precisely stylised No. The latter, older, form of theatre was originally an aristocratic amusement, and until after the Second World War remained primarily the theatre of the intelligentsia and the well-to-do. The No plays have a literary craftsmanship, intellectual challenge and ideological core quite lacking in the Kabuki.

The Japanese experience demonstrates that a region may be internationally recognised by more than one form of theatre unique to itself. It demonstrates that, although it is more usual for theatre to evolve out of the popular culture, by no means is this always necessarily so. It is also an example of the way most national theatres have developed, which is organically, over many generations.

The level of conscious intention on the part of many West Indian playwrights, to force-ripen a regional theatre, is possibly unparallelled in the history of world theatre. It springs from the particular circumstances of the region's experience, made more urgent by the perceived threat to regional identity from the rapid technological changes in the world today. Although, as we have seen, there are diverse views on the form such a regional theatre should take, and although there is a body of opinion that the West Indian theatre should be one of purely Afro-Caribbean roots, the larger consensus seems to be that, however it is presented, the West Indian theatre should evolve out of the region's pool of folk heritage, meaning the folk heritage of all the region's peoples.

Though both the theatre of realism and the theatre of the people mirror the region's cultural experience, ancestral as well as contemporary, neither stream has yet developed any distinctive presentational characteristics that make it uniquely West Indian, when compared with similar theatres around the western world. These two streams qualify as West Indian theatre only by virtue of the innate regional characteristics of the material: setting, themes, characters, dialogue. For many observers, such characteristics are more than adequate qualification for regional identity. And, for the foreseeable future, there will always be West Indian writers of popular drama and plays of realism. The latter in particular have an important role to perform in the enlarging of national consciousness.

However, for those who believe, with Errol Hill, that originality of form is essential for the definition of a national or regional theatre, only the two remaining streams seem likely, one or the other or in combination, to engender a distinctive West Indian theatre for future generations. These two are the stream of total theatre, with its increasingly recognised potential for creating form out of contemporary festivals, and the stream of theatre of ritual, which also draws on ancestral traditions, but with a more refined approach to form.

It may well be that, just as Japan has both the Kabuki and the No theatres, so the West Indies, too, will develop two unique theatres – the one perhaps a total theatre with a folk orientation, playing for the entertainment of the popular audience, the other a serious and more socially-conscious theatre of ritual, drawing form and symbolism from the same folk heritage, but created out of a more considered craftsmanship, and affording greater intellectual reward. The distinctive unifying West Indian element in both these theatres seems likely to be a form of role-playing within the play, at one or more levels.

The pioneering work of Errol Hill and his thesis of a Carnival theatre, with its emphasis on masquerade, point the way for both such forms. Hill himself, in the conclusion to his recently published *The Jamaican Stage 1655–1900*, foresees just such a dual development, which he describes as the streams of folk and of art theatre. 'The folk theatre enriches the art theatre, gives it validity and meaning, while the art theatre seeks to interpret folk performance, to give what is a communal, traditional form an individual and personal voice and vision.'[1]

Alwin Bully, Felix Edinborough, Roderick Walcott and Pat Cumper along with the Sistren group, are among the most notable of the region's contemporary playwrights to have moved in the direction of popular total theatre. Lennox Brown, Felix Cross, Rawle Gibbons, Earl Lovelace, Dennis Scott, Edgar White, and even Derek Walcott, are among those who have demonstrated the exciting potential range of a West Indian theatre of ritual.

NOTE

1 Errol Hill, *The Jamaican Stage 1655–1900*, University of Massachusetts Press, 1992.

SELECTED BIBLIOGRAPHY

Entries in the primary bibliography incorporate cross-references to all relevant bibliography sections 1 to 8. The first entry for each playwright gives full name, also year and country of birth, and of death, as available.

KEY TO COUNTRIES:

Ant Antigua; *Arg* Argentina; *Bah* Bahamas; *Bar* Barbados; *Bel* Belize, British Honduras; *Can* Canada; *Cay* Cayman Islands; *Col* Colombia; *Cur* Curaçao; *Dom* Dominica; *Gren* Grenada; *Gua* Guadeloupe; *Guy* Guyana, British Guiana; *Ire* Ireland; *Jam* Jamaica; *Mont* Montserrat; *Nig* Nigeria; *PR* Puerto Rico; *SC* St Croix; *Scot* Scotland; *SK* St Kitts; *SL* St Lucia; *SM* St Maarten; *ST* St Thomas; *Sur* Suriname; *SV* St Vincent; *Tob* Tobago; *Trin* Trinidad, Trinidad & Tobago; *UK* United Kingdom, England; *USA* United States of America; *WI* West Indies.

KEY TO OTHER ABBREVIATIONS (THE KEY TO PERIODICALS AND NEWSPAPERS IS LISTED IN SECTION 9):

ACTA	Association of Caribbean Theatre Artists
AFA	Annual Festival of Arts
BBC	British Broadcasting Corporation
BV	Best Village, Better Village
CanBC	Canadian Broadcasting Corporation
CBC	Caribbean Broadcasting Corporation
GBS	Guyana Broadcasting Service
GBU	Guyana Broadcasting Union
JAF	Junior Arts Festival
JBC	Jamaica Broadcasting Corporation
JF	Jamaica Festival
lc	literary competition
pc	playwriting competition
pr	production company
prem	première performance
NCC	National Cultural Council
NDF	National Drama Festival
NIFCA	National Independence Festival of Creative Arts
rec	recorded in (location, year)
RJ	Radio Jamaica
RT	Radio Trinidad
SSDF	Secondary Schools Drama Festival
TIE	Theatre Information Exchange
TTT	Trinidad & Tobago Television
tv	television
UCWI ED	University College of the West Indies Extramural Department, Mona, Jamaica, also alternative titles of this institution
UWI ESU	University of the West Indies Extramural Studies Unit, St Augustine, Trinidad, also alternative titles of this institution

A Primary bibliography

The primary bibliography, in sections 1 to 3, is greatly indebted to the research of Professor Errol Hill, in particular that published in *Bulletin of Black Theatre*, Nos. 2, 3 and 4, Washington, USA, 1972–3, and unpublished research. This bibliography is also indebted to Irma Goldstraw's *Derek Walcott: an annotated bibliography of his works, 1944–1980*, published New York, 1984.

1 PUBLISHED PLAYS

Abbensetts, Michael (*Guy*) *Sweet Talk*, 2 acts (London, 1973: Eyre Methuen; prem London, 1973).

——— see 4, also 8, *on Michael Abbensetts.*

Alladin, Mohammed Pharouk (*Trin*, 1919–80) *Brainser*, 1 act (in Alladin, *3 One-act Plays*, Trin. 1970: Alladin; prem Trin. 1945).

——— *Hosay*, 1 act (in Alladin, *3 One-act Plays*, prem Trin. 1946).

——— *The P.S.*, 1 act (in Alladin, *3 One-act Plays*, prem Trin. 1955).

Alleyne-Forte, Learie (*Trin*, 1947) *The Convention*, 1 act (Jam. 1977: *UWI Arts Review*).

——— *The Mongoose Trap*, 2 acts (extracts, Trin. 1975, 1979: Gayap; prem Jam. 1977).

——— see 2 and 8: *on Michael Abbensetts.*

Amoroso, Ronald Dunstan (*Trin*, 1935) *The Master of Carnival*, adapted from a story by Euton Jarvis, 1 act (in *Three Caribbean Plays* (ed. Hill), London, 1979: Longman Caribbean; prem Trin. 1973; first prize drama, NCClc, Trin. 1973; best original play, English-language drama festival, Caracas 1974; see 4).

——— see 2 and 4, also 8: *on Ronald Amoroso.*

Anon, *The Exile* (Jam. 1824–25; *Jamaica Journal & Kingston Chronicle*).

Anon, *I hear Jamaica*, adapted from Walt Whitman's poem, *I hear America* (Jam. c1957: Jamaica Times (Press) Ltd.).

Anon, *Jamaica – A Comedy* (Jam. 1824–25; *Jamaica Journal & Kingston Chronicle*).

Anon, *The New Jamaica* (Jam. c1946: Jamaica Welfare Ltd.).

Anon, *The Old Regime vs. the new; or, Colonial Prejudice – a farce in two acts* (Trin. 1881: *San Fernando Gazette*).

Anon, *Pelham – a drama in 5 acts*, adapted from the novel by Sir Edward Bulwer Lytton (Jam. 1847: R. J. De Cordova).

Anon, *Proverbe Creole – ca qui pas bon pour z'oies, pas bon pour canards* (Trin. 1847: *The Trinidad Spectator*).

Anon, *The Sailor's Opera, or A Trip to Jamaica* (London, 1745: printed for the author).

Anon, *A West India Scene* (Jam. 1824–25; *Jamaica Journal & Kingston Chronicle*).

Archibald, Rupert Douglas (Trin, 1919–93) *Anne-Marie*, 3 acts (Trin. 1967: UWI ESU; prem Trin. 1957; see 5).

——— *The Bamboo Clump*, 2 acts (Trin. 1967: UWI ESU; prem Trin. 1954).

——— *Defeat With Honour*, 3 acts (Trin. 1977: UWI ESU; see 5).

——— *Island Tide*, 3 acts (Trin. 1972: UWI ESU; see 5).

——— *Junction Village* (Jam. 1958: UCWI ED; in *Caribbean Plays v. 1* (ed. Hill), Jam. 1958: UCWI ED; new edition, Trin. 1967: UWI ESU; prem Trin. 1954; best play, Readers and Writers Guild, Trin. 1952; see 4).

——— *Old Maid's Tale*, 1 act (Trin. 1966: UWI ESU; see 4).

——— *The Rose Slip*, 3 acts (Trin. 1967: UWI ESU; prem Trin. 1962; Theatre Guild Foundation award, USA. 1962; see 4).

——— see 2, 3, 4, 5 and 6, also 8: *on Douglas Archibald.*

Archibald, William (*Trin*) *The Cantilevered Terrace* (New York, 1962: Samuel French; prem USA. 1957).

——— see 2 and 4, also 8: *on other playwrights.*

Arrivi, Francisco (PR) *Masquerade*, 3 acts, from *Vejigantes*, trans. Gabriel Coulthard (in *. . . a time and a season . . .* (ed. Hill), Trin. 1976: UWI ESU).

Arthur, Kevin Alan, *Violin on a Wet Horseback*, radio play (Bar. 1964: *Bim*, Vol. 10, #39, Jul–Dec).

Ashby, Osbourne (*Trin*) *The Doctor in spite of himself*, 1 act, adapted from Molière (Trin. 1966: UWI ESU; prem Trin. 1953).
——— *Sailors Ashore*, 1 act (Trin. 1966: UWI ESU).
——— see 3 Dykes, George, and . . .
Asmodeus, *The Two Governors*, duologue (in 3 parts, Jam. 1853: *The Morning Journal*).
Atkinson, Dermot (*Jam*, 1941) *The Meeting* (Jam. 1985: Atkinson).
——— see 2.
Baku, Shango (*Trin*) *One Bad Casa* (in *Baku: Three Plays of our time*, Trin. 1984: Baku Publications; prem Trin. 1986).
——— *Revo* (in *Baku: Three Plays of our time*, prem Trin. 1984; see 4).
——— *Ruby My Dear* (in *Baku: Three Plays of our time*, prem Tob. 1986).
Barker, John S. (*UK*) *Bond of Matrimony*, 1 act (Trin. 1955: UWI ESU; new edition, Trin. 1966: UWI ESU; prem Trin. 1953).
——— *Vulnerable Doubled*, 1 act (Trin. 1966: UWI ESU).
——— see 8: *on Derek Walcott, on other playwrights.*
Barraud, Fr. C. W., *Saint Thomas of Canterbury and St Elizabeth of Hungary: historical dramas*, two 5-act plays (London and New York, 1892).
Bourne, Tommy (*Guy*) *Hassa Curry, a Caribbean one act play* (Guy. 1958: Labour Advocate; prem Guy.1958).
Brathwaite, Edward Kamau (*Bar*, 1930) *Four Plays for Primary Schools*, containing *Anansi and the Dinner Drum*, *The Children's Gifts*, *The People that walk in Darkness* and *Rabbit at the Well* (London, 1964: Longman).
——— *Odale's Choice*, African adaptation of *Sophocles's Antigone* (London 1967: Evans Brothers Ltd; prem Ghana 1962; see 5).
——— see 6, 7 and 8: *general.*
Brown, Lennox (*Trin*, 1934) *The Captive*, 1 act (Can. 1966: Ottawa Little Theatre; as *Snow dark Sunday*, prem Toronto, 1965; first prize, the Karsh award and Birk's gold medal, national 1-act pc, Can. 1965).
——— *Devil Mas*, 3-act play in the cycle *Behind the Bridge* (in *Kuntu Drama* (ed. Harrison), New York, 1974: Grove Press; prem USA. 1976; see 4 and 5).
——— *Fog Drifts in the Spring*, 1-act play in the quartet *The Crystal Tree* (in Brown, *The Twilight Dinner and Other Plays*; prem New York, 1976; see 4 and 5).
——— *I have to Call My Father* (as *Jour Ouvert*, Can. 1968: Ottawa Little Theatre; in *Drama and Theatre*, Vol. 8, #2, New York, 1969–70: State University College; as *Jour Ouvert*, first prize, the Karsh award and Birk's gold medal, national 1-act pc, Can. 1968; first prize, National University Drama League competition, Can. 1969).
——— *The Meeting* (Can. 1965: Ottawa Little Theatre; in *Performing Arts in Canada*, Vol. VII, #4, Can. 1970; in Dutch translation, Holland 1972: Dutch Centre for Amateur Theatre; prem Can. 1972. second prize and Dorothy White award, national pc, Can. 1966; see 4).
——— *Summer Screen*, 1-act play in the quartet *The Crystal Tree* (in *Prism International*, Can. 1980: University of British Columbia; reading New York, 1978).
——— *The Trinity of Four*, 1 act (in *Caribbean Rhythms* (ed. Livingston), New York, 1974: Washington Square Press. prem New York, 1975).
——— *The Twilight Dinner* (in *Journal of Black Theatre*, USA. 1978: University of Illinois; in Brown, *The Twilight Dinner & Other Plays*; prem Illinois, USA. 1977; see 5).
——— *The Twilight Dinner and Other Plays*, containing *The Blood Promise of a Shopping Plaza*, *Fog Drifts in the Spring*, and *The Twilight Dinner* (Vancouver, 1981: Talonbooks).
——— see 2, 3, 4, 5 and 8: *on Felix Edinborough*, also 8: *on Lennox Brown.*
Browne, Charles (*Jam*) *Pas de Trois* (in *Three prizewinning plays of the 1966 Jamaica Festival*, Jam. 1966: Jamaica Festival Office; bronze medal, JFlc, Jam. 1966).

——— see 3.

Buenaventura, Enrique (*Col*) *Documents from Hell*; two vignettes, *The Funeral* and *The Orgy*, trans. Anthony Sampson (in . . . *a time and a season* . . . (ed. Hill), Trin. 1976: UWI ESU).

Bully, Alwin (*Dom*, 1948) *Good Morning, Miss Millie*, 1 act (in *Caribbean Plays for Playing* (ed. Noel), London, 1985: Heinemann; prem Bar. 1970).

——— *Nite Box* (mimeo Bar. 1980: TIE; prem Dom. 1977; see 5).

——— see 2, 4 and 5, also 8: *on Alwin Bully.*

Burke, Adrian (*Trin*) *Play Stick with the Devil*, 1 act (Trin. 1970: *S.A.G. 1*, Arts & the World, Vol. 1, #1).

Cambridge, Arnold A. (*Trin*) *Cockadoo* (Trin. 1967: UWI ESU; prem Trin. 1964).

——— see 2, also 8: *on other playwrights.*

Cameron, Norman E. (*Guy*) *Adoniya*, 3 acts (in Cameron, *Three Immortals*, Guy. 1953: F.A. Persick; prem Guy. 1943).

——— *Balthasar*, 5 acts (Guy. 1931: Argosy Co; prem Guy. 1931).

——— *Ebedmelech*, 3 acts (in Cameron, *Three Immortals*; prem Guy. 1952).

——— *Jamaica Joe*, 3 acts (Guy. 1962: De Souza's Printery; prem Guy. 1946).

——— *Kayssa, or Hear the Other Side*, 1 act (Guy. 1959: Adana Printing Service; prem Guy. 1959).

——— *The Price of Victory*, play in 2 parts (Guy. 1965: Labour Advocate Job Printing Department; prem Guy. 1965).

——— *Sabaco*, 3 acts (in Cameron, *Three Immortals*; prem Guy. 1947).

——— *The Trumpet*, 3 acts (Guy. 1969: Daily Chronicle Ltd.; prem Guy. 1969).

——— see 7 and 8: *general*, also 8: *on Norman Cameron.*

Campbell, George (*Jam*) *Play without scenery, a fantasy* (in *Focus Jamaica 1948* (ed. Manley), Jam. 1948: The City Printery Ltd; prem Jam. 1946).

Campbell, John (*Guy*) *Cuffy, the brazen*, 1 act (in *Writers in uniform, an anthology* (ed. Campbell), Guy. 1972: Guyana Police Force).

——— see 2.

Charles, Bertram I. A. (*Guy*) *The Alexin of our Cure*, 3 acts (Guy. 1969: Charles; prem Guy. 1969).

——— see 2.

Chevannes, Enid (*Jam*) *The Vision* (in *West Indian Plays for Schools*, Jam. 1979: Jamaica Publishing House; prem Jam. 1964; best serious play, JF, Jam. 1968).

——— see 2.

Collier, Dorothy (*Guy*) *Five Plays*, containing *Love is Blind*, *Married – yet happy*, *Marry in haste*, *Plain sailing* and *Quiverful* (Guy. 1948: Daily Chronicle Ltd.).

Collymore, Frank A. (*Bar*, 1893–) *An Evening with the Poets*, 1 act (Bar. 1945: *Bim*, Vol. 2, #5, February).

——— *Rough-on-Rats and Old Rags*, 1 act (Bar. 1943: *Bim*, Vol. 1, #3, December).

——— see also 8: *on other playwrights.*

Comma, Vivian (*Trin*) *The Case of Doris the Foolish Cook, a calypso operetta* (Trin. 1956).

Constance, Zeno (*Trin*, 1953) *Flight Through Fantasy (The Mark of the Beast)* (in Constance, *The Ritual & Flight Through Fantasy*, Trin. 1984: Jordan's Printing Service; prem Trin. 1983 SSDF; best original play, SSDF, Trin. 1983; see 4).

——— *The Ritual, or Friday Morning First Period* (in Constance, *The Ritual and Flight Through Fantasy*, in *Caribbean Plays for Playing*, (ed. Noel), London, 1985: Heinemann; prem Trin. 1978 SSDF; best original play, SSDF, Trin. 1978; see 4).

——— see 2 and 4, also 8: *on Zeno Constance.*

Cumper, Patricia (*Jam*, 1954) *The Rapist* (mimeo Bar. 1980: TIE; best new play, Jam. 1978; prem Jam. 1977).

——— see 2 and 5, also 8: *on Pat Cumper.*

Cundall, Dorothy, *Three Plays*, containing *Cousin Marta in the Judgement Seat*, *First Time go a' Kingston*, and *Hyacinth gets prosperous* (Jam. 1944: Printer's Ltd).

De Cordova, Raphael J. (Jam) *The Wit and Humour of the 70's*, six monologues

(Jam. 1939, written and performed Jam. 1859–88).
Dorant, St Clair Wesley (Bar, 1936) *Born to Live and A Moment With Fear* (mimeo Trin. 1973: Dorant).
——— *The Burning Question and Feelings* (Trin. 1978: Dorant).
——— *A Collection of Seven One-act Plays and One Sketch* (Trin. 1973: Dorant).
——— *Cry for Happiness*, 2 acts (Trin. 1986: Dorant; prem Trin. 1986).
——— *Hannah – the Domestic*, 3 acts (Trin. 1977: Dorant; prem Trin. 1977).
——— *My Son George*, 1 act (Trin. 1975: Dorant; prem Trin. 1978).
——— *Nearer to December*, 3 acts (Trin. 1975: Dorant; prem Trin. 1976).
——— *Panyard*, 2 acts (Trin. 1974: Dorant).
——— *Sleeping Dogs are Lying*, 2 acts (Trin. 1987: Dorant; prem Trin. 1988).
——— see 2, also 8: *on other playwrights.*
Douglas, Rodney (*Trin*) *Voice of the Ghetto, a play in one act* (New York, 1968; Samuel French Inc; prem New York, 1968; see 4).
Edgecombe, David (*Mont*, 1952) *Coming Home to Roost*, 2 acts (Mont. 1988: Summit Communications; prem Mont. 1978; revised, Montreal 1980; revised, SM. 1987).
——— *Strong Currents*, based on the novels *The Meeting Point* and *Storm of Fortune* by Austin Clarke (mimeo Bar. 1980: TIE; prem Nig. 1976 Festac).
——— see 2 and 5.
Ellis, Michael (*UK*) *Chameleon* (in *Black Plays* (ed. Brewster), London, 1987: Methuen; prem London, 1985).
——— see 2.
Fagon, Alfred (*Jam*, 1937–1986, UK) *Lonely Cowboy* (in *Black Plays* (ed. Brewster), London, 1987: Methuen; prem London, 1985).
——— see 2, 4 and 5.
Farrier, Francis Quamina (*Guy*,1938) *Manaka*, 1 act (Trin. 1978: UWI ESU; prem Guy. 1965; best local play, NDF, Guy. 1969; see 5).
——— *The Plight of the Wright*, 1 act (Guy. 1969: Farrier; prem Guy. 1966; best local play, NDF, Guy. 1972).
——— *The Slave and The Scroll*, 1 act (Guy. 1969: Farrier; prem Guy. 1964; see 5).
——— see 2, 4 and 5, also 8: *on Francis Quamina Farrier.*
Fatima College students and others, collective creation (*Trin*) *The Model*, mixed media play (Trin. 1978: *Kairi* 78; prem Trin. 1976; most original script, SSDF, Trin. 1976; see 4).
Fonrose, Veronica (*Trin*) *The Evil Spirit* (Trin. 1966: UWI ESU).
Forde, A. N. (*Bar*) *The Passing Cloud*, 1 act (Trin. 1966: UWI ESU).
——— see 5.
Forde-Smith, Honor, and Sistren, *Bellywoman Bangarang* (London 1986: New Beacon Books; prem Jam. 1978; gold medal, JF, Jam. 1978; first prize, mass media contest, OAS Commission of Women, Jam. 1978).
Foster, Denis (*Bar*) *The Snapper and the Doll*, 1 act (Jam. 1973: *Savacou* 7/8).
French, Stanley (*SL*, 1937) *Under a Sky of Incense* (SL. 1981: Government Printing Office; prem Jam. 1977).
——— see 2 and 5, also 8: *on other playwrights.*
Gabb, George (*Bel*) *Yellowtail, a symbolic drama in one act* (mimeo Bel. 1966: National Festival of Arts Committee; prem Bel. 1966).
Giddings, Rev. P. (*Guy*) *Quid Rides (Why do you laugh?)*, ten sketches (Guy. 1893).
Gilkes, Michael (*Guy*, 1933) *Couvade* (London 1974; Longman Caribbean; prem Guy. 1972 Carifesta).
——— see 2 and 8: *on Banyan, on other playwrights*, also 8: *on Michael Gilkes.*
Grannum, A. L. (*Guy*) *Desire in the Dust* (Guy: *Kaie*, Vol. 13, ##75–77, Guyfesta edition).
——— *Murder at Mahdia* (Guy: *Kaie*, Vol. 13, ##75–77, Guyfesta edition).
Greaves, George (*Trin*) *The Seance* (in *Vox Guyanae*, Vol. II, #2, 1956. Trin.: UWI ESU; prem Trin. 1953).
Griffith, Reginald (*Trin*) *Home on the Hills*, 1 act (Trin. 1967: International Authors Caribbean).
——— see 2, also 8: *on other playwrights.*
Hall, Henry W. (*Trin*) *Best Intentions, or*

Green Swizzle, a West Indian Comedy in three acts (Trin. 1945: Yuille's Printerie).
——— see 2.
Hamilton, Bruce (*Bar*) *Gettysburg Night*, 1 act (Bar. 1954: *Bim*, Vol. 6, #21, December).
——— *Smarty out-smarted, a perversion of the court scene from Shakespeare's Merchant of Venice*, 1 act (Bar. 1949; *Bim*, Vol. 3, #11, December).
Harris, William (*Guy*) *Aunt Esther* (mimeo Bar. 1981: TIE).
Hart, Lloyd (*Trin*) *Dorothy's Triumph* (Trin.: UWI ESU; prem Trin. 1955).
Hastings, Michael (*UK*, 1938) *Carnival War*, 2-act farce (in Hastings, *Carnival War, Midnite at the Starlite*, UK, 1981: Penguin; prem London, 1979).
——— *Gloo Joo*, (in Hastings; *Three Plays*, UK: Penguin; prem London, 1978; best comedy, *Evening Standard*, London, 1978; see 4).
——— see also 8: *on other playwrights.*
Henry, John (*UK*) *School for Soldiers, or The Deserter*, 4-act drama on military life in the colonies (Jam. c1783; prem Jam. 1781).
Hill, Errol Gaston (*Trin*, 1921) *Broken Melody* (Trin. 1966: UWI ESU; prem Jam. 1954).
——— *Dance Bongo, a fantasy in one act* (in *Caribbean Plays*, Vol. 2, (ed. Hill), Trin. 1965: UWI ESU; in *Caribbean literature: an anthology* (ed. Coulthard), London, 1966: University of London Press; Trin. 1972: UWI ESU; prem Trin. 1965; see 4).
——— *Dilemma* (Trin. 1966: UWI ESU; prem Jam. 1953).
——— *Man Better Man* (in *The Yale School of Drama presents* (ed. Gassner), New York, 1964: Dutton and Co; in *Plays for Today* (ed. Hill), UK, 1985: Longman Caribbean; prem Jam. 1957; revised with music, New Haven, USA. 1960; Theatre Guild Foundation award, USA. 1962).
——— *Oily Portraits*, 1 act (Trin. 1966: UWI ESU; as *Brittle and the city fathers*, prem Trin. 1947).
——— *The Ping Pong* (Jam. 1958: UCWI ED; in *Caribbean Plays*, Vol. 1, (ed. Hill), Jam. 1958: UCWI ED; Trin. 1966: UWI ESU; in *Carray!* (ed. Lee Wah), London 1977: Macmillan Caribbean; prem Trin. 1953; see 5).
——— *Square Peg*, 1 act (Trin. 1966: UWI ESU; prem Trin. 1949).
——— *Strictly Matrimony*, 1 act (Trin. 1966: UWI ESU; in *Black Drama Anthology* (ed. King and Milner), New York, 1972: New American Library; in *Whodunits, Farces and Fantasies*, USA. 1976: Hayden Books; prem Connecticut, USA. 1960; see 4).
——— *Wey Wey* (Jam. 1958: UCWI ED; Trin. 1966: UWI ESU; prem Trin. 1957; see 4).
——— see 2, 3, 7 and 8: *on Derek Walcott, general*, also 8: *on Errol Hill.*
Hill, Frank (*Jam*) *Betrayal*, 1 act (in *Focus Jamaica 1943* (ed. Manley), Jam. 1943: The City Printery Ltd.).
——— see 2.
Hill, Sonne (*Trin*) *Wild Cat Strike*, 1 act (Trin. 1952: Imperial Printing Company; prem Trin. 1985).
——— see 2.
Hillary, Samuel (*Jam*) *Chippy* (in *Caribbean Plays*, v. 2 (ed. Hill), Trin. 1965: UWI ESU; new edition, Trin. 1966: UWI ESU; prem Jam. 1961).
——— *Departure in the Dark* (Trin.: UWI ESU; prem Jam. 1960).
——— see 2 and 3, also 8: *on other playwrights.*
Hinkson, Anthony (*Bar*, 1943) *Teacher Teach 'er*, 3 acts (mimeo Bar. 1981: TIE; prem Bar. 1976).
——— see 2 and 4, also 8: *on Anthony Hinkson.*
Hippolyte, Kendel (*SL*) *The Drum-Maker* (in *Caribbean Plays for Playing* (ed. Noel), London, 1985: Heinemann).
Hopkinson, Clement Allan Slade (*Guy*, 1934–1993, Can) *The Onliest Fisherman*, 1 act (Trin. 1967: UWI ESU; prem Jam. c1960).
——— see 2 and 4, also 8: *on Slade Hopkinson.*
Hosein, F.E.M. (*Trin*) *Hyarima and the Saints, a Miracle Play and Pageant of Santa Rosa* (Trin. 1931: Hosein;

Pleasantville, Trin. 1976: Unique Services; prem Trin. 1931).

Inniss, Lewis Osborne, *Carmelita, the Belle of San José*, 4 acts (in Inniss, *Trinidad and Trinidadians*, Trin. 1910; prem Trin. 1897).

——— *Mura, the Cacique's Daughter*, 5 acts (in Inniss, *Trinidad and Trinidadians*, prem Trin. 1898).

Jairam, A. (*Trin*) *Jekkidy's Illness*, 1 act (Trin. 1971: *DE*).

James, Alexander MacGregor, *A Soul's Sacrifice, a domestic drama in one act of six scenes* (in *Four Stories and a Drama of Old*, prizewinner, Institute of Jamaica lc; prem Jam. 1926).

——— see 6.

James, Cyril Lionel Robert (*Trin*, 1901–1989, *UK*) *The Black Jacobins* (in . . . *a time and a season* . . . (ed. Hill), Trin. 1976: UWI ESU; as *Toussaint L'Ouverture*, prem London, 1936; revised as *The Black Jacobins*, Nig. 1967; see 4).

——— see 2, 6 and 7, also 8: *on C.L.R. James.*

John, Errol (*Trin*, 1924–1988, *UK*) *Force Majeure, The Dispossessed, Hasta Luego* (London, 1967: Faber & Faber).

——— *Moon on a Rainbow Shawl*, 3 acts (London, 1958: Faber and Faber; in *The Observer Plays*, London, 1958: Faber & Faber; new edition, London, 1963: Faber & Faber; New York, 1963: Grove Press; prem London, 1959; first prize, *Observer* playwrights' competition, London, 1957; see 3, 4, 5).

——— *The Tout*, 1 act (Trin. 1966; UWI ESU; prem Trin. 1949: see 4).

——— see 2, 3 and 4, also 8: *on Errol John.*

John, Ronald (*Trin*, 1947) *Cocktails at Seven* (extract, Trin. 1983: *TTR* Literary Supplement; prem Trin. 1983).

——— *The Dream*, 1 act (Trin. 1990: *New Voices*, Vol. XVIII, ##35/36; first prize, Tradewinds Collective competition, Trin. 1987; developed as *Welcome Home, Cousin Raphael*; see 2).

——— *Queen of the Boxboard Shacks* (Trin. 1988: *New Voices*; reading Trin. 1980; first prize, NCCpc, Trin. 1979).

——— see 2, 3, 5 and 8: *on Derek Walcott*, also 8: *on Ronald John.*

Joseph, Edward Lanza (*Scot*, –1840, *Trin*) *Adele, or the Dubious Widow*, 1 act (Trin. 1832: Mills and Stewart; prem Trin. 1832).

——— *Martial Law in Trinidad*, 2 act musical farce (Trin. 1833: Mills and Stewart; prem Trin. 1832).

——— *Past and Present*, 2 acts (Trin. 1833: Mills and Stewart; prem Trin. 1832).

——— see 2.

Joseph, Lorraine, *Simeon's Return* (mimeo Bar. 1981: TIE; prem SC. c1980).

Kissoon, Freddie (*Trin*, 1930) *Calabash Alley*, radio serial adapted (Trin. 1973: Hi-Grade Printery; prem Trin. 1972; see 4, 5).

——— *Mamaguy* (Trin.: UWI ESU; prem Trin. 1961; see 4).

——— *Zingay* (Trin. 1966: UWI ESU; prem Trin. 1961; second prize, Arts Festival, Trin. 1965; see 4).

——— see 2, 4 and 5, also 8: *on Freddie Kissoon.*

Kissoon, Freddie, and others, *Common Entrance*, 1 act (Trin. 1970: Granderson Bros; prem Trin. 1966; see 4).

Knox Summer School, *Sleepy Valley* (Trin. 1955: UWI ESU; prem Jam. 1952; see 4).

Labastide, Neville (*Trin*) *Cousin Adriana Coming* (Trin.: UWI ESU; prem Trin. 1963).

——— *One for the Road* (in *Caribbean Plays* v. 2 (ed. Hill), Trin. 1965: UWI ESU; Trin. 1966: UWI ESU; prem Trin. 1965; first prize, Arts Festival, Trin. 1965).

——— *Sans Everything* (Trin.: UWI ESU).

——— *Something Old, Something New* (Trin.: UWI ESU; prem Trin. 1961; see 4).

——— *Voice of the People* (Trin. 1978: UWI ESU).

——— see 2 and 4, also 8: *on other playwrights.*

Labatt, Philip Cohen, *Next of Kin, or Who is the Heir?*, 1 act farce (in *Selec-*

tions from miscellaneous posthumous works... (Jam. 1855: R.J.de Cordova).

Lee, Easton (*Jam*) *Tarshan Lace and Velvet*, 1 act (in *West Indian Plays for Schools*, Jam. 1979: Jamaica Publishing House; prem Jam. 1969).

——— see 2 and 4.

Lindo, Archie (*Jam*, –1990) *Under the Skin, a Jamaican play in three acts* (in *Bronze short stories, articles, a poem and a play*, Mandeville, Jam. 1944: College Press; prem Jam. 1943).

——— see 2, 6 and 8: *on Basil Dawkins, on Michael Reckord.*

Loague, Mark (*Jam*) *Reeds in the Wind* (in *Three Prizewinning Plays of the Jamaica Festival*, mimeo Jam. c1966: Jamaica Festival Office; silver medal, JFlc, Jam. 1966).

——— see 3.

Lovelace, Earl (*Trin*, 1935) *The Dragon Can't Dance*, novel adapted (in *Black Plays: Two* (ed. Brewster), London, 1989: Methuen; staged readings novel, Trin. 1978; workshopped Connecticut USA. 1984; prem Trin. 1986).

——— *Jestina's Calypso* (in Lovelace, *Jestina's Calypso and Other Plays*, London, 1984: Heinemann; prem Trin. 1978; best original play, NDF, Trin. 1985).

——— *My Name is Village* (in Lovelace, *Jestina's Calypso and Other Plays*; prem Trin. 1976 BV).

——— *The New Hardware Store* (in Lovelace; *Jestina's Calypso and Other Plays*; prem Trin. 1980).

——— see 2, 4, 6 and 8: *on Derek Walcott, general*, also 8: *on Earl Lovelace.*

Lyndersay, Dexter, and Umaru Ladan, *Shaihu Umar*, adapted from the novel by Alhaji Sir Abubakar Tafawa Balewa (in Hausa, Nig. 1974: Northern Nigerian Publishing Co.; in English, London, 1975: Longman; in Hausa, prem Nig. 1972; in English, Nig. 1982).

——— see 2 and 4, also 8: *on other playwrights.*

Lyons, Greta (*Jam*) *Out of many, one people – a pageant in ten episodes* (Jam. 1962: Government Printer).

——— see 2.

MacDermot, Thomas Henry (*Jam*, 1870–1933) *San Gloria*, 3 acts (in *Redcam: Orange Valley and other poems*, Jam. 1951: The Pioneer Press).

——— see 6, Redcam, Tom

Mais, Roger (*Jam*, 1905–1955) *The First Sacrifice* (in *Focus Jamaica 1956* (ed. Manley), Jam. 1956: UWI).

——— *George William Gordon* (in . . . *a time and a season* . . . (ed. Hill); Trin. 1976: UWI ESU).

——— *The Potter's Field* (in *Public Opinion*, Jam. 23 December, 1950).

——— see 2, 3 and 6, also 8: *on other playwrights.*

Maraj, Ralph (*Trin*, 1949) *The Missing File*, 5 acts (Trin. c1982: Rahaman Printery; prem Trin. 1982; best original play, NDF, Trin. 1982).

——— see 2 and 4, also 8: *on Ralph Maraj.*

Martin, Sidney (*Guy*) *'Enery Swankey: a tragedy in three acts* (in Martin, *Humour, etc.*, Guy.: F.A. Persick).

——— *Mrs Farrington's third husband* (Guy. 1916).

Masson, George H. (*Trin*) *The Social Barnacle* (Trin. 1903: *The Trinidad Miscellany*, Vol. 1, #12, December; prem Trin. 1903).

Matura, Mustapha (*Trin*, 1939) *As Time Goes By* (in Matura, *'as time goes by' and 'black pieces'*, London, 1972: Calder and Boyars; prem Edinburgh 1971; George Devine award, London, 1971; John Whiting award, London, 1971; see 5).

——— *The Coup* (New York, 1993; *American Theatre*, Vol. 9, #10, February; prem London, 1991).

——— *Dialogue* (in Matura, *'as time goes by' and 'black pieces'*; prem London, 1970).

——— *Independence*, 3 acts (in Matura, *Play Mas, Independence and Meetings*, London, 1982: Methuen; prem London, 1979).

——— *Indian* (in Matura, *'as time goes by' and 'black pieces'*; prem London, 1970).

——— *Meetings*, 1 act (in Matura, *Play Mas, Independence and Meetings*, New

York: Samuel French; prem New York, 1981).

——— *My Enemy* (in Matura, *'as time goes by' and 'black pieces'*).

——— *Nice*, monologue (in Matura, *Nice, Rum an' Coca Cola and Welcome Home Jacko*, London, 1980: Eyre Methuen; prem London, 1973; see 4).

——— *Party* (in Matura *'as time goes by' and 'black pieces'*; prem London, 1970).

——— *Play Mas*, 2 acts (in Matura, *Play Mas, Independence and Meetings*; prem London, 1974; most promising playwright, *Evening Standard*, London, 1974).

——— *Playboy of the West Indies*, adaptation of John Millington Synge's *Playboy of the Western World* (New York, 1989: Broadway Play Publishing; prem Oxford, UK, 1984; with music by André Tanker, New York, 1993; see 4).

——— *Rum an' Coca Cola* (in Matura, *Nice, Rum an' Coca Cola and Welcome Home Jacko*; prem London, 1976).

——— *Welcome Home Jacko* (in Matura, *Nice, Rum an' Coca Cola and Welcome Home Jacko*; prem London, 1979).

——— see 2 and 4, also 8: *on Mustapha Matura*.

Maxwell, Marina Omowale (*Trin*, 1934) *Play Mas* (in *Play Mas and Hounsi Kanzo*, mimeo: Maxwell; prem Jam. 1968; first prize, San Fernando Drama Guild pc, Trin. 1972).

——— *Hounsi Kanzo* (in *Play Mas and Hounsi Kanzo*).

McDonald, Ian (*Trin*, 1933) *The Tramping Man*, 1 act (in . . . *a time and a season* . . . (ed. Hill), Trin. 1976: UWI ESU; prem Guy. 1969).

——— see 4 and 6.

McField, Frank (*Cay*) *Time Longer dan Rope* (Cay. 1980: McField).

McTair, Roger (*Trin*, 1943) *The Chain*, 1 act (Trin. 1979: UWI ESU; 2nd prize, pc, Can. 1973).

——— see 2.

Mittelholzer, Edgar (*Guy*, 1909–1965, *UK*) *Before the Curtain Rose*, 1 act (Bar. 1959: *Bim*, Vol. 7, #28, Jan–June).

——— *Climate of Eden*, a 2-act dramatisation by Moss Hart of the novel *Shadows Move Among Them* (New York, 1953: Random House; prem New York, 1952).

——— *The Sub-Committee*, sketch (Bar. 1951: *Bim*, Vol. 4, #15, December).

——— see 3 and 6, also 7.

Moore, Ruth (*USA*) *Bones* (mimeo Bar. 1980: TIE; prem SC. 1977).

Nanton, Ronald (*Trin*) *Baucumar – the Carib*, 1 act (Trin. 1982: Ministry of Education).

Noel, Dennis O. (*Trin*) *Tears in the Gayelle* (in *Carray!* (ed. Lee Wah), London, 1977: Macmillan Caribbean; prem Trin. 1972 SSDF; best original play, SSDF, Trin. 1972).

O'Marde, Dorbrene E. (*Ant*, 1950) *Bad Play* (mimeo Ant. 1971: Harambee Open-Air Theatre; prem Ant. 1971).

——— *Fly on the Wall* (mimeo Ant. 1980: Harambee Open-Air Theatre; prem Ant. 1977; play of the year, Southwell Publishing Company, Ant. 1977; see 5).

——— *For Real*, 3 acts (mimeo Ant. 1976: Harambee Open-Air Theatre; prem Ant. 1976).

——— *Homecoming* (mimeo Ant. 1971: Harambee Open-Air Theatre; prem Ant. 1971).

——— *The Minister's Daughter*, musical comedy adapted from a novel by Obi Egbuna (mimeo Ant. 1980: Harambee Open-Air Theatre; prem Ant. 1980).

——— *Tangled Web* (mimeo Ant. 1979: Harambee Open-Air Theatre; prem Ant. 1979; see 5).

O'Marde, Dorbrene, and Shelly Tobitt, *We Nativity* (mimeo Ant. 1982: Harambee Open-Air Theatre; prem Ant. 1982).

Ogilvie, W.G. (*Jam*) *One Dollar for Dog* (in *West Indian Plays for Schools*, Vol. 1 (ed. Wilson), Jam. 1979: Jamaica Publishing House; prem Jam. 1964; bronze medal, JF, Jam. 1968).

——— see 2 and 3.

Phillips, Caryl (*SK*, 1958) *The Shelter* (UK. 1984; Amber Lane Press; prem London, 1983).
——— *Strange Fruit* (UK. 1981: Amber Lane Press; prem Sheffield UK. 1980).
——— *Where there is Darkness* (UK. 1982: Amber Lane Press; prem London, 1982).
——— see 4 and 6, also 8: *on Caryl Phillips.*
Pilgrim, Frank (*Guy*, –1989) *Miriamy*, 3 acts (Guy. 1963: B.G. Lithographic; Trin.: UWI ESU; mimeo Bar. 1981: TIE; prem Guy. 1962; see 4).
——— *Skeleton at the Party*, 1 act (London, 1954: Dean and Sons; prem London 1954).
——— see 2 and 5, also 8: *on Frank Pilgrim.*
Pinnock, Winsome (*UK*, 1961) *A Rock in Water* (in *Black Plays: Two* (ed. Brewster), London, 1989: Methuen; prem London, 1989).
——— see 2 and 4.
Price, B., *The First Anniversary of the Independence of Trinidad and Tobago*, written for Forest Reserve E.C. School, Texaco (Trin. 1964: PNM Publishing Company).
Quintero, Hector (*Cuba*) *The Booby Prize*, from *El Premio Flaco*, trans. Quintero and others (in *. . . a time and a season . . .* (ed. Hill), Trin. 1976: UWI ESU; prem Cuba, 1965; first prize, Cuban Theatre Center of the International Theatre Institute, Havana 1965; first prize, the Latinamerican Theatre Institute, Caracas, 1965; first prize, the International Theatre Institute, Paris 1968).
Reckord, Barry (*Jam*) *Skyvers*, or *I-man* (in *New English Dramatists 9*, London, 1966: Penguin Books; prem London, 1963).
——— see 2, 4 and 5, also 8: *on Barry Reckord.*
Reckord, Michael (*Jam*, 1943) *Sufferers*, two short plays, comprising *IYC: If You Cry* and *Man with Machete* ('Man with Machete' in *Exploring English in the Caribbean*, London, 1985: Macmillan; prem Jam. 1979; four awards, UWI Tallawah Drama Festival, Jam. 1979).
——— see 2, 3, 4, 5 and 8: *on Basil Dawkins, Ginger Knight*, also 8: *on Michael Reckord.*
Reckord, Michael and Drama Group, *Decisions* (Jam. 1977: Jamaica Drama Festival Committee; prem Jam. 1977).
Redhead, Wilfred (*Gren*, 1909) *Canaree and Pot* (Trin. 1966: UWI ESU; see 4).
——— *Goose and Gander* (in *Caribbean Plays*, Vol. 2 (ed. Hill), Trin. 1965: UWI ESU; Trin. 1966: UWI ESU; in *Carray!* (ed. Lee Wah), London 1977: Macmillan Caribbean; prem? Jam. 1957)
——— *Hoist Your Flag*, 1 act (Trin. 1966: UWI ESU; see 4).
——— *Now for Now* (in Redhead, *Three Comic Sketches*, prem? Gren. 1952).
——— *Three Comic Sketches*, containing *Just in Time*, *Now for Now* and *Thief from Thief* (Trin. 1956: UWI ESU; new edition, Trin. 1966: UWI ESU).
——— see also 8: *on other playwrights.*
Rhone, Trevor (*Jam*, 1940) *Old Story Time* (in Rhone, *Old Story Time and Smile Orange*, London, 1981: Longman; prem Nassau, 1979; most promising playwright, *Guardian*, London, 1984).
——— *School's Out* (in Rhone, *Two Can Play and School's Out*, London, 1986: Longman; prem Jam. 1975).
——— *Smile Orange* (in Rhone, *Old Story Time and Smile Orange*; prem Jam. 1971; see 4).
——— *Two Can Play* (Kentucky, USA. 1983?: Kentucky Education Television. in Rhone; *Two Can Play and School's Out*; prem Jam. 1982; as *Jeu pour Deux*, Paris 1985; best Jamaican play, Jamaican Cultural Development Committee national award, Jam. 1982; see 4).
——— see 2, 3 and 4, also 8: *on Trevor Rhone.*
Roach, Eric Morton (*Tob*, 1904–1974) *Belle Fanto*, 3 acts (Trin. 1967: UWI ESU; prem Trin. 1966; as musical adapted by Alwin Bully, Dom. 1982; see 5).
——— *Calabash of Blood*, 3 acts (Trin. 1971: UWI ESU; prem? Trin. 1975; see 5).

——— *Letter from Leonora*, 1 act (Trin. 1968: UWI ESU).
——— see 2, 3, 4 and 8: various, also 8: *on Eric Roach.*
Roberts, W. Adolphe (*Jam*) *Uncle Bernard*, 3 acts (in *Public Opinion Christmas Annual*, Jam. 1955; second prize, Jamaica 300 lc, Jam. 1955).
——— see 6.
Robinson, Carey (*Jam*) *The Runaway*, 2 acts (Trin.: UWI ESU; prem Jam. 1960).
——— see 2.
Rudet, Jacqueline (*UK*) *Basin* (in *Black Plays* (ed. Brewster), London, 1987: Methuen; prem London, 1985).
——— see 2.
Russell, A. D., *The Cave of Conscience*, with incidental music by Alice Pashley (Trin?.1927).
Sadeek, Sheik M. (*Guy*) *Fish Koker*, 1 act (Guy. 1967: Sadeek; prem Guy. 1965; Jagan gold medal, Guy. 1961).
——— *He*, 1 act (Guy. 1967: Sadeek).
——— *Namaste*, 1 act (Guy. 1965: Richard Noble; prem Guy. 1964; first prize, Theatre Guild pc, Guy. 1960; first prize, National History and Culture Council inter-school drama competition, Guy. 1964).
——— *Porkknockers, a Humour in One Act and One Scene* (Guy. 1959: *KOA*, #25, prem?, Guy. 1962).
——— *Savannah's Edge*, 1 act (Guy. 1968: Sadeek).
——— see 2 and 3.
Scott, Dennis (*Jam*, 1939–1991, *USA*) *The Crime of Anabel Campbell*, 1 act (in *Caribbean Plays for Playing* (ed. Noel), London, 1985: Heinemann; prem Jam. 1970).
——— *Dog* (mimeo Bar. 1981: TIE; prem Jam. 1978).
——— *Echo in the Bone* (in *Plays for Today* (ed. Hill), UK. 1985: Longman Caribbean; prem Jam. 1974).
——— *Sir Gawain and the Green Knight*, medieval poem adapted, commissioned by the O'Neill Center's National Theatre of the Deaf (USA. 1978: Anchorage Press in association NTD; prem Washington, USA. 1977).
——— *Terminus*, 1 act (Trin. 1966: UWI ESU; prem Trin. 1962; see 4).
——— see 2, 3, 6 and 8: *on Michael Reckord*, also 8: *on Dennis Scott.*
Sealy, John Clifford (*Trin*, –1991) *The Professor* (in *Caribbean Plays* Vol. 2 (ed. Hill), Trin. 1965: UWI ESU; Trin. 1966: UWI ESU; prem Trin. 1963; revised USA. 1966; see 4).
——— see 2 and 6, also 8: *on other playwrights.*
Selvon, Samuel Dickson (*Trin*, 1923) *El Dorado, West One*, radio series adapted by Susheila Nasta (Leeds, UK. 1988: Peepal Tree Press; see 5).
——— *Highway in the Sun and Other Plays* (ed. Susheila Nasta, Leeds, UK. 1989: Peepal Tree Press; see 5).
——— see 2, 3, 4, 5 and 6, also 8: *on Sam Selvon.*
Shand, Eden (*Trin*, 1939) *The Estates Within, A Docu-Drama* on the 1990 Muslim coup (Trin. 1992: Caribras Ltd).
——— see 3 and 8: *on Zeno Constance, Lester Efebo Wilkinson.*
Sistren (*Jam*, 1977), collective creation, *Bellywoman Bangarang*, see Forde-Smith, Honor, and . . .
——— *QPH* (London, 1986: New Beacon Books; prem Jam. 1981; national theatre critics award, Jam. 1981).
——— see 2 and 6, also 8: *on Sistren.*
Smith, M.G. (*Jam*) *The Leader* (in *Focus Jamaica 1943* (ed. Manley), Jam. 1943: The City Printery Ltd.).
Spense, Eulalie (*WI*) *Undertow* (in *Black Theatre USA: Forty-five Plays by Black Americans, 1847–1974* (ed. Hatch) New York, 1974: The Free Press; written 1929).
Spraggs, John Duff, *Malcolm and Alonzo, or The Secret Murder of Leonard, a tragedy in five acts* (Jam. 1880: George Henderson and Co.).
Springer, Eintou Pearl (*Trin*, 1944) *Anansi, Nansi, Anansi*, with music by David Rudder (London, 1991: Karia Press; prem Birmingham, UK. 1989 Kajoyo Festival of African Peoples Theatre).
——— see 2 and 8: *on Raoul Pantin*, also 8: *on C.L.R. James, on other playwrights.*

Stuart, Gladys (*Bel*) *Dog and Iguana* (in Lee Wah, *Carray!*, London, 1977; Macmillan Caribbean).

Sturgeon, Felix (*SV*) *Old Woman's Point, a legend of St Vincent* (SV: Reliance Printery; prem SV).

Teytaud, Anton C., *Sarah and Addie, 15 short West Indian plays* (SC. c1974: Crown? Printery Co.).

Tidd, Lincoln; *Small Matters* (Trin. 1966: UWI ESU; prem Trin. 1954).

Tipling, Carmen (*Jam*) *During lunch-time they had the revolution*, 1 act (in *Jamaica Journal*, Vol. 3, #3, Jam. 1969; bronze medal, JFlc, Jam. 1969).

——— see 2 and 3.

Towne, Richard (–1732) Prologue and epilogue to Crowne's *Sir Courtley Nice* (in *Caribbeana* (ed. Keimer), London, 1741; prem Bar. 1729).

Townshend, Mitzie (*Jam*, –1972) *Heavens Above* (in *West Indian Plays for Schools* (ed. Wilson), Jam. 1979: Jamaica Publishing House; high commendation, JFlc, Jam. 1965).

——— *The Job*, 1 act (in *Three prize-winning plays of the 1966 Jamaica Festival*, Jam. 1966: Jamaica Festival Office; silver medal, JF, Jam. 1966).

——— see 2.

Van Sertima, Sheila (*Guy*) *It's Brickdam!*, 1 act (in *KOA*, Vol. 8, #25, Guy. 1959)

——— see 5.

Veecock, Walter J. (*Guy*) *Phileron: the tragedy of a poet soul*, verse drama (Edinburgh 1896).

Von Kotzebue, August Friedrich Ferdinand (*Germany*) *The Negro Slave, a dramatic historical piece in three acts*, set in Jamaica (in English translation, London, 1796: printed for T. Cordell Jr, W. Davies and J. Edwards).

W.M.E.P., *Abassa, a play* (in *Abassa: a play, and poetical pieces*, Georgetown, 1883).

Waite-Smith, Cicely (Howland) (*Jam*) *Africa Sling Shot*, 1 act (Jam. 1958: UCWI ED; in *Caribbean Plays*, v. 1 (ed. Hill), Jam. 1958: UCWI ED; new edition, Trin. 1966: UWI ESU; in *Carray!* (ed. Lee Wah), London, 1977; Macmillan Caribbean; prem Jam. 1957).

——— *The Creatures*, 1 act (Trin. 1954: UWI ESU; in *Focus Jamaica 1956* (ed. Manley), Jam. 1956: UWI; new edition, Trin. 1966: UWI ESU; prem Trin. 1954).

——— *Grandfather is Dying* (in *Focus Jamaica 1943* (ed. Manley), Jam. 1943: City Printery).

——— *The Impossible Situation*, 1 act (Jam. 1957; Trin. 1966: UWI ESU).

——— *Return to Paradise*, 1 act (Trin. 1966: UWI ESU).

——— *Storm Signal*, radio play (in *Focus Jamaica 1948* (ed. Manley), Jam. 1948: The City Printery; see 5).

——— *Uncle Robert*, 3 acts (Jam. 1957: UCWI ED; new edition, Trin. 1967: UWI ESU; prem Jam. 1957).

——— *The Wild Horse*, 1 act (in *Public Opinion Christmas Annual 1955*, Jam. 1955; first prize, Jamaica 300 lc).

——— see 2, 3 and 6, also 8: *on other playwrights.*

Walcott, Derek Alton (*SL*, 1930) *Beef, No Chicken*, 2 acts (in Walcott, *Three Plays*, New York, 1986: Farrar, Straus and Giroux; prem Trin. 1981).

——— *A Branch of the Blue Nile*, 2 acts (in Walcott, *Three Plays*; prem Bar. 1983; revised Trin. 1985).

——— *The Charlatan, a Carnival comedy* (mimeo Trin.: UWI ESU; prem Jam. 1954; revised Trin. 1973; revised with music by Galt MacDermot, Los Angeles, USA. 1974).

——— *Dream on Monkey Mountain* (in Walcott, *Dream on Monkey Mountain and other plays*, New York, 1970: Farrar, Straus and Giroux; London, 1972: Jonathan Cape; prem Toronto, 1967; Obie award for most distinguished play off-Broadway, New York, 1971; see 4).

——— *Drums and Colours*, commissioned for the 1958 opening of the First Federal Parliament of the West Indies (Jam. 1961: *Caribbean Quarterly*, Vol. 7, ##1–2; as *Drums of Revolt*, extract on the Haitian Revolution in *West Indian Plays for Schools*, Vol. 1 (ed. Wilson), Jam. 1979: Jamaica Publishing House; prem Trin. 1958).

——— *Harry Dernier, a play for radio*

production (Bar. 1952: Advocate; adapted for stage, prem Jam. 1952; see 5).

——— *Henri Christophe, a chronicle* (mimeo 1949; Bar. 1950: Advocate; Trin.: UWI ESU; prem SL. 1950; see 5).

——— *In a Fine Castle* (extract Trin. 1971: *DE*, 24 October; prem Jam. 1970; see 5).

——— *Ione, a play with music* (Jam. 1957: UCWI ED; prem Jam. 1957).

——— *The Joker of Seville*, adaptation of Tirso De Molina's *El Burlador de Sevilla*, with music by Galt MacDermot (in Walcott, *The Joker of Seville and O Babylon*! New York, 1978: Farrar, Straus and Giroux; London, 1979: Jonathan Cape; prem Trin. 1974; record Trin. c1975: Semp Studios Ltd; cassette Trin. 1987).

——— *Jourmard, or a Comedy until the Last Minute*, 1 act (mimeo Trin; UWI ESU; prem SL. 1959; see 4, 5).

——— *The Last Carnival*, 2 acts (in Walcott, *Three Plays*; prem Trin. 1982; in Swedish, Stockholm 1992).

——— *Malcochon, or Six in the Rain* (as *Malcauchon*, in *Caribbean Plays*, Vol. 2 (ed. Hill), Trin. 1965: UWI ESU; as *Malcauchon*, Trin. 1966: UWI ESU; in Walcott, *Dream on Monkey Mountain and other plays*; prem SL. 1959; see 4).

——— *Marie Laveau*, with music by Galt MacDermot (extracts Trin. 1979: *TTR*, Christmas; prem ST. 1979).

——— *O Babylon!*, with music by Galt MacDermot (in Walcott, *The Joker of Seville and O Babylon!*; prem Trin. 1976).

——— *The Odyssey* (New York and Canada, 1993: Farrar, Straus and Giroux/HarperCollins Canada; prem London, 1992).

——— *Pantomime* (in Walcott, *Remembrance and Pantomime*, New York, 1980: Farrar, Straus and Giroux; prem Trin. 1978; see 4, 5).

——— *Remembrance* (in Walcott, *Remembrance and Pantomime*; prem SC. 1977).

——— *Robin and Andrea* (extract Bar. 1950: *Bim*, Vol. 4, #13, December).

——— *The Sea at Dauphin* (Trin. 1954: UWI ESU; Jam. 1958: UCWI ED; in *5 West Indian Plays*, Jam. 1958: UCWI ED; in *Caribbean Plays* Vol. 1 (ed. Hill), Jam. 1958: UCWI ED; in *Tamarack Review 14*, 1960; Trin. 1966: UWI ESU; in Walcott, *Dream on Monkey Mountain and other plays*; prem Trin. 1954; see 4, 5).

——— *The Snow Queen*, tv play (extract Trin. 1977: *People*, April).

——— *Ti-Jean and His Brothers* (in Walcott, *Dream on Monkey Mountain and other plays*; as a picture book adapted, hand-lettered and illustrated by Stuart Hahn, Trin. 1984: Paria Publishing; in *Plays for Today* (ed. Hill), UK. 1985: Longman Caribbean; as a ballet, prem SL. 1957; prem Trin. 1958; revised with music by André Tanker, Trin. 1970; revised New York, 1972; as *Ti-Jean Epi Fwe-y*, adapted by Alwin Bully, Dom. 1982; in Italian, Italy, 1993; see 4, 5).

——— see 2, 3, 4, 5, 6, 7 and 8: various, also 8: *on Derek Walcott.*

Walcott, Roderick (*SL*, 1930) *The Banjo Man* (in . . . *a time and a season* . . . (ed. Hill), Trin. 1976: UWI ESU; banned SL. 1958; prem SL. 1971).

——— *Cul-de-Sac*, 1 act (extracts in *A Shapely Fire*, Oakville, Can.: Mosaic Press; prem Can. 1981).

——— *Flight of Sparrows*, 1 act (Trin. 1966: UWI ESU; prem SL. 1958; best 1-act drama, JF, Jam. 1958).

——— *The Harrowing of Benjy*, 1 act (Jam. 1958: UCWI ED; Trin. 1966: UWI ESU; prem SL. 1956; best West Ind. comedy, JF, Jam. 1957; see 4, 5).

——— *Malfinis, or The Heart of a Child* (Trin. 1967: UWI ESU; in *Caribbean Rhythms* (ed. Livingstone), New York, 1974: Washington Square Press; prem SL. 1960; best long serious play, SL. 1960).

——— *Shrove Tuesday March*, 1 act (Trin. 1966: UWI ESU; prem SL. 1956; see 5).

——— *The Trouble with Albino Joe* (Trin. 1966: UWI ESU).

——— see 2, 3 and 8: *general.*

Walker, William (*Bar*, 1680–1726) *Marry or Do Worse* (London, c1710; prem London, 1703).
——— see 2.
White, Edgar (*Mont*, 1947) *The Boot Dance*, 2 acts (in White, *Redemption Song and other plays*, London and New York, 1985: Marion Boyars; prem London, 1984).
——— *The Burghers of Calais* (in White, *Underground, Four Plays*, New York, 1970; William Morrow; prem New York).
——— *Crucificado, two plays* (New York, 1973: William Morrow; prem? New York, 1978).
——— *Fun in Lethe* (in White, *Underground, Four Plays*; prem New York).
——— *I, Marcus Garvey (and the captivity of Babylon)* (in *Black Heroes* (ed. Hill), New York, 1989: Applause Theatre Book Publishers; prem Bar. 1987).
——— *Lament for Rastafari*, 3 acts (in White, *Lament for Rastafari and other Plays*, London and New York, 1983; Marion Boyars; prem New York, 1975).
——— *Les Femmes Noirs*, 11 scenes (in White, *Redemption Song and other plays*; prem New York, 1976; Ethnic Arts award, London 1981.
——— *Like Them That Dream (Children of Ogun)*, 3 acts (in White, *Lament for Rastafari and other Plays*; prem London, 1983).
——— *The Mummer's Play* (in White, *Underground, Four Plays*; prem New York, 1965).
——— *The Nine Night* (in White, *The Nine Night and Ritual By Water*, London, 1984: Methuen; prem London, 1983).
——— *Redemption Song* (in White, *Redemption Song and other plays*; prem London, 1984).
——— *Ritual By Water*, 3 acts (in White, *The Nine Night and Ritual By Water*; prem London, 1983).
——— *Trinity – The Long and Cheerful Road to Slavery* (in White, *Lament for Rastafari and other Plays*; prem London, 1982).
——— *The Wonderfull Yeare* (in White, *Underground, Four Plays*; prem, New York).
——— see 2, 3 and 6, also 8: *on Edgar White.*
Wilkinson, Lester Efebo (*Trin*) *To Confirm St Peter* (under pseud. Mwalimu Efebo, Trin. 1976, *Kairi 76*; first prize drama, NCCpc, Trin. 1976; see 4, 5).
——— see 2, 4 and 5, also 8: *on Lester Efebo Wilkinson.*
Wilson, Jeanne (*Jam*) *A Legacy for Isabel*, 1 act (London, 1967: Evans Bros; prem Jam. 1969).
——— *A Question of Loyalty*, 1 act (in *West Indian Plays for Schools* (ed. Wilson), Jam. 1979: Jamaica Publishing House; prem Jam. 1966 SSDF).
——— *No Justice in October*, 1 act (London, 1967: Evans Bros; prem Jam. 1961 SSDF).
——— see 2, 3 and 8: *on Michael Reckord, other playwrights.*
Wynter, Sylvia (*Jam*) *Maskarade*, Jonkunnu play (in *West Indian Plays for Schools*, Jam. 1979: Jamaica Publishing House; see 4).
——— see 2 and 6.
Young, Colville N. (*Bel*) *Riding Haas* (in *Carray!* (ed. Lee Wah), London, 1977; Macmillan Caribbean; prem Bel. c1969).
——— see 2.
Zephaniah, Benjamin (*UK*, 1958) *Job Rocking* (in *Black Plays: Two* (ed. Brewster), London, 1989: Methuen; prem London, 1987).
——— see 2, 5 and 6.

2 UNPUBLISHED PLAYS PRODUCED (WITH LOCATION AND YEAR OF PREMIÈRE PERFORMANCE).

Aaron, Philbert (*Dom*) 'Seven Seas' (Dom. 1989).
——— 'The Swine and the Pearl' (Dom. 1990).
Abhiram, Brent (*Trin*) 'Drugs' (Trin. 1984).
Adams, Aubrey (*Trin*) 'All Ah We is One, a West Indian Musical Comedy' (Trin. 1966).
——— 'Ambakaila' (Trin. 1972).

——— 'The Best of Everything', musical comedy, (Trin. 1961).
——— 'Carnival Madness, a Carnival Musical Comedy' (Trin. 1988).
——— 'The Dragon and the Dove', Carnival musical (Trin. 1992).
——— 'From Columbus to Calypso', musical comedy (Trin. 1992).
——— 'From Trinidad with Love', musical (Trin. 1965).
——— 'The Last Time I saw Paris', revue (Trin. 1958).
——— 'Piccadilly' (Trin. 1964).
——— see also 8: *on other playwrights.*
Adams, Aubrey and Nelson Caton, 'Bamboula, a carnival spectacle' (Trin. 1966).
Adams, Nambulumbu (*Ant*) 'Hidden Secret' (Ant. 1986).
Ahye, Richard (*Trin*) 'Behind the Wall' (Trin. 1992).
Aimable, Innocent (*SL*) 'The Statue' (SL. 1990).
Alleyne, Lystra (*Trin*) 'The Missing Ball' (Trin. 1965).
Alleyne-Forte, Learie, 'And Life Goes On – a West Indian play in six episodes' (as 'Bits and Pieces', Jam. 1976).
——— 'A Man for the Cocktail Crowd', 2 acts (Jam. 1976).
——— 'Newsmonger' (Trin. 1973).
——— 'Our Guest Mr Bocas', 1 act (Trin. 1970; prizewinner, Drama Guild pc, Trin. 1970).
——— see 1 and 8: *on Michael Abbensetts.*
American Company of Comedians, The, 'The Kingston Privateer', adaptation of 'Pillon: The Liverpool Prize' (Jam. 1781).
Amoroso, Ronald, 'Blood and Steel', folk musical (Trin. 1981 BV).
——— 'Blood Clot', 1 act (under pseud. Jim Grant, Trin. 1970).
——— 'The Brothers Five', 1 act (Trin. 1971; see 4).
——— 'Dragon's Mouth', 1 act (Trin. 1972).
——— 'The Dry Season' (Trin. 1975; as folk musical, Trin. 1989 BV).
——— 'The Finals', folk musical (Trin. 1983 BV).
——— 'Kid Sharkey', folk musical (Trin. 1988 BV).
——— 'Man Overboard', folk musical on the 1990 Muslim coup (Trin. 1991 BV).
——— 'Midnight Johnny', folk musical (Trin. 1980 BV).
——— 'Pan Rising', folk musical (Trin. 1992 BV).
——— 'Papa Brock', folk musical (Trin. 1984 BV).
——— 'The Probe' (Trin. 1980; workshopped ST. 1981: first Caribbean playwrights' conference).
——— 'Sangre Grande by Two', 2 acts (Trin. 1986; as folk musical 'The Man from Sangre Grande', Trin. 1986 BV; see 4).
——— 'The Stormers', folk musical (Trin. 1973 BV).
——— 'The Strike', folk musical (Trin. 1979 BV).
——— 'Tief from Tief', folk musical (Trin. 1985 BV).
——— 'Warrior Bois', folk musical (Trin. 1982 BV).
——— see 1 and 4, also 8: *on Ronald Amoroso.*
Anderson, Balfour (*Jam*) 'Hustler' (Jam. 1991).
——— 'King Root', Jamaican pantomime, with music by Noel Dexter (Jam. 1987).
——— 'Married Life' (Jam. 1989).
——— 'Rip Off' (Jam. 1990).
——— 'Worries' (Jam. 1989).
Anon: 'Alexander Hamilton of Nevis and the USA, a biographical sketch for presentation by the Charlestown Extra-Mural Club on Tuesday, 15 January, 1957' (Nevis.1957).
Anon: 'The Demerara Hobby', skit (Guy. 1817).
Anon: 'The Violet of Icacos' (Trin. 1897).
Applewhaite, Charles, 'Carenage O', musical (Trin. 1992 BV).
Applewhaite, Claudia, Ava Hutchinson-Agard and Sharon Marriott, as CAMA, 'De Maul Story, a musical portrayal of the prevalence of drugs in our society' (Trin. 1983; see 4).
——— 'Sons and Mothers' (Trin. 1984).
——— see also 8: *on other playwrights.*
Archibald, Charles Henry (*Trin*) 'A Surmise of Murder', 3 acts (Trin. 1978).

Archibald, Douglas, 'Back of Beyond', 2 acts (Trin. 1984).

——— see 1, 3, 4, 5 and 6, also 8: *on Douglas Archibald.*

Archibald, William, 'Carib Song, a musical play of the West Indies' (New York, 1945).

——— 'The Crystal Heart' (London, 1957).

——— 'Far Harbour, an opera' (New York, 1948).

——— 'The Innocents', adapted from the Henry James story 'The Turn of the Screw' (New York, 1950; see 4).

——— 'Portrait of a Lady', adapted from the novel by Henry James (New York, 1954).

——— see 1.

Arthur, Dwight (*Trin*, 1957) 'Behind Closed Doors, a domestic tragedy', third play in the trilogy 'Touch Me' (Trin. 1987).

——— 'Strangers', first play in the trilogy 'Touch Me' (Trin. 1985).

——— see 4, also 8: *on Dwight Arthur.*

Ashani, Stafford (Harrison) (*Jam*, 1953) 'Anancy and Unsung Heroes Out West', 12-act musical (Jam. 1978; gold medal, JFlc, Jam. 1977).

——— 'Foreign Mind', 2 acts (Jam. 1989).

——— 'Ma Ma Black Sheep', 1-act play based on letters from Patricka Dallas to her mother (New York, 1986).

——— 'Maskaradors', Jonkunnu musical (Jam. 1977).

——— 'The Quickie', 2 acts (Jam. 1975).

Ashani, Stafford, Melin Van Peebles and Kendrew Lascelles, 'Reggae', musical (New York, 1980).

Atkinson, Dermot, 'Shades' (Jam. 1990).

——— see 1.

Baisden, James (*Trin*) 'Fantasy Island' (Trin. 1987 SSDF).

——— 'The Last Bus', Christmas comedy (Trin. 1981).

——— 'Pay de Devil' (Trin. 1986).

——— 'The Pulley' (Trin. 1986 SSDF; best original play, SSDF, Trin. 1986).

——— 'Residue', musical (Trin. 1977).

Baksh, Walid (*Trin*) 'Christmas Spirits' (Trin. 1991).

Balgobin, Basil (*Guy*) 'Asra, a political play of India' (Guy. 1945).

Bansilal, Paul (*Trin*) 'Eternal Destination' (Trin. 1990).

Baptiste, David (*Trin*) 'The Good, The Bad and the Ugly', folk musical (Trin. 1992 BV; best script, BV Trophy Competition, Trin. 1992).

Barbados Writers' Workshop, 'God's Daughter' (Bar. 1974).

——— 'Rape' (Bar. 1976).

Bartels, Elisha (*Trin*, 1977) 'Cat. Tic. Tic. Tic . . . – a play about the environment', dramatised staging of a children's carnival band (Trin. 1991).

——— 'Meme Chose', dramatised staging of a children's carnival band (Trin. 1990).

——— 'Tryangles, Wreckedangles and Squeers', dramatised staging of a children's carnival band (Trin. 1992).

Bartels, Elisha, Keisha Barnett, and others, 'Dragon, Knight and the Pits and Gladys', dramatised staging of a children's carnival band (Trin. 1989).

Bascom, Harold A. (*Guy*, 1951) 'The Barrel', 2 acts (Guy. 1987).

——— 'Book and Key for Stolen U$', 2 acts (Guy. 1991).

——— 'The Butterline', 2 acts (Linden Guy. 1987; revised Guy. 1988).

——— 'Crisis Spell', 2 acts (Guy. 1989).

——— 'Family Budget', 2 acts (Guy. 1989).

——— 'Family Cutlash', 2 acts (Guy. 1990).

——— 'Home for Christmas', 2 acts (Guy. 1989).

——— 'Ol' Firewood', 2 acts (Guy. 1991).

——— 'TV Alley', 2 acts (Guy. 1988; best new Guyanese play, National Academy of Performing Arts, Guy. 1988).

——— 'TV Alley 2', 2 acts (Guy. 1988).

——— 'Tessa Real Girl and The Old Fool', 2 acts (Guy. 1990).

——— 'The Visa Wedding' (Guy. 1989; best Guyanese play, Theatre Arts award, Guy. 1989).

——— see 6, also 8: *on Harold Bascom.*

Bastien, Elliot (*Trin*, 1941) 'A Nancy Story, the inner journey of Jeun

Payee' (Toronto, 1971; revised Trin. 1982).
——— see also 8: *on Elliot Bastien.*
Beale, Paul (*Jam*) 'Unda Mi Nose 2' (Jam. 1991).
Beckles, Rodney (*Trin*) 'Choices' (Trin. 1986 SSDF).
——— 'Family Ties', 1 act (Trin. 1983 SSDF).
——— 'The King Nose Best' (Trin. 1987; best original script, SSDF, Trin. 1987).
Belgrave, Valerie (*Trin*) 'The Night of the Wolves', on the 1990 Muslim coup (Trin. 1991).
——— see 6, also 8: *on other playwrights.*
Bell, Vera (*Jam*) 'Easter Lilies', see Bennett-Coverly, Louise, and Extramural playmaking group.
——— 'Soliday and the Wicked Bird', Jamaican pantomime (Jam. 1943).
Bennett-Coverly, Louise (*Jam*, 1919) 'Anancy and Beeny Bud', Jamaican pantomime, with music and lyrics by Robert Lightbourne (Jam. 1956).
——— 'Anancy and Pandora', Jamaican pantomime, with music by Manny Ramirez (Jam. 1955).
——— 'Bredda Buck', see Fowler, Greta, and . . .
——— 'Busha Bluebeard', Jamaican pantomime, with music and lyrics by Barbara Ferland, additional lyrics by Orford St John (Jam. 1957).
——— 'Buzz Bizznizz' (Jam. 1956).
——— 'Queenie's Daughter', see Fowler, Greta, and . . .
——— see also 8: *on Louise Bennett.*
Bennett-Coverly, Louise and Extramural playmaking group, 'Easter Lilies', based on a story by Vera Bell (Jam. 1957).
Bennett-Coverly, Louise and Noel Vaz, 'Bluebeard and Brer Anancy', Jamaican pantomime, with lyrics by Orford St John, Louise Bennett and Barbara Ferland, music by Barbara Ferland (Jam. 1949).
Beouth, Joseph (*Trin*) 'Mysterious Ways', 1 act (Trin. 1985).
Berkeley, Wayne and John Mendes, 'Queen of the Bands', carnival musical, with music by John Mendes (Trin. 1987).
——— see also 8: *on other playwrights.*
Bickram, Richard (Ainsley) (*Trin*) 'Contemptuous Love' (Trin. 1988).
——— 'Phenomenal Purgatory' (Trin. 1989).
——— 'The Presidential Palace' (Trin. 1988).
——— 'Sentimental Honour' (Trin. 1989).
Bickram, Shane (*Trin*, 1959–93) 'The Coffin' (Trin. 1987; see 4).
——— 'Graves and Skeletons' (Trin. 1991).
——— 'Land of Soap and Story', on the 1990 Muslim coup (Trin. 1990).
——— 'The Old Woman who Lived in a Shoe' (Trin. 1992 SSDF).
——— 'The Poui Tree' (Trin. 1987; see 4).
——— 'The Pundit's House', based on Lorca, 'The House of Bernarda Alba' (Trin. 1991).
——— 'Say No to Eggnog', musical comedy (Trin. 1992 SSDF; best new playscript, SSDF, Trin. 1992).
——— 'Soap of the Day', Carnival street theatre (Trin. 1992).
——— 'Sunil's Baby ('The Pundit's House 2') (Trin. 1992).
——— 'The Unfinished Symphony' (Trin. 1985 SSDF).
——— 'The Way We Were,' Carnival street theatre (Trin. 1991).
——— 'Who Killed Pablo Sierra?' (Trin. 1989)
——— see also 8: *on other playwrights.*
Bim and Bam (pseuds. Ed Lewis and Aston Wynter, respectively) 'The Black Witch of Trout Hall' (Jam. 1964).
——— 'De Burial of A.B.' (Jam. 1943).
——— 'The Execution of Ras I' (Jam. 1963).
——— 'Extravaganza, a comical mock trial' (Jam. 1947).
——— 'Mr Ghost goes to Town' (Jam. 1948).
——— 'Rygin's Ghost' (Jam. 1949).
Bishop Anstey High School Drama Group, collective creation, 'Who Thief Me Vase' (Trin. 1957)
Bissundyal, Churumanie (*Guy*, 1950)

'From Ganges To Demerara' (York University, Can. 1988).
——— 'Migrants Error' (Guy. 1989).
Bobb, Kenetta (*Tob*) 'Unbroken Chains' (Tob. 1992 Heritage Festival).
Bonner, Vincent (*Jam*) 'Big Business' (Jam. 1968).
Boodhu, Kenneth (*Trin*) 'Market Wedding' (Trin. 1991).
——— 'School Project', 1 act (Trin. 1985).
Bourne, Kate (*Trin*) 'Love or Indulgence' (Trin. 1940).
——— 'Whose Captive', 5 acts (Trin).
——— 'You Shall Not' (Trin. 1939).
——— see 3.
Bourne, Luther (*Bar*) 'Bye Bye Papa' (SK. c1956).
——— 'The Waiting Room', skit (Bar. 1960).
——— see 5.
Bovell, Brian, Michael Buffong, Victor Romero Evans, Robbie Gee, Roger Griffiths, Gary MacDonald, Eddie Nestor, and Sylvester Williams, 'Pinchy Kobi and the Seven Duppies', with music by Felix Cross (London, 1992).
Brathwaite, Rudolph (*Bar*) 'Wild Emotions' (London, 1964).
——— see 4.
Brown, Lennox, 'A Ballet Behind the Bridge' (New York, 1972; see 5).
——— 'The Conversion', 2 acts (reading New York, 1974).
——— 'Prodigal in Black Stone', 2 acts (Connecticut, USA. 1972; prizewinner, Eugene O'Neill National Memorial pc, Connecticut, USA. 1972).
——— 'The Sisterhood of a Spring Night', 2 acts (New York, 1975).
——— 'The Throne in an Autumn Room', 1-act play in the quartet 'The Crystal Tree' (London, 1979; see 4. and 5).
——— 'The Winti Train', 2 acts (Hartford, USA. 1974; humanitarian art award, Hartford Connecticut American-West Indian Association, Hartford, USA. 1974).
——— see 1, 3, 4, 5 and 8: *on Felix Edinborough*, also 8: *on Lennox Brown*.
Brown, Patrick (*Jam*) 'Guava Jelly' (Jam. 1989).
——— 'Yard '89' (Jam. 1989).
——— 'Yard '90' (Jam. 1990).
Bully, Alwin, 'The Almost Forgotten Gift', children's play with music by Pearle Christian (Dom. 1982).
——— 'Folk Nativity', with music by Alwin Bully and Einstar LeBlanc (Dom. 1976).
——— 'Green Gold', stage adaptation of the radio serial (Dom. 1979; see 5).
——— 'McB', 4 acts (staged reading Jam. 1990).
——— 'Pelee', 2 acts (workshopped ST. 1981: first Caribbean playwrights' conference).
——— 'Pio-Pio', Carnival folk musical (Dom. 1978).
——— 'The Ruler', 3-act adaptation of G.C.H. Thomas's novel *The Ruler in Hiroona* (Dom. 1976).
——— 'Streak', 3-act musical (Dom. 1975).
——— see 1, 4 and 5, also 8: *on Alwin Bully.*
Bully, Alwin and Flora Spencer, 'Dedder and the Devil', 1 act (Bar. 1970).
Burke, Joy and Grace Diljohn, 'Boykin', 1 act (Trin. 1971 SSDF).
Cambridge, Arnold, 'Because of Lizzie, a West Indian play in one act' (Trin. 1967).
——— 'Jezebel, a West Indian play in one act' (Trin. 1967).
——— 'Sunflower', 3-act comedy with dance (Trin. 1966).
——— 'Thag Pundit, a West Indian play in one act' (Trin. 1967).
——— see 1, also 8: *on other playwrights.*
Cameron, Margaret Cheer (*UK*) 'A West Indian Lady's Arrival in London' (Jam. 1781).
Campbell, John, 'Come Back to Melda' (Guy. 1963).
——— 'Dhanwattie', 1 scene (Guy. 1966; second prize, Theatre Guild pc, Guy. 1966).
——— see 1.
Campbell, Parnell (*SV*) 'A-coming Home', 1 act (SV. 1969).
Camps, Helen (*Ire*) 'Ad', see Israel, Roger and . . .
——— 'Cinderama', see Edinborough, Felix and . . .

——— 'Rampanalgas Sunrise', see Israel, Roger and . . .
——— 'Snokone and the Seven Dwens', see Lyndersay, Mark and . . .
——— see also 8: *on other playwrights.*
Carew, Jan (*Guy*, 1925) 'Gentlemen, be seated' (Toronto, 1967).
——— 'University of Hunger', 3 acts (Guy. 1966; see 4, 5).
——— see 4, 5 and 6, also 8: *on Jan Carew.*
Caribbean Popular Theatre Exchange, collective creation, 'Ida Revolt Inna Jonkunnu Stylee', street theatre (Jam. 1985).
Carter, Peter (*Jam*) 'Come farm with me' (Jam. 1968).
Carter, Steve (*USA*, 1929) 'Eden', tribute to Marcus Garvey (New York?).
——— 'Nevis Mountain Dew' (New York, 1980).
——— 'Pecong', calypso musical, with music by Felix Cross (Chicago, USA).
Caudeiron, Daniel (*Dom*) 'Speak, Brother, Speak', folk musical (Dom. 1972).
Caudeiron, Mabel (*Dom*) 'How Johnny Break de Spell' (Dom).
——— 'Vernie' (Dom).
Cendrecourt, Esme (*Guy*) 'Grandpapa's Pride', 3 acts (Guy. 1942).
——— 'Romance of the Kaiteur', 3 acts (Guy. 1931).
——— 'Unmasked', 3 acts (Guy. 1944).
——— see 3.
Challenger, Veronica (*Ant*) 'Notlimah, a fantasy for children' (Hamilton, Can. 1971)
Chapman, Esther (*UK*) 'The West Indian', play in verse showing the historical development of the West Indies (Jam. 1936).
Charles, Bertram, 'Another Man', 2 acts (Guy. 1968).
——— 'Another Place, Somewhere', 2 acts (Guy. 1969).
——— 'The End of the Affair', 2 acts (Guy. 1968).
——— 'It Tolls Not for Thee', 1 act (Guy. 1970).
——— 'The Lost Husband', 1 act (Guy. 1971).
——— 'Of the Human Predicament', 1 act (Guy. 1971).
——— 'The Pains of Abortion', 1 act (Guy. 1967).
——— 'A Virgin Child', 2 acts (Guy. 1967).
——— 'Within our Narrow Walls', 5 acts (Guy. 1971)
——— see 1.
Charles, Rupert (*Ant*) 'Changing Times' (Ant. 1986).
——— 'The Landlord' (Ant. 1989).
Chase, Sam (*Guy*) 'The Collapsible Bridegroom' (Guy.).
——— 'The Dreamer and the Jar' (Guy.).
——— 'Gentlemen, the King' (Guy.).
——— 'Guardroom Jitters' (Guy.).
——— 'The Mare and the Bonds' (Guy.).
——— 'The Ruler and the Boo-boo Man' (Guy.).
——— see also 8: *on Sam Chase.*
Chattoram, Puran (*Guy*) 'A Bridle for the tongue: a sketch' (Guy. 1964).
Chen, William Laurence, 'Willi' (*Trin*) 'A Change of Heart', tv play adapted (Trin. 1986 SSDF; see 3).
——— 'Freedom Road' (Trin. 1985. workshopped first national playwrights' conference, Trin. 1985; see 4).
——— 'One Love' (Trin. 1989).
——— 'Tainted Blood' (Trin. 1987; see 4).
——— see 3, also 8: *on Willi Chen*
Cherrie, Errol S. (*Trin*) 'Among the Young', 3-act musical comedy (Trin. 1943).
——— 'Chamber in the Moon', 2 acts (Trin. 1944).
——— 'Of Life and Love', musical comedy (Trin. 1942).
Cherrie, Ralph (*Trin*) 'Music and Memories' (Trin. 1944).
Chevannes, Enid, 'The Root of all Evil', 1 act (Jam. 1956; best West Indian comedy, Drama Festival, Jam. 1956).
——— 'Superstition, a comedy' (Jam. 1960; best West Indian farce, Drama Festival, Jam. 1960; silver medal, JF, Jam. 1966).
——— 'Turned Tables' (Jam. 1957; high commendation, Drama Festival, Jam. 1957).
——— see 1.
Christian, Pearl, 'Song of the Cicero',

musical for year of environment (Dom. 1989).

Clarke, A.M. (*Trin*) 'Green Magic, a verse drama' (Trin. 1978).

——— 'The House of Love, a verse drama' (Trin. 1967).

——— 'Road to Glory, a verse drama' (Trin. 1964).

Clarke, Katie (*Jam*) 'Jamaican Moon', 3 acts (Jam. 1969; silver medal, JFlc, Jam. 1966).

Cobham, Cecil (*Trin*) 'The False Honeymoon, a comedy' (Trin. 1924).

——— 'The Fate of a Convent Girl' (Trin).

——— 'Retribution, a drama' (Trin. c1928).

——— 'Sold, but not lost, a tragedy' (Trin. c1926).

——— 'Suspicious Husband, a melodrama' (Trin. c1929).

Coley, Nolma (*Jam*) 'The Wedding' (Jam. 1991).

Collymore, George (*Trin*) 'Forever Yours Calvin' (San Fernando, Trin. 1992; special prize, National Petroleum pc, Trin. 1991).

Concanen, Matthew (*Jam*) 'Wexford Wells', comedy (Jam. 1732–1744).

Constable, John (*UK*) 'Black Mas', Anansi Carnival play (London, 1984).

Constance, Zeno (*Trin*, 1953) 'Adventure African' (Trin. 1986 SSDF).

——— 'The Agouti's Tale' (Trin. 1987 SSDF).

——— 'The Cinderella Syndrome' (Trin. 1986 JAF).

——— 'Death Row – (the nightmare continues . . .)' (Trin. 1984 JAF; best original play, SSDF, Trin. 1984; see 4).

——— 'Dorothy's Challenge – A Celebration' (Trin. 1985 JAF; best original play, SSDF, Trin. 1985).

——— 'Dragonslayer Dream' (Trin. 1990 SSDF; best original play, SSDF, Trin. 1990).

——— 'Duelling Voices' (Trin. 1984 SSDF; first prize, Ministry of Culture pc, Trin. 1985; see 4).

——— 'Ja Ja's Choice, or the bus is coming' (Trin. 1976).

——— 'King of the Jews' (Trin. 1975).

——— 'My Father's Child' (Trin. 1985; best original play, SSDF, Trin. 1985; see 4).

——— 'Patricia, a love story' (Trin. 1986 SSDF; as BV folk musical, Trin. 1989; best original play, SSDF, Trin. 1986).

——— 'The Pay Back' (Trin. 1976).

——— 'Reflections of a Nightmare' (Trin. 1979 SSDF; best original play, SSDF, Trin. 1982).

——— 'Swansong' (Trin. 1991 SSDF).

——— see 1 and 4, also 8: *on Zeno Constance*.

Constance, Zeno and Shrivinas Mohip, 'We Own Son' (Trin. 1973 SSDF).

Cooke, Aston and Barbara Gloudon, 'River Mumma and the Golden Table', Jamaican pantomime, with lyrics by Noel Dexter and Barbara Gloudon, music by Noel Dexter (Jam. 1986).

Coombs, Anthony (*Trin*) 'Success: The Destructive Version', folk musical (Trin. 1992 BV).

Corsbie, Ken (*Guy*, 1930) 'All Ah We', dramatisation of Caribbean writings (Guy. 1974).

——— 'Dem Two', dramatisation of Caribbean writings (Guy. 1973).

——— 'He One', dramatisation of Caribbean writings (Guy. 1973).

——— 'Jack and Jill' (workshopped Jam. 1988; ACTA).

——— 'My Name is Slave, a shamefully abbreviated documentary of the social and political history of the colony of British Guiana now called Guyana' (for Republic Celebration, Guy. 1970).

——— 'The Riddle of the Brain Coral, a Bajan musical comedy adventure' (Bar. 1986).

——— see 7 and 8: *on Frank Pilgrim, Derek Walcott*, also 8: *on other playwrights*.

Corsbie, Ken and Julia Senor, 'Barbados, Barbados', musical comedy (Bar. 1982).

Crawford, Thorma (*Trin*) 'The Man Who Lit Up the World', with music by Geraldine Connor (London, 1991).

Cross, Felix (*Trin*, 1953) 'Blues for Railton', novel adapted (London, 1985).

——— 'Glory!', musical (Derby, UK,

1990; first prize, London Weekend Television Plays on Stage competition, London, 1988).
——— 'Mass Carib', theatrical experience in music and dance commissioned by the Albany Empire, with book lyrics and music by Cross (London, 1987).
——— see 3, also 8: *on Felix Cross.*
Crosskill, Daryl and Jackson Martin, 'It's not my fault, Baby', based on an idea by Trevor Rhone (Jam. 1967).
Cummings, Mayeul (*Trin*) 'No Second Chance' (Trin. 1989 BV).
Cumper, Patricia, 'Benny's Song', an adaptation of Shakespeare's *Romeo and Juliet* (reading Jam. 1991).
——— 'Coming of Age' (reading Jam. 1984; Prime Minister's best play award, Jam. 1983).
——— 'Flame Heart', see Lewis, Maureen Warner and . . .
——— 'Jane and Louisa will soon come home', based on the novel by Erna Brodber (Jam. 1990).
——— 'Quadrille', in celebration of the 150th anniversary of 'Full Free' (workshopped Jam. 1988; ACTA).
——— see 1 and 5, also 8: *on Pat Cumper.*
Cumper, Pat and the Groundwork Theatre Company, 'De Fallen Angel and De Devil Concubine' (Jam. 1987).
Cumper, Pat and Lloyd Reckord, 'Sipplesilver', Jamaican pantomime, from a scenario by Dennis Scott, with music and lyrics by Noel Dexter (Jam. 1984).
Cumper, Pat and Sistren, 'Buss Out', based on Sistren's book *Lionheart Gal* (Jam. 1989).
Cunningham, Chris (*Jam*) 'Baby Father' (Jam. 1990).
Cupid, Jim and Loubelle Estrada, 'Creed and Race', on the Canboulay and Hosay riots (Trin. 1986 SSDF).
——— 'Water . . . . Fire . . . . ' (Trin. 1987 JAF).
Cupidon, Ernest M. (*Jam*) 'Jamaica Bandits', 3-act comedy, adapted from a short story by H.G. De Lisser (Jam. 1931).
——— 'Jane's Career', adapted from the novel by H.G. De Lisser (Jam. 1933).
——— 'Mock Trial of Dr Yen' (Jam. 1940).
——— 'Peaka Pow Mock Trial' (Jam. 1933).
——— 'Superior People' (Jam. 1936).
——— 'Susan Proudleigh', adapted from the novel by H.G. De Lisser (Jam. 1930).
D'Abreu, Gerard (*Trin*) 'Intelligent Life Reported In Trinidad' (Trin. 1992).
——— 'Out of the Corner of My Eye' (Trin. 1991).
D'Oliveira, Damon (*Trin*, 1964), Denyse Karn (*Can*), Jane Luk (*Can*), Alisa Palmer (*Can*), Dawn Roach (*Trin*) and Guillermo Verdecchia (*Arg*) 'I.D.' (Toronto, 1989; best new play for young audiences, Chalmers award, Canada 1989; best theatre production for young audiences, Dora award, Canada, 1989–90).
D'Olivieira, Evadne (*Guy*) 'The Scattered Jewels' (Guy. 1969).
Daniel, Azard (*Trin*) 'Dinner Time', short play set during the 1990 Muslim coup (Trin. 1992).
——— 'Full Credit for you', skit (Trin. 1983).
——— 'Kissandra', adapted from the novel by Michael Als (Trin. 1988).
——— 'Lunch Time', 1 act (Trin. 1989).
——— 'Why Me?' (Trin. 1991).
David, Hubert (*Trin*) 'Strange But True', 1 act (Trin. 1968).
Dawes, Carroll (*Jam*) 'The unravelled Sleeve, a projection of Lady Macbeth's troubled mind, adapted from William Shakespeare' (Jam. 1954).
Dawes, Kwaime (*Jam*) 'Song of a Wounded Stone' (Jam. 1989).
Dawkins, Basil (*Jam*, 1952) 'Champagne and Sky Juice', 2 acts (Jam. 1986).
——— 'Couples', 2 acts (Jam. 1984).
——— 'Flat Mate', 2 acts (Jam. 1980; bronze medal, JF, Jam. 1977).
——— 'Parson and Mrs Jones' (Jam. 1982).
——— 'Same Song, Different Tune', 2 acts (Jam. 1991).
——— see also 8: *on Basil Dawkins.*
De Coteau, Clifton (*Trin*) 'The Advice' (Trin. 1978 SSDF).

——— 'Who Fooling Who' (Trin. 1977; best original play, SSDF, Trin. 1977; see 4).
Denton, Michael (Jam, 1963) 'Dead-Lef' (Jam. 1986).
——— 'Hear sey' (Jam. 1989; see 4).
——— 'Lover Boy Ces'' (Jam. 1988).
——— 'Man in my Pyjamas' (Jam. 1991).
——— 'Night Nurse' (Jam. 1990).
——— 'Scandal' (Jam. 1985).
——— 'Some Like It Hot' (Jam. 1983).
——— see also 8: *on other playwrights.*
DeRiggs, Chris (*Gren*) 'Pan in Meh Blood' (Gren. 1990).
Domacasse, Pacheco (*Bonaire*) 'Tula' (Cur. 1973).
Donovan, Harold (*Trin*) 'Black Bondage' (Trin. 1987).
——— 'Never Lovers, Ever Friends' (Trin. 1983).
——— 'Never Lovers, Ever Friends Part 2' (Trin. 1984).
Dookie, Devindra (*Trin*) 'A Carol for Scrooge', adaptation of Charles Dickens' *A Christmas Carol* (Trin. 1986; see 4).
——— 'Play Your Balls White', revue (Trin. 1983).
——— 'The Rape' (Trin. 1975).
——— see also 8: *general.*
Dorant, St Clair Wesley, 'Back to Square One', 2 acts (Trin. 1989).
——— 'CornereD' (Trin. 1992).
——— 'Don't Do It', 1 act (Trin. 1975).
——— 'Love in the Family', 3 scenes (Trin. 1981).
——— 'Manwo' (Trin. 1990).
——— 'Say no more', 3 acts (Trin. 1959).
——— 'To-get-her-ness', 3 acts (Trin. 1981).
——— 'Too Many Voices' (Trin. 1991).
——— see 1, also 8: *on other playwrights.*
Dowlath, Hailes E. (*Trin*) 'The Trials of Growing up' (Trin. 1976 SSDF).
Drakes, S. A. (*Guy*) 'The Dead End' (Guy. 1963).
Duff, Michael (*Guy*) 'Asylum' (Guy. 1990).
——— 'Cathy Ann Possessed' (Guy. 1990).
——— 'Papa's Idol' (Guy. 1990).
——— 'The Tides that Bind' (Guy. 1990).
Duperly, Adrienne, 'The Dream Mountain' (Jam. 1989).
Dwyer, Ted (*Jam*) 'Bruckins', see Tipling, Carmen and . . .
——— 'Mansong', Jamaican pantomime, with lyrics by Ted Dwyer and Dennis Scott, music by Noel Dexter (Jam. 1980).
Edgecombe, David, 'The Bulletin' (reading, Montreal, 1977).
——— 'For Better For Worse' (Mont. 1973 Alliouagana Arts Festival; revised SM. 1988).
——— 'Heaven' (ST. 1991; revised SC. 1991).
——— 'Kirnon's Kingdom' (Mont.1981; workshopped ST. 1981 first Caribbean playwrights' conference; see 5).
——— 'Sonuvabitch' (Montreal, 1975; as 'Sunova', Cay. c1981; see 5).
——— 'A View from the Bridge', adaptation of Arthur Miller's play (Mont. 1979).
——— see 1.
Edghill, Barry (*Trin*) 'Heading for the Stars', pantomime (Trin. 1989).
Edghill, Barry, Lennox Lake and Davis, Glenn, 'The Spirit', revue (Trin. 1980).
——— 'Superheroes', revue (Trin. 1983).
——— 'Three Blind Mice', revue (Trin. 1981).
——— 'Two Flew into the Cuckoo's Nest', revue (Trin. 1979).
Edinborough, Felix (*Trin*, 1942) 'All Ah Dat is Carnival', Carnival show for Dimanche Gras (Trin. 1991).
——— 'Blight', skit (Trin. 1972 BV).
——— 'Calypsical', linking script for a retrospective of Superior's calypsos (Trin. 1985).
——— 'A Christmas Presence' (Trin. 1986).
——— 'Dat Ent Right', skit (Trin. 1977 BV).
——— 'Gene', musical (Trin. 1990).
——— 'Go To Hell', Carnival play with traditional music and original songs by Roger Israel (Trin. 1984; see also an adaptation by Godfrey Sealy, 'To Hell Wid Dat').
——— 'High Society' (Trin. 1978 BV; see 4).

——— 'J'Ouvert', Carnival play with traditional music and original songs by Roger Israel (London, 1982).
——— 'Jazz'll Dazzle', dance drama (Trin. 1981).
——— 'King Arthur and His Merry Men', Carnival play (Trin. 1987; see 4).
——— 'King Jab Jab', Carnival play with traditional music and original songs by Roger Israel (Trin. 1981).
——— 'Mas In Yuh Mas', see Keens-Douglas, Paul and . . .
——— 'Sugar Boy', skit (Trin. 1973 BV).
——— 'Visions', script for the opening ceremony of Carifesta V (Trin. 1992).
——— 'Who Fool Who', skit (Trin. 1974 BV).
——— see 5, also 8: *on Felix Edinborough.*
Edinborough, Felix and Helen Camps, 'Cinderama', pantomime with original score and lyrics by Roger Israel (Trin. 1980).
Edwards, Victor (*Trin*, 1954) 'Dead End' (Trin. 1983 SSDF).
——— 'For Sure This Time', Christmas play (Trin. 1981).
——— 'Games' (Trin. 1990 JAF; best original play, JAF, Trin.1990; best original play, SSDF, Trin. 1990).
——— 'Maniacs' (Trin. 1988 SSDF; best original play, SSDF, Trin. 1988).
——— 'The Sound of Thunder' (Trin. 1985 SSDF).
Elliott, Lorris (*Tob*) 'How Now Black Man' (Montreal, Can. 1971).
Ellis, Hall Anthony (*Jam*, 1936) 'Boopsy', comedy (Jam. 1986).
——— 'Conflict', on the trial of Marcus Garvey (Jam. 1987).
——— 'Country Time', comedy (Jam. 1986).
——— 'Don't Blame the Postman' (Jam. 1986).
——— '1888', historical play (Jam. 1988; National Journalist award).
——— 'Hurricane Baby', comedy (UK. 1988).
——— 'John Crow Note Book' (Jam. 1977).
——— 'Lament of a Dead Maroon', on Nanny of the Maroons (Jam. 1989).
——— 'Prescott', based on the tv series (Jam.; see 4).
——— 'Wedding Blues' (Jam. 1978).
——— see 4, also 8: *on other playwrights.*
Ellis, Michael, 'Starliner 2001, a Soap Odyssey' (London 1984).
——— 'A Temporary Rupture' (London, 1983).
——— see 1.
Ellis, Owen and the Groundwork Theatre Company, 'Pump up the Fun', with music by Winston Bell (Jam. 1990; best children's musical, Jamaica Music Industry, Jam. 1990).
Fagon, Alfred, 'Bristol Air-Raid Shelter' (reading, London, 1982).
——— 'Death of a Black Man' (London, 1975).
——— '11 Josephine House' (London, 1972).
——— 'Four Hundred Pounds' (London, 1983).
——— 'No Soldiers in St Paul's' (London, 1974).
——— see 1, 4 and 5.
Farray, Lincoln (*Trin*) 'Double Trouble', 1 act (Trin. 1968).
Farrier, Francis Quamina, 'Air Partner', 1 act (Guy. 1963; see 5).
——— 'Border Bridge', 1-act comedy (Guy. 1963).
——— 'Eyes', 1 act (Guy. 1968; see 5).
——— 'Freedom Trail', radio play adapted (Guy. 1971; see 5).
——— 'Gaylanda', 3-act musical comedy (Guy. 1966).
——— 'Journey to Freedom' (Guy. 1976; see 5).
——— 'Manaka', full-length play based on the short play (Guy. 1985; see 1).
——— 'Pal', 1 act (Guy. 1963).
——— 'Quitters', 1 act (Guy. 1965).
——— 'The Tides of Susanburg', adapted from the radio serial (Guy. 1985; see 5).
——— 'The Trumpeter', historical play commissioned by the Guyana Commemoration Commission to inaugurate the Guest Director series (Guy. 1984).
——— see 1, 4 and 5, also 8: *on Francis Quamina Farrier.*

Forsythe, Victor (*Guy*) 'Sweet Carila', radio play adapted (Guy. 1961; see 5).
——— 'The Waterfront', radio play adapted (Guy. 1969; see 3).
——— see 3.
Foster, Melville (*Trin*) 'Called to the Bar', 1 act (Trin. 1967 SSDF; best original play, SSDF, Trin. 1967; see 4).
——— 'Cinderella', children's pantomime (Trin. 1981).
——— 'The Departure', 1 act (Trin. 1971 SSDF; best original play, SSDF, Trin. 1971; Trin. 1971 SSDF).
——— 'For the Hell of It', monologue (Trin. 1975).
——— 'Limitation of Life', skit (Trin. 1974).
——— 'Not a Bed of Roses', tv play adapted (Trin. 1982; see 4).
——— 'Oh Silent Night', skit (Trin. 1972).
——— see 3, 4 and 5.
Fowler, Greta (*Jam*, 1901–78) 'Anancy and the Magic Mirror', Jamaican pantomime (Jam. 1954).
Fowler, Greta, Lois Kelly, Louise Bennett, and Derek Boughton, 'Bredda Buck', Jamaican pantomime, with music by Mapletoft Poulle, Hugh Moss-Solomon and Lois Kelly (Jam. 1964).
Fowler, Greta, Louise Bennett, Henry Fowler, Lois Kelly, Dennis Scott, and Ranny Williams, 'Queenie's Daughter', Jamaican pantomime, with lyrics by Greta Fowler, Louise Bennett, Dennis Scott and Noel Vaz, music by Mapletoft Poulle (Jam. 1963).
Fowler, Henry and Greta Fowler, 'Morgan's Dream', Jamaican pantomime, with lyrics by Greta Fowler, Orford St John and Louise Bennett, music by Sonny Bradshaw (Jam. 1965).
Francis, Fenrick (*Trin*) 'The Williams, the Bookers and the Ham' (Trin. 1991; third prize, National Petroleum pc, Trin. 1991).
Francis, Gabriel (*Trin*) 'Gone forever' (Trin. 1945).
——— see also 8: *on other playwrights.*
Francis, Nigel (*Dom*) 'Behind Closed Doors' (Dom. 1989).
Fraser, Godfrey Bobby (*SV*) 'Auntie and the preacher' (SV. c1967).
Fraser, Winslow (*Guy*) 'Andel', 1 act (Guy. c1959).
——— 'Auntie Annette', 1 act (Guy. c1959).
——— 'Bacra dead ah Backdam', 1 act (Guy. 1965; see 5).
——— 'Black Sheep', 1 act (Guy. 1970).
——— 'Body in the Lamaha', 2 acts (Guy. 1965).
——— 'Death Dream of Cassell Barry', 1 act (Guy. 1971).
——— 'Forbidden Love', 3 acts (Guy. 1966).
——— 'Inside the Forum', sketch (Guy. 1958).
——— 'Life is but an empty dream', 2 acts (Guy. 1970).
——— 'No. 55 Wildroot Alley', 1 act (Guy. c1965).
——— 'Our Last Job', 2 acts (Guy. c1962).
——— 'Professor John', 1 act (Guy. 1963).
——— 'Strange Secret', 1 act (Guy. 1964).
——— 'Valley of Tears', 4 acts (Guy. c1969).
——— 'Village Delinquent', 2 acts (Guy. 1968).
——— 'Winds of Change', 1 act (Guy. 1971).
French, Stanley, 'Ballad of a Man and Dog' (Jam. 1970?).
——— 'The Light and the Dark', 1 act (SL. c1971).
——— 'No Rain No Play', 2 acts (Jam. 1972).
——— 'The Rape of Fair Helen' (London, 1966; see 5).
——— see 1, also 8: *on other playwrights.*
Fullerton, Norvan (*Trin*) 'The Choice' (Trin. 1980 BV).
——— 'Dance Beryl Dance' (Trin. 1983 BV).
——— 'Obeah', calypso musical (Trin. 1986 BV; see 4).
——— 'The Visitor' (Trin. 1985 BV).
——— see 3, also 8: *on other playwrights.*
Gabourel, Glenford (*Bel*) 'The Black Belt of Darkness' (Bel. 1971 Festival of Arts).
Gaines, Phillip (*Trin*) 'Mother-in-law' (Trin. 1945).

——— 'Two Husbands, a domestic drama' (Trin. 1945).
Galt, Roy A. (*Trin*, 1922) 'A-musing we will go' (Trin. 1970; first prize, Arts Festival pc, Trin. 1957; fourth prize, Drama Guild pc, Trin. 1970).
——— see 3.
Gambrill, Tony (*UK*) 'All That Glitters', musical melodrama, with music by Peter Ashbourne (Jam. 1976).
——— 'Boonoonoonos', rock musical, with music by David Ogden (Jam. 1969).
——— 'Definitely the Last Eight O'Clock Jamaica Time', revue, with music by Peter Ashbourne (Jam. 1986).
——— 'Eight O'Clock Jamaica Time', revue, based on an idea by Jimmy Barton, with music and lyrics by Jimmy Barton (Jam. 1965).
——— 'Eight O'Clock Jamaica Time 2nd Edition', revue, with music and lyrics by Jimmy Barton (Jam. 1966).
——— 'Eight O'Clock Jamaica Time 3rd Edition', revue, with music and lyrics by Jimmy Barton (Jam. 1967).
——— 'Eight O'Clock Jamaica Time Again', revue, with music by David Ogden (Jam. 1972).
——— 'Eight O'Clock Jamaica Time Strikes Again', revue, with music by Brian Brodber (Jam. 1974).
——— 'Eight O'Clock Jamaica Time Strikes Back', revue, with music by Eddy Thomas (Jam. 1977).
——— 'Gunfight At The Last Chance Saloon', musical melodrama, with music by Eddy Thomas (Jam. 1978).
——— 'It's Time for Eight O'clock Jamaica Time', revue, with music by Peter Ashbourne (Jam. 1990).
——— 'The Last Eight O'Clock Jamaica Time', revue, with music by Peter Ashbourne (Jam. 1979).
——— 'Paradise Street', musical, with music by Eddy Thomas (Jam. 1971).
——— 'Rahtid', mixed media topical revue, with music by Eddy Thomas (Jam. 1968).
——— 'The Return of Eight O'Clock Jamaica Time', revue, with music by Peter Ashbourne (Jam. 1983).
Garcia, Anthony (Gary) (*Trin*) 'Jellilean' (Trin. 1992).
——— see 4.
Garvey, Marcus (*Jam*, 1887–1940) 'The Coronation of an African King', 3 acts (Jam. 1930).
——— 'Roaming Jamaicans' (Jam. 1930).
——— 'Slavery – from hut to mansion' (Jam. 1930).
——— 'Wine, Women and War' (Jam. 1932).
——— see also 7.
Gayle, Lois (*Jam*,1941) 'The Kings and the Star' (Jam. 1978).
——— 'The Prodigal' (Jam. 1963).
——— see 3.
George, Dykes E.H. (*Trin*) 'A Candle Glows', 2 acts (Trin. 1963).
——— 'Even a Beggar can give', Christmas play (Trin. 1962).
——— see 3.
George, Ralph (*Trin*) 'Common Entrance Eve', 1 act (Trin. 1981).
——— 'Miss Universe '82' (Trin. 1982).
——— 'Open for Business' (Trin. 1982).
Ghisays, Bobby (*Jam*, –1990) 'Is Everybody Happy?' (Jam. 1972).
Gibbons, Rawle (*Trin*, 1950) 'Ah Wanna Fall', calypso musical, 2nd in trilogy (Trin. 1992).
——— 'I Lawah' (Jam. 1985).
——— 'Shepherd' (Jam. 1981).
——— 'Sing De Chorus', calypso musical, 1st in trilogy (Trin. 1991; cassette and CD, Trin. 1992: Delos International).
——— 'Ten to One', calypso musical, 3rd in trilogy (Trin. 1993).
——— see 7 and 8: *on Errol Hill, Derek Walcott*, also 8: *on Rawle Gibbons*.
Gilbert, Joseph (*Trin*) 'Let No Man Put Asunder' (Trin. 1987).
Gilkes, Michael, 'In Transit', mixed media play (Guy. 1968).
——— 'A Pleasant Career (the life and fictions of Edgar Mittelholzer)', commissioned by the Royal Court Theatre, London (staged reading, London, 1988; Guyana prize for literature, Guy. 1992).
——— 'This Island Now', mixed media docu-drama (Bar. 1987).

——— 'Young Aesop', children's play (Guy. 1967).

——— see 1 and 8: *on Banyan, other playwrights*, also 8: *on Michael Gilkes.*

Gill-Murphy, Patricia, 'The Emancipators', 3 acts (SC. 1981; as 'Buddhoe', workshopped ST. 1981: first Caribbean playwrights' conference).

Gloudon, Barbara (*Jam*) 'A Carol for Moneybags' (Jam. 1989).

——— 'Fifty Fifty', Jamaican pantomime, with music by Grub Cooper, Noel Dexter, Peter Ashbourne, Marjorie Whylie, Joe Williams, Mapletoft Poulle and Barbara Ferland (Jam. 1990).

——— 'General B.', Jamaican pantomime, with music by Peter Ashbourne (Jam. 1983).

——— 'Hail Columbus', Jamaican pantomime, with music by Eddy Thomas (Jam. 1972).

——— 'Johnny Reggae', Jamaican pantomime, with music by Peter Ashbourne (Jam. 1978).

——— 'Man Dey Yah', Jamaican pantomime, with additional material by Trevor Fearon, music by Grub Cooper, also Noel Dexter and Pluto Shervington (Jam. 1991).

——— 'Moonshine Anancy', Jamaican pantomime, with music by Eddy Thomas (Jam. 1969).

——— 'The Pirate Princess', Jamaican pantomime, with music by Conroy Cooper (Jam. 1981).

——— 'Rabbit Punch' (Jam. 1989).

——— 'River Mumma and the Golden Table', see Cooke, Aston and . . .

——— 'Schoolers', Jamaican pantomime, developed from a concept by Owen Ellis (Jam. 1989).

——— 'Trash', Jamaican pantomime, with music by Grub Cooper (Jam. 1985).

——— 'The Witch', Jamaican pantomime, with music by Peter Ashbourne (Jam. 1975).

——— see 8: *on Louise Bennett, general.*

Gonzales, Anson (*Trin*) 'The Rice Mill', 1 act (Trin. 1968).

Gonzales, Roy (*Trin*) 'The Great Soup Story, or How Tiger saved the Forest', an Anansi play (Trin. 1990).

——— 'Watershed' (Trin. 1992).

Greaves, Hal (*Trin*, 1961) 'Gaps: Let the Fires Burn Again', play set during the 1990 Muslim coup (Trin. 1991).

——— 'The Graduation' (Trin. 1982 SSDF).

——— '90 Hoodlum Street' (Trin. 1983).

——— 'Once Upon A Wish' (Trin. 1982).

——— 'Others' (Trin. 1989).

——— 'Tief' (Trin. 1987; see 4).

——— 'Two Sides' (Trin. 1987 SSDF).

——— 'Upon the Sands' (Trin. 1986).

——— 'Victims' (Trin. 1985; see 4).

——— 'Walls and Fences' (Trin. 1988).

——— see 4 and 8: *general*, also 8: *on Hal Greaves.*

Greaves, Jim (*Trin*) 'Emma-Jean', 1 act (Trin. 1965).

Griffith, Reginald, 'Justina', folk musical (Trin. 1975 BV).

——— 'Levez Papa Niza Levez' (Trin. 1989 BV).

——— see 1, also 8: *on other playwrights.*

Groundwork Theatre Company, collective creation, 'Babsikysico', revue, incorporating work by Dennis Scott, Michael Reckord, Louise Bennett, traditional music and games (Jam. 1985).

——— 'Yuh Safe' (Jam. 1988).

Hackett, Daphne Joseph (*Bar*, –1988) 'Babes in the Wood, Bimshire 1970', Bajan pantomime (Bar. 1970).

——— 'Bathsheba Blowup, Bimshire 1967', Bajan pantomime (Bar. 1967).

——— 'Bimshire 1969', Bajan pantomime, based on *Alice in Wonderland* (Bar. 1969).

——— 'Rip van Brathwaite, Bimshire 1968', Bajan pantomime (Bar. 1968).

Hall, Anthony and others, '1937 Riots Street Theatre' (Trin. 1985).

——— see 8: *general.*

Hall, Anthony, Dennis Hall, Errol Fabien, Errol Sitahal, and others, 'Adult Sufferage', revue (Trin. 1986).

Hall, Billy (*Jam*) 'King Croton of Bouganvaille', children's pantomime (Jam. 1984).

——— 'Samantha and the Seven Do-Bees', children's pantomime (Jam. 1980).

Hall, Billy and others, 'Leviathan', children's pantomime (Jam. 1988).
Hall, Dennis (*Trin*) 'Adult Sufferage', see Hall, Anthony and . . .
——— 'Soca in Poetry' (Trin. 1983).
Hall, Henry W., 'Jumbie Doll', 1 act (Trin. 1954).
——— 'The Stiletto, a murder mystery' (Trin. 1949).
——— see 1.
Hamaludin, Mohamed (*Guy*) 'Much married Mary' (Guy. 1968).
Hanna, Cecilia (*Jam*) 'Animal Circus' (Jam. 1989).
Hanoomansingh, Peter (*Trin*) 'Dress Code in Effect' (San Fernando, Trin. 1991).
Harewood, Marva (*Trin*) 'We are the Future' (Trin. 1991 SSDF).
Harris, Amah (*Dom*) 'Anansi and Cooyah! She Changed Me into a Spider Man', children's musical (Toronto, 1984).
——— see also 8: *on other playwrights.*
Hazell, Bernard and Ricardo Nanton, 'Waves of Hope', a musical mime on the story of Christopher Columbus, with narration based on the poem *The Lost Sailor* by Beat Rettenmund (SV; revised Trin. 1992).
Hearne, John Edgar Colwell (*Can*, 1926) 'Freedom Man', 1 act (Jam. 1957).
——— see 6.
Henry, Jeff (*Trin*) 'Africa in the Caribbean' (Toronto, 1976).
——— see also 8: *on other playwrights.*
Henry, Robert, 'Fujamaad', musical based on Bantu tradition (Trin. 1973).
Hewan, C. and Keith Parkin, 'Hi, Celestina', musical play (Jam. 1970).
Heywood, Donald (*Trin*) 'Soucouyant', folk operetta (Trin. 1955).
——— see also 8: *on other playwrights.*
Hezekiah, Lloyd (*Trin*) 'The Breast of Heaven' (New York, 1967).
Hickling, Ann (*Jam*) 'Star Boarder', 1 act (Jam. 1956).
Hill, Errol, 'Dimanche Gras 1963, a carnival scenario' (Trin. 1963).
——— 'Whistling Charlie and the monster', Carnival show for Dimanche Gras (Trin. 1964).
——— see 1, 3, 4, 5, 7 and 8: *on Derek Walcott, general*, also 8: *on Errol Hill.*
Hill, Errol and Extra-mural Drama Workshop, Antigua, 'Priscilla's Wedding' (Ant. 1953).
——— see also 8: *on other playwrights.*
Hill, Frank, 'Upheaval', 3 acts (Jam. 1939).
——— see 1.
Hill, Sonne, 'The Last Will and Testament of a Parliamentarian' (Trin. 1991).
——— 'Murder in the Penthouse' (Trin. 1989).
——— see 1.
Hillary, Samuel, 'Banana Boy', Jamaican pantomime, with lyrics by Orford St John and David Lindo, music by Carlos Malcolm (Jam. 1961).
——— 'Koo-Koo, or Actor Boy', Jonkunnu play (Jam. 1967).
——— see 1 and 3, also 8: *on other playwrights.*
Hinkson, Anthony, 'Busman' (Bar. 1983).
——— 'City Man' (Bar. 1981).
——— 'God's Daughter' (Bar. 1979 NIFCA).
——— 'Jackpot' (Bar. 1982 NIFCA).
——— 'Laff-it-off 91' (Bar. 1991).
——— 'Laff-it-off 92' (Bar. 1992).
——— 'Nigger Yard' (Bar. 1978 NIFCA; see 4).
——— 'Round the Bend' (Bar. 1973).
——— 'Village Life', musical incorporating works by George Lamming and Paul Keens-Douglas (Bar. 1988).
——— see 1, also 8: *on Anthony Hinkson.*
Hinkson, Anthony, Ben Craig, Margaret Gill, Joseph Inniss, Robert Morris, and Earl Warner, 'Unchained, an experimental musical play' (Bar. 1972).
Ho-Lung, Fr. Richard, 'Rise Up', with music by Fr. Ho-Lung (Jam. 1990).
Ho-Lung, Fr. Richard and friends, 'David', musical (Jam. 1989).
Hopkinson, Slade, 'The Blood of the Family', 1 act (Jam. 1957).
——— 'Fall of a Chief', 9 scenes (Guy. 1965).
——— 'Sala' (as 'A Spawning of Eels', Guy. 1968; as 'Sala', Trin. 1975).
——— see 1 and 4, also 8: *on Slade Hopkinson.*

Hornby, Daisie L. (*Bel*) 'Troublesome Servants', 1 act (Bel. 1950; revised Bel. 1954).

Hyacinth, Steve (*Dom*) 'Snake Game' (Dom. 1989).

——— 'Times to Remember' (Dom. 1989).

Hyde, Evan X. (*Bel*) 'Haad Times' (Bel. 1971 Festival of Arts).

Imamshah, Marvin (*Trin*) 'A Killer in My House' (Trin. 1992).

——— 'Tempo Street' (Trin. 1990).

Ishmael, Marvin (*Trin*) 'The Revolutionist' (Trin. 1974).

Israel, Roger (Trin. 1954) 'Courtney and Me', musical (Trin. 1981).

——— 'Roger's Passion', a passion musical (Trin. 1979; see 4).

——— 'Terry, the True Story', musical (Trin. 1980).

Israel, Roger and Helen Camps, 'Ad', musical (Trin. 1982; revised as 'Rampanalgas Sunrise', Trin. 1983).

Jackman, Oliver (*Bar*) 'Stepchild, Stepchild', tv play adapted (Trin. 1969).

Jadoo, Wayne, 'The Greatest Gift of All', Christmas play (San Fernando, Trin. 1991).

James, C.L.R., 'Minty Alley', novel adapted by Eintou Pearl Springer (Trin. 1977).

——— see 1, 6 and 7, also 8: on *C.L.R. James.*

Jean-Baptiste, Deborah (*Trin*) 'A Spider Spins His Web' (Trin. 1986 SSDF).

——— see 8: *on Pat Cumper, Rawle Gibbons.*

Jhagroo, V. E. (*Trin*) 'Sammy's Hurt' (Trin. 1976 SSDF).

John, Errol, 'Easter and I'll Come For You' (London, c1985).

——— 'How then tomorrow', fantasy in 1 act, revised version of 'The Gateway' (Trin. 1947).

——— see 1, 3, 4 and 5, also 8: *on Errol John.*

John, Giftus (*Dom*) 'Great Great Story' (Dom. 1982).

John, Ronald, 'Irene's Song' (Trin. 1982).

——— 'Masquerade', calypso drama (Trin. 1991; second prize, National Petroleum pc, Trin. 1991).

——— 'Once Upon a Time' (Trin. 1990).

——— 'Welcome Home, Cousin Raphael', 3-act play developed from the 1-act 'The Dream' (Trin. 1985; workshopped, first national playwrights' conference, Trin. 1985; see 1).

——— 'The Wizard of Kandahar' (Trin. 1980; see 5).

——— see 1, 3, 5 and 8: *on Derek Walcott,* also 8: *on Ronald John.*

Johns, Vere (*Jam*) 'Dead and Wake' (Jam. 1969).

Johnson, C. (*Jam*) 'Waa-cu-yah' (Jam. 1969).

Jolly, Dorothy (*Dom*, 1931) 'The People' (Trin. 1989).

——— 'The Perfect Family', 1 act (Trin. 1989).

——— 'Speak Well of the Dead' (Trin. 1986; prizewinner, Drama Guild pc, Trin. 1971–72).

——— 'The Web Weavers' (Trin. 1992).

——— 'Will All The Looters Please Stand Up!', on the 1990 Muslim coup (Trin. 1991).

——— see 5, also 8: *on other playwrights.*

Jones, Clair (*Trin*) 'Voices of the Hills' (Trin. 1990 SSDF).

Jones, Evan (*Jam*, 1927) 'Go Tell it on Table Mountain', 1 act (Jam. 1970).

——— 'In a Backward Country', tv play adapted to 2 acts (Guy. 1964; see 4).

——— 'Inherit This Land' (Jam. 1950).

——— 'The Spectators' (UK. 1962).

——— see 4 and 6, also 8: *on other playwrights.*

Jorsling, Luke (*Trin*) 'West of Eden' (Trin. 1991; fourth prize, National Petroleum pc, Trin. 1991).

Joseph, Edward Lanza; 'Conscience', translation from German (Trin. 1831).

——— 'Kindred', translation from German (Trin. 1832).

——— 'The Novelist, or Superior Accomplishments', 1 act (Trin. 1832).

——— 'Post Mortem Will' (Trin. 1832).

——— see 1.

Joseph, Learie (*Trin*) 'Jean and Dina' (Trin. 1984).

Jubrasingh, Fr. Joseph (*Trin*) 'Our Sons – Their Power and Their Passion', passion play (Trin. 1991).

——— 'Women of Hope', passion play (Trin. 1990).

Keens-Douglas, Paul (*Trin*, 1942) 'Marriage of the Samaan', based on the story by Olga Comma-Maynard (Trin. 1985).
——— 'Ah Pan for Christmas' (Trin. 1982; see 4).
——— 'Tim Tim', annual series (Trin. 1975; see 4).
——— see 4 and 6, also 8: *on Paul Keens-Douglas.*
Keens-Douglas, Paul and Felix Edinborough, 'Mas In Yuh Mas', Carnival musical, with traditional music and original songs by Roger Israel (Trin. 1980).
Keens-Douglas, Ricardo (*Gren*) 'Caribbean Cindy' (Toronto, 1992).
——— 'The Obeah Man', musical comedy (Toronto, 1985).
——— see also 8: *on Ricardo Keens-Douglas.*
Kernahan, Jennifer (*Trin*) 'Illusions' (Trin. 1986).
Khan, Farida (*Trin*) 'Such is Life' (Trin. 1981).
Kinch, Don (*Bar*) 'Balm Yard' (London, c1987).
King, Hugh (*Jam*) 'Guzum' (Jam. 1990).
King, Lewis (*Trin*) 'Challenge' (Trin. 1963).
——— 'Drunk Artist' (Trin. 1963).
——— 'The Man Who Died at Twelve' (Trin. 1963).
——— 'The Striker Struck' (Trin. 1973).
King, Sheila (*Guy*) 'Fo' Betting or Worse, a two-act play in the vernacular' (Guy. 1966; third prize, Theatre Guild pc, Guy. 1966).
——— see 3.
Kirton, Enid and Wilston J. Campbell, 'A Family Crisis' (Trin. 1972 SSDF).
——— see 4.
Kissoon, Freddie, 'Beauty Contest', sketch (Trin. 1975; see 4).
——— 'Beulah Laughs Last', sketch (Trin. 1976; see 4).
——— 'Beulah's Boutique', 1 act (Trin. 1979).
——— 'Beulah's Dream', 1 act (Trin. 1979; see 4).
——— 'Boss Man', 1 act (Trin. 1974).
——— 'Crash workers', 1 act (Trin. 1973).
——— 'Do Your Home Lessons, Daddy', 1 act (Trin. 1968).
——— 'Doctor Beulah' (initial sketch, Trin. 1976; developed to full-length play, Trin. 1981).
——— 'Doo-Doo', 1 act (Trin. 1966; best original play, Arts Festival, Trin. 1965; see 4).
——— 'Food First', sketch (Trin. 1976; see 4).
——— 'Fugitive From the Royal Jail', 1 act (Trin. 1968; see 4).
——— 'Girls Wanted', 1 act, commissioned for the 50th anniversary of the International Labour Organisation (Point Fortin Trin. 1969; see 4).
——— 'God and Uriah Butler', 3-act historical drama commissioned for the 30th anniversary of the Oilfield Workers' Trade Union (San Fernando, Trin. 1967).
——— 'King Cobo', 3 acts (Trin. 1965; best full-length play, PNM 10th Anniversary lc, Trin.).
——— 'Licks Like Fire', sketch (Trin. 1976; see 4).
——— 'Like Hog Love Mud', 1 act (Trin. 1968; see 4).
——— 'Love me Carefully', 1 act (Trin. 1979).
——— 'Luisa Calderon' (Trin. 1992).
——— 'Lust for Power', 1 act (Trin. 1973).
——— 'The Miracle Man' (Trin. 1975).
——— 'Pahyol' (Trin. 1966).
——— 'Papa Look the Priest Passing', 1 act (Trin. 1967).
——— 'Police Woman Wanted', sketch (Trin. 1976; see 4).
——— 'Preston's Choice', 1 act (Trin. 1974).
——— 'Sally and Sam, part 1' (Trin. 1973).
——— 'Sally and Sam, part 2' (Trin. 1973).
——— 'The Servant', 1 act (Trin. 1979).
——— 'Shift System', sketch (Trin. 1976; see 4).
——— 'Twenty and Under', sketch (Trin. 1976; see 4).
——— 'We Crucify Him', passion play (Trin. 1967; see 4).

——— 'The Wedding', sketch (Trin. 1975; see 4).
——— 'The West Indies – Down and Under', 2 scenes (Trin. 1976).
——— 'What Party You Voting?' (Trin. 1987; see 4).
——— 'Woman Power', 1 act (Trin. 1975).
——— see 1, 4 and 5, also 8: *on Freddie Kissoon.*
Kissoon, Freddie and others, 'Mister Big Stuff', 1 act (Tob. 1970; see 4).
Knight, Ginger (*Jam*, 1951) 'Boy Blue' (Jam. 1987).
——— 'Dis-A-Reggae', musical (Jam. 1984).
——— 'Don-Man' (Jam. 1990).
——— 'Gilbert' (Jam. 1989).
——— 'Higglers' (Jam. 1988).
——— 'Part-time Lover' (Jam. 1986).
——— 'Poly-tricks' (Jam. 1985).
——— 'Return of the Don' (Jam. 1991).
——— 'Stepfather' (Jam. 1981).
——— 'Underwriters Undercover' (Jam. 1979).
——— 'Whiplash' (Jam. 1982).
——— see also 8: *on Ginger Knight.*
Koulirou Cultural Group, 'Riot' (Dom. 1989).
Krogh, Christen (*Trin*) 'A-Lad-In Space', pantomime (Trin. 1969).
——— 'Fun Cruise on the SS Go Brave' (Trin. 1992).
La Chapelle, Carol (*Trin*) 'Witness to Suicide' (Trin. 1991).
La Chapelle, Carol, Jemma Allong-Redman, and Geraldine Connor, 'Testimony' (Trin. 1990).
Labastide, Neville, 'A Bully Father' (Trin. 1951).
——— 'Love Thy Neighbour' (Trin. 1970; see 4).
——— see 1 and 4, also 8: *on other playwrights.*
Lamming, George (*Bar*, 1927) 'In the Castle of my Skin', novel adapted (Bar. 1981 Carifesta).
——— see 6.
Landrigen, Stephen (*USA*) 'The Pan Beaters' (London, 1993; first prize, London Weekend Television Plays on Stage competition, London, 1989).
——— see 3 Fullerton, Norvan and . . .
Lannaman, Gloria (*Jam*) 'Brashana O', Jamaican pantomime (Jam. 1976).
——— 'Dickance for Fippance', Jamaican pantomime, with music by Gloria Lannaman and Norman Rae (Jam. 1974).
——— 'Tantaloo', Jamaican pantomime, with music by Grub Cooper (Jam. 1982).
Laydoo, Lynette (*Trin*) 'Here We Go Gathering' (Trin. 1963).
Layne-Clark, Jeannette (*Bar*) 'Pampalam '89', revue (Bar. 1989).
Lee, Candid (*Tob*) 'Entrapment' (Trin. 1990 SSDF).
Lee, Easton (*Jam*) 'Pretty Medicine' (Jam. 1962; see 4).
——— 'The Rope and the Cross' (Jam.).
——— 'They That Mourn, a play in 3 acts for Easter' (Jam. 1963).
——— see 1 and 4.
LeFranc, Bolivar (*Jam*) 'Make the Drums talk' (London, 1966).
Leon, Gerardo (*Jam*) 'Experience, a play on prison life' (Jam. 1939).
Lewis, Arthur (*Trin*) 'Fallen Silence' (Trin. 1991 BV).
——— 'It's So hard to be You' (Trin. 1989 BV).
——— 'Workshopping' (Trin. 1990 SSDF; best original play, SSDF, Trin. 1990).
Lewis, Maureen Warner and Pat Cumper, 'Flame Heart', based on texts by Claude McKay (Jam. 1990).
Lezama, Brian (*Trin*) 'The Plan', calypso folk musical (Trin. 1983 BV).
Lezama, Michael (*Trin*) 'Coke and Dagger' (workshopped, first national playwrights' conference, Trin. 1985).
Lindo, Archie, 'Black Lightning', 5-act play based on Roger Mais's novel (Jam.).
——— 'Forbidden Fruit' (Jam. 1942).
——— 'The Maroon', adapted in four acts from Capt.Mayne Reid's novel (Jam. 1947).
——— 'The White Witch of Rose Hall', 3-act adaptation of Herbert G. De Lisser's novel (Jam. 1945).
——— see 1, 6 and 8: *on Basil Dawkins, on Michael Reckord.*

Little-White, Lennie (*Jam*) 'That golden necklace', a tragedy (Jam. 1966; first prize, JF, Jam. 1966?).
Lord, Daniel A., 'The Follies of 1939', musical (Jam. 1939).
Lord, Daniel and others, 'Jamaica Triumphant' (Jam. 1937).
Lovelace, Earl, 'The New Boss' (Rio Claro, Trin. 1962).
——— 'Pierrot Grenade' (Trin. 1977 BV).
——— 'The Seekers' (Trin. 1976 SSDF).
——— 'The Wine of Astonishment', novel adapted (Trin. 1988; workshopped first national playwrights' conference, Trin. 1985; best original play, NDF, Trin. 1988; see 4).
——— see 1, 6 and 8: *on Derek Walcott, general*, also 8: *on Earl Lovelace.*
Lovell, Glenville (*Bar*) 'A Silver Web' (Bar. 1989; workshopped ACTA, Jam. 1988).
——— 'When the Eagle Screams' (Trin. 1992).
Lyndersay, Kingsley William Dexter (*Trin*, 1932) 'After One Time . . . A Trinidad Wedding' (Nig. 1972).
——— 'Kolera Kolej', adapted from the novel by Femi Osofisan (Nig. 1975).
——— 'Mai Idris Alauma' (Nig. 1973).
——— 'Mr Three', adapted from the novel by William Butler (Nig. 1971).
——— see 1, also 8: *on other playwrights.*
Lyndersay, Dexter and Dani Lyndersay, 'Adamu Da Kyakkyawar Amarya Tasa', children's musical (in Hausa, Nig. 1974; in English, as 'Adamu and his Beautiful Wife', Nig. 1983).
——— 'The Hobbit', adaptation of J.R.R. Tolkien's book (Nig. 1971).
——— 'The Lion, the Witch and the Wardrobe', adaptation of C.S. Lewis's children's book (Nig. 1984).
——— 'The Piper Trio of Ikot X', adaptation of *The Pied Piper of Hamelin* (Nig. 1985).
——— 'Red Monkey works Overtime', adaptation of Ghanaian folk tale 'Anansi's Trick Does Double Work', collected by Carol Korty (Nig. 1983; as 'Kwa-oe-a-Kwa', Holland 1989).
——— 'Ruwan Bagaja', adaptation from the novel by Alhaji Abubakar Imam (in English under Hausa title, Nig. 1973; in English under Efik title 'Mmon Usobo', Nig. 1982).
——— 'The Search for Ata Utop', children's play (Nig. 1977; see 4).
——— 'Space Trek', children's play (Nig. 1970).
——— 'The Wisdom Trek of Onoyom', adaptation for children from the Mozart opera *The Magic Flute* (Nig. 1979).
——— 'The Wizard of Oz', adaptation from Frank Baum's book (Nig. 1972).
Lyndersay, Dexter, Okon Ekanem, and Imaikop Orok, 'The Successor' (Nig. 1976).
Lyndersay, Mark (*Trin*) 'A Christmas Vaps' (Trin. 1989).
——— 'The Perfect Prince', 1 act (Trin. 1990).
——— see 4 and 8: *various.*
Lyndersay, Mark, Helen Camps, and Robert Las Heras, 'Snokone and the Seven Dwens', pantomime, with original score and lyrics by Roger Israel (Trin. 1981).
Lyons, Greta, 'The Elopement' (Jam. 1960 SSDF).
——— 'On these Shores' (Jam. 1955 SSDF).
——— see 1.
MacAndrew, Wordsworth (*Guy*) 'Freedom Street Blues' (Guy. 1971).
Mahabir, Shekhar (*Trin*) 'The Struggle' (Trin. 1987; SSDF).
Mais, Roger, 'Atalanta in Calydon', 5 scenes (Jam. 1950).
——— 'Hurricane' (Jam. 1943).
——— 'Masks and Paper Hats' (Jam. 1943).
——— see 1, 3 and 6, also 8: *on other playwrights.*
Malloo, Anant (*Trin*) 'The Lurking Killer' (Trin. 1991 SSDF).
Maraj, Ralph, 'The Archbishop and the Prime Minister '(Trin. 1986).
——— 'The Broken Bridge' (in 1 act, Trin. 1985 SSDF; developed to 2 acts, Trin. 1989; best local play, NDF, Trin. 1989).
——— 'Cynthia Sweetness' (Trin. 1981).
——— 'Cynthia's Marriage' (Trin. 1985).

——— 'Easy in the Ashes' (Trin. 1981. see 4).
——— 'Far From the Madding Crowd'; adapted from Thomas Hardy's novel (Trin. 1976).
——— 'Flowers of the Nation' (Trin. 1987).
——— 'The Hardest Hard' (Trin. 1983).
——— 'The Heart of Laura' (Trin. 1981).
——— 'I Want to Stay with You' (Trin. 1982).
——— 'In the Office' (Trin. 1983).
——— 'The Last Competition' (Trin. 1973 SSDF; best original play, SSDF, Trin. 1973).
——— 'Lovers and Warriors' (Trin. 1983).
——— 'Oh Prime Minister!' (Trin. 1990).
——— 'Poison' (Trin. 1975).
——— 'Retreat-Return' (Trin. 1978).
——— 'The Saint' (Trin. 1984; see 4).
——— 'Sea Mystery' (Trin. 1985).
——— 'There Comes a Freedom' (Trin. 1981).
——— 'The Undefeated' (Trin. 1983).
——— 'Under The Sapodilla Tree' (as 'Under De Sapodilla Tree', Trin. 1980).
——— 'Wake it Up', musical (Trin. 1979; best original play, NDF, Trin. 1981).
——— see 1, also 8: *on Ralph Maraj.*
Marcano, Michael (*Trin*) 'From Columbus to Carnival' (Trin. 1970 BV).
——— 'Inside Out Upside Down' (Trin. 1984; third prize, TTT national pc, Trin. 1983).
——— 'Negotiations Break Down' (Trin. 1983).
——— 'Trap Gun', 3 acts (Trin. 1987).
Markham, E. Archie (*Mont*, 1941) 'Dropping out is Violence, part 1' (London, 1969).
Marriott, Louis (*Jam*, 1935) 'The Baiting of Reuben' (Jam. 1963).
——— 'The Last of the Jokers' (Jam. 1989).
——— 'Office Chase' (Jam. c1982).
——— 'One Stop Driver' see Rhone, Trevor and . . .
——— 'Over the Years', one man show (Jam. 1987).
——— 'Pack of Jokers', revue with music by Grub Cooper (Jam. 1978).
——— 'Public Mischief' (Jam. 1957).
——— 'The Shepherd', on Alexander Bedward (Jam. 1960).
——— see 5, also 8: *on Louis Marriott.*
Marson, Una (*Jam*, 1905–1965) 'London Calling', 3 acts (Jam. 1936).
——— 'Pocomania', 3-act play with music and dance (Jam. 1938).
——— see also 8: on *Una Marson.*
Marson, Una and Vaz, Horace, 'At What a Price', 1 act (London, 1933).
Martin, Ann Marie, 'A Pleasant Surprise' (Trin. 1993).
Martin, Dave (*Guy*) 'Raise Up', musical (Guy. 1989).
Martin, Gerald E. (*Trin*) 'Ramdass, the Battering-Ram', 1 act (Trin. 1989).
——— 'The Spider's Web' (Trin. 1992).
Martin, Paul (*Trin*) 'Nor Day, Nor Night' (Trin. 1974).
——— 'When Poui Blossom', play with music (Trin. 1975).
Martin, Paul and others, 'Cross Section', 1 act (Trin. 1981).
Mather, Jean, 'Market Interlude, a Jamaican play in one act using the Greek theories of drama' (Jam. 1956 SSDF).
Matthews, Marc (*Guy*) 'Independence Score for Rasspan', adapted by Ken Corsbie (Bar. 1985).
Matthews, Valton (*Trin*) 'Rainbows' (Trin. 1987 SSDF).
Matura, Mustapha, 'Another Tuesday' (London, 1978).
——— 'Bakerloo Line' (London, 1972; see 4).
——— 'Black Slaves, White Chains' (London, 1975).
——— 'Bread' (London, 1976).
——— 'A Dying Business' (London, 1980).
——— 'More, More' (London, 1978).
——— One Rule (London, 1981).
——— 'Trinidad Sisters', adaptation of Anton Chekhov's *Three Sisters* (London, 1988).
——— see 1, 4 and 5, also 8: *on Mustapha Matura.*
McGuire, Gregory (*Trin*) 'Ah Bag Ah Horrors', 1 act (Trin. 1987).
——— 'Crisis', 1 act (Trin. 1975).

——— 'Undercover', 1 act (Trin. 1977).

McIntosh, David (*Jam*) 'Nuh Put Eh Deh' (Jam. 1989).

McTair, Roger, 'Is the Carnival Over?' (workshopped Toronto, 1975).

——— see 1.

Meade, Ricardo (*Trin*) 'Shame and Scandal in the Family' (Trin. 1988 SSDF; best original play, SSDF, Trin. 1988).

Mills, Horace Leighton (*Tob*) 'Flora' (Tob. 1991).

Mills, Sonia and Don Mills, 'Anancy and Doumbey', Jamaican pantomime, with lyrics and music by Don Mills (Jam. 1968).

Minshall, Peter (*Guy*) 'Callalloo and the Crab', adaptation of the book *Callalloo* (Trin. 1984 BV)

——— 'Santimanitay', Carnival allegory (Trin. 1989).

——— see also 8: *on Peter Minshall.*

Mitchell-Allum, Bernadette (*Tob*) 'The Crime' (Tob. 1982).

——— 'The Rover' (Tob. 1981).

Mohamed, Paloma (*Guy*, 1967) 'Boo Legge', 1 act (Guy. 1987)

——— 'Jezebel', 2 acts (Guy. 1990; see 4).

——— 'Jezebel Too, the sequel', 2 acts (Guy. 1991).

——— 'Mammy', 2 acts (Guy. 1991).

——— 'Masquerade in Black', 2 acts (Guy. 1990; best new play, TAA, Guy. 1990).

——— 'Reggae Marley', 3-act musical docu-drama on the life of Bob Marley (Guy. 1989; best musical, TAA, Guy. 1989).

Moonasar, George A. (*Guy*) 'Double Trouble' (Guy. 1968).

Moreland, David (*Trin*) 'No God but God' (Trin. 1981).

Moze, Sonya (*Trin*, 1947) 'Woman Cleaning Brass', monologue (Trin. 1988; see 4).

——— 'The White Lady', monologue (Trin. 1988; see 4).

——— see also 8: *on other playwrights.*

Naipaul, Vidiadhar Surajprasad (*Trin*, 1932) 'B. Wordsworth', adaptation of the story from 'Miguel Street' (Jam. 1957; see 5).

——— 'The Blue Cart', adapted from 'Miguel Street' (Trin. 1986 SSDF).

——— 'The Case of Whisky' (Trin. 1960).

——— 'Miguel Street', adapted by Errol Sitahal (Trin. 1986).

——— see 6, also 8: *on other playwrights.*

Narine, Somnauth (*Guy*) 'Caribbean Driftwood' (Guy. 1989).

Nelson, Claire A. (*Jam*) 'Resident Alien' (Jam. 1990).

Nickie, Peter (*Trin*) 'Anancy, Snake and the Dragon' (Trin. 1989 BV).

——— 'Damn it in Hell', skit (Trin. 1975).

Nobrega, Cecile (*Guy*) 'Carib Gold', Jamaican pantomime (Jam. 1960).

——— 'Stabroek Fantasy, a musical extravaganza', 5 acts (Guy. 1956).

——— see also 8: *on other playwrights.*

O'Neill, Peter (*Trin*) 'Playing for Keeps' (Trin. 1967).

Oakley, Leo (*Jam*) 'A Stone's Throw' (Jam. 1965 SSDF).

Ogilvie, W. G., 'Jezebel', 3 acts (Jam. 1966; first prize, Jamaica 300 lc, Jam. 1955).

——— 'One Sojer Man', 3 acts (Jam. 1945).

——— 'The Sudden Guest', 1 act (as 'Star Boarder', Jam. 1962).

——— see 1 and 3.

Oginga, Kwesi (*Guy*, 1954) 'The Inheritance' (Guy.).

——— 'Jacko Come Back Tuh!' (Guy.).

——— 'The Rebellion' (Guy.).

——— ''Tiger' (Guy.).

——— To my Son, a Legacy' (Guy.).

——— 'Tengar' (Guy.).

Pantin, Raoul (*Trin*, 1943) 'The Ascot Recreation Club' (Trin. 1988; see 4).

——— 'The Best Family Ltd.', play with music (Trin. 1984; new local play award, NDF, Trin. 1984).

——— 'Hatuey' (Trin. 1980; see 4).

——— 'Paradise', skit commissioned by the Trinidad and Tobago Tourist Board (Trin. 1987).

——— 'Radio Republic 555' (Trin. 1981).

——— 'Sanctuary' (Trin. 1983; best original play, NDF, Trin. 1983; see 4).

——— 'Seasons' (*Trin*, 1986; workshopped first national playwrights' conference, Trin. 1985).
——— see 4, 6 and 8: various, also 8: *on Raoul Pantin.*
Pashley, Alice, 'The Children of Captivity', 3-act opera (*Trin*, 1941).
Paul, Lewis (*SL*) 'Vive La Revolution' (SL. 1982).
Payne, Tommy (*Guy*) 'Cinderella's Big Night, a pageant in one act' (Guy. 1970).
Peart, Moses (*Jam*) 'Me, You and Mi Taxi' (Jam. 1989).
Persad, Kanta (*Trin*) 'House for sale' (Trin. 1993).
Persad, Seeta (*Trin*) 'Dhan Deepak', or 'The Light of Knowledge' (Trin. 1990).
——— 'A New Beginning' (Trin. 1984).
——— 'Sitara' (Trin. 1993).
——— see also 8: *on other playwrights.*
Peters, Francis Urias (*Gren*) 'A New Beginning' (Gren. 1988).
——— 'Struggle, a West Indian play with music' (Gren. 1987).
——— 'Telephone', 1 act (Gren. 1990).
——— 'Who is the Servant?', 3 acts (Gren. 1987).
Philips, Thelma Knight (*Gren*) 'Back to Birth', pageant (Gren. 1971).
——— 'Historical pageant' (Gren. 1964).
——— 'Quiet in Paradise', 1 act (Gren. 1963).
——— 'Resurrection' (Trin. 1971).
Pilgrim, Bill (*Guy*) 'The Purchase', musical (Guy. 1980).
——— 'A Span of Time', historical pageant (Guy. 1976).
——— 'The Yard', musical comedy (Guy. 1981).
Pilgrim, Frank, 'Singing Rum', radio play adapted (Guy. 1964; see 5).
——— see 1, 4 and 5, also 8: *on Frank Pilgrim.*
Pilgrim, Frank and others, 'Again the Brink', revue (Guy.).
——— 'Brink Top', revue (Guy. 1965).
——— 'Brinkmanship', revue (Guy.).
——— 'On the Brink', revue (Guy. 1964).
——— 'Over the Brink', revue (Guy.).
——— 'So This is the Brink', revue (Guy. 1967).
Pinnock, Winsome, 'A Hero's Welcome' (reading London, 1986; revised, London, 1989).
——— 'Leave Taking' (UK. 1988).
——— 'Picture Palace' (UK. 1988).
——— 'The Wind of Change' (London, 1987).
——— see 1 and 4.
Questel, Victor (*Trin*, 1949–1982) 'De Doctor, He Dead' (Trin. 1974).
——— 'Improv, a ritual drama', revised version of 'Sufferer' (Jam. 1981; see also 'Sufferer's Song').
——— 'One Man and His Dog' (Trin. 1984).
——— 'Sufferer' (workshopped Jam. 1981; see 'Improv' and 'Sufferer's Song').
——— 'Sufferer's Song', tribute to Questel, constructed by Earl Warner and the Graduate Theatre Company from 'Sufferer' and 'Two Choices' (Jam. 1983; see also 'Improv').
——— 'Two Choices' (Jam. 1982; see 4; also 'Sufferer's Song').
——— see 3 and 8: *on Derek Walcott,* also 8: *on Victor Questel.*
Ramraj, Victor (*Guy*) 'The Dead Son', 1 scene (Guy. 1966; first prize, Theatre Guild pc, Guy. 1966).
Ramsawack, Al (*Trin*) 'The Devil's Ball of Fire' (Trin. 1972 SSDF).
Rand, Jimi (*Bar*) 'Anansi's Royal Quest' (London, 1983).
Raphael, Lennox (*Trin*) 'Che!' (New York, 1968).
——— 'Dracula the Dreamer' (Trin. 1980).
——— 'The Politicians' (Trin. 1981).
——— 'Rumpelstiltskin', children's play (Trin. 1980).
——— 'Waiting for Mick Jagger' (Trin. 1980).
——— see also 8: *on Lennox Raphael.*
Raphael, Marilyn (*Trin*) 'Looking Inwards' (Trin. 1992 BV).
Reckord, Barry, 'Beverly Hills Call Girls' (Jam. 1989).
——— 'Della' (Jam. 1954; as 'Flesh to a Tiger', London, 1958).

——— 'In the Beautiful Caribbean' (London; see 4).
——— 'Joshua v. Spiderman', satire (Jam.).
——— 'A Liberated Woman' (as 'Don't gas the Blacks', London, 1969).
——— 'Miss Unusual' (Jam. 1956).
——— 'Sugar D' (Jam. 1988).
——— 'The White Witch of Rose Hall' (Jam. 1977).
——— 'X', or 'Let it All Hang Out' (London, 1974).
——— 'You in your small Corner' (London, 1960).
——— see 1 and 5, also 8: *on Barry Reckord.*
Reckord, Lloyd (*Jam*) 'Sipplesilver', see Cumper, Pat, and . . .
Reckord, Maisie, 'Goodwell', 7 scenes (Bar. 1970).
Reckord, Michael: 'And So To Bed' (Jam. 1972; certificate of merit, JFlc, Jam. 1973).
——— 'Fete' (Jam. 1978; best play, best production, UWI Tallawah Drama Festival, Jam. 1976).
——— 'Flip Side: Death' (Jam. 1978).
——— 'The Hon. Allpurpus and the Dancing Princess', Jamaican pantomime, based on a fairy tale adapted by Pat Cumper, with music by Michael and Verena Reckord (Jam. 1979).
——— 'Musical Soup', musical comedy, with music by Tony Miller, Michael Reckord and Erica Brown (Jam. 1977).
——— 'Nanny Meets the Wicked White Witch', short play (Jam. 1986; Prime Minister's award, best short play, Jamaica 21 lc, Jam. 1984).
——— 'Shape' (Cay. 1985).
——— see 1, 3, 4, 5 and 8: *on Basil Dawkins, Ginger Knight*, also 8: *on Michael Reckord.*
Reckord, Michael, Rawle Gibbons, Dennis Scott, and Pierre Le Maire, 'Games', a programme of short plays including 'Prance' and 'Slide' by Michael Reckord (Jam. 1982).
Reckord, Verena (*Jam*, 1935) 'Twelve Million Dollar Man', Jamaican pantomime (Jam. 1977).
——— see 8: *general.*
Reid, Ian (*Jam*) 'Trixters' (Jam. 1990).
——— 'Twice My Age' (Jam. 1990).
Reid, Ronald (*Bar*) 'Return her to me' (Bar. 1970).
Reid, Victor Stafford (*Jam*, 1913–1987) 'Waterfront Bar', 1 act (Jam. 1959).
——— see 6.
Rhone, Trevor: 'Cinderella', pantomime (Jam. c1966).
——— 'Everyman', musical adaptation (Jam. 1981).
——— 'The Gadget' (Jam. 1969; silver medal, JFlc, Jam. 1969).
——— 'The Game' (Jam. 1985).
——— 'I'm human . . . right?', revue (Jam. 1968).
——— 'Music Boy', Jamaican pantomime, with additional material by David Ogden and Barbara Gloudon, music by Jackie Guy and Rex Nettleford (Jam. 1971).
——— 'Sleeper' (Jam. 1974).
——— see 1, 3 and 4, also 8: *on Trevor Rhone.*
Rhone, Trevor and Louis Marriott, 'One Stop Driver' (Jam. 1988).
Rhone, Trevor and Sonia Mills, 'Pepper', a musical commissioned by the Family Planning Association (Jam. 1989).
Rhys, Jean (*Dom*, 1894–1979, *UK*) 'Wide Sargasso Sea', novel adapted by Frances-Ann Solomon (Toronto, 1983).
——— see 6.
Roach, Eric, 'New Dancers in the Dooryard' (Trin. 1970; see 4).
——— see 1, 3, 5 and 8: various, also 8: *on Eric Roach.*
Roberts, Arthur Reginald (*Trin*) 'Divorce' (Trin.).
——— 'Fidelity' (Trin.).
——— 'Is It I?' (Trin.).
——— 'Obeah' (Trin.).
——— 'Retribution' (Trin.).
——— 'Romance Without Sanitation' (Trin.).
——— 'That Hospital!' (Trin. 1940).
——— 'Two Sides of the Picture' (Trin.).
——— 'War Gossip' (Trin. 1941).
——— 'When Wives Meet' (Trin.).
Roberts, Errol (*Trin*) 'Douendom – Carnival Baby' (Trin. 1986 SSDF).

Robinson, Aldwyn (*Trin*) 'No Easy Task', 1 act (Trin. 1968).
Robinson, Carey, 'Mountain Lion' (Jam. 1963; prizewinner, JF, Jam. 1963).
——— see 1.
Rodrigues, Basil (*Guy*) 'Kanima at Sun Mountain' (Guy. 1977).
Rodriguez, Arnaldo (*Trin*) 'Who She, study of the Afro Caribbean Woman in Song, Dance, Drama' (Trin. 1975).
Rogers, Chester (*SV*) 'The Obeah Man', 1 act (SV.1968).
Rogers, DeWilton (*Trin*, 1906–) 'Ace of Spades' (Trin.).
——— 'Blue Blood and Black' (Trin. 1936).
——— 'Silk Cotton Grove' (Trin. 1944).
——— 'Trickidad' (Trin. 1937).
Roller, Kendricks (*Dom*) 'Fear Pyro' (Dom. 1982).
Rudet, Jacqueline, 'God's Second in Command' (UK. 1985).
——— 'Money to Live' (London, 1984).
——— see 1.
Ryan, Finbar (*Trin*) 'Programmes' (Trin. 1983 SSDF).
——— 'Shadow of a Lion' (Trin. 1980; staged reading first national playwrights' conference Trin. 1985).
Sadeek, Sheik, 'Goodbye Corentyne', 1 act (Guy. 1965).
——— see 1 and 3.
St Hill, Errol (Stalk) (*Trin*) 'Black Man Black Gold', commissioned 40th anniversary history of OWTU (Trin. 1977).
——— 'Bush Medicine', 1 act (Trin. 1971; see 4).
——— 'Chicken Lickin' (Trin. 1991).
——— 'Dingolay's Mask', calypso operetta (Trin. 1975).
——— 'It Could Happen To You' (Trin. 1985).
——— 'Kom-E-Dee '84', skits including 'Danny's Dilemma', 'Who's Afraid of the Dark?', 'Man in Mih Own House', 'Super Salesman' and 'Bound to Drunk' (Trin. 1984; other 'Kom-E-Dee's 80, 81, 82, 83).
——— 'Life is a Stage' (Trin. 1983 BV).
——— 'A Suit for the Prime Minister' (Trin. 1985).
——— 'Thrifty Shirley' (Trin. 1991).
——— 'What are Friends for?' (Trin. 1991).
——— see 4.
St Louis, Norbert (*Trin*) 'Kathleen' (Trin. 1945).
Salmon, Kenny (*Jam*) 'Shades' (Jam. 1991).
Saul, Leon (*Guy*) 'For Better For Worse', two radio serials adapted (Guy. 1981).
Saunders, Ryan (*Trin*) 'Stone Walls and Iron Bars' (Trin. 1988 SSDF; best original play, SSDF, Trin. 1988).
Saunders, Winston (*Bah*) 'You Can Take a Horse to Water' (Bah. 1983).
Schwarz-Bart, Simone (*Gua*) 'Ton Beau capitane' (Gua. 1987; in English as 'Your Handsome Captain', Bar. 1993).
——— see also 8: *on other playwrights.*
Scott, Anne and Jack Scott, 'Red Riding Hood', pantomime (Trin. 1958).
Scott, Dennis, 'Breakfast with a Witch, a grim fairy tale' (Jam. 1964).
——— 'The Caged', 1 act (Jam. 1961).
——— 'Cold Equation', adapted from the story by Tom Godwin (Jam. 1959).
——— 'Games', see Reckord, Michael and . . .
——— 'The Inquisitors' (Trin. 1963).
——— 'Live and Direct from Babylon' (Jam. 1983).
——— 'Queenie's Daughter', see Fowler, Greta and . . .
——— 'The Ritual' (Trin. 1962).
——— 'A Short Story' (Jam. 1969).
——— see 1, 3, 4, 6 and 8: *on Michael Reckord*, also 8: *on Dennis Scott.*
Seaforth, Sylvia (*Trin*) 'Turning Point' (staged reading, first national playwrights' conference, Trin. 1985).
Sealy, Clifford, 'The Smell of Damp' (Trin. 1983; written 1968).
——— see 1 and 6, also 8: *on other playwrights.*
Sealy, Godfrey (*Trin*) 'Aida, the Wicked Wench of the World' (Trin. 1989).
——— 'Funny Business' (Trin. 1990).
——— 'Girlfriends', 2-act musical (Trin. 1989).
——— 'Home Sweet Home' (Trin. 1989).

——— 'How Pot Hound get he Name', 1 act (Trin. 1989).
——— 'Is There a Doctor in the House?' (Trin. 1990).
——— 'Limin' ', musical (Trin. 1985; see 4).
——— 'One of Our Sons is Missing' (Trin. 1988).
——— 'Play Yuh Mas!', Carnival musical (Trin. 1991).
——— 'Roll Call' (Trin. 1989; best original play, NDATT Cacique awards, Trin. 1990).
——— 'To Hell Wid Dat', Carnival musical based on and incorporating parts of Felix Edinborough's 'Go To Hell' (Trin. 1990).
——— 'You Never Miss the Water Till the Well run dry' (Trin. 1989).
——— see also 8: *on Godfrey Sealy.*
Sealy, Godfrey and John Isaacs, 'Yes We Can' (Trin. 1983).
Selim, Abdel Moneim, 'Marital Bliss' (Trin. 1984).
Selvon, Sam, 'Basement Lullaby', adapted from the story in 'Ways of Sunlight' (Trin. 1960; see 4, 5).
——— 'Brackley and the Bed', adapted from the story in 'Ways of Sunlight' (Trin. 1960; see 4).
——— 'A Brighter Sun', novel adapted by the Alternative National Theatre (Trin. 1985; see 4).
——— 'Switch' (London, 1977).
——— 'The Taming of the Show-Off', 1 act, story adapted by George Collymore (San Fernando, Trin. 1962; see 4).
——— 'The World of Sam Selvon', containing 'Basement Lullaby', 'Brackley and the Bed', 'The Calypsonian', 'The Old Moses', 'The Seagull', 'The Village Washer', 'Waiting for Aunty to Cough', and readings from 'A Brighter Sun', 'The Housing Lark' and 'I hear Thunder' (Trin. 1969; see 4).
——— see 1, 3, 4, 5 and 6, also 8: *on Sam Selvon.*
Senghor, Attiba (*Trin*) 'Mice don't roar' (Trin. 1990 SSDF).
Senior, Olive (*Jam*, 1941) 'Country of the One-Eyed God', short story adapted by Icil Phillips (Bar. c1992).
——— see 6.
Shanahan, Charles (*Jam*) 'The Mysteries of Vegetarianism', 1-act farce (Jam. 1853).
——— 'The Spanish Warrior', or 'The Death of Vasco Nunez', historical drama (Jam. 1853).
Singh, Rajkumari (*Guy*) 'The Sound of her Bells' (Guy. 1971).
——— see 3.
Sistren, collective creation, 'Bandoolu Version' (Jam. 1979; certificate of merit, OAS Commission of Women, Jam. 1979).
——— 'Buss Out', see Cumper, Pat and . . .
——— 'The Case of Iris Armstrong' (Jam. 1984).
——— 'Domestick' (Jam. 1982).
——— 'Downpression Get A Blow' (Jam. 1977).
——— 'Ida Revolt Inna Jonkunnu Stylee', see Caribbean Popular Theatre Exchange.
——— 'Muffet Inna All A We' (Jam. 1985).
——— 'Nana Yah' (Jam. 1980).
——— 'Sistren Song', musical (Jam. 1985).
——— 'Tribute' (Jam. 1983).
——— see 1 and 6, also 8: *on Sistren.*
Sitahal, Errol (*Trin*) 'Adult Sufferage', see Hall, Anthony and . . .
——— 'Bells', adaptation of Austin Clarke's novel *When I was Free and Young and Used to Wear Silks* (reading Toronto, 1980; Trin. 1982).
——— 'Jaahaji', play for Divali Nagar (Trin. 1988).
——— 'Let Man Live' (Trin. 1968).
——— 'The Mission Begins', play with dance (Trin. 1968).
——— 'Monster March' (Trin. 1987).
——— 'Sea Shango' (Toronto, 1978; workshopped Toronto, 1976).
——— see also 8: *on other playwrights.*
Smith, Jackie (*Guy*) 'A Bitter Memory' (Guy. 1968).
Smith, Ricardo (*Guy*) 'Guyana Legend', 3 acts, commissioned for 1966 Independence celebrations of Guyana (Guy. 1966).

——— 'Miss Phoebe', 1-act musical (Guy. 1963).

Soungie, Francis (*Trin*) 'The Lunatics', 1 act (Trin. 1983).

Spencer, Rhoma (*Trin*) 'Bois for Bois, a Folk Musicale' (Trin. 1987 SSDF).

——— 'Bullet in the Heart', 1 act (Trin. 1988).

——— 'Danse Macabre' (Trinidad, 1988 SSDF).

——— 'Judgement', gospel musical (Trin. 1989).

——— 'No Exit' (Trin. 1988 BV; second prize, Prime Minister's BV competition, Trin. 1988).

Springer, Eintou Pearl, 'Ti-Jean and Mariquite' (Trin. 1987).

——— 'The Trial', 1 act (Trin. 1979).

——— see 1 and 8: *on Raoul Pantin*, also 8: *on C.L.R. James, other playwrights.*

Springer, Marvin, 'Everybody is Somebody' (Trin. 1992).

Stevenson, Dennis (Trin) 'When You Dead You Done', 1 act (Trin. 1966).

Stone, Judy (*UK*, 1939) 'Old Mas, Pretty Mas', 2 acts (Trin. 1982).

——— see 3 and 8: various, also 8: *on other playwrights.*

Stuart, Joyce (*Guy*) 'Passport to Heaven, Revuedeville 1950', musical (Bar. 1950).

——— 'Revuedeville 1951, customs, culture and folklore of Trinidad, British Guiana, Jamaica and Barbados' (Bar. 1951).

——— 'Revuedeville 1952' (Bar. 1952).

——— 'Revuedeville 1953' (Bar. 1953).

Sukoorali, Hafeezul (*Trin*) 'A Little Soap and Water' (Trin. 1969 SSDF; best original script, SSDF, Trin. 1969).

Swift, Wayne (*Trin*) 'The Family', 1 act (Trin. 1983).

——— 'Man Must Live', 1 act (Trin. 1983).

Tafari, Ras Abdul Rahim (*Trin*) 'Columbus the Colonizer' (Trin. 1992).

——— 'From Chaka to Buthelezi' (Trin. c1990).

Tafari, Ras Ikael (*Bar*) 'Meet Me At Golden Square' (Barb. 1989).

Theobalds, Tom (*Jam*) 'A Climate of Concern', 3 acts (Jam. 1963).

Thomas, Davlin (*Trin*) 'The Play Within The Play' (Trin. 1991; first prize, National Petroleum pc, Trin. 1991).

——— 'Sans Humanite' (Trin. 1992).

——— see also 8: *on other playwrights.*

Thomas, Van (*Trin*) 'The Morocoy Man' (Trin. 1984).

Thomas, Vereen (*Mont*) 'The Long Holiday' (Mont. 1979).

Thompson, Flo (*Jam*) 'True Love Never Dies' (Jam. 1965; high commendation, JF, Jam. 1965?).

Thompson, Tony (*Bar*) 'Franny', musical (Bar. 1983).

——— 'Fuzzy's Sermon', musical (Bar. c1976).

Tipling, Carmen: 'The Delicately Wounded', 1 act (Missouri, USA. 1965).

——— 'Port Royal Ho!', see Dwyer, Ted and . . .

——— see 1 and 3.

Tipling, Carmen and Ted Dwyer, 'Bruckins', Jamaican pantomime, with music by Noel Dexter and Jon Williams (Jam. 1988).

Tjon, Henk and Thea Doelwijte (*Sur*) 'Stages', historical musical (Sur. 1981; workshopped ST. 1981: first Caribbean playwrights' conference).

Townshend, Mitzie, 'Apartment to Let' (Jam. 1966; first prize, JFlc, Jam. 1964).

——— see 1.

UCWI Summer School students, 'Naboth's Vineyard' (Jam. 1953).

Valz, Ian (*Guy*) 'Voodoo Verdict' (Guy. 1990).

Vignale, Ralph (*Trin*) 'Belle of the Harem' (Trin. 1924).

Wacca, Chaku (*Ant*) 'Time Bomb' (Ant. 1978).

Waite-Smith, Cicely, 'The Ravishers', 3 acts (Jam. 1958).

——— see 1, 3, 5 and 6, also 8: *on other playwrights.*

Walcott, Derek, 'Batai', Dimanche Gras Carnival show (Trin. 1965).

——— 'Crossroads', 1 act (Jam. 1954).

——— 'Cry for a Leader', 1-act verse play (SL. 1950).

——— 'Franklin, a Tale of the Islands', developed from 'The Wine of the Country' (Guy. 1969; revised, Trin. 1973; revised, Bar. 1990; prize-winner, Barbados Arts Council pc, Bar. 1968).
——— 'Ghost Dance' (Oneonta, USA. 1989; winner, College Play prize).
——— 'The Golden Lions', 3-act verse drama, developed from 'Dying Gods' (Jam. 1956; see 3).
——— 'Haytian Earth', commissioned by the St Lucia government (SL. 1984; see 4).
——— 'The Isle is Full of Noises' (Hartford, USA. 1982).
——— 'Let Resurrection Come', programme commissioned for the 25th anniversary of UWI St Augustine, compiled by Patricia Ismond of excerpts from *A Branch of the Blue Nile*, *Dream on Monkey Mountain*, *The Joker of Seville*, *Pantomime* and *Ti-Jean and His Brothers* (Trin. 1986).
——— 'The Price of Mercy', 1 act (SL. c1951)
——— 'Senza Alcun Sospetto', 1-act verse play (as 'Paolo and Francesca', SL. c1951; see 5).
——— 'Steel', with music by Galt MacDermot (Boston, USA. 1991).
——— 'Three Assassins', 1-act verse play (SL. c1951).
——— 'To Die for Grenada' (Cleveland, USA. 1986).
——— 'The Wine of the Country' (Jam. 1956).
——— see 1, 3, 4, 5, 6, 7 and 8: various, also 8: *on Derek Walcott.*
Walcott, Derek and Martin Carter, dramatised by Ernest Rodriguez, 'Journeys', based on Walcott's 'The Schooner Flight' and Carter's 'Poems of Resistance' (as 1-man show 'Schooner Flight', Jam. 1987; full show, Trin. 1988).
Walcott, Derek and others, 'Mammy Mammy Look Snow', children's play (Trin. 1980).
Walcott, Roderick, 'Carnival Revisited', Carnival show (SL. 1959).
——— 'Chanson Marianne', musical (SL. 1974).
——— 'Conte Mabouya, or The Guitar-Man's Song' (SL. 1989).
——— 'The Education of Alfie', 1 act (SL. 1964).
——— 'The Expatriates', full-length play (SL. 1963 AFA).
——— 'The Image of Canga Brown', 3-act play based on the poem by Eric Roach (SL. 1979).
——— 'The One-eye is King', 1 act (SL. 1956).
——— 'Papa Diable', musical (SL. 1977).
——— 'Romiel ec Violette', musical (SL. 1979).
——— see 1, 3, 4, 5 and 8: *general.*
Walker, Sullivan (*Trin*) 'Black Woman' (USA. 1983).
——— 'Boy Days' (New York, 1988).
——— 'Caribbean Woman', a collection of skits including 'De Man Ugly Too Much', '13th Child', and 'Wayside Vendor' (New York, 1982).
——— 'Down Trinidad Way' (USA. 1977).
——— 'Is We Own Ting', a montage of short stories, poems and sketches (New York, 1982).
——— 'The Journey', 9-scene monologue (first scene, New York, 1975; full work, USA. 1977).
——— 'Mother and Daughter', 3 acts (USA. 1976).
——— 'Piece for a King' (USA. 1975).
——— 'Requiem for ah Pan Mastah', 1 act (New York, 1981).
——— 'Two Soldiers at a Crossroad', 2 acts (USA. 1978).
——— see also 8: *on other playwrights.*
Walker, William, 'Victorious Love' (London, 1698).
——— see 1.
Wallace, Julius (*Trin*) 'Time for Truth' (Trin. 1971 SSDF).
Wallace, Rudolph (*ST*) 'The Philosopher Limer' (ST. c1982; workshopped ST. 1981: first Caribbean playwrights' conference).
Ward, Peter (*Trin*) 'The Devil on Calvary' (Trin. 1970).
Warner, Earl (*Bar*) 'Rock', musical created from works by Edward Kamau Brathwaite, Michael Gilkes, George

Lamming and Eric Roach (Bar. 1987).
——— 'Unchained', see Hinkson, Anthony and . . .
Warner, Earl, Stage One and others, 'Lights' (Bar. 1985).
——— 'Lights 2' (Bar. 1986).
——— see also 8: *on other playwrights.*
Watson, Anthony T, and the Wolmer's playmaking group. 'Joseph an' 'im Bredren' (Jam. 1957).
Webster, Paul (*Bar*, –1989) 'Under the Duppy Parasol', musical (New York, c1974).
Wells, Lesley-Ann (*Trin*) 'Danse', folk musical (Trin. 1992).
——— see also 8: *on other playwrights.*
West Indian Lady, A, 'Scandal Club, or Virtue In Danger' (Jam. c1781).
White, Edgar, 'The Defense' (New York, 1976).
——— 'Masada' (London).
——— 'Moon Dance Night', 3 acts (London, 1987)
——— 'Three Kings Darkly' (Jam. 1989).
——— 'Tres Cepas' (Cuba. c1987).
——— see 1, 3 and 6, also 8: *on Edgar White.*
Wickham, Elton (*Trin*) 'David Come Back' (Trin. 1974 SSDF).
——— 'Guilty as Charged' (Trin. 1978 SSDF).
——— 'Hamilton's Choice' (Trin. SSDF).
——— see also 8: *on other playwrights.*
Wight, Gerald, '3000 Years After' (Trin. 1926).
Wilkinson, Lester Efebo, 'Bitter Cassava', folk musical (Trin. 1979 BV; best written play, BV, Trin. 1979; best original play, NDF, Trin. 1984; see 4).
——— 'De Bocas is Mih Bound', BV folk musical (Trin. 1982 BV; best written play, BV, Trin. 1982).
——— 'Flag Woman', folk musical (Japan. 1989 International Amateur Theatre Association).
——— 'Is Who Kill Cock Robin?', folk musical (Trin. 1981 BV; best written play, BV, Trin. 1981).
——— 'It have King and King', children's play (Trin. 1977).
——— 'Lisa's Dream', children's play (Trin. 1978).
——— 'Same Khaki Pants', folk musical (Trin. 1980 BV; best written play, BV, Trin. 1980; see 4).
——— 'Santa Will Show You', children's play (Trin. 1978; see 4).
——— see 1, 4 and 5, also 8: *on Lester Efebo Wilkinson.*
Williams, Cecil A. 'Blazer' (*SV*) 'Backyard', 1 act (Bar.).
——— 'Bedroom not for Sleeping'.
——— 'Breaking of Chains'.
——— 'The Clearing'.
——— 'The Critics', 1 act (c1970).
——— 'Drawing Room' (Bar.).
——— 'I Don't Want to Bathe' (SV).
——— 'Nine Mornings' (SV. 1989).
——— 'War Delusions'.
——— 'The Woodworker', 2 acts.
Williams, Cecil and others, 'Do Mek Me See'.
Williams, Clement 'Bouncin'' (*SK*) 'It's Only For a Time'.
Williams, Maurice A. (*SK*) 'Hang Them High', 3 acts (SK. 1979).
Williams, Ranny (*Jam*) 'Blacks gone Wild' (Jam. 1929).
——— 'Jamaica Way', Jamaican pantomime (Jam. 1959).
——— 'King Belshazzar' (Jam. 1930).
——— 'Landing the landlord' (Jam. 1930).
——— 'Oh, what a wedding' (Jam. 1950).
——— 'Old black Joe' (Jam. 1930).
——— 'Perfectly satisfied' (Jam. 1930).
——— 'Quashie Lady', Jamaican pantomime, with lyrics and music by Robert Lightbourne and Eddy Thomas (Jam. 1958).
——— 'Queenie's Daughter', see Fowler, Greta and . . .
——— 'Robinson Crusoe', adaptation traditional pantomime (Jam. 1953).
——— 'Say it Singing' (Jam. 1930?).
——— 'She is a Sheba' (Jam. 1930).
Williams, Ranny and Phil Coppin, 'Ugly but good looking', sketch (Jam. 1930).
Wilson, E.N, 'Playing Truant' (Guy. 1949).
——— 'Purple Twilight' (Guy. 1946).
——— 'Star of Bethlehem' (Guy. 1951).
Wilson, Jeanne, 'The Heiress', 1 act (Jam. 1962 SSDF).

——— see 1, 3 and 8: *on Michael Reckord, other playwrights.*

Wilson, Peter, 'Harold Blakey' (Trin. 1957).

Worrell, Andy, 'Isabella', folk musical (Trin. 1991 BV).

——— 'The Root of all Evil', folk musical (Trin. 1992 BV).

Wynter, Sylvia, '1865 Ballad for a rebellion' (Jam. 1965).

——— 'Ssh . . . it's a wedding', musical (Jam. c1961).

——— see 1, 4 and 6.

Wynter, Sylvia and Alex Gradussov, 'Rockstone Anancy, a magical morality', Jamaican pantomime, with music by Joyce Campbell (Jam. 1970).

Yearwood, David Jr. (*Trin*) 'De Trail of the Brown and Scarlet Soucouyant' (Trin. 1989 BV).

Yearwood, Roland (*Trin*) 'I Created a Monster, or Rus the Mockasaurus', musical (Trin. 1990).

Yetming, Clive (*Trin*) 'An Echo of Drums' (Trin. 1966).

Young, Colville, 'Aggravatin' Pikni' (Bel. c1972).

——— 'Simon Lamb', 3 acts (Bel.).

——— 'Tiger Dead', folk musical (Bel. 1991).

——— see 1.

Young, Ethelbert, 'Basin Street Blues' (Trin. 1940).

——— 'Briars and Blossoms' (Trin. 1939).

——— 'Redemption' (Trin. 1939).

Zephaniah, Benjamin, 'Playing the Right Tune' (London).

——— 'Streetwise' (London, 1991).

——— see 1, 5 and 6.

Zindika, 'Paper and Stone' (London, 1990).

——— see also 8: *on other playwrights.*

3 PRIZE-WINNING PLAYS AND OTHER SCRIPTS OF HISTORICAL INTEREST, UNPUBLISHED AND UNPERFORMED

(in the absence of competition dates, the year given is for completion of manuscript, as available).

Archibald, Douglas, 'Sleep in Ashes Cold', 3 acts (original script 1956; revised 1974).

——— see 1, 2, 4, 5 and 6, also 8: *on Douglas Archibald.*

Ashani, Stafford, 'Bacchanal of Black Inventions', 2-act Carnival musical on the lives of Lewis Latimer and Granville Woods, originally commissioned by London's Battimamzel Productions under the title 'Man Who Lit up the World' (written 1991).

——— 'Bar Jonah', 2-act gospel musical on Alexander Bedward (written 1982).

——— 'Ites of Mar', 1 act (written 1983).

——— 'Nyahbinghi', full-length drama with song and dance (basis for research project into Rastafari, London 1987–91).

Benn, Denis Martin (*Guy*) 'Toussaint L'Ouverture, a struggle for freedom, an historical drama in verse', 5 acts (written 1968).

Bourne, Kate, 'Broken Chords'.

——— see 2.

Brown, Lennox, 'Fire for an Ice Age', 1 act (second prize, University of Toronto Drama Guild competition, Can. 1968).

——— 'The Night Class', 2 acts (runner up US Schubert Fellowship award, University of Michigan Theatre School, USA. 1970).

——— 'Night Sun' (first prize, the Karsh Award and Birk's Gold Medal, National 1-act pc, Can. 1967).

——— 'The Voyage Tonight' (second prize, Norma Epstein National Creative writing award, University of Toronto, Can. 1969).

——— 'Wine in Winter', originally titled 'King Kong', a 1-act play in the quartet 'The Crystal Tree'; see 5).

——— see 1, 2, 4, 5 and 8: *on Felix Edinborough*, also 8: *on Lennox Brown.*

Browne, Charles, 'Professor Saggy' (honourable mention, JFlc, Jam. 1964).

——— see 1.

Browne, Vincent B. (*Mont*) 'And on the Seventh Day', full-length play on the St Patrick's Day slave rebellion).

Callender, Timothy (*Bar*, 1946–89) 'The Lodger' (first prize, Esso pc, Bar. 1985).

——— see 6, also 8: *on other playwrights.*
Campbell, Ralph (*Trin*) 'Callaloo Suite'.
——— 'Death of a Crow', 3 acts (mimeo 1971).
——— 'Royal Visit' (c1964).
——— see 8: *on Derek Walcott*, also 8: *on other playwrights.*
Cendrecourt, Esme, 'Captain's party: a play'.
——— 'New probationer: a play in three acts'.
——— 'Night in the Caribbean: a play'.
——— see 2.
Chattoram, Paul (*Guy*) 'The Fall of an Idol' (prizewinner, Republic pc, Guy. 1970).
Chen, Willi: 'Cayu Cayenne, The Hunter', 4 acts (first prize drama, NCClc, Trin. 1981).
——— 'A Change of Heart', tv play (second prize, TTTpc, Trin. 1984; see 2).
——— see 2 and 4, also 8: *on Willi Chen.*
Creighton, Al (*Jam*) 'Your Witness', 1 act (certificate of merit, JFlc, Jam. 1967).
——— see 8: *on Harold Bascom.*
Cross, Felix, 'The Game of the Gods'.
——— 'La Trinite', sequel to 'Mass Carib', commissioned by Nottingham Playhouse.
——— see 2, also 8: *on Felix Cross.*
Cross, Felix and Lisa Forrell, 'Motortown Blues', musical.
Elder, Jacob D. (*Trin*) 'Cavalcade Caribbe, a pageant scenario'.
Figueroa, John (*Jam*, 1920) 'Jephtha's Daughter, a tragedy'.
——— 'The Straits of Aulis, a tragedy based on the Greek story of Agamemnon'.
Forsythe, Victor, 'Liberty Village', radio play (prizewinner, Demba radio play competition, Guy. 1966).
——— 'The Waterfront', radio play; see 2).
——— see 2 and 5.
Foster, Melville, 'Suffrage', tv play (third prize, Tradewinds Collective national lc, Trin. 1987).
——— see 2, 4 and 5.
Fritsche, Frank (*SL*) 'La Duchesse de Langeais', verse play.
Fullerton, Norvan, and Landrigen Stephen: 'Canboulay' (print USA. 1990).
——— see 2 and 4, also 8: *on other playwrights.*
Galt, Roy: 'Goodnight, Lisa, Goodbye' (third prize drama, NCClc, Trin. 1981).
——— 'The Secret' (first prize, Arts Festival pc, Trin. 1959).
——— see 2.
Gayle, Lois, 'Jonathan's Success' (certificate of merit, JFlc, Jam. 1969).
——— see 2.
George, Dykes and Osbourne Ashby, 'Make Me a Flower' (honorable mention, Theatre Guild Foundation, USA. 1962).
——— see 1 and 2.
Gonzales, Kit (*Trin*) 'Nine Months with Interest' (prizewinner, Drama Guild pc, Trin. 1971–72).
Hamilton, Norma (*Jam*) 'These People never learn' (bronze medal, JFlc, Jam. 1970).
Hernandez, Janice (*Can*) 'Corbeaux Carnival' (finalist, BBCpc, London 1993).
Hill, Errol, 'Freedom, brother, is . . . ', 6 scenes (mimeo 1970).
——— 'Happiness', adapted from Anton Chekhov's short story.
——— 'The silver palace', 3 acts (typescript 1956).
——— see 1, 2, 4, 5, 7 and 8: *on Derek Walcott, general*, also 8: *on Errol Hill.*
Hillary, Samuel, 'A Broken Wing' (high commendation, JFlc, Jam. 1965).
——— 'Favours of Lovers' (bronze medal, JFlc, Jam. 1966).
——— see 1 and 2, also 8: *on other playwrights.*
James, Cynthia (*Trin*) 'My Known Hero' (special prize, National Petroleum pc, Trin. 1991).
John, Errol, 'The Best of Times', tv comedy series (treatment written 1982).
——— 'Celebration', play (written 1982).
——— 'Census, a tale of terror and comic surprise', tv play (treatment written 1982).
——— 'Country Road Take Me Home', tv play (treatment written 1979).

——— 'Horseman Pass By', screenplay of 'The Exiles' (see 4).
——— 'House of Flowers', treatment and first draft screenplay of Truman Capote's novel (written 1969).
——— 'Rolling Stock', screenplay (written 1981–2).
——— 'Sarah', screenplay for a psycho-thriller (treatment written 1979, 35-page exposition 1980–82).
——— 'They say that Carnaval is a Creole Bacchanal', screenplay based on 'Moon on a Rainbow Shawl' (see 1, 4, 5).
——— 'Tryst, a meeting between an ageing woman and a youth', tv play (treatment written 1982).
——— see 1, 2 and 4, also 8: *on Errol John.*
John, Ronald, 'First Love' (second prize, Drama Guild pc, Trin. 1974).
——— 'Shalto's Dilemma' (first prize, Drama Guild pc, Trin. 1974).
——— 'Sun Queen' (first prize drama, NCCpc, Trin. 1978).
——— see 1, 2, 5 and 8: *on Derek Walcott,* also 8: *on Ronald John.*
King, Sheila, 'Wings to Two Mornings', radio play (second prize, Guyana Information Services Independence radio pc, Guy. 1966).
——— see 2.
King, Sidney (*Guy*) 'The Promised Land' (prizewinner, Drama Festival, Guy. 1965).
Loague, Mark, 'Breeze Blow' (prizewinner, JFlc, Jam. 1966).
——— see 1.
Lopez, Basil (*Jam*) 'In Another House' (Alcan award, JFlc, Jam. 1967).
Mais, Roger, 'Afternoon of the Gods', radio play, also 1-act play.
——— 'Apollo in Delos', 6 scenes (typescript 1943–50).
——— 'Before Philippi', play, also radio play (typescript 1943–50).
——— 'The Cloak', radio play.
——— 'The Cuckoo Clock' (typescript 1943–50).
——— 'Dragon's Teeth in the Ground'.
——— 'General Joshua', 3 acts, also radio play (typescript 1943–50).
——— 'The Golden Eagle', radio play.
——— 'The House of the Pomegranate', play, also radio play.
——— 'The Jest of Hassim', 5 scenes (typescript 1943–50).
——— 'Jorinda and Joringel', 1 act (typescript 1947–50).
——— 'Laughter on Olympus', radio play.
——— 'Lazarus' (typescript 1943–50).
——— 'The little green man', play, also radio play (manuscript 1947–50).
——— 'Love came in also', radio play.
——— 'Man about a squirrel'.
——— 'Moon over Ajalon'.
——— 'The Morning of Man', radio play.
——— 'The Naked Truth', play, also radio play.
——— 'The Old Mill Pool', play, also radio play.
——— 'Ordinary People' (typescript 1953).
——— 'Rosalind and Rolando' (manuscript 1947–50; as 'Rosamund and Rolando, a play in three acts', typescript 1943–50).
——— 'Samson' (typescript 1943–50).
——— 'Sinbad and Hindbad'.
——— 'Song for the Night', 1 act.
——— 'The Time of our Lives'.
——— 'The White Oxen', play, also radio play (manuscript 1947–50).
——— 'Wind over Aulus', 1 act.
——— 'You gotta go home', radio play (manuscript 1947–48).
——— see 1, 2 and 6, also 8: *on other playwrights.*
Manley, Carmen (*Jam*) 'Chi chi bud's love', tv play (Alcan award and certificate of merit, JFlc, Jam. 1967).
——— 'Coffee party' (certificate of merit, JFlc, Jam. 1970).
——— 'No Fool Like an Old Fool' (certificate of merit, JFlc, Jam. 1970).
——— see 5.
Manning, Lloyd (*Guy*) 'Cuffy, an historical drama in two acts' (2nd prize, Republic playwriting competition, Guy. 1970).
——— see 5.
McWilliams, Randhi (*Ant*) 'Sidewalk Sidney' (second prize, Manchester

Royal Exchange Theatre/Mobil Oil pc, UK. 1990).
Mittelholzer, Edgar, 'The Aloneness of Mrs Chatham, a sophisticated comedy' (mimeo).
——— 'Entirely Traditional' (written 1954).
——— 'Fears and Mirages'.
——— 'Ghosts at their Shoulders'.
——— 'No Guileless People'.
——— 'The Savannah Years'.
——— 'The Weather in Middenshot, a serio-comedy, dramatisation of the novel.'
——— see 1 and 6, also 7.
Momager, George (*Guy*) 'It Pays to Live an Independent Life', radio play (fourth prize, Guyana Information Services Independence radio pc, Guy. 1966).
Ogilvie, W. G., 'Hi, Miss Cleo', 3 acts.
——— 'His English Wife' (high commendation, JFlc, Jam. 1965).
——— 'The Legacy', 1 act.
——— 'Me Tief', 3 acts.
——— see 1 and 2.
Persaud, B. Darendra (*Trin*) 'Daughter's Dilemma', 2 acts (first prize, Theatre Guild pc, Trin. 1963).
Phillips, Anton (*Jam*) 'After three hundred' (Alcan award, JFlc, Jam).
Questel, Victor, 'Crossroads' (written 1980).
——— 'Countdown', 2-actor comedy (written 1979).
——— 'Dry Season Gods', Amerindian love story (written 1973).
——— see 2, 4 and 8: *on Derek Walcott*, also 8: *on Victor Questel.*
Ramchandani, Kay B. (*Trin*) 'You Need Contact See' (second prize drama, NCClc, Trin. 1981).
Reckord, Michael, 'Creatures of Habit' (silver award, JFlc, Jam. 1979).
——— 'Hello, I'm a Mermaid' (silver award, JFlc, Jam. 1983).
——— 'Jamaica Gold', adapted from the novel by Michael and Verena Reckord (bronze award, JFlc, Jam. 1979).
——— 'Nanny Meets the White Witch', full-length play (written 1988).
——— 'Rover' (bronze award, JFlc, Jam. 1979).
——— 'Uncoupling' (bronze award, JFlc, Jam. 1986).
——— 'Walk: A Romance' (bronze award, JFlc, Jam. 1983).
——— see 1, 2, 4, 5 and 8: *on Basil Dawkins, Ginger Knight*, also 8: *on Michael Reckord.*
Rhone, Trevor, 'The Blue Socks Blues' (bronze medal, JFlc, Jam. 1970).
——— see 1, 2 and 4, also 8: *on Trevor Rhone.*
Roach, Eric, 'The Corrigans' (first prize drama, UWI 25th anniversary lc, Jam. 1975).
——— 'Homecoming', domestic drama in verse.
——— see 1 and 2, also 8: *on Eric Roach.*
Sadeek, Sheik, 'Black Bush', radio play (prizewinner, Demba Radio play competition 1966).
——— 'Bound coolie', or 'Song of the sugarcanes' (written 1964).
——— see 1 and 2.
St Clair, Gandolph (*SL*) 'Just in Case' (second prize, BBC Caribbean Magazine radio play competition, London 1983).
Scott, Dennis, 'Chariots of Wrath' (gold medal, JFlc, Jam. 1966).
——— 'The Passionate Cabbage' (bronze medal, JFlc, Jam. 1969).
——— 'Quartet' (unfinished draft 1991).
——— see 1, 2, 4, 6 and 8: *on Michael Reckord*, also 8: *on Dennis Scott.*
Seaforth, Carol (*Guy*) 'Big Dilemma', 1 act (second prize, pc, Guy. 1963).
Selvon, Sam, 'The Lonely Londoners', screenplay adapted from the novel, commissioned by Robert Parish Enterprises (written 1958).
——— see 1, 2, 4, 5 and 6, also 8: *on Sam Selvon.*
Shand, Eden, 'The Temporary', tv play (prizewinner, NCClc, Trin. 1978).
——— see 1 and 8: *on Zeno Constance, Lester Efebo Wilkinson.*
Silvera, Maxwell St Aubyn (*Jam*) 'Shout First', 1 act (certificate of merit, JFlc, Jam. 1970).
Simmons, Dorothea, with A.J. and others, 'Wa Fe Do?, a Jamaican dialect play in three scenes' (c1937).
Singh, Rajkumari, 'Roraima', radio play

(prizewinner, Demba Radio play competition, Guy. 1966).
——— see 2.
Stone, Judy, 'Beausourire' (first prize drama, UWI 25th anniversary lc, Jam. 1975).
——— 'The Three Wives of Mahmoud the Saviour', radio play on the 1990 Muslim coup (typescript 1992).
——— see 2 and 8: various, also 8: *on other playwrights.*
Taylor, Lloyd (*Jam*) 'People's Business gi' me' (certificate of merit, JFlc, Jam. 1965).
Tipling, Carmen, 'The Comfortable Arrangement' (certificate of merit, JFlc, Jam. 1969).
——— 'Decision, Decision' (certificate of merit, JFlc, Jam. 1969).
——— 'The longest way is back', (silver medal, JFlc, Jam. 1968).
——— see 1 and 2.
Turner, T. E., 'Woman Take Two' (first prize drama, UWI 25th anniversary lc, Jam. 1975).
Waite-Smith, Cicely, 'The People's Champion', a play in 2 parts (typescript, 1957).
——— see 1, 2, 5 and 6, also 8: *on other playwrights.*
Wakeling, T. G., 'Ann Palmer of Rose Hall', 3-act historical drama (presented by the author to the Institute of Jamaica 1934).
Walcott, Derek, 'Another World for the Lost', 1-act verse play (written c1947).
——— 'Dying Gods', 1 act (typescript c1956; see 2: 'The Golden Lions').
——— 'Flight and Sanctuary', 1-act verse play (typescript 1946).
——— 'A Georgian House' (typescript c1954).
——— 'The Matadors', 1-act verse play (written c1947).
——— 'A Simple Cornada', 1-act verse play (written c1947).
——— 'Soso's Wake', 1-act comedy (typescript c1953).
——— 'A Sound of Hunting', 3-act play, revised version of 'A Georgian House' (mimeograph 1954).
——— see 1, 2, 4, 5, 6, 7 and 8: various, also 8: *on Derek Walcott.*
Walcott, Roderick, 'Cassian and Capricorn', 1 act Nativity play (written 1990).
——— 'Columbus and Guarionex'.
——— 'Field of Honour, an experiment in tele-theatre'.
——— 'I'll Remember Clifford', screenplay based on Clifford Brown.
——— 'The Legend of Tom Fool', 3-act musical comedy with score by Charles Cadet (mimeo, 1968).
——— 'Let Them Call It Jazz', 1-act play based on the short story by Jean Rhys.
——— 'Make a Joyful Sound', musical comedy.
——— 'Poucette, or The Devil with Love', fantasy in verse.
——— 'The Prowess of Ti-Jean, or, The Sound of a Wild Flute'.
——— 'Sugar Ray', screenplay on Sugar Ray Robinson.
——— 'Sweeeet Like Sugar', musical on Sugar Ray Robinson.
——— 'The Wonderful World of Brother Rabbit', musical comedy with score by Charles Cadet.
——— see 1, 2, 4, 5 and 8: *general.*
Waldron, Olutoye (*Bar*) 'The Price of Progress' (first prize, BBC Caribbean Magazine radio play competition, London, 1983).
White, Edgar, 'Abiku'.
——— see 1, 2 and 6, also 8: *on Edgar White.*
Wilmot, Cynthia (*Can*, 1921) 'Anancy and the Magic Calabash'.
——— 'Anancy Makes a Bargain'.
——— 'Benjie's Best Christmas'.
——— 'The Dancing Donkey of Old Rose Hall'.
——— 'The Lonely Lamb'.
——— see 5.
Wilson, Jeanne, 'No Medicine for Murder', 1 act (high commendation, JFlc, Jam. 1965).
——— 'No Truth at all', 1 act (certificate of merit, JFlc, Jam. 1966).
——— 'Reality is Relative', 1 act (high commendation, JFlc, Jam. 1965).
——— see 1, 2 and 8: *on Michael Reckord, other playwrights.*

4 FILM AND VIDEO

Abbensetts, Michael. *Crown Court*, 2 episodes of the tv series (UK: ITV).
——— *Empire Road*, 15-part tv serial (UK: BBC-TV).
——— see 1, also 8: *on Michael Abbensetts.*
Allfrey, Phyllis Shand (*Dom*, 1908–86) *The Orchid House*, 4-part tv series adapted by Jim Hawkins from the novel (UK. c1991; film, Dom. 1990).
——— see 6.
Amoroso, Ronald, *The Brothers Five*, stage play adapted (Trin. 1978: TTT; see 2).
——— *Manifesto*, tv play (Trin. 1978: TTT).
——— *The Master of Carnival*, stage play adapted (Trin. 1974: TTT; see 1).
——— *Sangre Grande by Two*, stage play adapted (Trin. 1987: TTT; see 2).
——— see 1 and 2, also 8: *on Ronald Amoroso.*
Applewhaite, Claudia, Ava Hutchinson-Agard, and Sharon Marriott, as CAMA, *De Maul Story*, stage play adapted (Trin. 1983: TTT; see 2).
Archibald, Douglas, *Junction Village*, stage play adapted (Trin. 1988: TTT; see 1).
——— *My Good Friend, Justice*, tv play (Trin. 1974: TTT).
——— *Old Maid's Tale*, stage play adapted (Trin. 1972: TTT; see 1).
——— *The Rose Slip*, stage play adapted (Trin. 1984: TTT; see 1).
——— see 1, 2, 3, 5 and 6, also 8: *on Douglas Archibald.*
Archibald, William and Truman Capote, *The Innocents*, screenplay based on Archibald's stage play (USA. 1961; see 2).
Arthur, Dwight, *Lagniappe*, tv series 15-minute episodes including *The Mystery Mauler*, *Following in Each Other's Footsteps*, *Sowing the Seeds* and *From Rags to Riches* (film, Trin. 1990–91).
——— see 2, also 8: *on Dwight Arthur.*
Baku, Shango, *Revo*, stage play adapted (Trin. 1985: TTT; see 1).
——— see 1.
Banyan Television Workshop, collective creation, *Carnival Callaloo*, tv revue (Trin. 1976: TTT).
——— *Christmas Callaloo*, tv revue (Trin. 1975: TTT).
——— *Classical Callaloo*, tv revue (Trin. 1976: TTT).
——— *Epiphany*, 4-episode tv series (Trin. 1982: TTT).
——— *Flashbacks*, tv revue (Trin. 1977: TTT).
——— *For Better or For Worse*, tv revue (Trin. 1977: TTT).
——— *Morral*, 12-episode tv serial (Trin. 1979: TTT).
——— *Sports Parang*, tv revue (Trin. 1976: TTT).
——— *The Wedding March*, tv revue (Trin. 1976: TTT).
——— *Who the C.A.P. fits*, tv series (Trin. 1977: TTT).
——— see also 8: *on Banyan.*
Bickram, Shane, *The Coffin*, stage play adapted (Trin. 1987: TTT; see 2).
——— *The Poui Tree*, stage play adapted (Trin. 1987: TTT; see 2).
——— see 2.
Brathwaite, Rudolph, *The Foreigners*, tv play (UK. 1964: ITV).
——— see 2.
Brown, Lennox, *A Clean Sweep*, tv play (Trin. 1977: TTT).
——— *Devil Mas*, stage play adapted (Trin. 1979: TTT; see 1, 5).
——— *Fog Drifts in the Spring*, stage play adapted (Trin. 1977: TTT; see 1, 5).
——— *Home is a Long Way*, stage play adapted (Trin. 1974: TTT).
——— *Last Dance in the Sun*, tv play (Trin. 1975: TTT; new version, Trin. 1987: TTT).
——— *The Meeting*, stage play adapted (Toronto, 1966: CBC-TV; see 1).
——— *The Throne in an Autumn Room*, stage play adapted (Trin. 1978: TTT; see 2, 5).
——— see 1, 2, 3, 5 and 8: *on Felix Edinborough*, also 8: *on Lennox Brown.*
Bully, Alwin, *Toto and the Town Visitors*, tv play based on *Amahl and the Night Visitors*, with music by Pearle Christian (Dom. 1982).
——— see 1, 2 and 5, also 8: *on Alwin Bully.*

Carew, Jan, *The Baron of South Boulevard*, tv play (London, 1963: BBC-TV).
——— *The Big Pride*, adapted from stage play *University of Hunger* (London, 1962: BBC-TV; see 2, 5).
——— *The Conversion of Tiho*, tv play (London, 1963: BBC-TV).
——— *The Day of the Fox*, stage play adapted (London, 1962: BBC-TV).
——— *No gown for Peter*, tv play (London, 1963: BBC-TV).
——— *The Smugglers*, tv play (London, 1963: BBC-TV).
——— see 2, 5 and 6, also 8: *on Jan Carew*.
Chen, Willi, *Freedom Road*, stage play adapted (Trin. 1986: TTT; see 2).
——— *Tainted Blood*, stage play adapted (Trin. 1987: TTT; see 2).
——— see 2 and 3, also 8: *on Willi Chen*.
Constance, Zeno, *Death Row*, stage play adapted (Trin. 1986: TTT; see 2).
——— *Duelling Voices*, stage play adapted (Trin. 1987: TTT; see 2).
——— *Flight Through Fantasy*, stage play adapted (Trin. 1988: TTT; see 1).
——— *My Father's Child*, stage play adapted (Trin. 1986: TTT; see 2).
——— *The Ritual, or Friday Morning First Period*, stage play adapted (Trin. 1979(part)/1983(complete): TTT; see 1).
——— see 2, also 8: *on Zeno Constance*.
De Coteau, Clifton, *Who Fooling Who*, stage play adapted (Trin. 1977: TTT; see 2).
——— see 2.
Decle, Larry (*Trin*, –1990) *The House*, tv play (Trin. 1979: TTT).
Denton, Michael, *Hear sey*, stage play adapted (Jam. 1991; see 2).
——— see 2, also 8: *on other playwrights*.
Dookie, Devindra, *A Carol for Scrooge*, stage play adapted (Trin. 1986: TTT; see 2).
——— see 2, also 8: *general*.
Dookie, Devindra and Ralph Maraj, *The Warning*, tv play (Trin. 1978: TTT).
Douglas, Rodney, *Voice of the Ghetto, a play in one act*, stage play adapted (New York, 1968: US-TV Channel 3; see 1).
Edinborough, Felix, *High Society*, stage play adapted (Trin. 1979: TTT; see 2).
——— *King Arthur and His Merry Men*, stage play adapted (Trin. 1987: TTT; see 2).
——— see 2 and 5, also 8: *on Felix Edinborough*.
Ellis, Hall Anthony, *Burnard Runatif*, tv play (Jam. 1984: JBC-TV).
——— *Great Junction*, 15-episode tv serial (Jam. 1980: JBC-TV).
——— *Ma Phiney*, tv play (Jam. 1981: JBC-TV).
——— *Prescott*, 23-episode tv soap opera (Jam. 1978: JBC-TV; see 2).
——— *Two Sisters*, tv play (Jam. 1979: JBC-TV).
——— *Woman Under Trial*, tv play (Jam. 1973: JBC-TV)
——— *Women in the Mountain*, tv play (Jam. 1973: JBC-TV).
——— see 2, also 8: *on other playwrights*.
Fagon, Alfred, *John Bull*, tv play (UK. 1969: HTV).
——— see 1, 2 and 5.
Farrier, Francis Quamina, *Operation Makonaima*, screenplay based on storyline by Henry W. Josiah (Guy. 1972).
——— see 1, 2 and 5, also 8: *on Francis Quamina Farrier*.
Fatima College students and others, collective creation, *The Model*, stage play adapted (Trin. 1976: TTT; see 1).
Foster, Melville, *Called to the Bar*, stage play adapted (Trin. 1976: TTT; see 2).
——— *Domestic Problems*, tv play (Trin. 1978: TTT; see 5).
——— *Not a Bed of Roses*, tv play (Trin. 1981: TTT; third prize, TTTpc, Trin. 1981; see 2).
——— *Ricinulei*, tv play (Trin. 1980: TTT).
——— see 2 and 3.
Fullerton, Norvan, *Obeah*, stage play adapted (Trin. 1987: TTT; see 2).
——— see 2 and 3, also 8: *on other playwrights*.
Garcia, Anthony, *Tommy*, tv play (Trin. 1980: TTT).
——— *Two Faces of the Dollar*, tv play (Trin. 1980: TTT).

——— see 2.

Gittens, Dominic (*Trin*) *Where Birds Fly*, tv play (Trin. 1976: TTT).

Greaves, Hal, *Let My People Go*, tv play (Trin. 1981: TTT).

——— *Tief*, stage play adapted (Trin. 1988: TTT; see 2).

——— *Victims*, stage play adapted (Trin. 1985: TTT; see 2).

——— see 2 and 8: *general*, also 8: *on Hal Greaves*.

Hastings, Michael, *Gloo Joo*, stage play adapted (UK. 1979; see 1).

——— see 1, also 8: *on other playwrights*.

Henzell, Perry, *The Harder They Come*, see Rhone, Trevor and . . .

——— see 6.

Hill, Errol, *Dance Bongo*, stage play adapted (Trin. 1976: TTT; see 1).

——— *Strictly Matrimony*, stage play adapted (Trin. 1974: TTT; see 1).

——— *Wey Wey*, stage play adapted (Trin. 1975: TTT; see 1).

——— see 1, 2, 3, 5, 7 and 8: *on Derek Walcott*, *general*, also 8: *on Errol Hill*.

Hinkson, Anthony: *Nigger Yard*, stage play adapted (Bar. 1978: CBC; see 2).

——— see 1 and 2, also 8: *on Anthony Hinkson*.

Hopkinson, Slade, *The Scent of Jasmines*, tv play (Trin. 1973: TTT).

——— see 1 and 2, also 8: *on Slade Hopkinson*.

Israel, Roger, *Roger's Passion*, stage play adapted (Trin. 1980: TTT; see 2).

——— see 2.

Jacob, Deborah (*USA*, 1953) *Sugar Cane Arrows*, 6-episode tv serial adapted from the novel *When the Ibis Flies Home*, with music by David Rudder (Trin. 1988: TTT, pr.Gemini TV).

——— see 6, also 8: *on other playwrights*.

James, C.L.R., *The Black Jacobins*, stage play adapted (Trin. 1979: TTT; see 1).

——— see 2, 6 and 7, also 8: *on C.L.R. James*.

James, Horace (*Trin*) *The Bully*, adaptation of Anton Chekhov's story *The Bear* (Trin. 1974: TTT).

——— *For Better Not Worse*, adaptation of Anton Chekhov's story *The Proposal* (Trin. 1974: TTT).

——— see 5, also 8: *on other playwrights*.

James, Horace and John Elliot, *Rainbow City*, 6-part tv series (UK. 1967: BBC-Midlands).

John, Errol, *The Dawn*, tv play (London, 1963: BBC-TV).

——— *The Exiles*, tv play (London, 1968: BBC-TV).

——— *The Insider*, tv play (London, 1969: ATV; writer's name withdrawn).

——— *Moon on a Rainbow Shawl*, stage play adapted (London, 1960: ATV; see 1, 3, 5).

——— *The Tout*, stage play adapted (Bar. 1972: CBC; see 1).

——— *Uhuru*, tv play (London: BBC-TV).

——— see 1, 2 and 3, also 8: *on Errol John*.

Johnston, Judy (*Trin*) *Christmas Magic*, tv play (Trin. 1989: TTT, pr. Video Associates).

Jones, Evan (*Jam*, 1927) *The Damned*, screenplay (UK, 1962).

——— *Eve*, screenplay (Venice, 1963).

——— *Funeral in Berlin*, screenplay, adaptation of Len Deighton's book (UK, 1966).

——— *The Fight Against Slavery*, tv series (London, 1976: BBC-TV).

——— *In a Backward Country*, tv play (London, 1959: BBC-TV; see 2).

——— *King and Country*, screenplay (UK. 1964).

——— *The Madhouse on Castle Street*, tv play (London, 1964: BBC-TV).

——— *The Man with the Power*, tv play (UK. 1977).

——— *Modesty Blaise*, screenplay (UK. 1966).

——— *Nightwatch*, screenplay (UK. 1975).

——— *The Racing Game*, 1st episode of tv series based on the novels of Dick Francis (UK. 1981).

——— *Return to Look Behind*, tv play (UK. 1963: ITV).

——— *Two Gentlemen Sharing*, screenplay (UK. 1969).

——— *The Widows of Jaffa*, tv play (London, 1957: BBC-TV).

——— see 2 and 6, also 8: *on other playwrights*.

Joseph, Gerard and Ria Joseph, *Men of Gray*, tv play (Trin. 1991: TTT, pr. Jomox; first place Pegasus Award for Entertainment and Variety, Greater Enid Video Festival, Oklahoma USA. 1990).
——— see also 8: *on other playwrights.*
Joseph, Helen (*Trin*) *A Descent into Madness* (Trin. 1981: TTT; second prize, TTTpc, Trin. 1981).
Keens-Douglas, Paul, *Fedon's Flute* (Trin. 1979: TTT).
——— *Ah Pan for Christmas* (Trin. 1979: TTT; see 2).
——— *Tim Tim*, stage show adapted (Trin. 1975: TTT; see 2).
——— see 2 and 6, also 8: *on Paul Keens-Douglas.*
Kirton, Enid, *The Breadwinner* (Trin. 1978: TTT).
——— see 2.
Kissoon, Freddie, *AIDS – It's Deadly Serious*, tv play (Trin. 1988: TTT).
——— *Aunt Agatha* (Trin. 1988: TTT).
——— *Beauty Contest*, stage play adapted (Trin. 1975: TTT; see 2).
——— *Beulah Laughs Last* (Trin. 1975: TTT; see 2).
——— *Beulah's Dream* (Trin. 1975: TTT; see 2).
——— *Calabash Alley* (half-hour adaptation of the stage play, Trin. 1972: TTT; 10-episode tv serial adapted from the radio serial, Trin. c1985: TTT; see 1 and 5).
——— *Doo-Doo*, stage play adapted (Trin. 1969: TTT; see 2).
——— *Food First* (Trin. 1974: TTT; see 2).
——— *Fugitive From the Royal Jail*, stage play adapted (Trin. 1975: TTT; see 2).
——— *A Gift for Father Francis*, tv play (Trin. 1974: TTT).
——— *Girls Wanted*, stage play adapted (Trin. 1974: TTT; see 2).
——— *He Died For Us*, adaptation of the stage play *We Crucify Him* (Trin. 1971: TTT; see 2).
——— *Licks Like Fire* (Trin. 1976: TTT; see 2).
——— *Like Hog Love Mud*, stage play adapted (Trin. 1970: TTT; see 2).
——— *Mamaguy*, stage play adapted (Trin. 1968: TTT; see 1).
——— *Police Woman Wanted* (Trin. 1976: TTT; see 2).
——— *A Promise for Christmas*, tv play (Trin. 1969: TTT).
——— *Shift System* (Trin. 1976: TTT; see 2).
——— *Time to be Serious, Father* (Trin. 1984: TTT).
——— *Twenty and Under* (Trin. 1976: TTT; see 2).
——— *The Wedding* (Trin. 1975: TTT; see 2).
——— *What Party You Voting?* (Trin. 1976: TTT; see 2).
——— *Zingay*, stage play adapted (Trin. 1966: TTT; see 1).
——— see 2 and 5, also 8: *on Freddie Kissoon.*
Kissoon, Freddie and others, *Common Entrance*, stage play adapted (Trin. 1979: TTT; see 1).
——— *Mister Big Stuff*, stage play adapted (Trin. 1988: TTT; see 2).
——— *The Right and the Wrong*, screenplay (Trin. 1970: Kumar).
Knox Summer School, *Sleepy Valley*, stage play adapted (Trin. 1985: TTT; see 1).
Labastide, Neville, *Love Thy Neighbour*, stage play adapted (Trin. 1972: TTT; see 2).
——— *Something Old, Something New*, stage play adapted (Trin. 1975: TTT; see 1).
——— see 1 and 2, also 8: *on other playwrights.*
Lee, Easton, *Gloria, a Jamaican Christmas play* (Jam. 1968: JBC-TV).
——— *Joy fe the whole worl', a Jamaican Christmas play for children* (Jam. 1967: JBC-TV).
——— *On the third day, a one-act play for Easter* (Jam. 1967: JBC-TV).
——— *Once in a manger, a Christmas play* (Jam. 1969: JBC-TV).
——— *Paid in Full* (Jam. 1965: JBC-TV).
——— *Pretty Medicine*, stage play adapted (Jam. 1966: JBC-TV; see 2).
——— see 1 and 2.
Lovelace, Earl, *The Wine of Astonishment*,

stage play adapted (Trin. 1988: TTT; see 2).

——— see 1, 2, 6 and 8: *on Derek Walcott, general*, also 8: *on Earl Lovelace.*

Lyndersay, Dexter and Dani Lyndersay, *The Search for Ata Utop*, stage play adapted (pr. Cross River State Film Unit: film, Nig. 1977; see 2).

——— see 1 and 2, also 8: *on other playwrights.*

Lyndersay, Mark, *The Christmas Spirit*, tv play (Trin. 1977: TTT; pr. Banyan).

——— see 2.

Maraj, Ralph, *Easy in the Ashes*, stage play adapted (Trin. 1985: TTT; see 2).

——— *The Saint*, stage play adapted (Trin. 1984: TTT; see 2).

——— see 1 and 2, also 8: *on Ralph Maraj.*

Matura, Mustapha, *Bakerloo Line*, stage play adapted (London, 1973: BBC 2; see 2).

——— *Black Silk*, tv drama series (London, 1985: BBC-TV).

——— *Nice*, stage play adapted (UK. 1987: Central; see 1).

——— *No Problem*, tv series (London, 1983–5: London Weekend Television Channel 4).

——— *Playboy of the West Indies*, stage play adapted (London, 1985: BBC-TV; see 1).

——— *There's Something Wrong in Paradise*, Kid Creole Christmas tv spectacular (UK. 1984: Granada).

——— see 1, 2 and 5, also 8: *on Mustapha Matura.*

McDonald, Ian, *The Hummingbird Tree*, 90-minute tv play adapted by Jonathan Falla from the novel (UK. 1992: BBC-TV).

——— see 1 and 6.

McLeod, Ian, *Obeah Man Agent*, stage play adapted (Trin. 1971: TTT).

Mohamed, Paloma, *Jezebel*, stage play adapted (Guy. 1991; see 2).

——— see 2.

Moze, Sonya, *Woman Cleaning Brass*, stage play adapted (Trin. 1988: TTT; see 2).

——— *The White Lady*, stage play adapted (Trin. 1988: TTT; see 2).

——— see also 8: *on other playwrights.*

Pantin, Raoul, *The Ascot Recreation Club*, stage play adapted (Trin. 1988: TTT; see 2).

——— *Avril*, screenplay (as *Obeah*, Europe c1991: film, Trin. 1975: Sharc Productions).

——— *Bim*, screenplay (Trin. 1974: Sharc Productions; special award, Carifesta, Jam. 1976).

——— *Hatuey*, stage play adapted (Trin. 1987: TTT; see 2).

——— *Sanctuary*, stage play adapted (Trin. 1983: TTT; see 2).

——— see 2, 6 and 8: various, also 8: *on Raoul Pantin.*

Phillips, Caryl, *Playing Away*, screenplay (UK. 1986: Film Four International).

——— see 1 and 6, also 8: *on Caryl Phillips.*

Pilgrim, Frank, *Miriamy*, stage play adapted (Trin. 1987: TTT; see 1).

——— see 1, 2 and 5, also 8: *on Frank Pilgrim.*

Pinnock, Winsome, *South of the Border*, 1 episode of the tv series (UK. 1988).

——— see 1 and 2.

Prescott, Alan (*Trin*) *Adventures of Bucky* (Trin. 1984: TTT; prizewinner, TTTpc, Trin. 1984).

Questel, Victor, *Two Choices*, stage play adapted (Trin. 1987: TTT).

——— see 2, 3 and 8: *on Derek Walcott*, also 8: *on Victor Questel.*

Reckord, Barry, *In the Beautiful Caribbean*, stage play adapted (London, 1972: BBC-TV; see 2).

——— see 1, 2 and 5, also 8: *on Barry Reckord.*

Reckord, Michael, *Lime Tree Lane*, tv series, sixty 5-minute sketches (Jam. 1988–90: JBC-TV).

——— *Lime Tree Lane*, tv series, 45-minute episodes (Jam. 1990–91: JBC-TV).

——— see 1, 2, 3, 5 and 8: *on Basil Dawkins, Ginger Knight*, also 8: *on Michael Reckord.*

Redhead, Wilfred, *Canaree and Pot*, stage play adapted (Trin. 1977: TTT; see 1).

——— *Hoist Your Flag*, stage play adapted (Trin. 1966: TTT; see 1).

——— see 1, also 8: *on other playwrights.*

Rhone, Trevor, *Smile Orange*, screenplay

based on the stage play (Jam. 1975: Knuts Productions Ltd; award, Cook International Film Festival; award, Virgin Islands Festival; see 1).

——— *Two Can Play*, stage play adapted (USA. 1983: Kentucky Education Television; see 1).

——— see 1, 2 and 3, also 8: *on Trevor Rhone.*

Rhone, Trevor and Perry Henzell, *The Harder They Come*, screenplay (Jam. 1972; award, Cook International Film Festival).

Rhone, Trevor and Glen Salzman, *Milk and Honey*, screenplay (Genie Award, Can.1989).

Roach, Eric, *New Dancers in the Dooryard*, stage play adapted (Trin. 1973: TTT; see 2).

——— see 1, 3, 5 and 8: various, also 8: *on Eric Roach.*

St Hill, Errol, *Bush Medicine*, stage play adapted (Trin. 1974: TTT; see 2).

——— *Memoirs*, tv play (Trin. 1977: TTT).

——— *The Ninth Chime*, tv play (Trin. 1976: TTT).

——— *Pan is for Panmen* (Trin. 1974: TTT).

——— *Surprise, Sonny, Surprise*, tv play (Trin. 1981: TTT).

——— *Yuletide Tidings*, tv play (Trin. 1979: TTT).

——— see 2.

St Hill, Errol and Bernard John, *Alvarado's House*, tv play (Trin. 1976: TTT).

Scott, Dennis, *Terminus*, stage play adapted (Trin. 1976: TTT; see 1).

——— see 1, 2, 3, 6 and 8: *on Michael Reckord*, also 8: *on Dennis Scott.*

Sealy, Godfrey, *Limin'*, stage play adapted (Trin. 1985: TTT; see 2).

——— see 2, also 8: *on Godfrey Sealy.*

Selvon, Sam, *Anansi, the Spider Man*, tv play (London, 1974: BBC 1).

——— *A Brighter Sun*, stage play adapted (Trin. 1986: TTT; see 2).

——— *Home, Sweet India*, radio play adapted (London, 1976: BBC 2; see 5).

——— *Selvon's England*, half-hour tv version of *The World of Sam Selvon*, containing *Basement Lullaby*, *Brackley and the Bed* and *Waiting for Aunty to Cough* (Trin. 1969: TTT; see 2).

——— *The Taming of the Show-off*, stage play adapted (Trin. 1975: TTT; see 2).

——— see 1, 2, 3, 5 and 6, also 8: *on Sam Selvon.*

Selvon, Sam and Horace Ove, *Pressure*, screenplay (London, 1978: British Film Institute).

Smith, John and Peter Smart, *A Day in the Life of a Fool* (Trin. 1977: TTT).

Sudan, Richard (*Trin*) *Survey the Wondrous Cross* (Trin. 1974: TTT).

Tom Yick, Kenneth (*Trin*) *To Catch a Thief* (Trin: TTT).

Walcott, Derek, *Dream on Monkey Mountain*, stage play adapted (Trin. 1970: TTT, pr.National Broadcasting Corporation, USA: filmed Trin. 1969; see 1).

——— *Hart Crane*, docu-drama on the American poet (USA. 1986: Public Broadcasting System: filmed SL. and USA).

——— *Haytian Earth*, stage performance filmed (SL. 1984; see 2).

——— *Jourmard*, stage play adapted (Trin. 1974: TTT; see 1, 5).

——— *Malcochon*, stage play adapted (Trin. 1972: TTT; see 1).

——— *Pantomime*, stage play adapted (Tob. 1978: TTT; see 1, 5).

——— *The Rig*, tv play (Trin. 1983: TTT, pr. Banyan: filmed Trin. 1982).

——— *The Sea at Dauphin*, stage play adapted (Trin. 1974: TTT; see 1, 5).

——— *Ti-Jean and His Brothers*, stage play adapted (video Bar. 1970: CBC; excerpts Black Journal, NET USA. 1971?: filmed Trin. 1971; adapted by Michael Gilkes, video Bar. 1979: Stage One for Ministry of Labour and Community Welfare Services; see 1, 5).

——— see 1, 2, 3, 5, 6, 7 and 8: various, also 8: *on Derek Walcott.*

Walcott, Roderick, *The Harrowing of Benjy*, stage play adapted (Trin. 1978: TTT; see 1, 5).

——— see 1, 2, 3, 5 and 8: *general.*

Wilkinson, Lester Efebo, *Bitter Cassava*, stage play adapted (Trin. 1980: TTT; see 2).

——— *Capital Death* (Trin. 1977: TTT; first prize drama, NCClc, Trin. 1977).
——— *Going Straight to Santa*, tv play (Trin. 1978: TTT; see 5).
——— *Same Khaki Pants*, stage play adapted (Trin. 1985: TTT; see 2).
——— *Santa Will Show You*, stage play adapted (Trin. 1979: TTT; see 2).
——— *To Confirm St Peter*, stage play adapted (Trin. 1976: TTT; see 1, 5).
——— see 2, also 8: *on Lester Efebo Wilkinson.*

Wilson, Horace (*Tob*,1943) *Back Bay*, tv play (Trin. 1981: TTT; first prize, TTTpc, Trin. 1981).
——— *Invocation*, tv play (Trin. 1982: TTT).
——— *The Love Song*, tv play (Trin. 1984: TTT).
——— *Meena*, tv play (Trin. 1987: TTT).
——— *Morning Visit*, tv play (Trin. 1983: TTT).
——— *No Boundaries*, tv series, 41 episodes (Trin. 1988(14), 1989(14), 1990 and 1991(13): TTT).
——— *Return to Back Bay*, tv play (Trin. 1982: TTT).
——— *Tangled Lives*, tv series, 6 episodes (Trin. 1990: National Aids Programme).
——— *Turn of the Tide*, tv series, 13 episodes (Trin. 1982: TTT, pr. Video Associates).
——— *Turn of the Tide – the movie*, screenplay (Tob. 1985: Cari-Film Company Ltd).
——— *What the Moon Saw*, tv play (Trin. 1980: TTT).
——— see also 8: *on other playwrights.*

Winkler, Anthony (*Jam*) *The Lunatic*, screenplay based on the novel (Jam. 1990).

Wynter, Sylvia, *Maskarade*, stage play adapted (Jam. 1973: JBC; see 1).
——— see 2 and 6.

5 RADIO

Archibald, Douglas, *Anne-Marie*, stage play adapted by Judy Stone (Trin. 1971: 610 Radio; see 1).
——— *Defeat With Honour*, stage play adapted (Trin. 1952: RT; see 1).
——— *Island Tide*, stage play adapted (Trin. 1978: RT; see 1).
——— *A Murmur of Wings*, radio play (Trin. 1979: RT).
——— see 1, 2, 3, 4 and 6, also 8: *on Douglas Archibald.*

Bourne, Luther, Leonore Harney, Stella St John, and Flora Squires Spencer, *The Brathwaites of Black Rock*, radio serial (Bar. 1965: CBC).

Brathwaite, Edward, *Odale's Choice*, stage play adapted by Ken Corsbie (Trin. 1971: 610 Radio; see 1).
——— see 1, 6, 7 and 8: *general.*

Brown, Lennox, *A Ballet Behind the Bridge*, stage play adapted (Can. 1971: CanBC; see 2).
——— *Devil Mas*, stage play adapted (Trin. 1973; see 1, 4).
——— *Fog Drifts in the Spring*, stage play adapted (Trin. 1971: 610 Radio; see 1, 4).
——— *Home is a Long Way*, radio play (Can. 1969: CanBC).
——— *Saturday's Druid*, radio play (Can. 1969: CanBC).
——— *Song of the Spear*, radio play (Can. 1969: CanBC).
——— *This Scent of Incense*, radio play (Can. 1972: CanBC).
——— *The Throne in an Autumn Room*, stage play adapted (Trin. 1971: CanBC; see 2).
——— *The Twilight Dinner*, stage play adapted (London, 1981: BBC World Service; see 1, 4).
——— *Wine in Winter*, stage play adapted by Albert Laveau (Trin. 1972: 610 Radio; see 3).
——— see 1, 2, 3, 4 and 8: *on Felix Edinborough*, also 8: *on Lennox Brown.*

Bully, Alwin, *A Dance in the Dark*, radio play (Dom. 1983; third prize, BBC Caribbean Magazine radio play competition, London, 1983).
——— *Green Gold*, 85-episode radio serial (Dom. 1978).
——— *Nite Box*, stage play adapted (Mont. 1979: Radio Antilles; see 1).
——— *Secrets of La Cloche*, 30-episode radio serial (Dom. 1980).
——— *Winds of Change*, 45-episode

radio serial (Dom. 1979).
——— see 1, 2 and 4, also 8: *on Alwin Bully.*
Bully, Alwin and O'Marde, Dorbrene, *Fire Go Bun*, 12-episode radio serial commissioned by the Caribbean Family Planning Affiliation (Mont. 1983: Radio Antilles).
Carew, Jan, *The Legend of the nameless mountain*, radio play (London, 1958: BBC).
——— *The River Man*, radio play (Jam. 1960: JBC).
——— *University of Hunger*, stage play adapted (London, 1961: BBC; see 2, 4).
——— see 2, 4 and 6, also 8: *on Jan Carew.*
Clarke, Gregory (*Trin*) *Queens Come Forth*, radio play (Trin. 1979: RT).
Clemendore, Claire (*Trin*) *Gifts of Love*, radio play (Trin. 1979: RT).
Cumper, Pat, *Aloysius*, radio serial (Jam: JBC).
——— *Legacy*, radio serial (Jam. 1992).
——— *Ma B's Family*, radio serial (Jam: JIS).
——— *Malvina's Revenge*, radio serial of 15-minute episodes (Jam. 1990–1991: JBC).
——— *Mortimer Simmonds*, radio serial of 15-minute episodes (Jam. 1980–1982: RJ).
——— see 1 and 2, also 8: *on Pat Cumper.*
De Lima, Janice (*Trin*) *The Rift*, radio play (Trin. 1979: RT).
Edgecombe, David, *Kirnon's Kingdom*, stage play adapted (London, 1989: BBC; see 2).
——— *Sonuvabitch*, stage play adapted (Mont. 1979: Radio Antilles; see 2).
——— see 1 and 2.
Edinborough, Felix, *The Journey*, radio play (Trin. 1973: RT).
——— see 2 and 4, also 8: *on Felix Edinborough.*
Fagon, Alfred, *Shakespeare Country*, radio play (London, 1974: BBC 2).
——— see 1, 2 and 4.
Farrier, Francis Quamina, *Air Partner*, stage play adapted (Guy. 1970: GBS; see 2).
——— *Backward March*, radio play (Guy. 1970: GBS).
——— *Echoes of the Savannahs*, radio play (Guy. 1970: GBS).
——— *Eyes*, stage play adapted (Guy. 1970: GBS; see 2).
——— *A Family Christmas*, radio play (Guy. 1964: GBS).
——— *Freedom Trail*, radio play on the Berbice Slave Rebellion, commissioned by the Guyana Broadcasting Service for the Co-operative Republic Anniversary celebrations 1971 (Guy. 1971: GBS; see 2).
——— *The Girl from Susanberg*, radio serial of 130 × 15-minute episodes, sequel to *The Tides of Susanberg* (Guy. 1968–69: GBS).
——— *Home is for Christmas*, radio play (Guy. 1964: GBS).
——— *In Memorial*, radio play (Guy. 1965: GBS).
——— *Journey to Freedom*, stage play adapted (Guy. 1986).
——— *Loafers' Lane*, radio play (Guy. 1967; third prize, Guyana Information Services Independence radio pc, Guy. 1966).
——— *Land of Beautiful Daughters*, radio play (Guy. 1970).
——— *Manaka*, stage play adapted (Guy. 1970: GBS; see 1).
——— *Rigor Mortis*, radio play (Guy. 1970).
——— *The Slave and The Scroll*, stage play adapted (Guy. 1970: GBU; see 1).
——— *Something to Live For*, radio play (Guy. 1967).
——— *The Tides of Susanburg*, radio serial of 78 × 15-minute episodes (Guy. 1966; see 2).
——— *Timberline*, radio play (Guy. 1966; first prize, Guyana Information Services Independence radio pc, Guy. 1966).
——— *To catch a Desperado*, radio play (Guy. 1970: GBU).
——— *A Walk in the Night*, radio play (Guy. 1970: GBU).
——— see 1, 2 and 4, also 8: *on Francis Quamina Farrier.*

Forde, A. N., *The Plot in the Garden*, radio play based on the story *Susannah and the Elders* (London, 1953: BBC).
——— see 1.
Forsythe, Victor, *Sweet Carila*, radio play (Guy. 1964: GBU; first prize, first national radio pc, Guy. 1958; see 2).
——— see 3.
Foster, Melville, *Food for Thought*, adapted from the television play *Domestic Problems* (Trin. 1979: RT; see 4).
——— see 2, 3 and 4.
Fraser, Winslow, *Backdam Murder*, adapted from the stage play *Bacra dead ah Backdam* (Guy. 1970; see 2).
——— see 2.
French, Stanley, *The Rape of Fair Helen*, stage play adapted by Judy Stone (Trin. 1972: 610 Radio; see 2).
——— see 1 and 2, also 8: *on other playwrights.*
Harris, Wilson (*Guy*, 1921) *The Crew from Sorrow Hill*, adaptation of the novel *Palace of the Peacock* (Can. 1971: CanBC: rec, Trin).
——— see 6 and 8: *general.*
Hill, Errol, *The Ping Pong*, stage play adapted (London, 1950: BBC; see 1).
——— see 1, 2, 3, 4, 7 and 8: *on Derek Walcott, general*, also 8: *on Errol Hill.*
James, Horace, *From the Frying Pan*, radio play (London, 1969: BBC).
——— see 4, also 8: *on other playwrights.*
John, Errol, *Moon on a Rainbow Shawl*, stage play adapted (as *Small Island Moon*, London, 1958: BBC; see 1, 3, 4).
——— see 1, 2, 3 and 4, also 8: *on Errol John.*
John, Ronald, *Tale of Tenor Pan Willie*, radio play (Trin. 1979: RT).
——— *The Wizard of Kandahar* (Trin. 1979; see 2).
——— see 1, 2, 3 and 8: *on Derek Walcott*, also 8: *on Ronald John.*
Jolly, Dorothy, *Always on Service*, radio play (Trin. 1980: RT).
——— see 2, also 8: *on other playwrights.*
Karamath, David (*Trin*) *Gossip* (Trin. 1980: RT).
Kissoon, Freddie, *Calabash Alley*, radio serial of 78 × 15-minute episodes (Trin. 1970–71: RT; see 1 and 4).
——— *The Don't Care Father*, radio play (Trin. 1979: Government Broadcasting Unit).
——— *Nine Months After*, radio play (Trin. 1978: Government Broadcasting Unit).
——— *Take Your Time*, radio serial of 4 × 15-minute episodes, commissioned by the Ministry of Health Population Programme (Trin. 1986: RT).
——— see 1, 2 and 4, also 8: *on Freddie Kissoon.*
Manley, Carmen; *My Brother's Keeper*, stage play adapted by Judy Stone (Trin. 1972: 610 Radio; as stage play, certificate of merit, JFlc, Jam. 1970).
——— see 3.
Manning, Lloyd, *The Miracle*, radio play (Guy. c1967: prizewinner, Demba radio pc, Guy. 1966).
——— see 3.
Marriott, Louis, *The Atom Bowlers*, radio play (Jam. c1962: JBC).
——— *Two Negatives*, radio play (Jam. c1960: JBC).
——— see 2, also 8: *on Louis Marriott.*
Matura, Mustapha, *As Time Goes By*, stage play adapted by Helen Camps (Trin. 1972: 610 Radio; see 1).
——— see 1, 2 and 4, also 8: *on Mustapha Matura.*
McLean, Dirk (*Trin*, 1956) *The House on Hermitage Road*, radio serial of 5 × 15-minute episodes (Toronto, 1991: CanBC).
——— see also 8: *on other playwrights.*
Naipaul, V.S., *B. Wordsworth*, story adapted by John Stockbridge and V.S. Naipaul (London, 1956: BBC; see 2).
——— see 2 and 6, also 8: *on other playwrights.*
O'Marde, Dorbrene, *Fly on the Wall*, stage play adapted (Mont.1978: Radio Antilles;. see 1).
——— *Tangled Web*, stage play adapted (Mont.1980: Radio Antilles; see 1).
——— see 1.
Pilgrim, Frank: *Christmas Reunion*, radio play (Guy. 1964).
——— *The Homecoming*, radio play (Guy. 1964).

——— *Singing Rum*, radio play (Guy. 1963; see 2).
——— see 1, 2 and 4, also 8: *on Frank Pilgrim.*
Ramon-Fortune, Barnabas (*Trin*) *A Lady in the Family*, radio play (Trin. 1980: RT).
——— *The Sentinels*, radio play (Trin. 1979: RT).
Reckord, Barry, *Adella*, radio play (London, 1954: BBC).
——— see 1, 2 and 4, also 8: *on Barry Reckord.*
Reckord, Michael, *The Idiot and the Fool*, radio series, 190 × 4-minute sketches (Jam. 1990–91: JBC).
——— see 1, 2, 3, 4 and 8: *on Basil Dawkins, Ginger Knight*, also 8: *on Michael Reckord.*
Roach, Eric, *Belle Fanto*, stage play adapted (Trin. 1971: 610 Radio; see 1).
——— *Calabash of Blood*, stage play adapted by Judy Stone (Trin. 1972: 610 Radio; see 1).
——— see 1, 2, 3, 4 and 8: various, also 8: *on Eric Roach.*
Roberts, Melville (*Trin*) *Food for Thought*, radio play (Trin. 1979: RT).
Rohlehr, Lloyd George (*Guy*, 1928) *Thousands Cheer* (Guy. 1964).
Sakal, Sirendra (*Trin*) *Nat's Son*, radio play (Trin. 1980: RT).
Samaroo, Daniel Joseph (*Trin*, 1927) *Taxi, Mister!*, story adapted by Wilbert Holder (Trin, 1972: 610 Radio).
——— see 6.
Selvon, Sam, *Basement Lullaby*, adapted by Peggy Wells from the story in *Ways of Sunlight* (London, 1957: BBC; see 2, 4).
——— *Bringing in the Sheaves*, radio play (London, 1969: BBC).
——— *Cry Baby Brackley*, radio play (London, 1972: BBC).
——— *El Dorado, West One*, 7-part adaptation of *The Lonely Londoners* (London, 1969: BBC; see 1).
——— *The Harvest in the Wilderness*, adaptation of *The Plains of Caroni* (London, 1972: BBC).
——— *Highway in the Sun*, adaptation of *A Brighter Sun* (London, 1967: BBC; see 1).
——— *Home, Sweet India*, adaptation of *An Island is a World* (London, 1970: BBC; see 4).
——— *Lost Property*, adaptation of *Eraser's Dilemma*, from *Ways of Sunlight* (London, 1965: BBC).
——— *Mary, Mary Shut Your Gate*, radio play (London, 1971: BBC).
——— *Milk in the Coffee*, radio play (London, 1975: BBC).
——— *Perchance to Dream*, adaptation of *Brackley and the Bed*, from *Ways of Sunlight* (London, 1966: BBC).
——— *Rain Stop Play*, adaptation of *The Cricket Match*, from *Ways of Sunlight* (London, 1967: BBC).
——— *Those Who Eat the Cascadura*, adaptation of *Johnson and the Cascadura*, from *Ways of Sunlight* (London, 1971: BBC).
——— *Turn Again Tiger*, novel adapted (London, 1970: BBC).
——— *Voyage to Trinidad*, radio play (London, 1971: BBC).
——— *Water for Veronica*, adaptation of *A Drink of Water*, from *Ways of Sunlight* (London, 1972: BBC).
——— *You Right in the Smoke*, radio play (London, 1969: BBC).
——— *Zeppi's Machine*, radio play (London, 1977: BBC).
——— see 1, 2, 3, 4 and 6, also 8: *on Sam Selvon.*
Van Sertima, Sheila, *Admit Joe*, radio play (Guy. 1964).
——— see 1.
Waite-Smith, Cicely, *Storm Signal*, radio play (Can: CanBC; see1).
——— see 1, 2, 3 and 6, also 8: *on other playwrights.*
Walcott, Derek, *Harry Dernier*, a play for radio production (London, 1952: BBC; see 1).
——— *Henri Christophe*, stage play adapted (London, 1951: BBC; see 1).
——— *In a Fine Castle*, stage play adapted (Can. 1973: CanBC; rec, Trin; see 1).
——— *Jourmard*, stage play adapted by Helen Camps (Trin. 1972: 610 Radio; see 1, 4).

——— *Pantomime*, stage play adapted (London, 1979: BBC Radio 3; see 1, 4).
——— *The Sea at Dauphin*, stage play adapted (Trin. 1971: 610 Radio; see 1, 4).
——— *Senza Alcun Sospetto*, radio play (London, 1950: BBC; see 2).
——— *Ti-Jean and His Brothers*, stage play adapted (Can. 1970: CanBC, rec, Trin; see 1, 4).
——— see 1, 2, 3, 4, 6, 7 and 8: various, also 8: *on Derek Walcott.*
Walcott, Roderick, *The Harrowing of Benjy*, stage play adapted (Trin. 1971: 610 Radio; see 1, 4).
——— *Shrove Tuesday March*, stage play adapted (SL. 1956: Radio Experimental; see 1).
——— see 1, 2, 3 and 8: *general.*
Wilkinson, Lester Efebo, *Going Straight to Santa*, tv play adapted (Trin. 1979: RT; see 4).
——— *To Confirm St Peter* (Trin. 1980: RT; see 1, 4).
——— see 2 and 4, also 8: *on Lester Efebo Wilkinson.*
Wilmot, Cynthia, *In Transit*, radio play (Jam: RJ).
——— *Mistress of the revels*, radio play (Jam. 1967: CanBC and RJ; Alcan award, certificate of merit, JFlc, Jam. 1967).
——— *Monster Among Us*, tv play adapted (Jam. 1968: CanBC and RJ; bronze medal, JFlc, Jam. 1968).
——— *Morning Encounter*, tv play adapted (Jam. 1968: CanBC and RJ; bronze medal, JFlc, Jam. 1968).
——— *The Phantom riders*, radio play (Jam. 1968: CanBC and RJ; bronze medal, JFlc, Jam. 1968).
——— *Visitors to tea*, tv play adapted (Jam. 1970: BBC and RJ; bronze medal, JFlc, Jam. 1970).
——— see 3.
Wilmot, Cynthia and Wilmot Fred, *Don't Leave it to George*, radio series (Can. 1945–55: CanBC).
Zephaniah, Benjamin, *Hurricane Dub*, radio play (London, c1989: BBC).
——— see 1, 2 and 6.

B Secondary Bibliography:

6 NOVELS, STORIES AND POETRY AND OTHER CREATIVE WRITING

(This section of the bibliography is indebted to the research of Professor Kenneth Ramchand, as published in *The West Indian Novel and its Background* (London, 1970: Faber and Faber).)

Allfrey, Phyllis Shand, *The Orchid House* (London 1953: Constable).
Archibald, Douglas, *Isidore and the Turtle* (Trin. 1977: UWI ESU).
Bascom, Harold, *Apata* (London 1986: Heinemann).
Belgrave, Valerie, *Ti Marie* (Oxford, UK. 1988: Heinemann).
Braithwaite, Edward: *Sun Poem* (Oxford, UK. 1982: Oxford University Press).
Brodber, Erna, *Jane and Louisa Will Soon Come Home* (London, 1980: New Beacon Books).
Brown, Stewart (ed.) *Caribbean New Wave – contemporary short stories* (Oxford, UK. 1990: Heinemann).
Callender, Timothy, *It So Happen* (Oxford, UK. 1991: Heinemann; first published 1975, Christian Journals Ltd).
Carew, Jan, *Black Midas* (London,1958: Secker and Warburg).
——— *The Last Barbarian* (London, 1961: Secker and Warburg).
——— *The Wild Coast* (London, 1958: Secker and Warburg).
De Lisser, Herbert G., *The Arawak Girl* (Kingston, 1958: Pioneer Press).
——— *The Cup and the Lip* (London, 1956: E. Benn).
——— *Jane, a Story of Jamaica* (Kingston, 1913: Gleaner).
——— *Jane's Career* (London, 1914: Methuen).
——— *Morgan's Daughter* (London, 1953: E. Benn).
——— *Psyche* (London, 1952: E. Benn).
——— *Revenge, a Tale of Old Jamaica* (Kingston, 1917: Gleaner).
——— *Susan Proudleigh* (London, 1915: Methuen).
——— *Triumphant Squalitone, a tropi-*

cal extravaganza (Kingston, 1917: Gleaner).
——— *Under the Sun, a Jamaican Comedy* (London, 1937: E. Benn).
——— *The White Witch of Rosehall* (London, 1929: E. Benn).
Harris, Wilson, *The Eye of the Scarecrow* (London, 1965: Faber and Faber).
——— *The Far Journey of Oudin* (London, 1961: Faber and Faber).
——— *Heartland* (London, 1964: Faber and Faber).
——— *Palace of the Peacock* (London, 1960: Faber and Faber).
——— *The Secret Ladder* (London, 1963: Faber and Faber).
——— *The Waiting Room* (London, 1967: Faber and Faber).
——— *The Whole Armour* (London, 1962: Faber and Faber).
Hearne, John, *The Autumn Equinox* (London, 1959: Faber and Faber).
——— *The Faces of Love* (London, 1957: Faber and Faber).
——— *The Land of the Living* (London, 1961: Faber and Faber).
——— *Stranger at the Gate* (London, 1956: Faber and Faber).
——— *The Sure Salvation* (London, 1981: Faber and Faber).
——— *Voices under the Window* (London, 1955: Faber and Faber).
Hearne, John and Morris Cargill, as John Morris, *Fever Grass* (London, 1969: Wm. Collins).
Henzell, Perry, *Power Game* (Kingston 1982: Ten-A Publications).
Howes, Barbara (ed.) *From the Green Antilles: Writings of the Caribbean* (London, 1967: Souvenir Press).
Jacob, Deborah as Amber Adamson, *When the Ibis Flies Home*, 32-part serialisation of a novel (Trin. 1985–86: *The Sun*, Nov–July).
James, Alexander MacGregor, *The Cacique's Treasure and Other Tales* (Kingston, 1920: Gleaner).
James, C.L.R., *Minty Alley* (London, 1936: Secker and Warburg).
Jones, Evan, *Lament of the Banana Man* (in *New Ships*, Jam. 1971: Savacou).
——— *Song of the Banana Man* (in *Breaklight*, London, 1971: Hamish Hamilton).
Keens-Douglas, Paul, *Tell Me Again* (Trin. 1979: Keensdee Productions).
——— *When Moon Shine* (Trin. 1975: Scope Publishing Caribbean).
Lamming, George, *The Emigrants* (London, 1954: Michael Joseph).
——— *In the Castle of My Skin* (London, 1953: Michael Joseph).
——— *Natives of my Person* (London, 1972: Longman Caribbean).
——— *Of Age and Innocence* (London, 1958: Michael Joseph).
——— *Season of Adventure* (London, 1960: Michael Joseph).
——— *Water with Berries* (London, 1971: Longman Caribbean).
Lamming, George (ed.) *Cannon Shot and Glass Beads* (London, 1974: Pan Books).
Lindo, Archie, *Bronze: short stories, articles, a poem and a play* (Mandeville, Jam. 1944: College Press).
——— *My Heart was Singing*, poems and short stories (Mandeville, Jam. 1945: College Press).
Livingston, James T. (ed.), *Caribbean Rhythms, the Emerging English Literature of the West Indies* (New York, 1974: Washington Square Press).
Lovelace, Earl, *A Brief Conversion* (Oxford, UK. 1988: Heinemann).
——— *The Dragon Can't Dance* (London, 1979: Andre Deutsch).
——— *The Schoolmaster* (London, 1968: Collins).
——— *While Gods are Falling* (London, 1965: Collins).
Mais, Roger, *And Most of All Man* (Kingston, c1945: City Printery).
——— *Black Lightning* (London, 1955: Jonathan Cape).
——— *Brother Man* (London, 1954: Jonathan Cape).
——— *Face and Other Stories* (Kingston, c1945: Universal Printery).
——— *The Hills were Joyful Together* (London, 1953: Jonathan Cape).
Maxwell-Phillip, Michel, *Emmanuel Apadocca*, a tale of the Buccaneers (1854).

McDonald, Ian, *The Humming-Bird Tree* (London, 1969: Heinemann).
McKay, Claude, *Banana Bottom* (New York/London, 1933: Harper and Brothers).
——— *Banjo: a Story without a Plot* (New York/London, 1929: Harper and Brothers).
——— *Gingertown* (New York/London 1932: Harper and Brothers).
——— *Home to Harlem* (New York/London, 1928: Harper and Brothers).
Mendes, Alfred H., *Black Fauns* (London, 1935: Duckworth).
——— *Pitch Lake* (London, 1934: Duckworth).
Mitchell, Adrian, *Man Friday* (London, 1975: Futura Publications).
Mittelholzer, Edgar, *The Adding Machine, a fable for capitalists and commercialists* (Kingston, 1954: Pioneer Press).
——— *The Aloneness of Mrs Chatham* (London, 1965: Library 33).
——— *Children of Kaywana* (London, 1952: Secker and Warburg).
——— *Corentyne Thunder* (London, 1941: Secker and Warburg).
——— *Eltonsbrody* (London, 1960: Secker and Warburg).
——— *The Harrowing of Hubertus* (London, 1954: Secker and Warburg).
——— *The Jilkington Drama* (London, 1965: Abelard-Schuman Ltd).
——— *Kaywana Blood* (London, 1958: Secker and Warburg).
——— *Kaywana Stock* (reissue of *The Harrowing of Hubertus*).
——— *Latticed Echoes* (London, 1960: Secker and Warburg).
——— *The Life and Death of Sylvia* (London, 1953: Secker and Warburg).
——— *The Mad MacMullochs* (London, 1959: Peter Owen Ltd).
——— *A Morning at the Office* (London, 1950: Hogarth Press).
——— *My Bones and My Flute* (London, 1955: Secker and Warburg).
——— *Of Trees and the Sea* (London, 1956: Secker and Warburg).
——— *The Piling of Clouds* (London, 1961: Putnam and Co.).
——— *Shadows Move Among Them* (London, 1952: Peter Nevill).
——— *A Tale of Three Places* (London, 1957: Secker and Warburg).
——— *Thunder Returning* (London, 1961: Secker and Warburg).
——— *A Tinkling in the Twilight* (London, 1959: Secker and Warburg).
——— *Uncle Paul* (London, 1963: Macdonald and Co.).
——— *The Weather Family* (London, 1958: Secker and Warburg).
——— *The Weather in Middenshot* (London, 1952: Secker and Warburg).
——— *The Wounded and the Worried* (London, 1961: Putnam and Co.).
Morris, Mervyn (ed.), *Contemporary Caribbean Short Stories* (London, 1990: Faber and Faber).
Naipaul, V.S., *A Bend in the River* (London, 1979: Andre Deutsch).
——— *Guerrillas* (London, 1975: Andre Deutsch).
——— *A House for Mr Biswas* (London, 1961: Andre Deutsch).
——— *In a Free State* (London, 1971: Andre Deutsch. Booker prize).
——— *Miguel Street* (London, 1959: Andre Deutsch; Somerset Maugham award).
——— *The Mimic Men* (London, 1967: Andre Deutsch; W.H. Smith award 1968).
——— *Mr Stone and the Knights Companion* (London, 1963: Andre Deutsch; Hawthornden prize).
——— *The Mystic Masseur* (London, 1957: Andre Deutsch; John Llewellyn Rhys Memorial prize).
——— *The Suffrage of Elvira* (London, 1958: Andre Deutsch).
Pantin, Raoul, *Journey* (Trin: Reprographic Consultants).
Phillips, Caryl, *Cambridge* (London, 1991: Bloomsbury Publishing).
——— *The European Tribe* (London, 1987: Faber and Faber).
——— *The Final Passage* (London, 1985: Faber and Faber).
——— *Higher Ground* (New York, 1989: Viking).
——— *A State of Independence* (London, 1986: Faber and Faber).

Redcam, Tom, *Becka's Buckra Baby* (Kingston, 1903: Jamaica Times).
——— *One Brown Girl and* – (Kingston, 1909: Jamaica Times).
Reid, V.S., *The Leopard* (London, 1958: Heinemann).
——— *New Day* (chapters, London, 1943, *Life and Letters*, Vol. 56, #127, March; complete, New York, 1949: Alfred A. Knopf).
——— *Sixty-Five* (London, 1960: Longman).
Rhys, Jean, *After Leaving Mr Mackenzie* (London, 1930: Jonathan Cape).
——— *Good Morning, Midnight* (London, 1939: Constable).
——— *The Left Bank* (London, 1927: Jonathan Cape).
——— *Quartet* (as *Postures*, London, 1928: Chatto and Windus).
——— *Sleep It Off Lady* (London, 1976).
——— *Tales of the Wide Caribbean* (Oxford, UK: Heinemann).
——— *Tigers are Better Looking* (London, 1968: Andre Deutsch).
——— *Voyage in the Dark* (London, 1934: Constable).
——— *Wide Sargasso Sea* (London, 1966: Andre Deutsch).
Roberts, W. Adolphe, *Brave Mardi Gras* (Indianapolis, NY. 1946: Bobbs-Merrill Co.).
——— *Creole Dusk* (Indianapolis, NY. 1946: Bobbs-Merrill Co.).
——— *The Haunting Hand* (London, 1926: Hutchinson).
——— *The Mind Reader* (New York, 1929: Macaulay Co.).
——— *The Moralist* (New York, 1931: Mohawk Press).
——— *The Pomegranate* (Indianapolis, NY. 1941: Bobbs-Merrill Co.).
——— *Royal Street* (Indianapolis, NY. 1944: Bobbs-Merrill Co.).
——— *The Single Star* (Indianapolis, NY. 1949: Bobbs-Merrill Co.).
Samaroo, Daniel (as Daniel Joseph), *Taxi Mister* (Bar. 1950: *Bim*, Vol. 4, #13, December).
Scott, Dennis, *Dreadwalk* (London, 1982: New Beacon Press).
——— *Strategies* (Jamaica, 1989: Sandberry Press).
——— *Uncle Time* (Jamaica, 1973: Pitt Press).
Sealy, Clifford, *A World Her Own* (Trin. 1977: *Voices*, Vol. 2, #4, April).
Selvon, Samuel, *A Brighter Sun* (London, 1952: Allan Wingate).
——— *Foreday Morning* (London, 1989: Longman).
——— *The Housing Lark* (London, 1965: MacGibbon and Kee).
——— *I Hear Thunder* (London, 1963: MacGibbon and Kee).
——— *An Island is a World* (London, 1955: Allan Wingate).
——— *The Lonely Londoners* (London, 1956: Allan Wingate).
——— *Moses Ascending* (London, 1975: Davis-Poynter; Danish translation, Denmark 1977: Kai Olsen and Olsen).
——— *Moses Migrating* (London, 1983: Longman).
——— *The Plains of Caroni* (London, 1970: MacGibbon and Kee).
——— *Those Who Eat the Cascadura* (London, 1972: Davis-Poynter).
——— *Turn Again Tiger* (London, 1958: MacGibbon and Kee; German translation, Germany, 1965: Deutsche Buch-Gemeinschaft).
——— *Ways of Sunlight* (London, 1957: MacGibbon and Kee).
Senior, Olive, *Summer Lightning* (London, 1986: Longman).
Sistren, *Lionheart Woman* (London, 1986: Womens Press).
Thomas, G.C.H., *Ruler in Hiroona* (Trin. 1972).
Waite-Smith, Cicely, *Rain for the Plains and other Stories* (Kingston, 1943: Gleaner).
Walcott, Derek, *Another Life* (New York/Canada 1973: Farrar, Straus and Giroux/Doubleday Canada).
——— *The Arkansas Testament* (New York, 1987: Farrar, Straus and Giroux).
——— *The Castaway and Other Poems* (London, 1965: Jonathan Cape).
——— *Epitaph for the Young: XII Cantos* (Barbados, 1949: Advocate).
——— *The Fortunate Traveller* (New York, 1981: Farrar, Straus and Giroux).

——— *The Gulf* (New York, 1970: Farrar, Straus and Giroux).
——— *The Gulf and Other Poems* (London, 1969: Jonathan Cape).
——— *In A Green Night: Poems 1948–1960* (London, 1962: Jonathan Cape).
——— *Midsummer* (New York, 1984: Farrar, Straus and Giroux).
——— *Omeros* (New York/Can., 1990: Farrar, Straus and Giroux/Collins).
——— *Poems* (Kingston, 1951: City Printery).
——— *Sea Grapes* (London, 1976: Jonathan Cape).
——— *Selected Poems* (New York, 1964: Farrar, Straus and Company).
——— *The Star-Apple Kingdom* (New York, 1979: Farrar, Straus and Giroux).
——— *25 Poems* (Trin., 1948: Guardian Commercial Printery).
White, Edgar, *The Rising* (London/New York, 1988: Marion Boyars).
Wynter, Sylvia, *The Hills of Hebron* (London, 1962: Jonathan Cape).
Zephaniah, Benjamin, *The Dread Affair* (London, 1985: Arrow Books).

7 TEXTS

Anthony, Michael, *Parade of the Carnivals of Trinidad 1839–1989* (Trin. 1989: Circle Press).
Baugh, Edward, *Derek Walcott* (London, 1978: Longman).
Bodu, Jose, *Trinidadiana* (Port of Spain, 1890).
Bolingbroke, Henry, *A Voyage to Demerara* (ed. Roth, Georgetown, 1947).
Brathwaite, Edward, *The Development of Creole Society in Jamaica 1770–1820* (Oxford, UK. 1971: Clarendon Press).
Brook, Peter, *The Empty Space* (New York 1968: Avon Books).
Cameron, Norman, *The Evolution of the Negro* (Guy. 1929, Vol I, 1934, Vol II: Argosy Company Ltd).
Corsbie, Ken, *Theatre in the Caribbean* (London, 1984: Hodder and Stoughton).
Cowell, Joseph, *Thirty Years passed among the Players in England and America* (New York, 1844: Harper and Brothers; facsimile, Hamden, USA. 1979; The Shoe String Press Inc.).
Craig, E. Quita, *Black Drama of the Federal Theatre Era* (Amherst, USA. 1980: University of Massachusetts Press).
Cundall, Frank, *Historic Jamaica* (London, 1915).
Ernst, Earle, *The Kabuki Theatre* (Oxford, UK. 1956: Oxford University Press).
Froude, James Anthony, *The English in the West Indies* (London, 1887).
Gibbons, Rawle, 'Traditional Enactments of Trinidad – Towards a Third Theatre' (unpublished, M.Phil thesis 1979: University of the West Indies, St Augustine Trin).
Goldstraw, Irma E., *Derek Walcott, an annotated bibliography of his works, 1944–1980* (New York, 1984: Garland Publishing Inc., Critical Studies on Black Life and Culture, Vol. 14, Garland Reference Library of the Humanities, Vol. 279).
Hill, Errol, *The Jamaican Stage 1655–1900* (Amherst, USA. 1992: University of Massachusetts Press).
——— *Shakespeare in Sable* (Amherst, USA. 1985: University of Massachusetts Press).
——— *The Trinidad Carnival, mandate for a national theatre* (Austin, USA. 1972: University of Texas Press).
Hyatt, Charles, *When me was a boy* (Jam. 1989: Institute of Jamaica).
James, C.L.R., *Beyond a Boundary* (London, 1963: Hutchinson and Co.).
——— *Mariners, Renegades and Castaways* (London, 1985: Allison and Busby).
Johnston, Robert A., *The Theatre of Belize* (Massachusetts, 1973: Christopher Publishing House).
Keimer, Samuel, *Caribbeana* (London, 1741).
Kingsley, Charles, *At Last: A Christmas in the West Indies* (London, 1874: Macmillan).
Long, Edward, *History of Jamaica*, 3 vols (London, 1774).
Martin, Tony (ed.), *African Fundamentalism: A Literary and Cultural Anthology of Garvey's Harlem Renaissance* (USA, 1990: Majority Press).

Mitchell, Loften, *Black Drama* (New York, 1967: Hawthorn Books).

Nettleford, Rex, *Dance Jamaica: Cultural Definition and Artistic Discovery* (New York, 1985: Grove Press Inc).

Newson, Linda A., *Aboriginal and Spanish Colonial Trinidad*, A Study in Culture Contact (London, 1976: Academic Press).

Nunley, John W. and Bettelheim, Judith, *Caribbean Festival Arts* (Seattle/London, 1988: The Saint Louis Art Museum in association with University of Washington Press).

Omotoso, Kole, *The Theatrical Into Theatre*, A Study of the Drama and Theatre of the English-speaking Caribbean (London, 1982: New Beacon Books).

Quevedo, Raymond, *Atilla's Kaiso: A Short History of Trinidad Calypso* (Trin. 1983: University of the West Indies).

Ramchand, Kenneth, *The West Indian Novel and its Background* (London, 1970: Faber and Faber).

Rohlehr, Gordon, *Calypso and Society in Pre-Independence Trinidad* (Trinidad, 1991: Rohlehr).

——— *My Strangled City and other essays* (Trin. 1992: Longman Trinidad Ltd.).

Schomburgh, Robert H., *History of Barbados* (London, 1848: Longman, Brown, Green and Longman).

Seymour, A. J., *Edgar Mittelholzer, the man and his work* – the 1967 Edgar Mittelholzer Lectures (Guy. 1968: National History and Arts Council).

Walcott, Derek: *The Antilles : Fragments of Epic Memory* – The Nobel lecture. (New York and Canada, 1993: Farrar, Straus and Giroux/HarperCollins Canada).

Walsh, William, *Commonwealth Literature* (Oxford, UK. 1973: Oxford University Press).

Wright, Richardson, *Revels in Jamaica 1682–1838* (New York, 1937: Dodd, Mead and Co.).

8 ARTICLES AND REVIEWS

(This section of the bibliography is indebted to Irma Goldstraw's *Derek Walcott, an annotated bibliography of his works, 1944–1980* (New York, 1984), and to Victor Questel's bibliography of the Trinidad Theatre Workshop (Trinidad, 1976: *Kairi* 76).)

on Michael Abbensetts:

Alleyne-Forte, Learie; 'Sweet Talk' – review (Trin. 1982: *Gayap*, 1982).

Lyndersay, Mark, 'Nude scenes? No, Sweet Talk is just commercial' – review (Trin: *TG*, 24 July, 1981).

on Ronald Amoroso:

Stone, Judy, 'Impressive record for a modest Ronnie Amoroso' – interview (Trin: *TG*, 13 May, 1986).

——— 'Present "Master" musical has creaky joints' – review, *Master of Carnival* (Trin: *TG*, 9 March, 1988).

——— ' "Sangre Grande by Two" wins a smile and sympathy' – review (Trin: *TG*, 28 May, 1986).

on Douglas Archibald:

Searl, D.M., 'A Force To Be Reckoned With' – review, *Junction Village* (Trin: *Evening News*, 8 March, 1954).

Stone, Judy, 'Drama of the joys and sorrows of a neglected people' (Trin; *TG*, 18 October, 1983).

Walcott, Derek, 'It's Life . . . I Beg You to See It' – review, *The Bamboo Clump* (Trin: *SG*, 29 April, 1962).

——— 'Miss Bruno tops in "The Rose Slip" ' – review (Trin: *SG*, 28 October, 1962).

Walke, Olive, 'New Company Stages Local Play' – review, *Junction Village* (Trin: *The Port of Spain Gazette*, 9 March, 1954).

on Dwight Arthur:

Ramchand, Kenneth, ' . . . behind (the) complex doors' – review (Trin: *TG*, 25 November, 1987).

Stone, Judy, 'Dwight scoffs at superstition' (Trin: *TG*, 13 November, 1987).

——— 'Excellent drama behind closed doors: Dwight Arthur triumphs with his play on incest' (Trin: *TG*, 18 November, 1987).

on Banyan:

Gilkes, Michael, 'Inside the people tv: Banyan' (Trin: *TG*, 24 September, 1991).

Lyndersay, Mark, 'Moving Pictures, Still Pictures' – review, *Epiphany* (Trin: *TTR*, Easter, 1982).

Mauby (pseud. Judy Stone), 'Banyan: For better or for worse?' – review (Trin: *TG*, 1 February, 1977).

——— 'Clever Maurice strikes again' – review, *The Wedding March* (Trin: *TG*, 21 December, 1976).

——— '. . . of Banyan's timely food for thought' – review, *Christmas Callaloo* (Trin: *TG*, 30 December, 1975).

——— 'A rich and spicy "Carnival Callaloo" ' – review (Trin: *TG*, 15 June, 1976).

——— 'Romeo and Juliet à la Callaloo' – review, *Classical Callaloo* (Trin: *TG*, 23 November, 1976).

——— ' "Sports Parang" designed for the wrong medium' – review (Trin: *TG*, 28 October, 1976).

Stone, Judy, 'New horizons open for popular Banyan' (Trin: *TG*, 8 February, 1977).

Taylor, Jeremy, 'The Banyan Experiment' (Trin: *People*, November–December, 1976).

on Harold Bascom:

Bacon, Lee, 'T.V.Alley – Second uproarious triumph for Harold Bascom' (Guy: *Sunday Chronicle*, 3 April, 1988).

Creighton, Al, 'Social Hysteria In A TV Culture' – review, *TV Alley* (Guy: *Stabroek News*, 2 April, 1988).

Wintz, Desiree, 'Though The Critics Carp Harold Bascom Keeps Pulling Them In At The Box Office' – interview (Guy: *Stabroek News*, 30 September, 1989).

on Elliot Bastien:

Asein, S. O., 'Bastien's Anancy Story: A Critique' (Toronto, 1972, *Black Images*, Vol. 1, #2).

Chambers, Geanine, 'A Look at another Caribbean Workshop presentation' – review, *A Nancy Story* (Toronto, 1971, *Contrast*).

Lyndersay, Mark. ' "A Nancy Story" – thinly sketched but full of chat' – review (Trin: *TG*, 1 February, 1982).

Maharaj, Vashti, 'Vital themes woven into "A Nancy Story" ' – review (Trin: *TG*, 20 January, 1982).

Pantin, Raoul, ' "A Nancy Story": A tale of Yore' – review (Trin: *DE*, 27 January, 1982).

on Louise Bennett:

Gloudon, Barbara, 'The Hon. Louise Bennett, O.J. – Fifty Years of Laughter' (Jam: *JJ*, Vol. 19, #3, 1986).

on Lennox Brown:

Foreman, Ellen, 'The Trinity Of Four/ Fog Drifts in The Spring' – review (New York: *New York Recorder*, Vol. 24, #3, 28 February, 1976).

Lewis, Emory, 'Play Brings Caribbean Ghetto to Life' – review, *A Ballet Behind the Bridge* (New Jersey, USA: *The Record*, 15 March, 1972).

McGinnis, Juliette, 'Two Plays By Lennox Browne Explore Depths of The Mind' – review, *The Trinity of Four, Fog Drifts in the Spring* (New York: *Voice*, 27 February, 1976).

Newton, Edmund, ' "Dinner" has vibrant talk and little action' – review, *The Twilight Dinner* (New York: *New York Post*, 19 April, 1978).

Paddington, Bruce, 'Four failures far from home' – review, *Home is a Long Way* (Trin: *TG*, 2 December, 1974; see also 9 December).

Schier, Marge, 'Becoming major forces in world theatre' – interview (Trin: *TG*, 25 August, 1972).

Stone, Judy, 'Calypsonians are our dramatists of the future, says Lennox Brown' (Trin: *TG*, 18 November, 1986).

——— 'Calypsonians will be the action' – interview (Trin: *TG*, 4 June, 1985).

Taylor, Jeremy, 'It's a very Long Way from Home' – review, *Home is a Long Way* (Trin: *DE*, 2 December, 1974).

Whitbeck, Doris, 'You must pit yourself against the universe' – interview (Trin: *TG*, 22 July, 1974).

Whittaker, Herbert, 'Theatre' (Toronto: *Globe and Mail*, 11 June, 1973).

on Alwin Bully:

Barratt, Harold, 'Ruler in Hiroona and the Picaroon Hero', review of the G.C.H. Thomas novel (Trin: *Voices*, Vol. 2, #4, April, 1977).

Lyndersay, Mark, 'Thrilling "Nite Box" mystery by promising UWI players' – review (Trin: *TG*, 8 April, 1982).

Stone, Judy, 'A multi-talented Caribbean man' – interview (Trin: *TG*, 29 January, 1985).

on Norman Cameron:

Loncke, Joycelynne, 'The Price of Victory: the Plays of Norman Cameron' (Guy: *Kaie*, 1977, #13, Guyfesta 1975 and 1977).

on Jan Carew:

Birbalsingh, Frank, 'Interview with Jan Carew' (Guy: *KOA*, #37, December, 1987).

Jardine, Monica, 'University of Hunger' – review (Guy: *New World*, 19 September, 1966).

on Sam Chase:

Josiah, H. W., 'How Sam Chase Operates' (Guy: *KOA*, Vol. 8, #25, June, 1959).

on Willi Chen:

Johnson, Kim, '1950s time warp – and a good time had by all' – review, *Freedom Road* (Trin: *SE*, 22 March, 1992).

Ramchand, Kenneth, 'Not a police station but a madhouse' – review, *Tainted Blood* (Trin: *TG*, 6 May, 1987).

Stone, Judy, 'Creditable first effort by Willi Chen' – review, *Freedom Road* (Trin: *TG*, 21 November, 1985).

——— ' "One Love" a more sophisticated piece of theatre' – review (Trin: *TG*, 26 June, 1989).

——— ' "Tainted Blood", a front runner for this year's Original Play Award' – review (Trin: *TG*, 12 June, 1987).

on Zeno Constance:

Bassant, Reynold, 'Bringing incest out into the open' – review, *My Father's Child* (Trin: *TG*, 18 March, 1986).

Jaikaransingh, Ken, ' "Death Row . . . The Nightmare Continues" ' – review (Trin: *SE*, 8 June, 1986).

——— 'Schools Drama Festival perks up' – review, *Duelling Voices* (Trin: *DE*, 17 November, 1987).

Shand, Eden, 'Fantasy Flight Crashes' – review (Trin: *TG*, 15 June, 1984).

Stone, Judy, 'Constance play as a folk musical? Yes!' – review, *Patricia* (Trin: *TG*, 10 July, 1989).

——— 'Zeno may inspire Teachers in Theatre' – review, *Deathrow . . . the Nightmare Continues* (Trin: *TG*, 3 June, 1986).

Taylor, Jeremy, ' "Flight Through Fantasy" was just too slow' – review (Trin: *DE*, 14 June, 1984).

on Felix Cross:

Brown, Tim, 'Glory!' – review (London: *The Guardian*, 23 February, 1990).

Diamond, Rodger, 'The Glory and the Cross' – interview (London: *Artrage*, Spring/Summer, 1990).

Gilbey, Liz, 'The dish washer who just "fell into acting" ' – interview, Oscar James (Leicester: *Leicester Mercury*, 16 February, 1990).

Hammerton, Geoff, 'Glorious hopes for latest show' – review (Derby: *Derby Evening Telegraph*, 19 February, 1990).

Hammerton, Geoff, 'Glory be!' – review (Derby: *Derby Evening Telegraph*, 17 February, 1990).

Lloyd, Kevin, 'A glorious production' – review (Derby: *Derby Express*, 22 February, 1990).

Raymond, Judy, 'For Felix, it's a kind of homecoming' – interview (Trin: *SE*, 28 March, 1993).

Stone, Judy, 'Warner reaping fame and "Glory!" in London' (Trin: *TG*, 3 September, 1990).

Sweeting, Adam, 'Glory!' – review (London: *The Guardian*, 28 April, 1990).

on Pat Cumper:

Armitstead, Claire, 'Fallen Angel and the Devil Concubine' (London: *Financial Times*, 20 July, 1989).

Jean-Baptiste, Deborah, 'Sensitive and precise performance by Jamaican cast'

– review, *The Fallen Angel and the Devil Concubine* (Trin: *SG*, 3 June, 1990).
Ross, Leone, 'Play on Sistren! Play on!' – review, *Buss Out* (Jam: *Sistren*, Vol. 11, #1, 1989).
Stone, Judy, 'An education to welcome Sistren' – review, *Buss Out* (Trin: *TG*, 12 June, 1989).
——— ' "Fallen Angel" not to be missed' – review, *The Fallen Angel and the Devil Concubine* (Trin: *TG*, 5 June, 1990).
——— 'Rebellion with mother drives the rapist' – review (Trin: *TG*, 12 October, 1988).

on Basil Dawkins:
Campbell, Jenni, 'Dawkins struck gold with "Same Song Different Tune"!' (Jam: *The Jamaica Record*, 24 March, 1991).
Cromwell, Liz, 'Champagne, Sky Juice: Panorama of moods, emotions' – review (Cay: *Newstar*, July, 1987).
Lindo, Archie, 'Good Entertainment Value', review, *Champagne and Sky Juice* (Jam: *The Star*, 29 October, 1986).
McKnight, Franklin, 'Thought-provoking and funny' – review, *Champagne and Sky Juice* (Jam: *The Star*, 5 January, 1987).
Reckord, Michael, ' "Champagne" sparkles' – review, *Champagne and Sky Juice* (Jam: *Daily Gleaner*, 12 November, 1986).
——— ' "Same Song" destined to be a hit' – review, *Same Song, Different Tune* (Jam: *Daily Gleaner*, 16 April, 1991).

on Felix Edinborough:
Brown, Lennox, 'Honour for some unsung heroes' – review, *King Arthur and his Merry Men* (Trin: *Mirror*, 1 March, 1988).
Johnston, Christine, 'Why "J'Ouvert"'s one of the best' (Trin: *TG*, 11 February, 1991).
Stone, Judy, 'Gene would have been proud of "Gene" ' – review (Trin: *TG*, 2 July, 1990).
——— 'King Arthur takes on a zesty new life' – review (Trin: *TG*, 10 February, 1988).
——— 'Malick's King Arthur needed more rehearsal for opening' – review (Trin: *TG*, 7 September, 1987).
——— 'Spectacular Reopening for L'il Carib' – review, *Mas in Yuh Mas* (Trin: *TG*, 23 January, 1980).
Taylor, Jeremy, 'It really was Mas In Yuh Mas – review (Trin: *DE*, 20 January, 1980).

on Francis Quamina Farrier:
Agard, John, 'Operation Makonaima gets away with Murder' – review (Guy: *Caribbean Entertainer*, Vol. 1, #2, October, 1972).
Searwar, Lloyd, 'Make Films for the World' (Guy: *Caribbean Entertainer*, Vol. 1, #2, October, 1972).

on Rawle Gibbons:
Ali, Shereen, 'Feast for fans of long-time kaiso' – review, *Ah Wanna Fall* (Trin: *SE*, 9 February, 1992).
Hughes, Brenda, 'When less sometimes means more' – review, *Sing De Chorus* (Trin: *TG*, 4 February, 1991).
Jean-Baptiste, Deborah, 'All the humour, wit and imagery in calypso present in "Ah Wanna Fall" ' – review (Trin: *SG*, 9 February, 1992).
——— 'Night "de audience" sang "de Chorus" – review (Trin: *TG*, 25 January, 1991).
——— 'Right at home "singing de chorus" – review (Trin: *SG*, 3 March, 1991).
Lee, Simon, ' "Ten to One" makes Three' – review (Trin: *SG*, 24 January, 1993).
Lyndersay, Mark, 'Warm and respectful, but too much of a good thing' – review, *Sing De Chorus* (Trin: *TG*, 25 January, 1991).
Marshall, Willys, 'Dog and Shepherd truly deserve the accolades' – review (Trin: *People*, October, 1981).
Ramchand, Kenneth, 'Drama of the jamet bands' – introduction and overview, *I Lawah* (Trin: *TG*, 10 June, 1987).
Ramcharitar, Raymond, 'Sing on, Sparrow', review, *Ten to One* (Trin: *SE*, 7 February, 1993).
Ravi-Ji (Ravindranath Maharaj), 'Come

back home kaiso, come back home!' – review, *Ah Wanna Fall* (Trin: *SG*, 23 February, 1992).

Raymond, Judy, 'Modern kaiso put to shame' – review, *Ten to One* (Trin: *SE*, 31 January, 1993).

Stone, Judy, ' "I Lawah" has little sense of continuity' – review (Trin: *TG*, 5 June, 1987).

——— 'Rawle Gibbons makes time to direct' – interview (Trin: *TG*, 22 July, 1986).

Taylor, Jeremy, 'Sing de Chorus' – review (Trin: *Galerie*, Vol. 1, #1, 1991).

on Michael Gilkes:

Hill, Errol, 'An Introduction to "Couvade" ' (in *Couvade*, London, 1974: Longman Caribbean).

Hosein, Alim, 'Couvade: the birth of a dream' – review (Guy: *Starbroek News*, 29 May, 1993).

Wintz, Desiree, 'Couvade: a community on stage' – review (Guy: *Starbroek News*, 27 May, 1993).

on Hal Greaves:

Stone, Judy, 'The originality of "Upon the Sands" ' – review (Trin: *TG*, 26 November, 1986).

——— ' "Others" a pioneer in community theatre' (Trin: *TG*, 18 September, 1989).

——— ' "Others" : Breaking the cycle of abuse' – review (Trin: *TG*, 18 October, 1989).

——— 'Tief throws theatre's preaching rule to the winds' – review (Trin: *TG*, 18 November, 1987).

——— ' "The Victims" – fast-paced and painfully funny' – review (Trin: *TG*, 4 July, 1985).

on Errol Hill:

Blyth, Alan, 'Bewitching and fun' – review, *Man Better Man* (London: *Daily Express*, 1 October, 1965).

Coton, A. V., 'Neat play by actors from Trinidad' – review, *Man Better Man* (London: *Daily Telegraph*, 1 October, 1965).

Gibbons, Rawle, 'Review, Trinidad Carnival Mandate for a National Theatre' (Trin: *Kairi*, 1976).

Hill, Errol, 'Is "Man Better Man", Mr Walcott' (Trin: *TG*, 3 February, 1965).

Jacobs, Carl, 'We lead the Hemisphere in cultural affairs, says Hill' – interview (Trin: *SG*, 11 January, 1970).

Kerensky, Oleg, 'Trinidad's Julian Slade' – review, *Man Better Man* (London: *Daily Mail*, 1 October, 1965).

Kerr, Walter, 'Too Much Too Soon?' – review, *Man Better Man* (New York: *New York Times*, 13 July, 1969).

Lewis, Emory, 'Captivating Rhythm Of Calypso' – review, *Man Better Man* (New Jersey, USA: *The Record*, 3 July, 1969).

Mauby, 'Rerun for Man? Some obeah might help' – review, *Man Better Man* (Trin: *TG*, 12 September, 1975).

Novick, Julius, 'Man Better Man' – review (New York: *Village Voice*, 10 July, 1969).

Parker, T. H., 'Man Better Man' – review (Hartford, USA: *The Hartford Courant*, 28 January, 1962).

Redpath, William M., 'Man Better Man' – review (Hartford, USA: *Yale Daily News*, 22 April, 1960).

Roach, Eric, 'The Gentiles reap the rich reward' – review, *Man Better Man* (Trin: *EN*, 1 September, 1965).

Shepard, Richard F., 'A Refreshing Calypso Tale' – review, *Man Better Man* (New York: *New York Times*, 3 July, 1969).

Tallmer, Jerry, 'Witch Doctor Meets His Downfall' – review, *Man Better Man* (New York: *New York Post*, 3 July, 1969).

Walcott, Derek, 'Interview with an actor' – Errol Jones in *Man Better Man* (Trin: *TG*, 13 October, 1965).

——— 'S. Grande tonight; Broadway next' – review, *Man Better Man* (Trin: *TG*, 27 January, 1965).

Wyke, Marguerite, 'Man Better Man' – review (Trin: *The Nation*, 8 October, 1965).

on Anthony Hinkson:

Mauby, 'Young Bajan actors star at Little

Carib' – review, *Teacher, Teach 'er* (Trin: *TG*, 5 August, 1977).

Stone, Judy, 'Dynamic level of stagecraft' – review, *Village Life* (Trin: *TG*, 5 June, 1989).

on Slade Hopkinson:

Anthony, Michael, 'Conversation with Slade Hopkinson' (Trin: *SG*, 9 August, 1970).

Lee Wah, James, 'For Slade' (Trin: *Gayap*, 1973–74).

Mauby, 'Dilemma of an educated country boy' – review, *Sala* (Trin: *TG*, 16 October, 1975).

Parvatan, Vibert, 'Fall of a Chief' – review (Guy: *New World*, 20 August, 1965).

Walcott, Derek, 'Actor Slade Hopkinson gives a farewell interview' (Trin: *TG*, 14 July, 1965).

——— 'Energetic Guild comes to Town' – review, *Fall of a Chief* (Trin: *TG*, 19 May, 1965).

Waterman, Kathy Ann, 'A man called Slade' – interview (Trin: *SE*, 9 June, 1985).

on C.L.R. James:

Glaberman, Martin, 'C.L.R. James – The Man and his Work' (Guy: *New World*, #31, 7 January, 1966).

Mauby, 'Answer to dramatic cry from Minty Alley' – review, Springer's adaptation (Trin: *TG*, 19 December, 1977).

Rohlehr, Gordon, 'Our Truest Ancestor' (Trin: *TTR*, Vol. 11, #9, June, 1989).

Stone, Judy, 'Yard Theatre triumphs in "Jacobins" ' – review, *Black Jacobins* (Trin: *TG*, 3 August, 1979).

on Errol John:

Ifill, Wendy, 'Errol John. Now his wish is to make a Carnival film' (Trin: *People*, Vol. 1, #2, September, 1975).

Jaikaransingh, Ken, ' "Moon" a Caribbean classic' – review (Trin: *SE*, 9 June, 1985).

John, Deborah, 'John's Moon shining on' – review (Trin: *DE*, 26 May, 1988).

Reyes, Elma, 'Now even calypso is different' – interview (Trin: *DE*, 3 September, 1973).

Roach, Eric, 'Let's air some more home-made drama' – review, *Moon on a Rainbow Shawl* (Trin: *TG*, 12 September, 1973).

——— 'Mrs Adams – The Heroine' (Trin: *TG*, 19 April, 1967).

Stone, Judy, 'Spectacular lighting, sound in "Moon on a Rainbow Shawl" ' – review (Trin: *TG*, 10 May, 1988).

Tallmer, Jerry, 'Theatre: Moon on a Rainbow Shawl' – review (New York: *The Village Voice*, 25 January, 1962).

Taylor, Jeremy, 'Cuts weaken Errol John's Moon' (Trin: *DE*, 17 November, 1973).

Walcott, Derek, 'Errol John – Busy Man with a dual career' (Trin: *SG*, 30 July, 1961).

Watson, Neil, 'Errol John' – obituary (London: *The Times*, 16 July, 1988).

on Ronald John:

Jaikaransingh, Ken, 'Irene's Song – a promising beginning' – review (Trin: *DE*, 7 June, 1988).

Ramcharitar, Raymond, ' "Masquerade" – a bad play with music' – review (Trin: *TG*, 6 April, 1992).

Raymond, Judy, 'Tempo high with John's Masquerade' (Trin: *DE*, 18 June, 1991).

Stone, Judy, 'Here is where the grass is greener' – review, *Welcome home, Cousin Raphael* (Trin: *TG*, 25 November, 1985).

——— 'What kind of play is "Irene's Song"?' – review (Trin: *TG*, 13 June, 1988).

Taylor, Jeremy, 'The wizard is a jailbird' – review, *The Wizard of Kandahar* (Trin: *DE*, 8 July, 1980).

on Paul Keens-Douglas:

James-Bryan, Meryl, 'No laughing matter' – interview (Trin: *Entertainer*, April, 1983).

Mauby, 'Now Creola enters with successful "Tim Tim" ' – review, *Tim Tim* (Trin: *TG*, 17 September, 1975).

Raymond, Judy, 'Loving the Language' (Trin: *SE*, 28 January, 1990).

Stone, Judy, 'Paul's more than a writer' – interview (Trin: *TG*, 5 February, 1985).

——— 'Spectacular Reopening for L'il Carib' – review, *Mas in Yuh Mas* (Trin: *TG*, 23 January, 1980).
Taylor, Jeremy, 'It really was Mas In Yuh Mas' – review (Trin: *DE*, 20 January, 1980).

on Ricardo Keens-Douglas:
Auguste, Arnold A., 'Obeah's our Dr Faustus' – review, *The Obeah Man* (Toronto: *Share*, 27 June, 1985).
Carfagnini, Paul, 'Obeah Man a story for all' – review, *The Obeah Man* (Toronto: *Share*, 27 June, 1985).
Harvey, Robin, 'Dancers create magic in musical' – review, *The Obeah Man* (Toronto: *Sunday Star*, 30 June, 1985).

on Freddie Kissoon:
Blood, Peter Ray, 'Calabash Alley Live and Direct' – review (Trin: *The Sun*, 8 March, 1988).
Cuffy, David, 'Big 35 for Strolling Players' (Trin: *TG*, 7 June, 1992).
Elcock, Dave, 'Freddie Kissoon is "Strolling" Along' (Trin: *SE*, 13 September, 1987).
Marshall, Willys, 'Freddie Kissoon: Theatre is the audience' (Trin: *People*, April, 1982).
Mauby, 'To Woman yes, but with love?' – review (Trin: *TG*, 22 November, 1975).
——— 'TTT's Fugitive needs an electric charge' – review (Trin: *TG*, 2 October, 1975).
Melser, John, 'There's no view outside the window' (Trin: *TG*, 24 June, 1969; see also 25 June, 1969).
Roxburgh, Kit, 'Freddie Kissoon – the great local hope' (Trin: *SG*, 14 June, 1981).
Stone, Judy, 'Non-stop laughter at "Another 5 Beulah Plays" ' – review (Trin: *TG*, 5 June, 1990).
——— ' "We Crucify Him" – a simple but great story' – review (Trin: *TG*, 15 June, 1988).
Strolling Players, *Silver Jubilee Magazine* (Trin. 1982).
Walcott, Derek, 'Company of Players Tries' – review, *Mamaguy* (Trin: *SG*, 2 July, 1961).
——— 'A Laventille Crookback' – review, *King Cobo* (Trin: *TG*, 1 February, 1966).

on Ginger Knight:
Reckord, Michael, 'Knight's powerful "Whiplash" ' (Jam: *Daily Gleaner*, 1 October, 1983).
Stone, Judy, 'Jamaicans' "Whiplash" proves entertaining' – review (Trin: *TG*, 22 August, 1987).

on Earl Lovelace:
Armistead, Claire, 'This dragon couldn't dance on the stage' – review, *The Dragon Can't Dance* (London: *Financial Times*, 6 July, 1990).
Blood, Peter, 'The Wine – an astonishing play' – review (Trin: *The Sun*, 1 June, 1988).
Keeling, Julian, 'The New Hardware Store' – review (Croydon, UK: *Plays and Players*, May 1985).
Lynch, Hugh, ' "The Dragon" is dancing in London' – review (Trin: *SE*, 22 July, 1990).
Pantin, Raoul, 'Bringing the "Dragon" back to life' – review (Trin: *DE*, 6 February, 1986).
Raymond, Judy, 'A writer explores Caribbean rhythms' – interview (Trin: *SE*, 4 August, 1991).
Scott, Lawrence, 'Earl Lovelace's "Store" a success in London's West End' – review, *The New Hardware Store* (Trin: *SE*, 28 April, 1985).
Stone, Judy, 'Astonishment gives life to drama festival' – review (Trin: *TG*, 14 June, 1988).
——— ' "Dragon" has all the elements but needs lot more polish' – review (Trin: *TG*, 10 February, 1986).
——— 'Lovelace's play speaks to people' – interview (Trin: *TG*, 21 January, 1986).
——— 'Play that thinks a little too hard' – review, *Jestina's Calypso* (Trin: *TG*, 3 July, 1985).
——— ' "Wine of Astonishment" moves with the hop-and-halt pace of a crapaud' – review (Trin: *TG*, 26 May, 1988).

on Ralph Maraj:

Jaikaransingh, Ken, ' "Broken Bridge" – another play from Ralph Maharaj' (Trin: *DE*, 15 August, 1988).

Lyndersay, Mark, 'Easy in the Ashes – grade B movie – grade A dialogue' – review (Trin: *DE*, 28 October, 1980).

Maraj, Ralph, 'Meeting a mandate in "The Saint" ' (Trin: *TG*, 12 November, 1990).

Ravi-Ji, ' "The Saint" bowls them over' – review (Trin: *TG*, 3 December, 1990).

Stone, Judy, ' "The Broken Bridge" – another Drama Guild hit' – review (Trin: *TG*, 2 September, 1988).

——— 'Maraj brings us his own brand of satirical farce' – review, *Flowers of the Nation* (Trin: *TG*, 2 December, 1987).

——— ' "Missing File" – a satisfying production' – review (Trin: *TG*, 30 June, 1987).

——— 'Ralph Maraj in a style all his own' – review, *The Archbishop and the Prime Minister* (Trin: *TG*, 17 July, 1986).

——— 'Ralph Maraj returns to "something important" ' – interview (Trin: *TG*, 25 October, 1983).

——— 'Revolution of sorts in Oh Prime Minister' – review (Trin: *TG*, 13 August, 1990).

——— ' "Sapodilla" gives Ralph another winner' – review, *Under the Sapodilla Tree* (Trin: *TG*, 6 April, 1988).

——— ' "Wake It Up" tackles social problem' – review (Trin: *TG*, 6 November, 1979).

Taylor, Jeremy, 'Gutsy play by Maraj' – review, *Under de Sapodilla Tree* (Trin: *DE*, 23 June, 1980).

on Louis Marriott:

Stone, Judy, 'Where's the box office for this quality?' – review, *Office Chase* (Trin: *TG*, 28 May, 1990).

Wilson, Michelle R.A., 'Marriott: No sign of theatre recovery' (Jam: *Sunday Gleaner*, 21 April, 1991).

on Una Marson:

Smilowitz, Erika, 'Una Marson, Woman Before Her Time' (Jam: *JJ*, Vol. 16, #2, May, 1983).

on Mustapha Matura:

Caulfield, Holden (pseud.George John), 'Around the Town' – review, *Rum and Coca Cola* (Trin: *DE*, 30 June, 1980).

Lynch, Hugh, 'Three sisters: from Russia to Trinidad' – review, *Trinidad Sisters* (Trin: *SE*, 13 March, 1988).

——— 'A Trinidad Coup stemming from two others' – review, *The Coup* (Trin: *SE*, 4 August, 1991).

——— 'You can take a play out of Ireland but . . . ' – review, *Playboy of the West Indies* (Trin: *SE*, 27 May, 1984).

Lyndersay, Mark, 'Bloodless passion of Matura's Independence' – review (Trin: *TG*, 20 August, 1991).

——— ' "Rum and Coca Cola" not too strong' – review (Trin: *Catholic News*, 22 June, 1980).

Maharaj, Vashti, 'Playwright looks homeward' – interview (Trin: *TG*, 18 August, 1981).

Milne, Anthony, 'Mamapoule to sweetman' – review, *Playboy of the West Indies* (Trin: *DE*, 18 May, 1985).

Neil, Heather, 'All for the love of the language' – interview (London: *The Times*, 10 July, 1991)

Nightingale, Benedict, 'Fulfilment found with monkeys' – review, *Meetings* (London: *The Times*, 16 March, 1991).

Pantin, Raoul, 'A Piece of our Landscape' – review, *Independence* (Trin: *DE*, 19 August, 1981).

Stone, Judy, 'Authentic Trinidad in "Playboy" ' – review (Trin: *TG*, 9 July, 1985).

——— 'Mustapha creates a Trinidadian playboy out of the Irish' (Trin: *TG*, 14 May, 1985).

Taylor, Jeremy, 'Matura packs both comedy and tragedy' – review, *Rum and Coca Cola* (Trin: *DE*, 16 June, 1980).

Wardle, Irving, 'The Playboy of the West Indies' – review (London: *Sunday Times*, 23 February, 1984).

on Peter Minshall:

Aguillo, Xavier, interview (Barcelona: *La Gente*, 5 May, 1992).

Chee Mooke, Robert, 'Minshall immor-

talises the spirit of Mother T and T' (Trin: *SE*, 22 May, 1988).
——— 'Peter Minshall brings theatre to the streets' (Trin: *SE*, 15 May, 1988).
Minshall, Peter, 'A call for grads to be honest with selves' (Trin: *SE*, 28 July, 1985; continues 29 July, 'Enough of roots, let's grow some branches').
——— 'The Doctor of Mas' (Trin: *SE*, 10 November, 1991).
Patrick, Gail, 'Minshall: From Port of Spain to Spain, look where mas' reach' (Trin: *TG*, 3 November, 1991).
Raymond, Judy, 'Minshall stirs up richer Callaloo' (Trin: *SE*, 31 January, 1993).
Scott, Lawrence, 'Not just mas' – interview (Trin: *Entertainer*, April, 1983).
Stone, Judy, 'Minshall staging mas' at the National Stadium' – interview (Trin: *TG*, 4 January, 1989).
——— 'Santimanitay: What was Minshall trying to do?' (Trin: *TG*, 21 February, 1989).
Tait, Simon, 'A white man's carnival' (London: *Daily Telegraph*, 21 August, 1988).
Walcott, Derek, 'Minshall's settings the one bright spot' (Trin: *SG*, 19 December, 1965).

on Raoul Pantin:
Jaikaransingh, Ken, 'Radio 555: relevant, grim wit' – review (Trin: *DE*, 16 July, 1981).
Pires, B.C., 'Waiting for Bimsingh' – review, *Bim* (Trin: *SE*, 20 December, 1992).
Raymond, Judy, 'After 1990, Raoul Pantin entering a hermit phase' – interview (Trin: *SE*, 16 June, 1991).
Solomon-Armour, Elizabeth, ' "Bim" is back' (Trin: *SE*, 13 December, 1992).
Springer, Pearl Eintou, 'More serious side of "Radio Republic 555" – review (Trin: *SE*, 28 April, 1985).
Stone, Judy, ' "Hatuey" set space lacking but challenging script endures well' – review (Trin: *TG*, 10 July, 1987).
——— ' "Seasons" warms the second time around' – review (Trin: *TG*, 2 July, 1986).
Taylor, Jeremy, ' "Hatuey" brightened up bleak Labour Day' – review (Trin: *DE*, 23 June, 1980).

on Caryl Phillips:
Bartholomew, Kelroy, 'Caryl Phillips' (London: *The Voice*, 6 November, 1982).
Coveney, Michael, 'The Shelter' – review (London: *Financial Times*, 7 September, 1983).
Evans, Laurie, 'Telling no white lies' – profile (London: *The Leveller*, 22 January–4 February, 1982).
Fenton, James, 'Theatre' – review, *Where There is Darkness* (London: *Sunday Times*, 14 February, 1982).
Raymond, Judy, 'Writing to maintain his sanity' – interview (Trin: *DE*, 29 December, 1991).
Yarde, Rosalind, 'Black against white . . . past and present' – review, *The Shelter* (London; *Acton Gazette*, 15 September, 1983).

on Frank Pilgrim:
Corsbie, Ken, 'Brink Top' (Guy: *New World*, 1 October, 1965).
John, Deborah, ' "Miriamy" is endless bacchanal!' – review (Trin: *DE*, 21 January, 1981).
Lyndersay, Mark, 'Belly laughs galore in "Miriamy" ' – review (Trin: *TG*, 17 February, 1981).

on Victor Questel:
Milne, Anthony, 'Victor Questel: Poet of the People' (Trin: *SE*, 25 April, 1982).
Rohlehr, Gordon, 'Victor Questel: A Homage' (Trin: *TTR*, Vol. 5, #9, High Season, 1982).
Stone, Judy, 'A stunning piece of theatre' – review, *Two Choices* (Trin: *TG*, 16 June, 1986).
——— 'Tribute to a young writer' (Trin: *TG*, 12 May, 1982).

on Lennox Raphael:
Ackrill, Lesley, 'Lennox Raphael is sure that Trinidad has literary potential to astonish the world' – interview (Trin: *People*, January, 1981).
Clarke, LeRoy, 'Rumpelstiltskin spells

Rummpellstillskkiin' – review, (Trin: *DE*, 26 May, 1980).
Greenberger, Howard, 'The Naked Stage – Lennox Raphael and Che!: The Symbolism of Sex' – interview (in *Greenberger: The Off-Broadway Experience*, Englewood Cliffs, USA: Prentice-Hall Inc., 1971).
Lyndersay, Mark, 'Lennox gives us a much larger joke that's difficult to laugh at' – review, *The Politicians* (Trin: *TG*, 8 October, 1981).
——— 'Rumpelstiltskin' – review (Trin: *Catholic News*, 1 June, 1980).
Marshall, William Doyle, 'Picking up the pieces after politics' – interview (Trin: *TG*, 6 January, 1993).
Taylor, Jeremy, 'Bloodsuckers' – review, *Dracula the Dreamer* (Trin: *SE*, 15 June, 1980).
——— 'A puzzle . . . an experience . . . ' – review, *Waiting for Mick Jagger* (Trin: *DE*, 13 February, 1980).
——— ' "Rumpel" is a real romp – review, *Rumpelstiltskin* (Trin: *SE*, 9 May, 1980).

on Barry Reckord:
Walcott, Derek, 'About a Jamaican playwright' – on *Skyvers* (Trin: *TG*, 23 February, 1967).

on Michael Reckord:
Lindo, Archie, 'Weekend Theatre' – review, *Flip Side Death* (Jam: *The Star*, 18 March, 1978).
Morris, Mervyn, 'September pantomime?' – review, *Musical Soup* (Jam: *Daily Gleaner*, 22 September, 1977).
Scott, Dennis, 'A lovely entertainment' – review, *The Hon. All Purpus* (Jam: *Jamaica Daily News*, 9 January, 1980).
Wilson, Jeanne, 'Lime Tree Lane' – review (Jam: *The Weekend Star*, 10 May, 1991).

on Trevor Rhone:
Gussow, Mel, 'Two Can Play' – review (New York: *New York Times*, 16 April, 1985).
Hay, Malcolm, 'Old Story Time' – review (Croydon, UK: *Plays and Players*, November, 1985).
Ince, Laurel B., 'Smile Orange – Profound social commentary' – review (Trin: *SG*, 16 September, 1979).
Jaikaransingh, Ken, ' "School's Out" a dark, alarming vision' – review (Trin: *DE*, 16 November, 1988).
Mauby, 'Some solid laughs in heavy-handed souffle' – review, film *Smile Orange* (Trin: *TG*, 16 January, 1976).
Mietkewicz, Henry, 'Dramatist: The true voice of Jamaica' (Trin: *SG*, *'Two Can Play' Supplement*, 3 July, 1983).
Morris, Mervyn, 'Interviews Trevor Rhone' (Jam: *JJ*, Vol. 16, #1, 1983).
Parnell, Jeanne, "Two Can Play" ' – review (New York: *Black American*, Vol. 25, #16, 18 April, 1985).
Stone, Judy, 'A lot of fun things with "Old Storytime" ' – review (Trin: *TG*, 19 June, 1986).
——— 'Sell-out start for Dinner Theatre . . . audience joins in Rhone's Old Story Time' (Trin: *TG*, 7 June, 1979).
——— 'Trevor's "Orange" is Caribbean's comedy' – review (Trin: *TG*, 7 September, 1979).
Thompson, Elaine, 'Trevor Rhone: Maverick playwright' – interview (Trin: *SG* *'Two Can Play' Supplement*, 3 July, 1983).

on Eric Roach:
Phelps, Karen, ' "Belle Fanto" much too confined' – review (Trin: *SG*, 17 April, 1966).
Stone, Judy, 'Fast action and audience appeal in "Calabash of Blood" – review (Trin: *TG*, 19 June, 1985; see also 25 June, 1985).

on Dennis Scott:
Douglas, Karl, 'Requiem on Tape for a Lost Soul' – review, *The Caged* (Trin: *TG*, 13 May, 1962).
Gianetti, Danielle, 'Journeys' – interview (Trin: *TTR*, Vol. 8, ##1 and 2, Independence, 1982).
Marshall, Willys, 'Dog and Shepherd truly deserve the accolades' – review (Trin: *People*, October, 1981).
Stone, Judy, 'Dog depicts vicious contempt for poor' – review (Trin: *TG*, 28 October, 1987).

Walcott, Derek, 'Derek Walcott Grabs at a Thread, the Terse Mr Scott is still in the Dark' (Trin: *SG*, 15 July, 1962).
——— Miss Lee Wah to the rescue! So ambitious a programme but . . . ' – review (Trin: *TG*, 11 November, 1961).

on Godfrey Sealy:
Jaikaransingh, Ken, 'Certainly not "Home Sweet Home" ' – review (Trin: *DE*, 12 October, 1989).
——— 'A Situation gone Astray' – review, *Roll Call* (Trin: *DE*, 29 July, 1989).
Khelawan, Vernon, ' "Girlfriends" hit at (whew) Roxy' – review (Trin: *SG*, 9 July, 1989).
Ramcharitar, Raymond, 'Farce or ole mas . . . ?' – review, *Three's a Crowd* (Trin: *TG*, 9 April, 1992).
——— 'One of Our Sons is Missing' (Trin: *Galerie*, Vol. 1, #2, 1992).
——— 'Police storm AIDS play at theatre' (Trin: *SG*, 20 September, 1992).
Raymond, Judy, 'Maybe it was too life-like' – review, *Roll Call* (Trin: *The Sun*, 23 June, 1989).
——— 'Worthy revival of wordy play' – review, *One of Our Sons is Missing* (Trin: *SE*, 13 September, 1992).
Stone, Judy, 'Disco fantasy highlights musical' – review, *Limin'* (Trin: *TG*, 5 June, 1985).
——— 'Frank piece about sex and drugs' – review, *Roll Call* (Trin: *TG*, 19 June, 1989).
——— 'Good for business, this Comedy' – review, *Funny Business* (Trin: *TG*, 14 May, 1990).
——— ' "One of our sons is missing" – a brutally explicit play' – review (Trin: *TG*, 2 September, 1988).
——— 'Problems in "Home Sweet Home" – review (Trin: *TG*, 16 October, 1989).

on Sam Selvon:
Melser, John, 'Basement proves a genius for comedy' – review, *The World of Sam Selvon* (Trin: *TG*, 21 March, 1969).
Roach, Eric, 'Return to sanity' – review, *The World of Sam Selvon* (Trin: *TG*, 11 March, 1969).
Roxburgh, Kit, 'Conversation with a writer' (Trin: *SG*, 31 March, 1985).
Stone, Judy, 'Take "A Brighter Sun" to Secondary Schools' – review (Trin: *TG*, 13 April, 1985).

on Sistren:
Ford-Smith, Honor, 'Sistren at Work' (Jam: *Carib*, #4, 1986).
Ross, Leone, 'Play on Sistren! Play on!' – review, *Buss Out* (Jam: *Sistren*, Vol. 11, #1, 1989).
Stone, Judy, 'An education to welcome Sistren' – review, *Buss Out* (Trin: *TG*, 12 June, 1989).

on Derek Walcott:
Augustus, Earl, 'In a fine Castle' – review (Trin: *SE*, 7 November, 1971).
Babb, John, 'Walcott wins Nobel' (Trin: *TG*, 9 October, 1992).
Barker, J. S., 'A Canvas Too Large For Walcott's Brush' – review, *Henri Christophe* (Trin: *TG*, 30 November, 1954).
——— 'Not the Stuff For A W.I. National Theatre' – review, *The Sea at Dauphin* (Trin: *TG*, 18 August, 1954).
Brown, Lloyd, 'Dreamers and Slaves – The Ethos of Revolution in Walcott and Leroi Jones' (Jam: *CQ*, Vol. 17, ##3 and 4, September/December, 1971).
Brown, Wayne, 'Chow time, King Kong' – on *Dream on Monkey Mountain* (Trin: *DE*, 21 March, 1985).
——— 'Derek Walcott, poet and playwright: Wayne Brown talks with Albert Laveau' (Trin: *SG Magazine*, 18 October, 1992).
——— 'A Home for Mr Walcott' (Trin: *SG*, 22 November, 1992).
Campbell, Ralph, 'The Birth of Professional Theatre in Trinidad' (Trin: *SG*, 22 July, 1973).
——— 'To whom can the playwright turn?' (Trin: *SG*, 5 August, 1973).
Clarke, LeRoy, ' "Marie La Veau" – an artificial resurrection' – review (Trin: *DE*, 18 June, 1980).

Coke, Lloyd, 'Walcott's Mad Innocents' (Jam: *Savacou*, #5, June, 1971).

Corsbie, Ken, 'Play which deserves the award' – review, *A Branch of the Blue Nile* (Bar: *The Nation*, 29 November, 1983).

The Crusader: 'Derek Walcott' – commemorative edition (SL: *CPC*, Vol. 29, #42, October, 1992).

Dockray, Brian, 'A most significant musical contribution' – review, *Ti-Jean and his Brothers* (Trin: *TG*, 27 June, 1970).

Douglas, Karl, ' "Charlatan" Scores – Comedy Wise' – review (Trin: *TG*, 10 December, 1962).

Douglas-Smith, Aubrey, 'Henri Christophe' – review (Bar: *Bim*, Vol. 3, #12, June, 1950).

Espinet, Adrian, ' "Drums and Colours" Seeks to Trace WI Consciousness' – review (Trin: *SG*, 27 April, 1958).

——— 'Undistinguished – That's The Word for "Ti-Jean" ' – review, *Ti-Jean and His Brothers* (Trin: *TG*, 1 July, 1958).

Falcon, John, 'The spiritual agony of an old coal-burner' – review, *Dream on Monkey Mountain* (Trin: *TG*, 5 August, 1974).

Fields, Sidney, 'A Gift for Words' – review, *Ti-Jean and His Brothers* (New York: *New York Daily News*, 20 June, 1972).

Flanagan, Brenda, 'An Interview with Derek Walcott' (Michigan, USA: *Voices of the African Diaspora*, Vol. VII, #2, 1991).

Gibbons, Rawle, 'O Babylon! – A Review' (Trin. 1976: *Kairi*, 1976).

Gocking, W. E., 'Henri Christophe – a review' (Trin: *TG*, 8 September, 1950).

Graham, Roland, 'An art of wind upon water of wave upon shore' – reply to Clarke's critique of *Marie Laveau* (Trin: *DE*, 28 June, 1980).

Grimes, John, 'Company of Players Win Praise for "Ione" ' – review (Trin: *TG*, 9 November, 1957).

Gunness, Christopher, 'White man, black man' – review, *Pantomime* (Trin: *People*, June, 1978).

Hawley, David, ' "Pantomime" very funny, but lacks comic bombshells' – review (St Paul, USA: *St Paul Sunday Pioneer Press*, 27 March, 1983).

Hill, Errol, 'No Tears for Narcissus' – review, *Batai* (Trin: *TG*, 7 March, 1965).

Hilton, Anne, 'Brave Banyan effort but story hard to follow' – review, *The Rig* (Trin: *SG*, 22 January, 1984).

Hosein, Clyde, 'Lack of Appreciation drives one to Madness', interview (Trin: *TG*, 10 June, 1971).

——— 'Stormy Applause Well Deserved' – review, *Ti-Jean and his Brothers* (Trin: *TG*, 27 June, 1970).

Ismond, Pat, 'The Joker of Seville: Breaking Myths and Maidenheads' (Trin: *Tapia*, Vol. 5, ##20 and 22, 18 May and 1 June, 1975).

Jacobs, Carl, 'Bajans Are Still Very Insular and Prejudiced' – interview (Trin: *SG*, 23 July, 1967).

——— 'Spiritual Crippling from an absence of Vision' – interview (Trin: *SG*, 31 August, 1974).

——— 'There's No Bitterness in our Literature' – interview (Trin: *SG*, 22 May, 1966).

James, Dalton, 'Ti-Jean and his brothers: A brilliant effort – but why was Queen's Hall half-filled?' (Trin: *SE*, 7 November, 1971).

Jenkin, Veronica, 'Drums and Colours' – review (Bar: *Bim*, Vol. 7, #27, July–December, 1958).

John, Deborah, 'Marie La Veau, and the people who really had my sympathy' – review (Trin: *The Sun*, 6 June, 1980).

John, Ronald, 'Errol Jones remembers . . . ' (Trin: *TG*, 29 July, 1987).

Jones, Marilyn, 'Striking a blow for Women's Lib' – review, *The Joker of Seville* (Trin: *TG*, 12 December, 1974).

Juneja, Renu, 'Derek Walcott' (in *Post-Colonial English Drama* (ed:King), London: *St Martin's Press*, 1992).

Konwalina, Trudy, 'West Indian Drama – In The Hands Of An Expert Guardian' – review, *The Sea at Dauphin* (Trin: *EN*, 16 August, 1954).

Lee, Simon, 'Walcott on writing' (Trin: *SG*, 11 October, 1992).

Lee Wah, James, 'Ti-Jean and his Brothers At Point Fortin' – review (Trin: *Gayap*, 1973–74).

Lovelace, Earl, 'The Last Carnival' – review (Trin: *SE*, 25 July, 1982).

Lowhar, Syl, 'Another Station of the Cross' (Trin: *Tapia*, #23, 26 December, 1971).

——— 'A Struggle for Freedom' (Trin: *Tapia*, #8, 9 August, 1970).

Lyndersay, Mark, 'Pantomime is still a joy' – review (Trin: *DE*, 14 October, 1980).

——— 'You want jokes? I'll give you jokes – review, *Beef, no Chicken* (Trin: *TG*, 12 May, 1981).

Mauby: 'Charlatan? Yes, Walcott is still with us' – review (Trin: *TG*, 20 January, 1977).

——— 'Now the Joker's laugh is mature and polished' – review (Trin: *TG*, 24 October, 1975).

——— 'O Babylon, do Mafia play with beach balls?' – review (Trin: *TG*, 1 April, 1976).

Melser, John, 'A similar quality could be achieved' – review, *Malcochon* (Trin: *TG*, 25 April, 1969).

Mentus, Ulric, 'The Little Workshop's Mammoth Task of 5 Plays a Year' (Trin: *Sunday Mirror*, 8 May, 1966).

——— 'Nobody wants to be a West Indian' – interview (Jam: *Jamaica Daily News*, 7 December, 1975).

Milne, Anthony, 'I prefer the building to the Nobel Prize' (Trin: *DE*, 20 November, 1992).

Mills, Therese, 'Conversation with Derek Walcott' (Trin: *SG*, 20 June, 1971).

——— 'Don Juan was a Stickman' – interview (Trin: *SG*, 18 November, 1973).

——— 'No "Stardust" Just the polish of Hard Work' (Trin: *SG*, 23 July, 1967).

——— 'This is an experiment in courage' – interview (Trin: *SG*, 15th April, 1973).

Mombara, Sule, 'O Babylon! – Where it went wrong' – review (Bar: *CC*, Vol. 4, #2, May, 1976).

Pantin, Raoul, 'The amazing "Joker of Seville" ' – review (Trin: *SE*, 6 April, 1975).

——— 'Back to Africa theme: Walcott at it again' – review, *O Babylon*! (Trin: *Tapia*, Vol. 6, #13, 28 March, 1976).

——— 'O Babylon!' – review (Bar: *CC*, Vol. 4, #1, April, 1976).

——— 'Once a (pun) a time' – review, *Beef, no Chicken* (Trin: *SE*, 3 May, 1981).

——— ' "Talk is Free": The Amazing "Joker of Seville" ' – review (Trin: *DE* 6 April, 1975).

——— 'We Are Still Being Betrayed' – interview (Bar: *CC*, Vol. 1, ##7 and 8, July and August, 1973).

Phelps, Karen, 'Where Actors and Audiences Share Same Level' (Trin: *TG*, 12 January, 1966).

Questel, Victor, ' "Dream on Monkey Mountain" in Perspective' – review (Trin: *Tapia*, Vol. 4, #35, 1 September, #36, 8 September, #37 15 September, #39, 29 September, 1974).

——— 'From the horses mouth' (Trin: *Tapia*, Vol. 3, #31, 5 August, 1973).

——— 'The Horns of Derek's Dilemma' (Trin: *Tapia*, Vol. 3, #12, 25 March, 1973).

——— 'Marie Laveau – disappointing, uneven' – review (Trin: *TTR*, Governor Plum, 1980).

——— 'Remembrance : An inspiring elegy for the Afro-Saxon' – review (Trin: *TG*, 3 July, 1979).

——— 'Trinidad Theatre Workshop, A Bibliography' (Trin: *Kairi 76*, 1976).

——— 'Will Walcott have the last laugh on his Joker?' – review (Trin: TG, 6 December, 1974).

Ramchand, Ken, ' "It have compassion in the end" ' – on *The Sea at Dauphin* (Trin: *TG*, 7 January, 1993).

Rampersad, Krishendaye, 'Walcott, Great talent in Caribbean' (Trin: *TG*, 27 July, 1991).

Raymond, Judy, 'Future site of Walcott School for Arts?' (Trin: *SE*, 22 November, 1992).

——— 'Lending hand for national theatre' (Trin: *SE*, 3 January 1993).

Riley, C., 'A Black Man's Dream of Freedom' (New York: *New York Times*, 4 April, 1971).

Roach, Eric, 'Experiment in establishing

the West Indian theatre' – review, *Franklin* (Trin: *TG*, 18 April, 1973).
——— 'It must be an agonising place to act, the Basement Theatre' (Trin: *EN*, 17 January, 1966).
——— 'This musical fuses both traditions of folk legend' – review, *Ti-Jean and his Brothers* (Trin: *SG*, 28 June, 1970).
——— 'Walcott makes fine Castle of hate, fear' – review, *In a Fine Castle* (Trin: *TG*, 1 November, 1971).
Rothwell, Miles, 'Faulty script but fine talent in "Franklin" ' – review (Bar: *Weekend Nation*, 2 February, 1990).
Russell, Kathlyn, 'Give me film, says Derek Walcott' (Trin.: *DE*, 4 September, 1983).
——— 'Walcott's light and the TTT bushel' – review, *The Rig* (Trin: *SE*, 8 January, 1984).
Samuel, Kennedy, 'The Vision and The Reality' – review, *The Haytian Earth* (SL: *The Weekend Voice*, 1984).
Smith, Keith, 'O Babylon! an adventure in Reggae Theatre' – review, (Trin: *People*, April, 1976).
Solomon, Denis, ' "Ape and Essence" ' (Trin: *Tapia*, #7, 19 April, 1970).
——— ' "Can Walcott deal with the poor of our society?" ' (Trin: *DE*, 4 and 5 January, 1972).
——— 'Liberation and Libido' (Trin: *Tapia*, Vol. 4, #39, 8 December, 1974).
Stone, Judy, 'At last, masterpiece on the middle class' – review, *Remembrance* (Trin: *TG*, 13 July, 1979).
——— 'Death of our dodos in "The Last Carnival" ' – review (Trin: *TG*, 15 July, 1982).
——— 'Memorable "Ti-Jean" setting at St Augustine' – review (Trin: *TG*, 2 April, 1987).
——— 'Nigel's moment in "Hart Crane" all too brief' – review (Trin: *TG*, 21 October, 1986).
——— 'Sitahal follows the footsteps of Olivier' – review, *Franklin* (Trin: *TG*, 2 April, 1990).
——— 'Warner's "Beef, No Chicken" an inspired Production' – review, *Beef, No Chicken* (Bar: *CC*, June, 1985).
——— 'What Corsbie did to Walcott's "Pantomime" ' (Trin: *TG*, 5 February, 1981).
Swanzy, Henry, 'Henri Christophe' – review (Bar: *Bim*, Vol. 5, #17, December, 1952).
Taitt, Andy, 'Andy Taitt interviews Michael Gilkes' – on *Franklin* (Bar: *Together Magazine*, 26 January, 1990).
Taylor, Jeremy, 'Banyan and Walcott team up on "The Rig" ' (Trin: *SE*, 1 August, 1982).
——— 'A beautifully simple dramatic idea . . . ' – review, *O Babylon*! (Trin: *DE*, 24 March, 1976).
——— 'Caught in the dilemma of exile' – review, *Franklin* (Trin: *TG*, 16 April, 1973).
——— ' "The Joker of Seville" – actors give grand performance' – review (Trin: *DE*, 4 December, 1974).
——— 'Walcott nudging up to Broadway – review, *Marie Laveau* (Trin: *DE*, 2 June, 1980).
——— 'Walcott's "Steel" hammered in US' (Trin: *SG*, 28 April, 1991).
Vaughan, Peter, 'Holder brings a tropical coolness to "Pantomime" role – interview, Wilbert Holder (Minneapolis, USA: *Minneapolis Star and Tribune*, 25 March, 1983).
——— '2 "Pantomime" actors excel in magical verbal ballet' – review (Minneapolis, USA: *Minneapolis Star and Tribune*, 1 April, 1983).
Walcott, Anna, 'Walcott on Walcott' – on *The Odyssey* (Trin: *SG*, 19 July, 1992).
——— 'Walcott goes home' (Trin: *SG*, 22 November, 1992).
Walcott, Derek, 'Derek Walcott Grabs at a Thread, the Terse Mr Scott is still in the Dark' (Trin: *SG*, 15th July, 1962).
——— 'Derek's "most West Indian play" ' – on *Ti-Jean and His Brothers* (Trin: *SG Magazine*, 21 June, 1970).
——— 'Down by the old gas pump'(Trin: *TG*, 12 May, 1965).
——— 'The Joker: Closer to continuous theatre' (Trin: 22 March, 1975).

——— 'Makak symbolises Workshop' (Trin: *TG*, 1 August, 1974).
——— 'Mixing the Dance and the Drama' (Trin: *TG*, 18 April, 1972).
——— 'Of Masks and Men' (Trin: *TG*, 12 October, 1967).
——— 'Soul Brother to "The Joker of Seville" ' (Trin: *TG*, 6 November, 1974).
——— 'Talks about "The Joker of Seville" ' (Jam: *Carib*, #4, 1986).
——— 'The Theatre Workshop at the Crossroads' (Trin: *SG Magazine*, 29 September, 1968).
——— 'Their naturalness is more than mimicry' (Trin: *TG*, 4 March, 1969).
——— 'Trinidad's 1st Repertory Season opens next month' (Trin: *SG*, 11 September, 1966).
——— 'What the Twilight Says: An Overture', introduction to *Dream on Monkey Mountain and Other Plays* (London: Jonathan Cape, 1972).
——— 'Why this astigmatism towards the Workshop's white actors?' – on *Franklin* (Trin: *TG*, 19 April, 1973).
Walcott, Derek, with Terrence Chandler, Pamela Franco, Wilbert Holder, Stanley Marshall, John Melser and Judy Stone, 'The Seven Year Itch' (Trin: *Art and Man*, Act II Scene II, June, 1969).
Washburn, Martin, 'A likeable devil and a hellish president' – review, *Ti-Jean and His Brothers* (New York: *New York Post*, 14 August, 1972).
Watt, Douglas, ' "Ti-Jean and Brothers" Comes to Central Park' – review (New York: *Daily News*, 28 July, 1972).
Wickham, John, 'Dream on Monkey Mountain' – review (Bar: *Bim*, Vol. 12 #48, Jan–June, 1969).
——— 'Now that the poet is 60' – interview (Bar: *Daily Nation*, 29 January, 1990).
Wight, Benedict (pseud.Owen Baptiste) 'Benedict Wight Talks to Derek Walcott' (Trin: *SE Independence Magazine*, 31 August, 1969).
——— 'The success of Derek Walcott' (Trin: *Express*, 16 February, 1970).

on Edgar White:
Bruckner, D.J.R., ' "Trinity", Three One-Acts' – review, *Trinity* (New York: *New York Times*, 17 December, 1987).
Stone, Judy, 'Edgar White moves base from London to Caribbean' – interview (Trin: *TG*, 31 July, 1987).
——— ' "I Marcus Garvey", best bit of theatre this year' – review (Trin: *TG*, 16 July, 1987).
——— New realisations the essence of "Like Them That Dream" ' – interview, Earl Warner (Trin: *TG*, 11 October, 1983; see also 22 and 29 November, 1983).
Wickham, John, 'Marcus Garvey at Frank Collymore' – review, *I Marcus Garvey* (Bar: *Sunday Sun*, 12 April, 1987).

on Lester Efebo Wilkinson:
Reyes, Elma, 'Same Khaki Pants in August – review (Trin: *The Sun*, 29 May, 1985).
Shand, Eden, 'Bitter Cassava – a sweet start' – review (Trin: *TG*, 1 June, 1984).
Stone, Judy, 'Theatrical excitement from "Same Khaki Pants" ' – review, Wilkinson's musical (Trin: *TG*, 17 July, 1985).

on other playwrights:
Adams, Aubrey, 'The night of the wolf' – review, Belgrave's play (Trin: *SG*, 15th September, 1991).
Ainsworth, John, 'Going, Going, Gone! "Soucouyant" Is Sold' – review, Heywood's musical (Trin: *TG*, 7 October, 1955).
Allum, Helena, 'Dancing out your anger' – review, Schwarz-Bart's *Your Handsome Captain* (Trin: *CN*, 4 July, 1993).
Andersen, Peter, 'Portrait of an Artist: Ken Corsbie' (Guy: *New World*, 19 February, 1965).
Barker, J.S., 'Not the Stuff For A W.I. National Theatre' – review, Antigua's *Priscilla's Wedding*, Waite-Smith's *Sleepy Valley* (Trin: *TG*, 18 August, 1954).
Bassant, Reynold: ' "Dhan Deepak" and the East Indian girl' – review, Persad's play (Trin: *TG*, 7 November, 1990).
——— 'A parade of closet-type characters' – review, Bickram's *Graves and*

Skeletons (Trin: *TG*, 18 November, 1991).

Baugh, Edward, 'Frank Collymore, A Biographical Portrait' (Jam: *Savacou*, ##7/8, January/June, 1973).

Baytop, Adrianne Roberts, 'James Baldwin and Roger Mais' (Jam: *JJ*, #42, 1978).

Blood, Peter, 'All-woman team comes good in Danse' – review, Wells's play (Trin: *SE*, 22 March, 1992).

——— 'Uncle Horace bows out' – tribute to Horace James (Trin: *DE*, 30 October, 1992).

Cromwell, Liz, 'Hilarious look at immigrant's problems' – review, Hastings's *Gloo Joo* (Trin: *The Sun*, 9 September, 1980).

Feay, Suzi, 'Paper and Stone' – review, Zindika's play (London: *Time Out*, 28 February 1990).

Fido, Elaine Savory, 'Samuel Hillary's Yard Play' – review, *Departure in the Dark* (Bar: *Bim*, Vol. 18, #70, 1986).

Forbes, Deirdre, 'What's in a name?' – interview, Zindika (London: *The Voice*, 20 February, 1990).

Gilkes, Michael, 'Sonya on stage in Barbados' – review, Moze's *Sonya* (Trin: *TG*, 21 May, 1990).

Hughes, Brenda, 'Scouting's New York trip a turning point' – interview, Sullivan Walker (Trin: *TG*, 6 March, 1991, see also 7 and 8 March, 1991).

Jacob, Debbie, 'Jolly's got a good hobby' – interview, Dorothy Jolly (Trin: *DE*, 3 March, 1989).

——— 'Now the movie, Turn of the Tide' – on Wilson's film (Trin: *DE*, 6 June, 1986).

James, Royson, 'Play closes on successful note' – review, Harris's *Anansi and Cooyah*! (Toronto: *Toronto Star*, 2 April, 1985).

Konwalina, Trudy, 'West Indian Drama – In The Hands Of An Expert Guardian' – review, Antigua's *Priscilla's Wedding*, Waite-Smith's *Sleepy Valley* (Trin: *EN*, 16 August, 1954).

Lee, Simon, 'The narrow road to the small screen', interview James, on Wilson's *No Boundaries* (Trin: *SG*, 11 October, 1992).

Lee Wah, James, 'Dinner Theatre serves witty, delightful farce' – review, Stone's *Old Mas, Pretty Mas* (Trin: *TG*, 4 February, 1982).

Lyndersay, Mark, 'Finbar steals show in many roles' – review, Stone's *Old Mas, Pretty Mas* (Trin: *TG*, 28 January, 1982).

——— 'Gabriel Francis is sure his radio plays will not be a brief love affair' (Trin: *People*, July, 1979).

——— 'Gloo Joo' – review (Trin: *Catholic News*, 14 September, 1980).

Martin, Angela, 'Rudder stars in TV series' – on Jacob's *Sugar Cane Arrows* (Trin: *DE*, 23 September, 1988).

Mauby, ' "Justina" – A Spirited Communal Effort' – review, Griffith's *Justina* (Trin: *TG*, 6 January, 1976).

Nobrega, Cecile, 'Genesis of Stabroek Fantasy' (Guy: *KOA*, Vol. 8, #25, June, 1959).

Noel, Peter, 'Trinidad playwright laments Carib clichés' – interview, Sullivan Walker (New York: *NY Amsterdam News*, 25 September, 1982).

Pryce, Vinette, 'Sullivan Walker Takes You Back to Boy Days with Caribbean Theatre' (New York: *Caribbean News*, week ending 2 November, 1981).

Ramchand, Ken, 'A man with a sound colonial education' – on Clifford Sealy (Trin: *TG*, 12 November, 1992).

Ramcharitar, Raymond, ' "The Coffin" – definitely not a dead play' – review, Bickram's play (Trin: *TG*, 7 September, 1992).

——— 'Cultural reality reflected in theatre' – review, Schwarz-Bart's *Your Handsome Captain* (Trin: *TG*, 5 July, 1993).

——— 'Eggnog laced with satire' – review, Bickram's *Say No to Eggnog* (Trin: *SG Magazine* 31 January, 1993).

——— 'Trinidad stage is real hell' – review, Thomas's *Sans Humanite* (Trin: *TG*, 16 October, 1992).

Raymond, Judy, 'Dirk McLean: Hoarder and harvester of memory' (Trin: *SE*, 10 November, 1991).

——— 'A Full-Time Artist – Valerie

Belgrave . . . ' (Trin: *SE*, 21 July, 1991).
——— 'Two plays offer strong women's roles' – review, Schwarz-Bart's *Your Handsome Captain* (Trin: *SE*, 27 June 1993).
Roach, Eric, '. . . of Creole T'dad's dance and drama' – review, Labastide's *One for the Road* (Trin: *TG*, 12 December, 1972).
Scott, Lawrence, 'Born in the wrong continent' – interview, Helen Camps (Trin: *Entertainer*, April, 1983).
Smith, Michael, 'Theatre: The Cantilevered Terrace' – review, Archibald's play (New York: *The Village Voice*, 25 January, 1962).
Stone, Judy, ' "The Coffin" is full of surprises, but "Separate Tables" needs more' – includes review, Bickram's play (Trin: *TG*, 28 June, 1988).
——— 'David Rudder relieved the tedium of Madness' – review, Adams's *Carnival Madness* (Trin: *TG*, 8 March, 1988).
——— ' "De Maul Story" rich in catchy lyrics' – review, Cama's musical (Trin: *TG*, 12 April, 1985).
——— 'Drama for the young and young at heart' – review, Springer's *Ti-Jean and Mariquite* (Trin: *TG*, 18 December, 1987).
——— 'Group that's trying to get back to the basics' – interview, Helen Camps (Trin: *TG*, 28 June, 1983).
——— 'Human frailty and corruption in We's "Guilty as Charged" ' – review, Wickham's play (Trin: *TG*, 8 November, 1983).
——— 'Jeff's Fountainhead gives Toronto a taste of Caribbean drama' – interview, Jeff Henry (Trin: *TG*, 7 May, 1985).
——— ' "Jennifer's Curse" shows up Dorant's writing weakness' (Trin: *TG*, 25 June, 1987).
——— 'Lively "Obeah" at the Carib' – review, Fullerton's musical (Trin: *TG*, 5 March, 1987).
——— 'Lyndersay: Lifetime of varied theatrical achievement' – on Dexter Lyndersay (Trin: *TG*, 4 September, 1989).
——— ' "March" has quality script but too much speechifying' – review, Sitahal's *Monster March* (Trin: *TG*, 6 October, 1987).
——— ' "Men of Gray" plays a role in Joseph's dream of boosting local film industry' (Trin: *TG*, 27 August, 1990).
——— 'My gods are in the audience says Dexter Lyndersay' (Trin: *TG*, 20 January, 1987).
——— 'Now we can enjoy our soap opera' – review, Wilson's *No Boundaries* (Trin: *TG*, 21 October, 1988).
——— 'Pablo Sierra: Entertaining and palatable' – review, Bickram's *Who Killed Pablo Sierra?* (Trin: 12 June, 1989).
——— ' "Queen of the Bands", not Carnival not a musical' – review, Berkeley's musical (Trin: *TG*, 16 July, 1987).
——— 'Stage One can be proud of "Lights" ' (Trin: *TG*, 30 July, 1986).
——— 'Sullivan is back in town' – on Sullivan Walker (Trin: *TG*, 2 December, 1986).
——— 'Why Gerard Joseph stands out in "Men of Gray" (Trin: *TG*, 20 August, 1990).
——— 'A worthy experiment at UWI' – on dramatisation of Naipaul's *Miguel Street* (Trin: *TG*, 8 April, 1986).
Tanna, Laura, 'Evan Jones, Man of Two Worlds' (Jam: *JJ*, Vol. 18, 1985).
Taylor, Jeremy, ' "All Ah We" missing something' – review, Corsbie's show (Trin: *DE*, 3 June, 1975).
——— 'Gloo Joo – a battle of wits' – review, Hastings's play (Trin: *DE*, 19 August, 1980).
——— 'Old mas, pretty mas' – review, Stone's play (Trin: *TG*, 10 February, 1982).
——— 'Perfect blend of music and dance' – review, Labastide's *One for the Road* (Trin: *DE*, 11 December, 1972).
Walcott, Derek, 'Author deserves another service' (Trin: *TG*, 20 August, 1965).
——— 'Broadway success is disappointing, yet . . . With all its faults, It Deserves a Sellout' (Trin: *SG*, 8 July, 1962).
——— 'Enter Another Playwright' – on

Campbell's *Royal Visit* (Trin: *TG*, 8 April, 1964).
——— 'Enter Kirkley and Pitts – And A Promise Is Kept' – review, pantomime *Puss in Boots* (Trin: *TG*, 17 December, 1964).
——— 'Henry's "Goose" is my pick for Drama win' – review Redhead's *Goose and Gander* (Trin: *TG*, 3rd August, 1961).
——— 'Not so fast, Mr Cambridge!' – review, Cambridge's three plays (Trin: *TG*, 31 May, 1967).
——— ' "Piccadilly": A Thing of Shreds And Bright Patches' – review, Adams's revue (Trin: *SG*, 31 May, 1964).
——— 'U.C.W.I. Players 1 hour late but an attack on "Chippy" saves day' – review, Hillary's play (Trin: *TG*, 10 August, 1961).
Walker, Bert, 'Caribbean theater opens season with 1-man show' – review, Walker's *The Journey* (New York: *Daily News*, 26 September, 1982).
Whyte, T.K., 'Night Nurse – "great crowd pleaser" – review, Denton's play (Jam: *Daily Gleaner*, 24 May, 1990).
Wilmot, Fred, 'Roger Mais' (Guy: *KOA*, #20, 1955).
Wilson, Jeanne, 'Better local productions promised' – review, Ellis's *Lament for a Dead Maroon* (Jam: *Daily Gleaner*, 29 October, 1990).

general:
Barnett, Sheila, 'Pitchy Patchy' (Jam: *JJ*, #43, 1979).
Bassant, Reynold, 'Censorship in theatre obsolete' – interview, Devindra Dookie (Trin: *TG*, 22 June, 1981).
Benjamin, Joel, 'The Early Theatre in Guyana' (Guy: *KOA*, #37, December, 1987).
Bennett, Wycliffe, 'The Jamaican Theatre' (Jam: *JJ*, Vol. 8, ##2 and 3, 1974).
Bettelheim, Judith, 'The Jonkonnu Festival – its relation to Caribbean and African masquerades' (Jam: *JJ*, Vol. 10, ##2, 3 and 4, 1976).
Brathwaite, Edward Kamau, 'Chronicles of Unchaos', review, Nettleford's *Dance Jamaica* (Jam: *JJ*, Vol. 18, #4, 1985).
Brown, Wayne, 'Carnival jottings' (Trin: *DE*, 13 February, 1991).
Cameron, Norman E., 'Building tradition in drama' (Guy: *KOA*, Vol. 8, #25, June, 1959).
——— 'Drama in British Guiana' (Guy: *KOA*, Vol. 1, #1, 1945).
Chen, Julie, 'Jamaica's annual pantomime a Christmas tradition' (Trin: *TG*, 21 December, 1990).
Chun, Diane, 'Raw Talent and Vibrant Personalities Fuel Trinidad Drama' (Gainesville, USA: *Gainesville Sun*, 5 September, 1982).
Danny, Phoolo, 'It's a battle against evil – Hindus celebrate Ram Leela' (Trin: *SE*, 23 September, 1990).
Dummett, Joan (ed), 'A Guyanese National Theatre?', panel discussion (Guy: *New World*, ##23, 24 and 25, 1965).
Gloudon, Barbara, 'Twenty Years of Theatre' (Jam: *JJ*, #46, 1982).
Greaves, Hal, 'Dollars and cents approach destroying Best Village' (Trin: *Magnum*, *TG*, 20 October, 1990).
Hall, Anthony, 'Commitment' (Trin: *Gayap*, 1973–74).
Hanson, Francis, 'Preface to The Laws of Jamaica Passed by the Assembly and Confirmed by His Majesty in Council, 23 February, 1683' (London, 1683).
Harris, Wilson, 'Guyana Prize Address' (Guy: *KOK*, #38, June, 1988).
Harrison, Ron, 'The Drama League an inspired art movement' (Jam: *Sunday Gleaner*, 11 June to 9 July, 1989).
Hill, Errol, 'The Beginnings of Regional Theatre' (Jam: *ACT*, Vol II, ##1 and 2, Vol. III, #1, 1990–91).
——— 'Calypso and War' (Bar: *Bim*, Vol. 18, #70, 1986).
——— 'Calypso Drama' (USA: *Theatre Survey*, Vol. IX, #2, 1968).
——— 'The Emergence of a Caribbean Aesthetic' (Bar: *Bim*, Vol. 17, ##66 and 67, 1983).
——— 'The Emergence of a National Drama in the West Indies' (Jam: *CQ*, Vol. 18, #4, 1972).

——— 'The First Playwrights of Jamaica' (Jam: *Carib*, #4, 1986).
——— 'Plays of the English-speaking Caribbean, Part I: Jamaica' (Washington: *Bulletin of Black Theatre*, Vol. 1, #2, 1972).
——— 'Plays of the English-speaking Caribbean, Part II: Guyana' (Washington: *Bulletin of Black Theatre*, #3, 1973).
——— 'Plays of the English-speaking Caribbean, Part III: Trinidad and Tobago' (Washington: *Bulletin of Black Theatre*, #4, 1973).
——— 'The Role of the Arts in Nation-building', 5th Dr Eric Williams Memorial Lecture (Trin: Central Bank, 1987).
——— ' . . . a time and a season. . . ', introduction (Trin: UWI ESU, 1976).
——— 'Traditional Figures in Carnival: their preservation, development and interpretation' (*CQ*, Vol. 31, #2, 1985).
Hill, Errol and William Talbot, 'Blackface vs. Whiteface on Stage' an exchange of letters (Washington: *Bulletin of Black Theatre*, #3, 1973).
Hyatt, Charles, 'Actor and Folklorist', interview (Jam: *JJ*, #45, 1981).
John, George, 'Carifesta' (Trin: *Galerie*, Vol. 1 #1, 1991).
Jones, Bridget, 'Theatre in the French West Indies' (Jam: *Carib*, #4, 1986).
Lee Wah, James, 'Does anybody care about the state of the arts?' (Trin: *SG Independence Supplement*, 30 August, 1981).
Lovelace, Earl, 'Artists as Agents of Unity' (Trin: *SE*, 27 September, 1992).
——— 'Theatre and Audiences' (Trin: *SG*, 1 May, 1966).
——— 'Why we need Carifesta now' (Trin: *SE*, 19 January, 1992).
Lyndersay, Mark, ' '81 in the Arts . . . a perspective' (Trin: *TTR*, New Year's, 1982).
——— 'Theatre of Mas' (Trin: *TTR*, Kaiso, 1982).
McArthur, Tom, 'Caliban' (in *The Oxford Companion to the English Language*, Oxford, UK: Oxford University Press, 1992).
Menezes, Sr. M. Noel, 'Portugese Drama in Nineteenth Century British Guiana' (Guy: *KOA*, 1989).
Morris, Mervyn, 'Literature: Some Trends' (Jam: *JJ*, #46, 1982).
Nri, Monique, 'Back to our Future – African Caribbean Theatre in Britain' (London: *Artrage*, Spring/Summer, 1990).
Poynting, Jeremy, 'At Homes, Tagore and Jive – ethnic identity and the British Guiana Dramatic Society' (Guy: *KOK*, #37, December, 1987).
Ramchand, Ken, 'Don't Mess with the Carnival' (Trin: *TG*, 18 October, 1990).
——— 'What is art, and what is cultural confidence?' (Trin: *TG*, 3 September, 1992).
——— 'What is really Indianness? – WI writer Lovelace poses the question' (Trin: *SG*, 21 October, 1979).
Raymond, Judy, 'The Lost Tribe: the forgotten Jewish community of Trinidad' (Trin: *DE*, 6 February, 1990).
Reckord, Verena, 'Reggae, Rastafarianism and Cultural Identity' (Jam: *JJ*, #46, 1982).
Rohlehr, Gordon, 'Trophy and Catastrophe' (Guy: *KOK*, #38, June, 1988).
Ryman, Cheryl, 'Jonkonnu – A Neo-African Form' (Jam: *JJ*, Part I, Vol. 17, #1, Part II, Vol. 17, #2, 1984).
St Hill, C.A.P., 'Down memory lane . . .' (Trin: *SG Magazine*, 11 August, 1991).
Seymour, A.J., 'A note on Literature and Caribbean Society' (Guy: *Kaie*, #8 December, 1971).
Stone, Judy, 'CARIBUSTE Promises bright era for theatre' (Trin: *SG Independence Supplement*, 26 August, 1979).
——— 'Danger of forcing nationalism on our art' (Trin: *TG Independence Supplement*, 28 August, 1977).
——— 'National Theatre wanted' (Trin: *Trinidad and Tobago Review*, December, 1977).
Tanna, Laura, 'Anansi – Jamaica's Trickster Hero' (Jam: *JJ*, Vol. 16, #2, 1983).

Tewarie, Kamla D., 'Ram Leela in Trinidad since Indentureship' (Trin: *SG Divali Supplement*, 14 October, 1990).

Walcott, Derek, 'The Answer is not Festivals' (Trin: *SG*, 22 April, 1964).

——— 'Beyond the Backyard' (Trin: SG, 11 December, 1966).

——— 'Carnival: The Theatre of the Streets' (Trin: *SG*, 9 February, 1964).

——— 'Education Through The Theatre' (Trin: *TG*, 15 January, 1964).

——— 'Emperor's Orphans' (Trin: *SG*, 14 August, 1960; see also *TG*, 15 August, 1960).

——— 'Future of Art Promising' (Trin: *SG Independence Supplement*, 31 August, 1963; see also 26 August 1962).

——— 'Gift of Comedy West Indian Gaiety – Our Most Successful Role' (Trin: *SG Magazine*, 22 October, 1967).

——— 'The Kabuki . . . Something to Give To Our Theatre' (Trin: *SG*, 16 February, 1964).

——— 'National Theatre is the Answer' (Trin: *TG*, 12 August, 1964).

——— 'Need for a Little Theatre in Port of Spain' (Trin: *SG*, 10 July, 1960).

——— 'A Need for Supporters' (Trin: *TG*, 25 December, 1963).

——— 'On the Theatre' (Trin: *TG*, 30 January, 1967).

——— 'The Outlook For A National Theatre' (Trin: *SG*, 22 March, 1964).

——— 'Principle must be questioned' (Trin: *TG*, 2 September, 1965).

——— 'Problems of Exile' (Trin: *TG*, 13 July, 1966).

——— 'Professional Vs. the Amateur' (Trin: *TG*, 12 January, 1966).

——— 'The Prospect of a National Theatre' (Trin: *SG*, 6 March, 1966).

——— 'Public Debut for Theatre Workshop' (Trin: *SG*, 25 March, 1962).

——— 'Sparrowdrama! A Solution to the Dimanche Gras Flops?' (Trin: *TG*, 2 March, 1966).

——— 'Spreading our Culture Abroad' (Trin: *SG*, 8 November, 1964).

——— 'Theatre in Guyana' (Trin: *SG Magazine*, 21 November, 1965).

——— 'The Theatrical Feel now at R.V.I.' (Trin: *TG*, 10 February, 1965).

——— 'There's Ample Room For A Theatre' (Trin: *TG*, 16 December, 1964).

——— 'Time to Talk and a Time to Act' (Trin: *TG*. 13 January, 1965).

——— 'Villages Are Really The Heart of Port of Spain' (Trin: *SG*, 12 July, 1964).

——— 'We must Dig Deeper into the Sources' (Trin: *TG*, 4 September, 1962).

——— 'West Indian Farce Fires Put Into Festival' (Trin: *TG*, 9 June, 1961).

——— 'Why is our theatre so tame?' (Trin: *SG*, 30 April, 1967).

——— 'Why We do Shakespeare Badly' (Trin: *SG*, 8 March, 1964).

Walcott, Roderick, 'Call for a Federated West Indian Theatre' (Trin: *Trinidad Chronicle*, 10 March, 1957).

Wickham, John, 'Some Reflections on the State of Theatre in the Caribbean' (Bar: *Bim*, Vol. 17, #65, 1979).

Williams, J. C., 'Responsibility of Caribbean Festival Arts' (Trin: *TG*, 8 May, 1989; see also 24 April, 1 May, 1989).

9 PERIODICALS AND NEWSPAPERS

key:

ACT *ACTA News* (The Association of Caribbean Theatre Artists (Jamaica), c/o Groundwork Theatre Co., 3 Oxford Terrace, Kingston 5, Jamaica).

American Theatre (Theatre Communications Group Inc., 355 Lexington Avenue, New York, NY 10017–0217).

Animations (Puppet Centre Trust, Battersea Arts Centre, Lavender Hill, London SW11 5TJ).

Art and Man (defunct, 1968–69 Trinidad).

Artrage (28 Shacklewell Lane, London E8 2EZ).

The Beacon (defunct, 1931–33 Trinidad).

Bim (c/o The Editors, Ferney, Atlantic Shores, Christ Church, Barbados).

Carib (Jamaica).

CC *Caribbean Contact* (P.O. Box 616, Bridgetown, Barbados).

CQ *Caribbean Quarterly* (Department of Extramural Studies, University of the West Indies, Mona, Jamaica).

Caribbean Review (Florida International University, Tamiami Trail, Miami, Florida 33199).

CN *The Catholic News* (31 Independence Square, Port of Spain, Trinidad).

The Cosmopolitan (defunct, 1928–31 Jamaica).

CPC *The Crusader* (The Crusader Publishing Company, 19 St Louis Street, Castries, St Lucia).

DE *Daily Express* (35–37 Independence Square, Port of Spain, Trinidad).

Drama, Quarterly Theatre Review (British Theatre Association, 9 Fitzroy Square, London W1P 6AE, UK).

Dramatics (The International Thespian Society, 3368 Central Parkway, Cincinnati, Ohio 45225, USA).

The Entertainer (defunct, 1983 Trinidad).

EN *The Evening News* (22–24 St Vincent Street, Port of Spain, Trinidad).

Galerie (MacLean Publishing Ltd., Suite 4, 1a Dere Street, Port of Spain, Trinidad).

Gayap (San Fernando Arts Council, c/o Torrance Mohammed, Maritime Life, Carlton Centre, San Fernando, Trinidad).

JJ *Jamaica Journal* (Institute of Jamaica Publications Limited, 2a Suthermere Road, Kingston 10, Jamaica).

Kaie (National History and Arts Council, Ministry of Information and Culture, Georgetown, Guyana).

Kairi (defunct, 1974–78 Trinidad).

KOA *Kyk-over-al* (1945–61, revived 1984, Ian A. McDonald, c/o Guysuco, 22 Church Street, Georgetown, Guyana).

New Voices (P.O. Box 3254, Diego Martin, Trinidad).

New World (defunct, Guyana).

New World Quarterly (Jamaica).

People (defunct, 1975–83 Trinidad).

Plays and Players (Brevet Publishing (UK) Ltd., 43b Gloucester Road, Croydon, London CR0 2DH, UK).

Prince (defunct, Antigua).

S.A.G. (defunct, 1970–71 Trinidad).

Savacou (P.O. Box 170, Mona, Kingston 7, Jamaica).

Sistren (Sistren Theatre Collective, 20 Kensington Crescent, Kingston 5, Jamaica).

Spare Rib (27 Clerkenwell Close, London EC1R 0AT).

SE *Sunday Express* (35–37 Independence Square, Port of Spain, Trinidad).

SG *Sunday Guardian* (22–24 St Vincent Street, Port of Spain, Trinidad).

Tapia (now the *Trinidad and Tobago Review*).

TTR *Trinidad and Tobago Review* (24 Abercromy Street, Port of Spain, Trinidad).

Trinidad Chronicle (defunct, Trinidad).

Trinidad Courant and Commercial Gazette, for the year 1818 (defunct, Trinidad).

TG *Trinidad Guardian* (22–24 St Vincent Street, Port of Spain, Trinidad).

Voices (defunct, Trinidad).

INDEX